THE PIRATE'S SECRET BABY

HIGH SEAS #3

DARLENE MARSHALL

THE PIRATE'S SECRET BABY (High Seas #3)

Copyright © 2014, 2018 by Eve D. Ackerman
ISBN Print: 9780692132708
ISBN Ebook:9780463714904
Cover Art © 2014 Trace Edward Zaber

PUBLISHED IN THE UNITED STATES OF AMERICA BY: EVE D. ACKERMAN

❧ Created with Vellum

THE PIRATE'S SECRET BABY

..."What is it you want?" Macdavid said, looking about the deck at his shabby little vessel, which looked like a flounder alongside the sleek, sharklike *Prodigal.*

Robert gestured at the trio coming abovedecks.

"Her."

"You! Reprobate! Wastrel! Knave! Scoundrel! Libertine! Villain!" Miss Burke sputtered to a finish having run out of epithets for the moment. The two crewmen escorting her looked at her with new respect, but she needed a few weeks aboard a pirate vessel. That would add salt to her vocabulary.

A slow smile curled his lips. The governess's ugly linen cap was absent. While her hair was pinned tightly against her head, it shone in the sun, a glorious shade of chestnut with highlights of russet and gold. A few wisps escaped to curl across her forehead, with enough amber depths that it made one itch to unpin the mass and see all the colors gathered there. No wonder the little hedgehog kept it covered! Hair like that would inspire naughty thoughts in her employers and jealousy in their wives.

She was also younger than he'd suspected when he first

encountered her, pegging her age at around twenty-five years old. The day just became that much more interesting.

"You missed me, didn't you, Miss Burke?"

"Why have you stopped this ship? What do you want with me?"

Anger looked good on her. The gray sack she wore hurt his eyes though. He'd have to do something about that.

Robert turned back to the hapless captain of the *Clementine*.

"This is what I came for..."

PRAISE FOR DARLENE MARSHALL

"I seriously doubt that any summer experience can possibly be more delightful than sitting on the beach while reading *The Pirate's Secret Baby*."—Smart Bitches, Trashy Books

"Pirates, a shipboard romance, a new father upended by his unexpected responsibilities and a woman who manages to keep her head and agency? Sign me up, Captain."—Dear Author Reviews

"A Great Read--I would totally stow away on any ship Darlene writes about."—Book Binge

"5 Stars!.. *The Pirate's Secret Baby* is a well-researched historical romance spiced with humor. The story of Robert, Lydia, and Marauding Mattie weaves an invisible spell that tugs at your heart strings, and I particularly liked Robert's non-violent, but oh-so-typically-piratical solution to thwarting Lydia's nemesis...I've read several of Marshall's previous pirate tales, but this is the best written and most intriguing one..."—Pirates and Privateers Newsletter

ALSO BY DARLENE MARSHALL

DEDICATION, NOTES & THANKS

If anyone has ever wondered why my pirate captain is Robert St. Armand instead of the more correct Robert St. Amand, blame Canada.*

Thanks go to Diana Gabaldon, who graciously gave me permission to use The Impetuous Pirate *and her characters "Tessa" and "Valdez."*

My editor, Catherine Snodgrass. You help bring my words to life.

Raphael T. Rosenblatt, math teacher extraordinaire, who allowed me to guest lecture to his economics class at Harvard using a passage from The Bride and the Buccaneer *to illustrate how the barter system approximates commodity currency in a market economy. That is so going on my resumé! Reader, any math mistakes in this book are mine. He tried his best to assist me.*

Nathalie Fossé, PhD, LMT for help with French phrases and words.

The Beaumonde (Regency) chapter of Romance Writers of America. They're always there for me when I need answers.

The Alachua County (Florida) Library District, zooming through the 21st century.

My beta readers, Janice, Connie, and Amarilis. Any mistakes are mine, not theirs.

Captain Charles Johnson's A General History of the Robberies & Murders of the Most Notorious Pirates *is still very much in print and enjoyed by pirates young and old.*

*There is a tiny hamlet in Quebec named St. Armand, but the correct English spelling of the saint's name is St. Amand. A municipality in New York repeated the mistake when their town was named after the Quebec town. Then it got worse—a lovely destination in Florida named St. Armand's Key continued the error. From Wikipedia: "A Frenchman named Charles St. Amand bought property on the island in 1893. His name was misspelled in land deeds, and this misspelled name is still used today."

I happened to be sitting in a cafe on St. Armand's Key sipping wine** and working on Castaway Dreams *when I exclaimed aloud, "What this book needs is pirates!" Since I was enjoying myself so much at St. Armand's Key, I decided to call my pirate "St. Armand." It's probably a good thing I wasn't in Yeehaw Junction or Sopchoppy when I had this brainstorm. It never occurred to me St. Armand's Key was a historic typo, so I merrily wrote along. I realized the error while doing research for this book, and bring it to your attention so readers (even—or especially—Canadian ones) wouldn't send me letters saying, "That is not a real name in French!"*

**I earned that wine. I walked over the bridge to St. Armand's Key from the mainland to see if I could overcome my fear of high bridges. It worked, and I've made that hike a number of times since.

CHAPTER 1

1820

*T*he room reeked of stale perfume, spilled liquor, hashish, the effluvia of multiple bodies and a hint of…donkey?

Not possible.

To be honest, it was possible, but not likely.

Robert St. Armand scratched his balls and sighed contentedly, an arm thrown over his eyes to block the sliver of sunlight daring to insert itself through the shuttered windows. Had there ever been a better morning? He thought not. He recalled other visits to Madame Olifiers's establishment, evenings of bacchanalian delights contributing to his near-legendary reputation, not just on tiny St. Martin, but throughout the entire Caribbean. It was well-known in certain circles a man could get nearly anything he desired at the exclusive brothel, even things he did not know he desired until they were offered to him.

Robert ceased his scratching. What *had* he desired last evening? For the life of him he could not remember who shared his bed (though the donkey was a slim possibility, at best). Was it Francine, that naughty minx whose round bottom was made for spanking? Raul, whose limpid eyes and soft curls reminded one of a most luscious faun? Francine and Raul?

Now, there was a vision!

He moved his hand up, resting it against the part of his anatomy risen like a bowsprit parting the waves. He felt a tad tender in that area. Even if he could not recall the details, he knew the evening's activities has been vigorous, prolonged, and one assumed, satisfying for all involved. He'd spent the last fortnight in the brothel as a favored customer and had a reputation to maintain.

"I'm surprised there's life in you yet, m'boy, after the night you've had," he murmured.

Still, his morning condition owed as much to nature's call as his desires. This required movement and eye-opening, two activities he'd hoped to avoid for a few hours more, but with a sigh he forced himself out of the bed and made use of the pot beneath.

It was a lengthy process given the amount of liquor he'd consumed the previous night, so when the door burst open he only glanced over his shoulder and said, "Be with you in a moment, love."

He'd registered that an unknown woman stood there, which was good because had it been an unknown man he would have gone for his sword. Considering his current activity, it would create a mess which Cornelia Olifiers would take out of his hide and his pocket.

Eventually he was drained and tottered back into bed, leaning up against the carved headboard to face his visitor.

"If you're here for my morning fuck, sweetheart, you'll have to come back later. I don't think I'm up to it right now," he said in French, glancing down. "Then again, like Lazarus I could be persuaded to rise from the dead for a pretty face and a skilled mouth."

"Are you Captain St. Armand?" she demanded in English.

He looked up, eyeing his visitor more closely. He wouldn't call her face pretty, but it was certainly colorful, that bright crimson in her cheeks, the white lines around her mouth, the narrowed gaze with a flash of green. The rest of her was neither colorful nor pretty. The woman wore a gray dress of uncertain styling, baggy where it should be fitted, resembling a sack. A white cap without a touch of lace to soften it covered her hair. Clearly she was not in the usual style of Cornelia's girls. Must be one of the specialty doxies, and he could guess what that specialty was.

"I did not request a mistress of discipline last night, did I?"

His brow furrowed as he thought, a painful process given the state of his head.

She advanced two steps closer, fists clenched by her sides.

"Get up, you...you reprobate!"

"No, seriously, sweetheart, you will have to find another customer." He looked at her critically. "Some men like the stern English governess act, but I think you would do better in a leather corset."

"I *am* an English governess, you disgusting piece of offal, your daughter's governess!"

The combination of liquor and hashish and sex had left his brain like tapioca, but even so, a small part of what she said penetrated his consciousness.

"You are not here for my morning fuck?"

She grabbed the nearest object containing liquid and dumped it over his head. Fortunately for him, it was the dregs of the wine and not the chamber pot. Robert was too stunned to do anything but sit there, dripping, as the unknown woman turned on her heel and stomped out of the room.

~

LYDIA BURKE LEANED against the papered wall, her hand at her throat as she tried to catch her breath.

When Nanette told her of her darling captain, she had somehow formed an image of a grizzled sea-scoundrel, every bit of his dissolute life visible in his face. The reality was nothing like she'd envisioned.

Robert St. Armand was the most beautiful man she'd ever seen. He had a face and form made for sculpting in marble, the artist's hands lovingly carving out the long lines of his lithe frame, sleek muscles and shoulders broad enough to swing a cutlass or a dance partner with ease.

His face would have been too perfect, with those cheek-bones sharp enough to reflect sunlight and a cleft chin, had his nose not been broken at some point. That small flaw did not detract, but rather made him look more human, more approachable, and therefore more dangerous to any woman with breath in her body.

Nonetheless, he was a disgusting piece of offal. Poor Mathilde! What kind of life could she have with a pirate who fornicated his way through the brothels of St. Martin, and possibly the brothels of every island in the Caribbean?

As if to punctuate her thoughts, one of the whores strolled by at that moment. When she saw at whose door Lydia stood, she winked.

"The captain is a mighty lover, is he not? No wonder you look pale! You should eat some oysters to restore your strength, *cherie*."

The woman's words restored color to Lydia's face. She smoothed down her faded muslin skirt.

"I am only a visitor here, *mademoiselle*. I have no knowl-edge of Captain St. Armand's activities."

She snapped her jaws shut as the woman critically

assessed her total appearance in a manner unique to French-women of any station. She wore a deep pink cotton wrapper, lovely against skin the color of rich caramels, her bare feet poking out beneath. She was abundantly curved and had a dimpled smile.

"You have good bones," she said. "With a bit of color in your face and a proper hair styling you might do well for yourself, if you decide to stay."

"Thank you, Miss—"

"I am Francine Dubois." The girl dropped a pert curtsey, holding her robe shut to keep herself covered.

"Thank you, Miss Dubois. I am Lydia Burke and I already have employment," Lydia said dryly. She pushed herself off of the wall as Francine gave her a Gallic shrug.

"This is a good house," she said. "Madame takes care of the girls, so if you find yourself not liking your house you should reconsider."

Lydia opened her mouth to correct the girl, then closed it. She was, after all, only trying to be helpful.

"Thank you for your advice. Can you direct me to Madame Olifiers?"

"She is in the parlor downstairs, the one with the windows that get morning light."

Lydia nodded and turned to leave. She glanced over her shoulder and saw Francine enter Captain St. Armand's room, exclaiming in French, "Captain Robby! You look so unhappy! And wet!"

A slight smile turned up the corner of Lydia's lips as she went to search out Madame.

CHAPTER 2

Robert paused in the doorway of the morning room, plastering on a smile for the two women seated there. It never hurt to make a good entrance. He had sent Francine to get him hot water to wash off the wine and the remnants of their busy night and he took his time dressing. If he was going to face that harpy again he wanted to have all his weapons available to him, his wardrobe and good looks being every bit as useful in certain encounters as sword and pistols. He knew he looked more than adequate. He paid his tailor well to ensure he would, and his looking glass reassured him daily. The message he sent was that he was master of the notorious *Prodigal Son*, a captain whose reputation preceded him. His white linen shirt was unfastened at the neck, his coat of rich cobalt silk was his own design, the polished brass buttons drawing the eye to his shoulders and trim waist, while the diamond weighing down the lobe of his ear carried its own message of status and wealth. He seated himself at the breakfast table and poured a cup of coffee, remarking mildly, "*My* nurse used to warn me if I scowled like that my face would freeze in that position."

"Miss Burke was explaining to me that she spoke with you this morning, Captain," Cornelia Olifiers said. Madame looked her usual competent and attractive self, her silvered chestnut hair neatly arranged in a bun at her neck, and her smoke-blue eyes twinkled at him over the steam rising from the cup she raised to her lips. Her cap was a confection of Brussels lace, enhancing her appearance, not like the rag atop the head of the woman next to her.

"I confess I was not at my best this morning and may have given Miss…Burke?…a less than coherent response," Robert said, fixing a look that had charmed him out of many difficult situations.

Gray, faded and bland Miss Burke only stared at him, unmoved, but he was not willing to concede defeat or change tactics just yet.

Cornelia rose, and Robert did as well.

"I will leave the two of you to talk in private," she said, taking her cup with her as she left the room.

Robert helped himself to the shirred eggs and airy pastries on the table, as well as a slice or two of ham. Cornelia kept an excellent kitchen and he was not about to let some scowling spinster ruin his appetite.

He expected her to start haranguing him while he ate, but she stayed silent. To his dismay he began to feel nervous, wondering what was going through her head. Finally, when the thick atmosphere became more than he could stand, he set down his knife and fork and watched her calmly drinking her coffee.

"I thought you had a tirade you wished to share with me, Miss Burke. Was that all resolved earlier?"

She dabbed at her lips and pushed her plate away, fixing her eyes on him. They were the same shade as a malachite carving in his cabin, a fierce little goddess of Aztec origin who'd been in the possession of a Spanish merchant. The Spanish brig had an encounter with *The Prodigal Son* west of Cuba and Robert kept the smooth stone figurine as a memento of a profitable day.

"I realize you were befuddled by alcohol and your wretched excesses of the previous night, but do you recall anything I said, Captain? Anything at all?"

He sipped his own coffee, trying to think. She'd called him names, dumped a pitcher over his head, refused to fuck him…

"Daughter. You said *my daughter*. A ridiculous statement, since I have no children. I am quite careful in such matters."

"Not careful enough," the woman snapped. "Nanette Lestrange bore your child and before you protest, once you see Mathilde you will see for yourself she is yours."

Robert set down his cup, his fingers gone nerveless.

"Impossible. Nanette would inform me if such a thing happened. I would have made arrangements for a child."

The governess raised her eyebrows. She appeared surprised that he'd assume financial responsibility for any by-blows.

"Nanette said you left her well able to take care of herself," she grudgingly admitted. "She took the money you gave her and opened a dress shop that was popular and profitable in Philipsburg."

"Where is Nanette now?"

Miss Burke swallowed, and when she looked up at him there was a shadow in her eyes.

"Nanette is dead?"

She nodded, and Robert found his appetite gone.

"Nanette Lestrange," he said. "She was good to me when I first arrived in the islands."

He remembered the Frenchwoman who was soft and welcoming, patient with a youngster who did not know nearly as much as he thought he did, but knew a great deal more about life, and pleasing women, and pleasing himself by the time Nanette finished instructing him. A few rich strikes at sea and he'd returned to buy out Nanette's contract with Madame and set her up in her own quarters until they parted on friendly terms.

"An illness carried Nanette off last summer. Now I have a new position awaiting me and I can no longer care for Mathilde," the governess said.

"I would pay you," he said quickly. "You could continue to care for the child."

Miss Burke's look at this statement came close to freezing Robert's guts.

"You have not even met your daughter and already you wish to be rid of her? I am not Mathilde's mother, nor am I her father. She is your responsibility, Captain St. Armand. Loathe as I am to leave her with a pirate wastrel, she is still your daughter."

"I am not a wastrel," Robert muttered, his mind awhirl at the thought of a child in his care. He knew himself well enough that he could think of few people less suited to raise offspring.

She rose from the table and Robert jumped up.

"Where are you going?"

"I am saying farewell to Mathilde, and then I am leaving this establishment," she said, her tight mouth puckering at the idea of spending a minute longer in a bawdy house than absolutely necessary.

"Wait! No, you cannot leave! Who will take care of the child?"

"*Mathilde* is eight years old, Captain, in case you are unable to do the arithmetic. She is quite capable of dressing herself and if you provide her with food, she can feed herself as well. She is an intelligent child and will grow up to be a warm and caring individual, despite her paternity. Nanette was an excellent mother," she finished softly.

Robert stared at the governess, as if he could hold her in place with his gaze alone.

"Let me come with you when you say farewell. It will be better if you are there when I meet her for the first time."

Miss Burke looked at him keenly and Robert fought the urge to step back. He had not backed down from a fight since —well, in a long time—and he was not about to be cowed by a drab, dusty governess.

Nonetheless, he fought hard not to fidget.

"That may be best."

She turned to leave, and Robert followed in her wake, the little food he'd eaten sitting like round shot in his stomach as he accompanied the governess outside to the detached kitchen. The few ladies up and about at this hour chirped out greetings in a variety of languages, French, English, Spanish and Dutch. St. Martin was tiny but a busy crossroads, and the ship traffic kept the women well employed and the house's owner comfortable.

"Perhaps Cornelia knows a family who could take her in."

He'd spoken to himself, but the governess rounded on her heel and glared at him.

"You would leave your daughter's care to a brothel keeper?"

"You do not know me, Miss Burke, and you do not know my associates. If I asked Cornelia to find the child…"

"Mathilde. Your daughter's name is Mathilde, Captain St. Armand."

"If I ask her to find Mathilde a suitable home, she will."

"Wait here," the woman commanded him.

Robert stood with his arms crossed over his chest, his boot tapping nervously at the flagstones. He heard voices within the kitchen, then she emerged, a child holding her hand.

Robert looked down at a miniature version of his mother.

Mathilde's black curls clustered about her head, she had eyes as deep a blue as the ocean surrounding the island, and a firm little chin with a dimple that would someday be a small cleft. Her skin was golden, a legacy from Nanette, but Miss Burke was correct. There was no doubt the child was his offspring.

"Greet your father, Mathilde," the woman murmured.

The child looked up at the governess, then curtsied prettily.

"Good morning, Captain St. Armand. Miss Burke says you are my papa. Is that so? Am I coming to live with you now?" the girl said, looking up at him curiously.

Robert's mouth opened, then closed. He squatted on his heels to bring himself down to her level. A glance at the governess showed he'd finally done something of which she approved.

"We must talk together about that, Mathilde."

He put his fingers out, brushing his knuckles against the edge of her face. The skin was so soft he feared his hand might bruise the child, even with a thistledown touch. He could see his mother's bones beneath the baby roundness of her cheek, the same bones that looked back from his shaving glass each morning.

"For now, is there anything you need? Are you hungry?"

"The cook gave me milk, and a roll, and I played with the new kittens. Would you like to see the kittens, Captain?"

"Perhaps later," he said, clearing his throat around the obstruction there. "And you may call me papa, if you wish."

"Do the other pirates call you Captain St. Armand? I want to be a pirate too!" the child said enthusiastically.

Robert rose to his feet and glared at the governess.

"Someone has been telling tales."

She pursed her mouth and looked off at the bougainvillea rioting around the back door to the main house.

"Nanette liked to entertain Mathilde with adventure tales. I'm sure she exaggerated."

Robert feared rather than exaggerate, Nanette had told the truth—at least as she knew it.

"Will we live aboard your ship, Papa? Do you have lots of guns and swords aboard ship?"

He looked down again at the bloodthirsty moppet. Her enthusiasm was a good sign, as he had no wish to deal with was a crying, whiny infant. He had no wish to deal with a child at all, but she was clearly his butter-stamp.

"I am leaving for England, Mathilde. Do you want to come with me, or would you like me to find you a kind family for you to live with here?"

"I want to live with my papa," she said firmly, sticking her chin out in a fashion that looked familiar to him. "I want to be a pirate."

"We will discuss your aspirations later. Stay here with the kittens while Miss Burke and I talk."

"You will not leave without saying goodbye, will you, Miss Burke?" Mathilde asked in a small voice, clinging now to the governess's skirts, some of her bravado diminished.

"I will come and see you before I leave so we may say goodbye properly."

The girl watched her for a long moment, then nodded. "That is a promise isn't it?"

"Yes, Mathilde, that is a promise. I will not leave without saying goodbye, and your father is here now to care for you. You are not alone."

The child relaxed her shoulders and turned to the kitchen and the attractions of the kittens without a glance back.

"Do you always do as you promise, Miss Burke?" he asked as they started for the house.

Her steps were sedate, steady, a drab gentlewoman to the core. Only the flash of her green eyes when she turned her head and looked at him gave a hint of the steel also at her core.

"To the best of my ability, yes, I always keep my promises, Captain. Children in particular need assurance that adults mean what they say. A child wants a foundation she can build upon, people who are dependable and responsible. You may not see signs of her distress, but like any child, Mathilde was devastated by the loss of her mother. She needs to know she can depend on the remaining adults in her life."

The look she gave him rather pointedly said she had her doubts about the person she gazed on now.

He escorted her back into the breakfast parlor, pausing to ask one of the girls to have fresh coffee and pastries sent. Miss Burke seated herself, her spine never touching the chair as she poured coffee for them both. Robert cradled the deep cup in his hand, inhaling the fragrance. People assumed he stayed at Madame Olifiers when he was in St. Martin for rather obvious reasons, but her coffee was almost as great an inducement as her talented staff.

He fortified himself now with the dark beverage and watched her add cream and sugar to hers, her movements graceful and sure.

"I suppose I should apologize for my remarks to you this morning, ma'am."

"You suppose you should? Is that what passes for an apology amongst pirates, Captain St. Armand?"

"Pirates do not apologize. They let their gun speak for them," he snapped. "See here, Miss Burke—I do not know what tales Nanette Lestrange told you about alleged piratical activity. All you need to know is that I am the captain and owner of *The Prodigal Son*, a merchantman.

He slouched back in his chair and crossed his booted foot over his knee.

"As for how I addressed you, this is, after all, an establishment where the women are employed in tasks other than governessing."

The color flagging Miss Burke's cheekbones showed she had not spent nearly as much time in these types of establishments as Robert had.

"Nanette instructed me to bring Mathilde here. She said Madame Olifiers would keep her safe until you returned, as this was your...domicile...when you are in St. Martin."

"She seems rather poised for a child her age."

"Do you know many youngsters?"

"I have had ship's boys not much older than my daughter, and I was once a child myself, so I do have some experience."

"She is a bright child, Captain. I was not only Nanette's friend, but she hired me to school Mathilde, particularly in English." She toyed with her coffee, then set it down. "She expected some day she would bring Mathilde to you, or at least make you aware of her, and that the girl might have a dowry from her father enabling her to make a good marriage. She is especially gifted in languages and mathematics, though I have no complaints about her grasp of reading or her deportment. It is in traditional female skills where she is less than outstanding, showing no patience for needlework, though she does well on the pianoforte. Nanette hoped Mathilde would be able to take over her shop someday."

"My daughter will not work as a dressmaker."

"Even if she is not your legitimate offspring? You have no obligation to support her, after all."

He frowned at the woman sitting across from him. "Why

are you not dressed with more style, if you were close to Nanette?" It was a rude comment, but he could not imagine Nanette Lestrange letting a sack like that out of her shop.

"I am about to start a new position, and the last thing the mistress of the house wishes is to see the governess dressed more fashionably than she is dressed," Miss Burke said dryly.

Naïve woman. The last thing the mistress of the house wishes is to see is her husband swiving the help in her bedchamber, but this bristly hedgehog posed little threat. Everything about her was colorless. Except for those eyes. One could look into those verdant eyes and see forest glades, emeralds, rivers sparkling in the sunlight. With proper outfitting, a touch of kohl, she could be made passable.

That, however, was not his problem.

"This other position as a governess—I will need someone to care for the child—"

"Mathilde."

"For Mathilde on the voyage. I will pay you double whatever this other family is paying if you accompany us to England."

"Back to England? I cannot return to England," she paled at the thought.

"Why not? I realize the climate there is atrocious, but they tell me there are warm and sunny days. At least one or two a year." He drummed his fingers on the table. "If you take the voyage with us I will pay for return passage to the Indies, if you desire."

Her fingers trembled as she set down her cup. Was she afraid of traveling on the water? That made no sense since she was in the islands and the only way to get about was to get on a boat.

"I cannot return to England," she said with finality. "I told Mrs. Milton I will be in Charlotte Amalie in the beginning of the month. I have already accepted money for my passage."

"You are not tempted by my offer to double your wages?"

"A foolish gesture," she said. While she didn't smile, her mouth lost some of its thin-lipped stiffness. "What if I told you I was earning twenty pounds a year?"

"I'd tell you that you should consider employment here with Madame Olifiers. Better wages, easier hours and you'd be off your feet." He ignored her gasp and swallowed his coffee, thinking fast.

"I will pay you one hundred pounds to work your passage across the Atlantic as Mathilde's governess, and then pay your passage back if you wish."

"That is a fortune for a few weeks of work! However, I gave my word, and will head to St. Thomas."

He looked at her, consideringly.

"Given my changed circumstances I will be returning to my vessel rather than stay here, Is there a way to contact you in town if I have any questions about Mathilde before we leave?"

She bit her lip, as if gauging whether to release the information to him. It left her lips reddened and he found himself looking at her mouth while she spoke. That small gesture sparked…something. It was likely only an aftereffect of the previous night's debauchery.

"I am boarding with the widow Dupre. You can leave a message for me."

"Are the child's belongings there?"

"No, because I expected to leave Mathilde here if you were not in residence. Madame has them. Nanette and I shared lodgings over the shop, and when she died I found a buyer for the property. The remaining money from Nanette's estate is also with Madame. Nanette trusted her, so I had no reason not to."

He waved his hand negligently.

"Keep the money. You earned it taking care of Nanette and Mathilde."

She shook her head.

"I cannot keep what does not belong to me, Captain St. Armand."

"You would make a poor pirate with that attitude."

Unlike Mathilde, she just sniffed at the idea of a pirate's life, then rose from the table and he stood also. "I will say goodbye to Mathilde now."

She hesitated, then straightened her back and clasped her hands at her waist.

"Mathilde is a good girl, Captain. Lively, intelligent, eager to learn new things. You are a fortunate man to have such a daughter, and I hope you will remember that. I will miss her," she added softly.

He'd never considered it, but caring for other people's children might be the closest a governess such as the plain Miss Burke would come to having children of her own.

"Are you certain I cannot convince you to come to England?"

"I am certain. I will not return to England."

"Then this is goodbye, Miss Burke." He stepped closer to her and noticed the pulse fluttering at her neck, just above the ugly gown. It seemed she was not as impervious to him as she wished to appear. He took her hand from where it was clasped at her waist and she released it into his hold with a small intake of breath, a tiny puff of nervousness. Never taking his eyes off of hers, he leaned down and at the last moment turned the slim hand over. She made a movement as if to tug it from his grasp, but it was half-hearted at best. He lowered his lips to her wrist where the pulse raced, and he smiled inwardly before placing a soft kiss there. If the tip of his tongue darted out and licked the sensitive skin it was surely an accident.

She snatched her hand back and cradled it as though it burned, starting at him through eyes gone large as jade teacups.

"Captain St. Armand!"

"*Adieu*, Miss Burke. Meeting you has been memorable."

He gave her a small bow, and she hurried out as Madame Olifiers walked in, carrying a sheaf of papers. She nodded at the younger woman as they passed.

"Cornelia, do you know where I can find a governess?"

"I believe one just came close to running me down, Robert."

"Miss Burke does not want to return to England." He sighed. "And I must take the child and return to the *Prodigal*."

She went to a cabinet, unlocking it and returning with a valise.

"These are the child's belongings and Nanette's funds."

Madame refreshed their coffee, then pushed over the papers.

"I suspected you'd be leaving us. Here is an accounting of your time in the house."

He took the list from her and couldn't help feeling warm with pride. His reputation was secured. And to his relief, there was no mention of a donkey.

"A night with the twins? I do not recall spending the night with Dawn and Dusk."

"There was also opium that night, and a great deal of rum. You do not get your money refunded for not remembering. I am considering reproducing that account in needlework and hanging it on the parlor wall. I doubt I'll ever see the like again."

She looked up at him with eyes gone serious.

"You will not return, will you, Robert?"

He wanted to reassure her nothing would keep him away from the islands, but he knew better. Changed circumstances

—and the discovery of a child was only part of it—meant his time in paradise was coming to a swift end.

"I had a good run, Cornelia. Fair winds and loyal friends, my coffers enriched. I cannot complain. Now that the wars are finally ended it seems prudent to retire from this life and begin anew elsewhere."

"As you say, Robert, it is a different world than when you arrived here. Your belongings will be sent to the ship." She set her cup down and stood. "Fortunately, what I sell is always in demand. If it's not successful pirates coming here, then I can count on the merchants and planters to keep the house busy."

She took his hand in hers and he held it. He remembered when her hair did not have silver in it, her soft eyes unlined at the corners. Like Nanette, she'd brought comfort when he needed it. Sometimes it was only the opportunity to speak with a friend and unburden himself that brought him to Madame Olifiers's establishment, and that was more than enough.

"Goodbye, Cornelia," he leaned down and kissed her on her cheek.

She reached up and patted him on his own cheek.

"Goodbye, Robert. I wish you luck in all your future endeavors. Raising a daughter, you will need it," she finished dryly.

He left her there and walked out to the kitchen. Mathilde sat at the wooden table, peeling vegetables for the cook. There were tear tracks on her round cheeks, but he said nothing, and her face lit up at the sight of him. *It had been eons since anyone had been so thrilled at the sight of Robert St. Armand*, he thought ruefully.

"Look, Captain! This is a sharp knife I am using."

"Good," he said, clasping his hands behind his back. "One's blades should always be sharp and ready for action."

Probably not the typical advice for a father to give his daughter, but it was true.

"Are you ready to go now, Mathilde?"

"Yes, Papa. Cook says I can have one of the kittens? May I take one? I will take good care of it."

"No, no cats," he said, more firmly than was needed because her lower lip began to quiver and he began to panic.

"We cannot have a cat because cats make me sneeze, Mathilde. However, when we are in England we will discuss your having a dog."

The lip stopped quivering and she fixed him with a look he'd seen on the faces of the shrewd ladies who sold baskets in the market.

"Is that a promise, Papa?"

"It is a promise we will discuss it in England."

"I will not forget," she swore.

"Neither will I, child. Shall we shake on it?"

She liked this idea, and stuck her hand out. He gave it a firm shake, then picked up her bag.

"Say goodbye, and thank you to the cook."

"Goodbye, Lucille. Thank you for letting me help."

A grin split the cook's wrinkled face, gleaming from the heat of the day and the cooking fires.

"Farewell, Mam'zelle Mathilde. You be good for your papa now."

Mathilde nodded vigorously.

"If I don't he might make me walk the plank!" she said with enthusiasm.

As they stepped out into the sunlight, Robert looked around, but the governess was gone.

"Did Miss Burke say farewell?"

Some of the light went out of Mathilde's small face.

"Yes, sir. I will miss her very much."

They headed out to the road, the ladies calling farewells

that Robert returned with a wave. It was a pleasant day and Mathilde's mood lightened as she skipped alongside him, chatting as they walked down to the Marigot harbor. Her voice was a charming blend of island lilt and French accented English.

Her dress was neat, but simple in its design. The flowered pink muslin was appropriate for a young girl, but he could see a good two inches of wrist showing at the ends of the sleeves. It appeared his daughter would inherit his height as well as his looks.

For some odd reason he thought of the governess. She was only of average height and when he'd stood close to her she'd had to tilt her head back, which made her resemblance to an annoyed hedgehog even more pronounced, looking up at him from close to the ground.

"'Walk the plank'? Wherever did you get that idea, child?"

"*Maman* told me stories of the buccaneers and the pirates who live in the islands. She said my papa was the fiercest pirate of all!"

He wasn't about to deny such a sterling character reference.

"Fiercest of all, am I? Hmmm…it occurs to me that if you are going to join the crew of my ship we need to give you a pirate name."

She stopped skipping and looked up at him, and one would think he'd just handed her the moon on a platter.

"A pirate name! Oh yes, please!"

They resumed walking and he thought about it, swinging her valise as he walked. She began skipping again.

"Not that there is anything wrong with Mathilde," he assured her. "It is a perfectly lovely name for a young lady. It strikes me though as not being piratical. Women who are pirates have names that are simple, but do not detract from their fierceness. Girls like Anne Bonny and Mary Read."

"There are girl pirates?" If she looked happy before, he feared now she would explode with excitement.

"Yes, indeed there are. I will show you Captain Johnson's book of pirates when we're aboard the *Prodigal Son*. So. What shall your name be?"

"What is your pirate name, Papa?"

"I find being Captain St. Armand is sufficient in the course of a day's work," he said dryly. "For you...what about Tilly?"

She thought about this, her steps slowing as she tried the name out.

"No, Papa, not Tilly. If you give me that name, people might call me 'Silly Tilly' and that would not be a good pirate name."

"An excellent point," he said. They were now in town and people called out greetings to them, some even fit for the ears of an impressionable child. He ignored most of it and concentrated on the task at hand.

"I have it!" he snapped his fingers and looked at her. "Mattie! You will be Mattie! How does sound? Marauding Mattie, scourge of the West Indies!"

She stopped again to try out the name, then grinned up at him. "I like that name! Marauding Mattie! It is fierce!"

"Indeed. It suits you."

She muttered the name to herself as they walked along, clearly pleased with her new *nom de guerre*.

"If I am going to be Marauding Mattie I will need a sword, Papa. And pistols too!"

"What? Was swordplay included in your lessons with Miss Burke?"

Mattie giggled at this question.

"No, Miss Burke with a sword would be silly. She would say it is not ladylike behavior."

"No doubt she would. Hmmm...aboard my ship the crew

has to earn the right to use the weapons, Mattie. And remember, a weapon is a tool and we always take care of our tools and stow and use them properly. Perhaps we can start with a clasp knife and I will see how you care for it and use it before I issue you a brace of pistols."

"A clasp knife? Of my own?" She threw her arms around his legs and hugged him, nearly causing him to stumble and fall in the street. He held his hand over her head and then rested it on her curls. So soft, like thistledown. Usually glib, he found he could say nothing as she looked at him with shining eyes.

"You are the best pirate in the entire world!"

He did not disagree, but took her hand in his as they walked along. There was a tooth missing in her smile. Was he supposed to do something about that? As best he could recall, his own teeth at that age loosened and fell out without any assistance, followed by new teeth. He felt that chill again, the one he'd felt when he was first told he had an unknown child. He knew nothing about caring for a little girl and needed help, desperately.

"Papa, there is the boarding house where I stayed with Miss Burke." The child pointed to a modest dwelling where an older woman dressed in black and wearing a black bonnet sat on the veranda sewing. She waved back at the pair as Mattie called out a cheerful, "*Bonjour*, Madame Dupre!"

The governess was not about, but Robert noted the location in case he needed to speak with her again.

By the time they were at the docks Mattie's steps were lagging but she did not complain, and perked up when he said, "There's our vessel, Mattie, the *Prodigal Son*."

The schooner gleamed, its brightwork shining in the tropical sunlight. The crew was at their tasks, which was only as he expected. He ran a tight ship, a well disciplined and prepared crew making for more effective forays. Too many people who styled themselves pirates had slack standards and sloppy habits, making them the dregs of the sea lanes. Robert St. Armand had a reputation to maintain.

They came aboard and were met by the mate.

"Welcome back, Cap'n," the older man said. He looked down at Mattie holding Robert's hand and craning her neck to try and take in all of the busy activity aboard the vessel. When Mattie looked at Horace Fuller, his eyebrows went up.

"Looks like you have a memento of your time in the islands, Captain."

"Mattie, make your curtsey to Mr. Fuller."

She looked up at her father, puzzled.

"Do pirates curtsey, Papa?"

Fuller coughed into his fist and looked at Mattie.

"Perhaps a handshake will do, miss."

"I am Mathilde St. Armand," she said, dropping the expected curtsey from habit if not circumstances. "But my pirate name is Marauding Mattie, Mr. Fuller."

She glanced up at her papa.

"Can I be Mathilde St. Armand instead of Mathilde Lestrange? I want everyone to know I have a papa."

The mate looked at his captain.

"Nanette Lestrange?"

Robert just shook his head slightly, not wanting to ruin Mattie's good mood.

"Mattie St. Armand here will be joining the crew, Mr. Fuller. She will sleep in my cabin tonight but be thinking about where she can have her own quarters with room for a governess as well."

"Papa, pirates do not have governesses. I will not have one!" She stuck out her lower lip and crossed her arms over her chest, causing the mate to murmur, "The resemblance is uncanny, Captain."

"Mr. Fuller," Robert said sternly. "Instruct the newest

crewmember of the punishment for disobeying the captain's orders!"

Fuller looked at him, and Robert shrugged his shoulders slightly.

"Oh. Well, Mattie, we save the floggings and keelhaulings for the most serious offenses, but you must do as instructed aboard ship or—or you might not get your ration of grog—I mean pudding," he amended at his captain's scowl. "After all, we can't have the crew questioning orders during battle, can we?"

Her forehead scrunched up as she thought on this.

"I understand, Mr. Fuller. And I was rude. I am sorry, Captain Papa."

Mr. Fuller looked out to sea, scratching his nose until he had control of himself.

"Norton!"

A cheerful young sailor with freckles scattered across his face came at the call.

"Mattie here is the newest member of the crew. Take her below to the captain's cabin and see her settled."

"Aye, Mr. Fuller. Come, Mattie."

The child went docilely enough. She'd tried to hide a yawn behind her hand, but Robert suspected she would be napping in his bunk shortly.

"Well now," Fuller said, watching as they went below. "There's a complication we weren't expecting. And where the hell are you going to find a governess?"

"I have a plan, Mr. Fuller."

"A plan, eh? I'm not going to like it, am I?" the mate asked rhetorically, but he followed his captain to the stern to hear his latest scheme.

CHAPTER 3

*L*ydia looked down at the shoe in her hand and realized she'd been scowling at it for a good ten minutes. She sighed and tossed the inoffensive footwear onto the narrow boarding house bed. The room had been cramped with Mathilde's trundle bed. Now it was more spacious, but empty of life.

Was the child missing her as much as she missed Mathilde? Lydia hoped not. Mathilde needed to get on with her life and Lydia needed to get on with hers. She could not take care of the child, not while she was employed to care for other peoples' children. She'd considered asking Captain St. Armand for his direction in England so she could write to Mathilde, but refrained. In England Mathilde would have a different life, and reminders she'd been raised by a former whore turned modiste, and a governess who—

She quashed that dangerous thought. No good would come from dwelling on the past. It was enough that nightmares disturbed her sleep. Time now to focus on Mrs. Milton and the young charges awaiting her in St. Thomas, the Milton daughters. Lydia's references passed scrutiny and she was optimistic it would be a good position, perhaps one she could enjoy for ten years or more since the younger daughter was only seven years old. If she was careful with her money she might even be able to set aside enough to buy herself a tiny cottage when she was too old to work.

The captain's offer jumped into her mind again but she brushed it away. She'd be lying to say she wasn't tempted by the generous offer, but there was too much risk involved. Risks of all sorts. She blushed anew as she recalled his naked form when she first glimpsed him. She'd never considered whether a man's backside was exceptionally attractive or not, but the view of Captain St. Armand from behind shifted her brain's functions into dangerous areas, areas where she had no business spending time.

Especially not when there was packing to finish so she could board the *Clementine*, a New Brunswick brig traveling to St. Thomas. Captain Macdavid instructed her to be ready at dawn and said he'd send a man to escort her and get her gear. His vessel was small and cramped and smelled of salt-fish, but she could not be choosy about her passage. Ships sailed at the whims of the wind and the tide, and she couldn't wait for a better, and more expensive, mode of transport.

Lydia ate a solitary supper off of a tray and washed herself thoroughly before putting on her night rail, knowing from experience fresh water would be a luxury, even on short hops among the islands. Captains filled their holds with goods to be sold, not comforts for passengers and crew, and it was important to arrive in St. Thomas at her best. She sighed, looking at the gray dress hanging for her to wear in the morning. She had two colors in her everyday wardrobe— dark blue and gray. Her one good dress was a faded beige silk, years out of fashion. No wonder St. Armand looked at her with disdain.

There had been a time when, if their paths crossed, he

might have looked at her differently. Now they were just two more of England's children in the islands where the cast-offs of many nations washed ashore like so much flotsam and jetsam. It was the appropriate milieu for him, and for her as well.

She had done what she could for Mathilde in bringing her to her father. Would he be good to her? Would he listen to her prayers at night and find someone to care for her with affection, if not love?

While it was now out of her hands Lydia could not help feel she was abandoning the child to a horrible fate.

CHAPTER 4

"*A*gain, Papa, throw the knife again! Hit him in the eye this time!"

Robert paused, the knife held lightly with his thumb resting on the flat of the blade. "As entertaining as it is to stab someone from a distance, always remember, Mattie… If you throw your knife you no longer have a knife you can use, and it could even be used against you. You must have a backup weapon. What did I tell you is the first rule of knife fights?"

"Kill your enemy from a distance and avoid knife fights."

"Second rule?"

"Bring a pistol."

"That's correct. If your opponent brings a knife, you bring pistols, with your own knife as backup."

"Aye, sir."

"Also," he added in a pedantic fashion, "my victim is painted on wood. A real person would be moving, or yelling, or trying to harm you. If he's just standing there one could simply cosh him over the head with a belaying pin. Of course, *you* would have to stand on a chair to do that."

Mattie put her hand up over her mouth and giggled at the

image. She'd adjusted to life aboard ship in a fashion that made him proud and more convinced than ever she was his child. Maxwell the boatswain, known to all as Sails, cut down clothing to fit her, trousers and a shirt, and she looked right at home as she scampered barefoot across deck. Mr. Fuller gave her chores to do and while she grumbled about scrubbing the decks, she only did so because all the pirates grumbled about it and she wanted to fit in with the crew.

For their part the crew made efforts to keep their more salacious shanties to themselves and sing work-songs suitable for the ears of an eight-year-old, but Robert could tell Mattie's vocabulary was undergoing a sea change as she learned the ways of the *Prodigal Son*. At some point he would have to inform her that "By King Neptune's Damp Balls!" was not a suitable oath for a young lady, no matter how often she heard Conroy say it.

"A sail, Captain!" Conroy yelled now from aloft.

Robert easily threw the knife, hitting the wooden form square in his eye patch. He pulled his knife out and tucked it back in his boot.

"Go below, Mattie, and fetch my spyglass."

"Aye, Captain," the littlest crew member said, running off to do his bidding.

Robert went to the rail and looked out over the turquoise seas. His gut told him the prey he sought was out there wallowing across the water, just waiting for him to swoop down and pluck it like a Christmas goose.

Spyglass in hand, he focused on the ship, then smiled to himself. Fuller took the glass from him and gave a grunt of confirmation when he saw it more closely.

"Mr. Fuller, clear the decks for action."

"Against *that*?"

"Just do it."

"Papa, are you going to blow them out of the water? Will

you put burning fuses in your hair like Blackbeard to scare them?"

Fuller looked down at the tyke, then back at his captain.

"I told you reading Captain Johnson to her was a bad idea."

Robert rested his hand atop his daughter's curls. "If all goes as planned my being a bad influence on the child will be less of an issue. Run up the colors, Norton!"

The banner of Mexico flapped easily in the wind and Mattie looked up at it and frowned.

"That is not a skull-and-crossbones."

"It keeps the lawyers happy, Mattie. We have a letter of marque from the rebels in Mexico that makes us respectable."

"If Britain gets word you're attacking their merchantmen that piece of parchment won't be good for anything but wiping your arse, Captain."

"Language, Mr. Fuller. Don't you have weapons to distribute?"

The crew of the *Prodigal Son* enthusiastically prepared for action, as Robert St. Armand had a deserved reputation for sniffing out good hauls. The men were cheered by the thought of returning to England with more booty, although one or two did remark, out of Mr. Fuller's hearing, that the brig they were bearing down on did not look exactly like a Spanish treasure ship, now did it? In fact, it looked more likely to be carrying salt cod than silver.

When they were within hailing distance Robert took the speaking trumpet from the mate.

"Ahoy, *Clementine*! Heave to and prepare to be boarded!"

Robert watched the frantic activity aboard the *Clementine* with satisfaction. Captain Macdavid was no fool, and the small arms he carried to fend off brigands in port were no match for the *Prodigal's* guns. Like most captains in the

Caribbean, he'd do the prudent thing and not try to outrun the schooner.

"Put out fenders and make fast to that vessel, Mr. Fuller. I'm going aboard. Send Paget aloft with a rifle to cover the deck." He patted Mattie on the head. She was clinging to the gunwale, watching everything with wide eyes.

"I will be back soon, Mattie. Mind Mr. Fuller while I'm gone."

"Do not worry, Papa! I have my knife and if any of them try to come aboard, I'll gut them!"

"Charming."

Robert and his men boarded the vessel with the ease of experienced banditti and soon had the crew up on deck under the watchful eyes and well-armed men of the *Prodigal*. Captain Macdavid offered no resistance, though if he were any angrier steam would be coming from his ears. The Canadian captain knew Robert by reputation if not personal acquaintance.

"I heard you were shipping out for England, Captain St. Armand," Macdavid growled.

"I am enroute, but you have something I need. If I get it, we should be able to part company without bloodshed or difficulty," Robert said cheerfully.

"What is it you want?" Macdavid said, looking about the deck at his shabby little vessel, which looked like a flounder alongside the sleek, sharklike *Prodigal*.

Robert gestured at the trio coming abovedecks.

"Her."

"You! Reprobate! Wastrel! Knave! Scoundrel! Libertine! Villain!" Miss Burke sputtered to a finish having run out of epithets for the moment. The two crewmen escorting her looked at her with new respect, but she needed a few weeks aboard a pirate vessel. That would add salt to her vocabulary.

A slow smile curled his lips. The governess's ugly linen

cap was absent. While her hair was pinned tightly against her head, it shone in the sun, a glorious shade of chestnut with highlights of russet and gold. A few wisps escaped to curl across her forehead, with enough amber depths that it made one itch to unpin the mass and see all the colors gathered there. No wonder the little hedgehog kept it covered! Hair like that would inspire naughty thoughts in her employers and jealousy in their wives.

She was also younger than he'd suspected when he first encountered her, pegging her age at around twenty-five years old. The day just became that much more interesting.

"You missed me, didn't you, Miss Burke?"

"Why have you stopped this ship? What do you want with me?"

Anger looked good on her. The gray sack she wore hurt his eyes though. He'd have to do something about that.

Robert turned back to the hapless captain of the *Clementine.*

"This is what I came for."

"You want her?" Captain Macdavid looked at her and scratched his beard, puzzled. "Well, all right, go ahead and take her."

Miss Burke gasped, and pulling free of the men holding her, marched over to Macdavid. "You don't protest this man kidnapping a passenger from your vessel?" she angrily pointed at St. Armand in case there was any question exactly who she meant.

Macdavid shrugged. "Your passage is already paid, so it's all the same to me. I never guaranteed a safe journey, miss."

She stood nearly toe to toe with the older man, her fists clenched. "Return my money!"

"I never promised that neither!" he protested, and Robert stepped forward and took the governess by the arm before there was bloodshed.

"What a prudent attitude, Captain Macdavid. You are also, no doubt, eager to show your gratitude for my not attacking your ship. How grateful is the captain, Norton?" he asked the sailor who'd just emerged from the hold.

"Macdavid wants to show his gratitude in the form of Cuban cigars and rum, Cap'n."

"What? Now see here, taking the woman is one thing, but you can't take my cargo too!"

"Why would you make such a foolish claim that I am *taking* your cargo? Rather, say in earshot of all these witnesses that you're *giving* me those gifts. Then I will refrain from accidentally sinking your pestilent scow. After all, I have what I came for, so it's all the same to me."

Robert grinned broadly at the captain, but apparently it wasn't the friendliest smile in his repertoire, for Macdavid gulped and nodded jerkily.

"Of course, Captain St. Armand! It would be my pleasure to give you these gifts!"

"Excellent!" Robert turned back to his crewmen.

"Go with Norton and fetch our gifts from Captain Macdavid, then meet me aboard the *Prodigal*. Fetch Miss Burke's trunks and gear as well."

She just stood there, looking down at the deck, pale and numb from her change in status from paying passenger to pirate booty. Ah well, he had no doubt she'd perk up when she saw Mattie.

"Do not despair, ma'am. I can offer you far better accommodations aboard my vessel than what you have on this hulk," he said. At least when she looked at him she was angry again, and not wan and frightened as she'd looked moments ago. Angry was better.

"If you make me travel to England, I will tell the authorities when we arrive."

"You don't want to do that. People who try to inform on

me have tragic and fatal accidents. You do not wish to have a tragic and fatal accident, do you, Miss Burke?"

"Are you *threatening* me?"

"I never threaten. Instead, I share information which leads people to make prudent and healthy decisions, not tragic and fatal ones."

He smiled at her again, the "dashing pirate rogue" smile that prompted an amazing roundness in the heels of the women he used it on. Miss Burke appeared impervious and when she drew close to him he saw her eyes were not solid green, but emerald flecked with warm tones of citrine. They nearly distracted him from her next statement.

"I cannot return to England."

"Cannot or will not?"

She did not speak, but glared at him.

"Why can you not return to England? My heavens, did you murder someone?"

"I am contemplating murder at this moment, Captain St. Armand," she said through her teeth. "Leave me alone to continue to St. Thomas!"

"That *I* cannot do."

She gasped as he hoisted her in his arms.

"I suggest you cease struggling and put your arms around my neck, Miss Burke, unless you fancy crashing to the deck or falling into the ocean."

She did as he instructed and he grabbed the line tossed to him by one of his men, then easily swung over to his ship. Now there was a move calibrated to impress starched-up spinsters! Whether from fear or simply overcome with the thrill of being in his arms—he had to assume the latter was the case—she clung to him for dear life. Robert's senses registered that the bundle of womanhood he carried smelled clean, like soap, not like the heavily scented whores and ladies he was used to having in his arms.

Clean was pleasant. Showed she wouldn't instill slovenly habits in his daughter. He set Miss Burke on her feet where she wobbled before putting her hand up to her scalp. Some of her pins had come loose and so had her hair, now flying about in the breeze.

Robert eased the pins into his coat pocket.

"Avast, ye scurvy dog! Strike your colors or I'll...I'll... What will I do, Mr. Turnbull?"

"Say, 'I'll scupper your ship and use your guts for garters, ye lily-livered—oh. Captain, sir!" Turnbull knuckled his forehead and said, "Um, I have to be off now, Mattie," before scurrying below.

Mattie looked up then and spotted the governess, her face lighting up. She ran over and Lydia Burke squatted down on the deck to open her arms to Mattie's embrace.

"Miss Burke! Miss Burke! I am so happy to see you again!"

"I am happy to see you too, Mathilde. I missed you," she said fiercely, hugging the child to her chest. Mattie drew back her head and looked at her.

"I am not Mathilde anymore, Miss Burke. Now I'm Marauding Mattie, the terror of the West Indies!"

"Are you indeed, miss?"

She stood, still holding Mathilde. While her words were icy, if she were a dragon she'd be breathing flame to protect the child. Rather than make Robert angry, he found it promising she would champion her welfare. Mathilde needed someone to watch her back because while there were few things in the world he was certain of, he knew pirates did not die of old age in bed. At least, not their own beds.

"Mathilde, you know I said you needed a governess."

"Papa did say that, miss. He said my governess would keelhaul me if I disobeyed her commands."

"Wha—no, I did not say that!" He glanced around the

deck for rescue. "Mr. Fuller! Is the cabin ready for Miss Burke?"

"Aye, Captain, and we're almost done here."

"Very good. Prepare to get under way. Miss Burke, may I escort you to the cabin you'll be sharing with Mattie?"

She set Mattie back on her feet and brushed down her garment before clasping her hands at her waist and taking a deep breath.

"I see I will accomplish nothing by discussing my"—she looked down at the child who was watching her—"my situation, but we will talk this evening."

"I am certain any evening spent in your company can be nothing but delightful, Miss Burke."

Robert kept his smile fixed as he went below. She thought she had the weather gage, but the day was not yet over. He did need a governess, but he was not about to stand down on his own ship. She was a servant, kidnapped to care for Mathilde. He was the captain and enjoyed all the privileges of that position. He flung open the door to Fuller's cabin, then stopped still.

"My goodness," Miss Burke said as she peered around his back. "This was not what I expected."

Someone had raided the captain's cabin while he was out, carrying off the booty. There were two bunks, narrow, but awash in embroidered and jewel-toned silk pillows of crimson, amber, sapphire, turquoise and emerald. A fine rug on the deck promised comfort to bare feet padding about during the night. He knew from experience how cozy, deep and luxurious the silken pile of that rug felt, a gift from a grateful Turkish pasha.

The raiders had not carried off his deep mattress or the mirror fastened to the wall, or the rose satin coverlet, but it was a near thing. They had taken the ivory-inlaid chest, the brass lantern from Morocco, his chest of drawers set in silver, and for all he knew, his chamber pot with the King of Spain's portrait on the bottom, a special gift from the Mexican rebels.

The cabin was cramped for two people, even if one was a little girl, but it looked much more inviting than when Mr. Fuller occupied it. Miss Burke walked into it in a daze, looked around, and then turned and did the strangest thing. She smiled at him.

Robert blinked. He knew his smiles were devastating, but that was to be expected, given his charm, amazing good looks, fashion sense, *savoir faire,* and his practice sessions before his looking glass, but to find such loveliness behind her drab exterior…

"Most unexpected indeed," he murmured.

"You told me the accommodations aboard your vessel would be finer, but really, Captain St. Armand, I never would have imagined this!"

She reached onto the bunk and picked up—dammit, those scrubs had taken his sable pillow!—his favorite pillow and caressed it with her slim hand. A ripple of pleasure crossed her face, quickly suppressed. It appeared the governess had a touch of the sensualist within her and he filed the information away in his mind, one more weapon he might use to his advantage.

He crossed his arms over his chest, one of his favorite poses.

"This is satisfactory then? You will be sharing the cabin with Mattie."

"Mattie the Marauder?" she asked dryly. "Yes, I think the littlest pirate and I can be quite comfortable here."

She looked about to say something else, but he forestalled her with a raised hand.

"I recognize that look. Before you ring a peal over my head, I'll leave and spare myself. I really do not care to hear it. The men will bring you your gear. Get what you need for now, and the rest will be put in the hold to give you more room here. Supper is at six bells and you and Mattie will join me, Miss Burke."

"Is that an order?"

"When I say you *will* do something, you may take it as an order. It is safer that way."

He favored her with another look, the one that sent his men scurrying for the relative safety of the rigging, but she just sniffed in a governessy fashion and said, "Send Mattie to me, Captain, and we will organize our cabin and discuss our schedule."

"Until later then, ma'am."

Robert returned to his own cabin, now considerably barer than before. He examined himself in the looking glass, but he did not look any different to his own eyes. Why then was Miss Burke impervious to his charm? It was a mystery.

It was not important, he told himself firmly. She was here to take care of Mattie, and the last thing he needed was a lovesick governess swooning over his good looks when she should be teaching. He would take her to England, pay her, buy her passage back to the Indies if she desired, and he and Mattie would move on with their lives.

He pulled out the hairpins he'd stolen from the lady's hair and put them in a carved box inside his sea chest.

WHEN MATTIE ENTERED the cabin she looked around and said, "All of Papa's nice things are here now."

Lydia stopped from where she was folding her dress. "These items belong to your father?"

Mattie nodded, running her finger over the silver hairbrush. "I slept in Papa's cabin when he brought me aboard.

39

He has a very large bed, but he hung a hammock for himself and I slept in the bed with all these pillows."

Lydia could imagine the pirate captain in a very large bed surrounded by all the pillows, his bronzed body gleaming against the satin. She'd seen men in the islands whose skin was roughened by weather and time, but Captain St. Armand wore his color as if a loving sun had kissed him all over, laving a gold sheen across the expanse of his muscles and sinews. He was covered now, but the glimpse she'd had of him on St. Martin was enough to allow her imagination free rein, and she knew, to her own regret, that her imagination was quite well developed.

"Which bunk should I take, Miss Burke?"

Lydia shook herself and looked down at her charge. Mathilde—or Mattie as she preferred—was once again her responsibility and she would not shirk from that responsibility, even if it came at gunpoint, more or less.

"I will take the bunk closer to the door, Mattie. Are you enjoying your life aboard this boat?"

Mattie giggled. "The *Prodigal Son* is not a boat, Miss Burke! It is the finest schooner and the most feared pirate ship in the Caribbean!"

"That is as may be, but my responsibility is to you, not to this ship. I am not a pirate, I am your governess."

"Wouldn't you rather be a pirate?"

"Pirates—" Lydia was about to say pirates usually ended their careers on a hangman's rope, but that might distress the child, who'd already lost a mother.

Mattie was looking down at her bare toe, scuffing across the deck. "I did not want a governess, Miss Burke. Oh, I like you ever so much, but I want to be a member of the *Prodigal's* crew and I cannot do that if I have to do needlework and practice my handwriting."

"It seems to me, Mattie, those would be useful skills

aboard ship. For example, who made those clothes you are wearing? You did not sew them yourself, did you?"

Mattie giggled again. "No, I cannot sew this well, ma'am. You know that. Sails made them for me. He is also making me a jacket of pink satin with quilting that will keep me warm on the trip!"

"Where would a pirate get pink satin?"

"Papa says a French sloop gave it to them when they stopped to exchange greetings."

Lydia kept her thoughts on the provenance of French satin to herself and continued with her teaching. After all, one did not spend one's life in the classroom, so learning occurred in the world where one would be living every day.

She'd learned life's most important lessons outside of the classroom and her goal now was to prepare Mattie for her own life. She wondered what that life in England would be, and why Captain St. Armand was so committed to going there. One would think life in the islands would be more suited to his sybaritic tastes.

"There is my point exactly then. Mr. Sails has skills he put to use for you, skills vital to this vessel. I always saw men mending sails and their clothing on the ships where I was a passenger."

"I help too. I can scrub the deck and peel potatoes and I am learning how to tie proper knots."

"All of those are excellent skills, Mattie. Think of how much more you would have to offer if you became good with a needle, and if your handwriting was clear enough that you could make entries in the log and write letters."

"Letters ordering people to surrender to the *Prodigal*?"

"I was thinking more of letters about your life aboard ship. Do you not think it would be an interesting story to tell?"

"It will be interesting if there are guns and swordplay and

booty. You should read Captain Johnson's book! It even has lady pirates!"

Lydia added "appropriate reading material" to her list of items to discuss with Captain St. Armand. In fact, she should be making a list of issues to raise with the pirate. That way she was less inclined to be distracted by strong arms and cleft chin. She continued to unpack her belongings as the youngster arranged her dolls on her bunk. A new doll with a china head was part of the crew and Mattie addressed them in a low voice as she played.

"And you must always obey the captain's orders or else she'll maroon you!"

"Perhaps we can have a tea party with your friends there?" Lydia said a touch frantically. "If you cooperate and have your lessons with me each morning, and do your chores, we will have a tea party later in the voyage."

"Pirates don't have tea parties, Miss Burke, that would be silly."

"I believe pirates will come to a tea party if we invite them."

The girl looked at her for a long moment, assessing her words. Her expression was so similar to what she'd seen on Captain St. Armand's face she was struck anew by the resemblance. To his credit, he had not denied Mattie was his own daughter, but Lydia could not help but wonder what the captain would have done had the child not looked like a tiny version of her father.

"I would like that, ma'am."

"Then we have a bargain, Mattie. No more talk about not doing your lessons with your governess, and we will plan a tea party. With pirates."

"We have to invite my papa too."

In her experience, men avoided spending time with their children, especially daughters. She expected now that

Captain St. Armand had kidnapped himself a governess, he would mostly ignore his small responsibility.

So much had occurred in the space of a few hours that she had not had time to analyze her own situation. Every league they traveled across the Atlantic brought her closer to England, and dismay at the prospect caused her breath to catch. There was nothing to be done for it now, but if she were careful she might be able to escape again. This time she would head to Canada or the United States. If her captor came through with her promised funds she could assume a new name, find herself a new life where no one knew her.

Lydia ran her hand over a pillow, a shiver of sensation running down her spine at the lush fur beneath her fingers. The ship was aptly named *The Prodigal Son*, for the captain had been lavish outfitting it with luxuries for his pleasure. She could well imagine how such an object might enter into lustful encounters inside the pirate's cabin. She suspected he would be a selfish lover, but he did have an eye for creating an inviting environment. That put him ahead of most of his gender who were happy to shove a woman up against a table and toss her skirts over her head.

That last thought brought back to mind those moments in the captain's arms, his hard body plastered against hers as she held on for dear life while he effortlessly swung them aboard his ship. He'd smelled of limes and salt and male, a change from being subjected to the unwashed captain and crew of the *Clementine*. There was no doubt the man was an accomplished libertine who thought he knew his way around women. This voyage promised danger of many levels, not the least of which being the caught between the handsome blue-eyed devil and the deep blue sea.

Her shoulders relaxed as she looked at Mathilde ordering her toys about, the bunk acting now as a ship on the ocean for the hearty crew of rag animals and doll babies. There was no denying that seeing Mathilde again, holding her in a warm embrace, feeling her soft childish curls against her cheek was indescribably wonderful.

"I have teaching materials in the larger trunk, Mattie. Would you help me organize them so we can prepare your lessons?"

Mattie gave her crew a final admonishment to behave and joined Lydia in unpacking slates and chalk and books, pencils and an ink pot and some pens, and with a sigh pulled out the sewing kit for her needlework lessons.

"Do not despair, Matttie. I know needlework is not your favorite, but wouldn't you like to make something for your father? You could embroider a handkerchief for him with his initials?"

"Captain Papa also likes to wear a kerchief around his neck when working on deck, Miss Burke. Can I embroider a new one for him?"

"A kerchief for your father is an excellent idea. We will begin work on it this afternoon," Lydia said, buoyed by the resumption of instructing her favorite pupil.

CHAPTER 5

*R*obert examined his now sadly bare cabin and sighed. He watched Paget's efforts to lay out the service properly and took some small comfort in being able to still set a fine table. The sailor had aspirations to be in service in a grand house when he left the sea and Mr. Fuller assisted him, instructing him on what would be required of him if he became a footman.

"That fork goes on the other side, Paget."

"Aye, Mr. Fuller."

Promptly at six bells there was a knock at the cabin door and Robert welcomed in Mattie, her face freshly scrubbed and her hair combed, and Miss Burke, looking her usual drab self. She was also wearing a noxious cap atop her head. He was going to have to do something about that. It was ugly enough aboard this ship now that his cabin was ransacked, and he did not intend to put up with more ugliness than was absolutely necessary. He'd picked out the sapphire satin shirt he was wearing because he knew it enhanced his eyes and had a devastating effect on susceptible women. He said nothing about her attire, but bowed over her hand.

"So pleased you could join us this evening, Miss Burke."

Then he took his daughter's hand, inspected the nails with a critical "Hmmmm..." that made her giggle, and kissed her hand as well.

"So pleased you could join us this evening, Marauding Mattie."

She giggled again and he glanced to the side to see the governess smiling down indulgently. Her starchiness did not carry over into her interactions with the child as it did with the child's father, and he was glad of it. He knew too well how easily a youngster could be warped by disapproving adults, battered by beatings and canings, made to feel worthless and not fit for civilized company. Those youngsters oftentimes ended their short lives on a rope, or if they were lucky, grew up to be pirates.

He seated the ladies and Fuller joined them, with Paget waiting on the table assisted by Conroy. Miss Burke's eyes widened when she saw the silver dinner service and fine china.

"Not what you expected, Miss Burke?"

"It is certainly a change from what I experienced aboard the *Clementine* and on my voyage out to the islands, Captain St. Armand," she confessed. "You live quite well aboard your vessel."

Robert shrugged. "It is my home, and naturally I wish my home to be as comfortable as possible. The fact that we're at sea makes it even more important to me to enhance my small spaces with items that stimulate the senses and enhance each moment."

Her eyes glanced over at his bunk, the rose satin coverlet neatly tucked in, and a brush of matching color filled her cheeks. He'd spoken blandly enough, but he could tell his statement regarding "stimulating the senses" took root in her imagination.

For a brief moment he thought about the propriety of seducing his daughter's governess. It would be so very wrong. Then he took that niggling remnant of conscience and did with it what he'd done so often over the years— metaphorically shoved it over the rail to fall deep into the ocean and not bother him again.

"Some wine, Miss Burke?"

She hesitated, then nodded. "A small amount."

He poured for her while Mattie chatted with Fuller about what her dolls had been up to that afternoon, and how Miss Burke had unpacked all sorts of interesting items for her shipboard schoolroom. Fuller listened gravely, nodding when Mattie reminded him he'd promised to show her how to hone her knife for the best edge.

Miss Burke's lips tightened as she caught the trailing edge of that conversation, then she looked at Robert. "I would like to set a schedule for Mathilde's lessons, Captain. What duties does she have aboard ship? I don't want to interfere with your routine. I understand if Mathilde is part of your crew she has obligations to the vessel as well as to her lessons with me."

Mattie straightened up, her small shoulders back, spine straight. "You see, Papa? Miss Burke knows the importance of everyone aboard ship pitching in. I told you she was a fine governess."

"So you did, Mattie. Let us work out our schedule this way… The mornings you will spend in your lessons with Miss Burke. After luncheon there will be a siesta period, then in the late afternoon we will have weapons. After that you will do whatever chores Mr. Fuller has assigned for you that day—in the galley or picking oakum or whatever he feels is needed—and after supper your evenings will be your own until your bedtime."

"Will you still read to me at bedtime now that Miss Burke is here?"

"Do you want me to read to you?"

She nodded vigorously.

"I like it when you read to me, Papa. You do pirate voices very well!"

The governess's eyebrows hovered upward at the idea of the pirate reading bedtime stories to his child, but she gave a nod of her own.

"It sounds like an excellent schedule. While I cannot fully approve of weapons practice for a young lady, I am a proponent of regular and vigorous exercise for children."

"And what about yourself, Miss Burke. Are you a proponent of regular and vigorous exercise for adults?"

"I am a proponent of *appropriate* exercise for adults as well, Captain. Of course, one is limited in the small space of a vessel. There are only so many times you can stroll around the deck without becoming dizzy from going in circles," she finished with a smile.

He was about to say something dazzlingly witty when he paused, thrown off stride by what that smile did to the governess's face. She had a charming gap in front, *"les dents du bonheur."* Her "teeth of happiness" changed her as no cosmetic or fashionable attire could, rendering her approachable and attractive. She saw some of what he was thinking in his face because the smile disappeared as quickly as a flower chopped from its stem.

"I will do my best to ensure you get all the regular and vigorous exercise you could possibly desire," he finished.

He really was going to have to work on his "dashing rogue" smile because she seemed singularly unaffected.

They dined on swordfish fritters and peas, a pie of crab-meat, and, for Mattie, fresh goat's milk from the four-legged crewmembers. She made a face but dutifully drank it when

Mr. Fuller solemnly assured her the most bloodthirsty of the buccaneers all drank their milk as lads. The meal ended with cheeses from St. Martin and the last of the fresh bananas.

In response to Miss Burke's question, Robert confirmed there were ample oranges and limes aboard to stave off illness.

"If we make the passage in good time that fruit will be part of what we sell in England. Fresh fruit from the tropics can bring a good return for a businessman."

Miss Burke paused from where she poked at her cheese. "I remember my grandfather's orangery. The fruit from those trees always seemed like little bubbles of sunshine in the winter."

She appeared about to say more, then stopped abruptly. It was too late, for Robert's mind was already speculating on how a threadbare governess had a grandsire who could afford to maintain an orangery.

She was silent for the rest of the meal, only responding to Mattie's queries about lessons and what was planned for the morrow. Robert studied the puzzling woman. Well spoken and well mannered, as one would expect from an English governess. Was she some gentleman's daughter fallen on hard times? There were few options for gentlewomen who did not marry, and becoming a governess was the most respectable of those options. Following Nanette's path did not seem like an activity suited to the lady, though with that stern demeanor he still felt she could offer specialized service in certain establishments.

Unwrapping the mysterious package that was Miss Lydia Burke promised diversion on what could otherwise be a tedious Atlantic crossing.

As the ladies rose so Mattie could be put to bed, Robert said, "Do not forget, Miss Burke, you wished to talk with me this evening. I will await you in my cabin."

Her back pokered up, but before she could respond Mattie chimed in. "Papa, you said you would read to me at bedtime. That was a promise."

"So it was, child. You get under your covers and I will be in shortly."

After the females left, the talk revolved around ship's business until Robert thought enough time had passed. He scanned the few books in his cabin. None of them were really suitable for a child—especially the illustrated ones—but he could edit while he read.

He entered the ladies' cabin without knocking, but regretfully did not catch Miss Burke disrobing. She was still fully clothed, sitting on her bunk.

"Do you wish me to wait above while you read to Mattie?"

"Oh, stay and listen with us, Miss Burke!"

"Yes, do stay, Miss Burke."

Robert sat on Mattie's bunk next to her. She was propped up against the bulkhead, her hands around her knees. He angled the lantern for more light, then cleared his throat.

"I believe we left off with the story of the pirate Captain Davis, Mattie. Ah, here we are... 'Early in the morning, the man at the mast-head espied a sail. It must be observed, they keep a good lookout, for, according to their articles, he who first espies a sail, if she proves a prize, is entitled to the best pair of pistols on board, over and above his dividend...'"

"Really, Papa?" Mattie's grew wide. "If I'm the lookout and spot a prize I will get a brace of pistols? Your best ones?"

There was some rather obvious throat clearing from the bunk across the cabin, but he ignored it.

"Either Mr. Fuller or I decide who shall be the lookout, Mattie. When the time comes for you to take on that task I will expect you to serve as zealously and capably as any other crewmember aboard the *Prodigal Son*. That will *not* happen until you are ready for the responsibility. Is that clear?"

"Aye, Captain," she said, but that bottom lip jutted out. He continued reading of the exploits of Captain Davis, then closed *A General History of the Robberies & Murders of the Most Notorious Pirates*. More tales of mayhem would wait for another evening.

"You have a busy day tomorrow, so I'll say goodnight."

"Tuck me in, Papa?"

"Always, Marauding Mattie."

She scooted down and he tucked the covers around her, then she raised her arms for a kiss goodnight, which he gave her on each cheek.

When he straightened, the governess was watching him with an unreadable expression, and Robert felt warmth in his own cheeks. He could kiss whomever he chose from his crew. He was the captain, after all.

Miss Burke leaned over to kiss Mattie on the forehead, reminding him of his other reason for stepping in here this evening.

"When you are finished, Miss Burke, report to my cabin."

LYDIA BRUSHED moist palms down the skirts of her gray gown. Taking a deep breath, she raised her hand, but before she could knock a voice said, "Stop dithering and come in, Miss Burke."

She stepped over the threshold of the cabin and when he said, "Close the door," she clasped her hands before her.

"If it is all the same to you, I would leave the door open, Captain St. Armand."

"It is not all the same to me. Close the door."

His back was to her as he returned his book to the railed

shelf above his compact desk. His pantaloons must have been carefully tailored to give him such a close fit, the lines of his long thighs and the muscles they displayed all too evident.

"If you are done admiring my backside, let's chat," he said, turning with a grin.

"I am not—you cannot speak to me that way!"

"I just spoke to you that way. It was not difficult at all. Take a seat, Miss Burke."

Lydia sat at the table where they'd dined, and did her best to keep her face expressionless. The captain found cat-and-mouse games entertaining, did he? He was not the first charming rogue who'd crossed her path, and if she couldn't outfight him, she was confident she could outthink him.

She relaxed, clasping her hands in her lap again, but not from nerves this time. He took his time pouring them each a glass of wine in delicate goblets that looked out of place aboard a ship at sea. The wine caught ruby glints in the soft lamplight, the same light caressing his face and form, making the satin that strained across his shoulders gleam.

He seated himself across from her and took a sip of his own wine.

"Now that is a vintage worth stealing. Confess, Miss Burke, you are pleased to be aboard a vessel where you have fewer concerns the food will kill you."

"I did not come here to discuss wine, Captain St. Armand. I am here to discuss Mathilde's lessons, and then I wish to seek my bed."

As soon as the words left her mouth she knew they'd been a mistake. One should never say "bed" in this man's proximity. It raised too many images and issues. She plowed on.

"Mathilde has a good head for numbers and is ready to learn her multiplication, Captain. Her penmanship needs improvement, and it is not too early for her to learn some history and geography, especially since she will be moving to

England. I teach by incorporating all aspects of study as a whole, using natural philosophy, mathematics, geography, history and literature together around themes, such as the ocean and travel. Since we are at sea, and since you are already sharing some of your nautical wisdom with Mattie, it only makes sense to continue along those lines. However," she added dryly, "I would prefer you keep lessons of blood-shed and mayhem to a minimum."

"Do you believe in beating children who do not do their lessons?"

For a moment Lydia was stunned silent. "I would never strike a child for not studying! If you think that is an effective teaching method, you have kidnapped the wrong governess!"

She stood to leave, but he only nodded, his face serious for a change.

"Sit down, Miss Burke. As it happens, I agree with you. I said, sit down. Please."

He stroked his chin as he thought, those long fingers reminding her of the sensual furnishings she now enjoyed in her cabin, furs and silks once caressed by his hands.

"That sounds like a good course of study for the child. It is hard for me to remember my own lessons from when I was her age, but I trust your judgment. I do want Mattie to learn mathematics and a range of other subjects. Too often girls' education is neglected, but someday Mattie will receive funds from me and she should know how to do more than embroider cushions."

"That is a liberal attitude—" she paused.

"For a pirate?"

"I was going to say, 'for a father.' Many men are solely concerned with their daughters making a good marriage, so they wish governesses to focus only on the womanly arts and not fill their heads with what they consider 'useless book-learning.' Mattie should learn those arts as well, but rich or poor she'll need to know how to manage a household, and that takes a variety of skills."

"Did your father want you to only learn the womanly arts, Miss Burke?"

She sipped her wine, then looked at him. "My background is not up for discussion here."

"If I were hiring you, I would need to know your background and get letters of reference as well."

"If you were hiring me, I would share that information with you. You kidnapped me, Captain St. Armand."

She rose, and he stretched his long legs out before him.

"Miss Burke, you have an annoying habit of jumping up and trying to leave when I am talking to you. I do not wish to rise every time you do."

"Never fear, sir, the last thing I look for in a pirate is gracious manners."

"Sit."

It was his tone rather than his words that had her obeying like a well-trained spaniel.

"Much better. You have the run of the ship, but do your best to stay out of the way of the men as they work at their tasks. Is there anything else you need for this voyage that you did not bring with you?"

"No, I have all my supplies for teaching Mattie."

"You and Mattie will take your meals with me, unless I say otherwise. I am up with the morning watch, so you may miss me at breakfast."

Her face must have reflected her thoughts because he added, "No, I do not sleep until noon, at least not when I am aboard my vessel. If you find I've overslept, feel free to come into my cabin and wake me. Do not send Mattie. I sleep in the nude. You blush easily, Miss Burke."

"I know that," she snapped, and this time when she stood,

she was determined to leave. He'd have to physically restrain her to keep her here a moment longer. The idea of being restrained by this pirate only made her face heat up more, but he took pity and rose himself to open the cabin door.

This had the unfortunate effect of bringing them too close together in the confines of his cabin, inches apart as he reached around her to open the door, brushing against her in the process. Lydia looked straight ahead, but out of the corner of her eye she saw him distracted by his own mirror as he paused to look at himself. She scurried away to her cabin, but couldn't resist one final glance back over her own shoulder. A thick lock of hair cascaded down over her ear, slipping from beneath her cap, and she made a sound of annoyance.

The pirate stood in his doorway, watching her. He gave her a short nod and a smile before closing his own door again.

Lydia reached up to tuck her wayward hair back under, and realized more hairpins had gone missing while she was in the pirate's cabin. He'd pretended to be distracted by his own pretty face to rob her again. She was about to pound on his door and demand he return what he'd stolen, but stopped, reminding herself to outthink, not outfight him.

Fortunately, in a contest of wits, she was better armed than the pirate.

CHAPTER 6

"Try again, Mattie. You had it almost perfect this time."

"This is not fun, Miss Burke! Pirates do not need to learn multiplication tables!"

Lydia fixed her charge with a stern eye and put her finger in the text to mark her place. The author of *The Young Ladies' New Guide to Arithmetic* clearly had been focusing on teaching household account skills rather than division of pirate booty, but numbers were numbers and Lydia never gave up on a recalcitrant pupil.

"Mathilde, we had an agreement. You were not to argue about lessons. Back to your recitation, miss."

Mattie sighed as if her world conspired against her, but began reciting. "Two times two is four, two times three is six, two times four is eight…"

When she recited all the way through to the twelves without a mistake Lydia said, "Well done. Let us stretch our legs, and I will show you interesting tricks about multiplication."

Mattie looked skeptical at the offered treat, but jumped

up. Lydia knew this child was so full of energy she would not tolerate sitting still for long. When Captain St. Armand arrived in England, she hoped he would find the right governess for the child, one who would not seek to suppress Mathilde's enthusiasm and energy.

The thought of the child's future brought a flutter of anxiety as she contemplated her own future, but she did her best to push it aside. There was nothing for it now, and while she could plan and scheme, nothing would happen until they reached England. Then her task would be to get back out of the country as quickly and quietly as possible, and she could only hope St. Armand would not stand in her way.

Lydia stretched her own limbs, deeply inhaling the salt air. It was such a lovely day out on the ocean one simply could not stay below in the cramped and dank cabin, not when there was sunshine and fresh air and the temperature left tropical memories to be cherished on colder, darker days ahead. Mattie chatted with Paget, who paused in his task to show the child how to tie a complicated knot. Lydia admitted to herself that these rough men were not what she envisioned when she thought about pirates. Despite their coarse language and unschooled manners, they treated Lydia with respect and seemed genuinely fond of the girl who had the run of the ship.

Glancing now back to the stern where Captain St. Armand talked with Mr. Fuller, she suspected discipline was more important than she would have suspected, and that for all his fashionable airs, the captain ran a tight ship. The men here seemed better fed and less downcast than the sailors aboard the *Clementine*.

Today the fashionable captain was dressed for working, his raven locks secured beneath a red bandana to keep them from getting in his face. He'd stripped down as the day warmed, leaving off the snowy white linen shirt and leather vest he'd worn at breakfast. He paused from speaking to Fuller and looked at her, his azure gaze daring her to say something so he could respond in a way that would make her uncomfortable.

Lydia turned her back on the distracting captain and shook out her skirts, taking advantage of the break in routine to move about the deck, stepping carefully around the gear where the men worked. Mattie was still talking with Paget, who described the schooner's rigging to the bright-eyed youngster. Mattie nodded, the straw hat shading her head bobbing up and down as she gestured at the collection of ropes and cloth that appeared so arcane to Lydia, but whose configuration made sense to the sailors.

Lydia put her hand atop her own straw bonnet, plain but for the faded blue ribbons securing it beneath her chin. The edges of her cap ruffled about her face in the stiff breeze and as she brushed them back she frowned. When she went to don her cap this morning there were only two in her luggage. She knew there were three when she started her journey, and could not imagine what happened to the third cap. She wasn't careless with her wardrobe, as she had to scrimp and save her wages to buy or make what she had, and she hoped the missing cap would turn up at a later date.

Thinking of her wages reminded her there were still lessons to be taught this morning, and she called her charge back.

"Miss Burke, do you know what they call the boy who climbs aloft to fix the fouled lines? A rigging monkey! I could do that! I just need to practice climbing aloft and then I can be a rigging monkey and I'll spot ships and win a brace of pistols!"

"There will be no climbing until your pa—your captain or Mr. Fuller allows it, young lady. As you know, a good crewmember follows orders, and your orders this morning are to study your multiplication. Now, fetch your slate and I will show you those tricks with numbers I mentioned."

Mattie sat crosslegged next to her in the shade provided by an awning thoughtfully rigged by Mr. Fuller. Lydia sat on an overturned box, with a pillow atop it from the collection on their bunks, more comfortable than if she'd been forced to sit on the deck with her legs akimbo and her skirts hiked up. She could only imagine what kind of comments from the captain that might generate!

"You know all your twos are even numbers when multiplied. There are more ways to know whether you're multiplying correctly. Recite your fives for me, please."

Mattie did, then looked at her governess.

"Now, what do those numbers have in common?"

"All of them end in five, or zero."

"That is one way you know you're multiplying your fives correctly—the answer, or product, must end in five or zero. Now, pass me your slate and I will show you another trick."

Lydia took the slate and scratched on it.

"What do you notice about the product of these numbers, Mattie?"

Mattie studied the three examples. "All of them have factors of nine?"

"Yes, but they have something else in common. Look again."

Mattie stared at the numbers, her brows pulled down in a frown. "I think—I see! When you add the numbers in the product it's nine! Fifty-four is nine times six, but five and four is nine! Eighteen is nine times two, but eight and one is nine!"

"Bugger the bishop, she's right!"

Lydia twisted her head around. Turnbull and Nash stood behind her, looking over her shoulder at Mattie's slate.

"I never knew that, Miss Burke," Nash said. "Show us some more number tricks!"

Turnbull elbowed Nash and guffawed.

"You're going to need help if she shows you anything over..." his brow furrowed. "Eighteen. You ain't having enough fingers and toes to count higher."

Lydia was about to correct Turnbull's addition when she realized he was right. Nash was missing two fingers on his left hand.

"Yes, ma'am, show us some more!"

Mattie's enthusiasm for arithmetic was ramped up by the pirates' interest. Anything that helped her charge study her lessons was a good thing, and the piratical approval seemed to help.

"Very well, Mattie, gentlemen. Let's look at the number three."

She worked over the slate, then showed it to her rapt audience. The men were now seated crosslegged on the deck alongside her pupil.

"Three is, as you know, a prime number and a factor of nine. But what also makes three interesting is the rule that anything divisible by three must have digits that add to a value divisible by three. For example, we know fifty-four is divisible by three because five plus four equals nine, which is divisible by three."

She wrote another number.

"This is larger than what you're working with now, Mattie, but just to show you... Five hundred and seventy-six must also be divisible by three, because five plus seven plus six equals eighteen, which is divisible by three."

"And eighteen is nine times two and one plus eight equals nine and three goes into nine three times!"

"Swive me sideways! The sprat is right!" Turnbull exclaimed.

Lydia winced, but the language aboard the *Prodigal Son* was fast becoming a lost cause for her. She would be earning all of that extraordinary salary Captain St. Armand promised her if she could keep Mattie from repeating too much of what she learned from the sailors.

"This is what we will work on now, Mattie. I want you to practice with your slate, and be sure to write your numbers with a clear hand."

"That's right, sprat," said Turnbull. "If you're dividing up the booty and your shipmates think you're cheating or holding back you could find yourself on the wrong end of a blade."

Mattie's eyes widened at the hidden dangers of multiplication, and Lydia hoped the twinge behind her own eye would not develop into a full blown headache. When she'd contemplated being a governess she'd never considered pirates and their economic systems as part of her teaching methodology.

Turnbull and Nash were looking at her expectantly.

"Gentlemen?"

Nash snickered at that, but Turnbull said, "Do you have extra slates we could use, Miss Burke? We could try our hands at the problems."

Lydia was about to beg off but she saw how Mattie's face glowed at the idea of the pirates joining in her lessons.

"To be honest," she started, then paused to think. "Mr. Nash, Mr. Turnbull—you must understand that I do not teach unless I am compensated for my labors."

Nash looked at Turnbull, who said, "She wants her share."

"Well, that's only right." Nash nodded. "So what do teachers get? Jewels? Gold? I've a good Spanish dagger I'd be willing to trade for lessons."

"And I have a mummified head from the Sandwich Islands. You could have that, ma'am," Turnbull said.

"Take the head! I've seen it and it's disgusting!" Mattie enthused.

"It *sounds* disgusting, but thank you, no. What I want, gentlemen, is for you to join us at a tea party to be held at a future date."

Nash looked at Turnbull, who said, "I reckon we'd have to drink tea."

"Thought so," Nash said gloomily. "But if that's what it takes, I'll do it."

He spat into his hand, then held it out to Lydia. "Shake on it, and it's a bargain, Miss Burke."

Lydia gamely took Nash's hand, promising herself she could scrub later. She glanced over at Mattie, who wore an awed expression, and Lydia allowed herself a satisfied smile.

"If you gentlemen will wait here with Mattie, I'll fetch some slates."

Lydia was about to push herself to her feet when a firm hand beneath her elbow effortlessly hoisted her up. Nash and Turnbull jumped to their own feet in the captain's presence, as did the youngest crewmember.

Captain St. Armand still had his hand wrapped about her arm, and she could feel the warmth of the contact through the thin fabric of her gown. She tried to subtly maneuver out of his grip, but he seemed content to keep her there. Standing so close to him she reflexively inhaled, and she was glad he steadied her. It had been ages since she'd wanted to lean in and get closer to a man because her nose told her it was a fine idea, and this was definitely the wrong man to set off olfactory responses and bring her skin and senses to life.

"Miss Burke?"

"Miss Burke was teaching us number tricks, Papa."

"I was addressing the lady," he said mildly, which brought a "Sorry, sir," from Mattie and silence from the rest of the crew standing there.

"We were having lessons, Captain," Lydia said.

"These two weren't a distraction?"

"On the contrary, it is a pleasure to teach eager pupils of any age."

"I would let you teach me a thing or two, Miss Burke," he murmured close to her ear. She ignored this and continued.

"The men asked if they could sit in on the lessons, their schedules permitting. Mattie approves of the idea as well, and I've found that sometimes a pupil's learning is stimulated by the presence of other students."

She looked up at the captain, whose eyebrows arched at the idea of Nash and Turnbull as classroom compatriots, but he said, "If Mr. Fuller agrees, then I have no objection."

The two men thanked their captain and hurried off, arguing over how to check sums. This discussion involved allusions to Turnbull's parentage and to Nash's hygiene, so Lydia was relieved when they took themselves off.

Somewhat relieved. She still had Captain St. Armand standing too close to her, crowding her and intruding in her breathing space. She wanted to step back away from him, but at the same time, she did not want to. Regardless, retreat displayed cowardice and it was not the best response with him, no matter the provocation.

He smiled down at her as if he could parse all these thoughts, then stepped back himself, his slender fingers gliding down her upper arm as he released her, a shiver lingering along that too sensitive flesh in their wake.

"I came to alert you ladies it is time for luncheon. May I escort you below?"

He cocked an arm, but offered it to Mattie, rather than Lydia. The girl giggled and took her father's hand.

"You are too tall for me to hold your arm, Papa. This is a better fit."

"As you say, Marauding Mattie. And this way your knife hand is free."

They both turned at the garbled noise that worked its way out of Lydia's throat.

"Never mind," she muttered, following behind as father and daughter went below.

CHAPTER 7

*H*er remaining caps were missing, and she knew positively she'd put them in her trunk. Their absence could only mean the mysterious cap thief had visited while she slept.

Her blood ran cold at the thought of one of the men stealing into her cabin, then her brain began working properly and her blood heated up. There was only one suspect, the only one daring enough to enter the cabin where the captain's daughter slept, never mind her governess!

She braided her hair because her remaining hairpins also were not to be found. Really, it was the outside of enough! She tied off the thick braid and tossed it back over her shoulder. She might not be able to pin her hair properly atop her head, but she would not wear two braids like a schoolgirl.

Lydia fumed through breakfast, responding in short words to Captain St. Armand and Mr. Fuller, even though she bore the mate no ill-will. Fortunately, Mattie did not seem to notice that her governess was glowering, and chatted with Mr. Fuller about the change in weather and her new pink jacket.

"Now I am rigged out for foul weather, Mr. Fuller. It is important to have the proper gear during a blow," Mattie told him solemnly.

"I have heard that said, Miss Mattie," Fuller responded, passing the biscuits around. Lydia rapped hers on the table to encourage any wildlife inside to leave. Weevils in her food were one of the harsh realities of sea life she'd come to grips with on her first voyage, and now she ignored them even as she longed for more wholesome fare. At least there were still oranges from the islands. A luxury in England, she intended to enjoy them while she could.

After breakfast Lydia said, "Mattie, would you gather your books and wait for me? I need to speak to your father."

Mr. Fuller took one last biscuit with him, stuffing it into his coat, and said, "I'll help you with your books, Mattie."

"I can climb without help, Mr. Fuller!"

He ushered her out of the cabin, closing the door firmly behind them.

"I too have to get to my work, Miss Bur—"

"This will not take long, Captain," Lydia interrupted, and to emphasize her point she took a stance in front of the door, blocking his passage. His lips quirked up at the corners, but he leaned against the table and threw his arms wide.

"I am all yours."

In his dreams. She sniffed at his insouciant manner, but his pose brought his well-muscled arms to her attention, which was, of course, his goal. Today he was wearing one of his knit shirts, similar to that worn by the sailors aboard the *Prodigal Son*. The difference was his shirt was of a much finer weave and shaped itself to his shoulders and arms. His fore-arms were left bare, browned from the sun and corded with strength. She remembered his backside as being a lighter shade, also muscled, sleek muscles that flexed with his move-ment, not like the muscles that bulged across his shoul—

He snapped his fingers.

"Miss Burke? I have a ship to command, if you recall."

She shook herself and remembered why she was there. The anger helped her focus.

"Captain St. Armand, *someone* came into our cabin and stole my caps!"

"I'm shocked, Miss Burke, shocked, that anyone would steal something as hideous as your silly caps! I give my crew credit for having better taste than that."

He had the audacity to smile like it was all a joke to him.

"I have heard rumors that Sails likes to wear women's undergarments. Perhaps you should ask him if he took your caps?"

She dismissed this nonsense with a sneer.

"My hairpins are missing as well."

"I find your new coiffure quite charming, Miss Burke. Very feminine and *de jeune fille.* I approve."

"I do not want your approval," she said through her teeth. "I want my hairpins and caps returned to me!"

"Ridiculous," he said, pushing himself off the table and coming closer. Lydia wasn't aware she'd moved until her back was against the door, and then she couldn't move any farther. He kept coming, until he could reach out and tug her braid forward, across her shoulder, his hand gliding down the length like it was a string of pearls.

"So silken," he murmured. "And the color is glorious, a rich sienna that frames your face and makes your eyes glow. I cannot imagine why you would wear those caps, hiding this glory unless…are you in disguise, Miss Burke? Why would a governess hide from prying eyes? Did you steal the family silver? Murder a former employer?"

"You are the only person who would say that like it's praiseworthy."

"I confess, as interesting as I already find you, your being

67

a murderess would make you even more fascinating to me on this tedious voyage."

"May I remind you that I am responsible for teaching your daughter, Captain St. Armand?"

"If what I'm conjecturing is correct, I hope you will teach her effective ways to hide the bodies of your victims," he finished with a boyish grin, stepping back, finally, and allowing her to pull air into cramped lungs.

"No, I did not kill any—why am I defending myself to a scoundrel like you? I want my belongings returned to me! I want to know I can sleep unmolested at night aboard your vessel!"

"Miss Burke, I can assure you none of the crew will molest you, asleep or awake."

He said nothing about the captain and she was about to accuse him, but he was still talking, "As far as your ugly caps and pins are concerned, I will mention it to Mr. Fuller and if anything resembling them turns up, I will be certain you are told. Now, don't you have lessons with Mattie?"

He reached around her and opened the door, helping her into the passageway before she could protest.

ROBERT COULD ALMOST SEE steam seeping under his door from where the little hedgehog bristled on the other side. She had a temper, Lydia Burke did. Needling people into losing their tempers purely for the entertainment value of it had ever been one of Robert's besetting sins.

He was still smiling as he opened his box and gazed upon his new collection of hairpins, secreted from her cabin in the dark. He'd indulged himself last night, admiring the sleeping woman's form. She'd kicked off the covers and her night rail was tangled up around her legs, not far enough to satisfy

Robert, but far enough to assure him his suspicions were correct. She had neat ankles and shapely calves. His imagination was good enough for him to assume the rest of her form would be equally shapely. While he was a connoisseur of all things lovely, he found most women beautiful in their own way. A good eye, a winning smile, a long neck, all had something to commend them. Whether they were rounded and buxom or sleek and slender, all had attractions. Miss Burke— Lydia—had more than average looks if she'd let herself properly display it. Those snapping eyes like the green flash of a tropical sunset, the rich chestnut hair, the shapely parts, oh yes, the lady was hiding herself away.

But hiding from what? Murder? Theft? Robert believed with the right provocation she would shoot him, and heaven knew he could be provoking, but she did not strike him as the sort to plot out a premeditated murder. She also did not seem a probable thief. So what—or who—was she hiding from? A former employer? A jealous husband?

This last thought made him frown, but only for a moment. Disposing of people who were in his way was nothing new. If Miss Burke left a husband behind in England, she no doubt had good reasons. If he needed to be done away with so she could live her own life, then Robert was the man for the job. No false modesty, he was good at what he did and he considered how utterly appreciative a young widow might be for his assistance.

He had substantial complications in his life these days, a situation which did not sit well with him. Robert knew himself well enough to understand avoiding complications kept him on an even keel. However, one of those complications was a delightful moppet who made his heart ache, and the other complication was a prickly lady who made his balls ache. Complications, yes, but there were rewards from having them in his life and he hoped to get quite well rewarded indeed if he took care of Miss Burke's own complications.

As he prepared to join his crew up top, Robert paused to check himself in the mirror, smiling at what he saw. Truly, it was only a matter of time before the lady found herself with a whole new set of complications in the comfort of his berth.

MATTIE PREENED in her new jacket in the brisk sea air. It was styled as the men's jackets were, but hers was a deep rose that set off her curls charmingly and made her eyes look even bluer. The jacket was quilted and of a substantial weight, and Lydia shivered in her garments more suited to the occasional cool breeze of the tropics than for sea travel.

"You need your own heavy weather gear, Miss Burke," Mattie said as her father stepped over to join them and admire Mattie's coat.

"Quite correct, Mattie. Do not argue with me, Miss Burke. You would be no good to us if you came down with an ague from being inadequately clothed. If you're ill I would have to move you to my cabin and nurse you so Mattie would not be exposed to your contagion. Surely you do not wish that to happen?"

"Surely not," Lydia said promptly. "Being in your cabin is a fate I do not wish to contemplate, Captain."

She was such a fibber, but she'd gotten good at it over the years, though the captain just smiled at her firm response.

"Then I will instruct Sails to make you a jacket. If you have a spencer you can spare, he can use that as the pattern."

"Do you plan to dress me in pink satin as well?"

He shuddered. "My dear Miss Burke, you would not be at your best in pink, satin or otherwise. No, you should be dressed in colors of the forest, with the addition of the deep blues and purples of an autumn afternoon at sunset. And you should never wear gray, at least not up around your face. It makes you look positively sallow."

"You would look good in pink, Papa."

"True, Mattie, but I have all the heavy weather gear I need and I do not wish to overburden Sails. I will hold onto your suggestion though. What do you think? Perhaps I'll purchase a rose silk waistcoat? It would look good beneath a blue jacket."

Lydia ignored the question, knowing no good would come of her commenting on how anything the captain wore would look stunning on him. He was enough of a peacock already and did not need her to add to his preening and strutting. Instead she turned back to her charge.

"Mattie, would you like to recite your multiplication tables for your father?"

Mattie looked unsure, but at a nod from her papa she took a deep breath.

"Two times two is four, two times three is six, two times four is eight…"

She stumbled over the sevens but managed to finish without making an error and Lydia beamed with pride. It was a delight to teach such a bright and eager pupil, what every teacher longed for.

Mattie's papa stood silently, his face grave as he examined his child.

"I recall it took me longer to memorize my tables, Mathilde, and I was older when I did. You have an excellent mind."

He looked at Lydia next, as serious as she'd ever seen him.

"Hold nothing back from Mathilde, Miss Burke. I want her to learn everything you are capable of teaching her. I want her to learn…" he paused. "She has a sharp mind and it needs to be exercised."

A warm glow bloomed in Lydia's chest, close to the region of her heart. Too often she'd dealt with parents who only wanted their daughters to learn the minimum amount necessary to snag a husband. Anything else would be a waste, or horror of horrors, have them labeled bluestockings.

"It is and will be my pleasure, Captain St. Armand."

"Then I will leave you ladies to your lessons, and return to my duties. Ma'am, Mathilde."

"I will see you later, Papa," Mattie chirped. Her face glowed at her father's praise and Lydia thought how wonderful it was to have someone who did not chastise you for not being like everyone else.

Mattie returned to her lessons with new enthusiasm, and they were joined by Turnbull and Nash. They brought the slates they'd been using for practice, and Lydia was pleased to see they'd assisted each other.

"You learn when you teach, Mr. Turnbull. Learning together will reinforce the lessons for both of you."

"Aye, it does seem easier when I can ask Nash to check my work, miss. And this bast—looby has a good head for numbers when he uses it."

"Hey! Remember those girls at the tavern in Santa Rosa? They were negotiating in pesos and you were lost trying to figure out what the cost would be for adding in the special trick with the honey and the parrot—ooof."

"Miss Burke does not want to hear about that, you idiot," Turnbull snarled as he removed his elbow from Nash's stomach.

Lydia ignored this byplay and turned the subject around to their lessons for the following day.

"Of course, miss, you know that we could suddenly find ourselves in um, contact with another vessel and be too busy for arithmetic. Or there could be a squall."

"I do understand, Mr. Nash. The needs of the ship come

first. But I am also confident our lessons are progressing well enough that I can begin to plan for our promised tea party."

The two men looked at each other and sighed, resignedly.

"As you say, miss. We made an agreement, and we'll keep it."

They rose to their feet and excused themselves, and Lydia looked over at Mattie, who was eyeing the mainmast of the *Prodigal Son*.

"That is a tall mast, Miss Burke," she said out of the blue. "Norton told me it's taller than houses up to the top."

Lydia looked up at the top of the mast, swaying gently, then pulled her eyes away. She was a good voyager, but there was no point in risking her stomach's equilibrium unnecessarily.

"It is tall, and while I do not know much about sailing, I imagine a tall mast allows the canvas up at the top to capture more wind and increase speed. A short mainmast would be more like a skiff, correct?"

Mattie didn't respond to the question, but studied the mast, a frown on her face.

"Mattie?"

"Sorry, ma'am. I was thinking. I would like to learn more about sailing. Can we include Papa in our lessons and he can teach us?"

Lydia mulled this over. "Perhaps…but as your papa is the captain, he may feel there is someone better suited to teaching you. Mr. Fuller makes many of the decisions about when to add or remove canvas, does he not? He may be the person to ask. We can discuss it at our meal."

Mattie was quiet during the midday meal, but Lydia did not dwell on it. She was following the discussion between Mr. Fuller and the captain over selling the goods filling the hold of the *Prodigal Son*. Everything she knew about pirates was about their bad habits, dangerous lives and lack of morals. She'd never thought about the *business* of being a pirate, how once you took a ship you had to have buyers for your booty.

"The oranges and lemons alone make this voyage worthwhile, Captain."

"They will bring a tidy profit, but be sure the men continue to take their lime juice. I want everyone shipshape when we dock in Liverpool. Contact Josiah Talbot as soon as we drop anchor and deal with the harbormaster. He'll want first choice and is willing to pay top money for the best we have."

Mr. Fuller made some notes to himself and Lydia could not contain her curiosity.

"What are you carrying on your ship, Captain?"

He took a sip of his wine and looked at her over his glass. She'd heard the expression "a twinkle in his eyes" but she'd never known a grown man who could look so much like a mischievous lad. That would not be a problem in itself, but he also looked too much like a man whose idea of mischief involved an oversized bed and fur pillows.

"I have select goods for discerning consumers, Miss Burke. Brandy, silks and satins from France—"

"Seems a long way for them to travel, Captain, considering France's proximity to England."

"They may have originally been destined for America, or the islands, but when I negotiated with the ships carrying the freight they saw a better outcome for them if I had their goods."

How the man could make statements like that with a straight face amazed her. Not a twinge of guilt, no remorse, and even Mr. Fuller, who seemed to have some morality imbued in him ignored it and cut at the goat meat in his stew. One of the ship's animals had been injured and had to be destroyed. Lydia was concerned over the loss of the goat's milk for Mattie, but there were still two nannies that might not go dry before they made landfall. Mattie's shipboard chores included caring for some of the livestock and she'd insisted on a brief memorial service for the unnamed animal now gracing their plates. However, she was a pragmatic child, her mother's daughter, and took the loss of her ship-mate and its appearance at table in stride.

"I will miss eating goat when I am in England," Lydia said. "I became rather used to it in the islands."

"You may be able to keep goats where you settle, depending, of course, on what you decide."

"Are you leaving me, Miss Burke?" Mattie asked in dismay.

"You know it was my intention to stay in the islands, Mattie," she said gently. "I will certainly be with you for the near future and help you when you arrive in England, but I am sure your father has plans of his own and they do not include me."

"Regarding the goods aboard ship, Miss Burke, we also have other products from the islands—rum, sugar, the fruit, spices, coffee. All of these things are welcome in England and will ensure Mattie has plenty of pink jackets in her future."

Lydia looked up, grateful for his stepping into the conversational breech. Every now and then he evidenced flashes of sensitivity that surprised her, coming as they did from a man of his background, habits and piratical ways. She wondered again what his plans were when he reached England. Would he set sail to plunder shipping in areas of the world thrown into disarray by the end of the long war with France? Would he have to hide from the authorities? Would he abandon Mattie with some worthy relatives?

She wanted to ask him all these things, to talk with him without feeling on edge. That was impossible. Every time she was near him she was too aware of his presence, of her body's unwelcome response to his appeal. His sensual nature and amazing looks, even the smell of him, it all conspired against her to make her want what she should not want and could not have without dire consequences.

She'd gone down that road once already, the road leading to ruin, disgrace and hiding. Lydia liked to think she learned from her mistakes, the hard won knowledge separating her from the bad choices in her past. Too many people made the same errors of judgment over and over, leading to financial ruin, or jail, or disgrace, or life in a bottle of gin. She demanded better of herself, and would not be led off the path of common sense by a pirate, no matter how beautiful he was, or how much she longed to touch that smooth chest, run her fingers through the hair on his head that looked as silken as the coverlet on his dangerous bed.

When the meal was finished Mattie and Lydia excused themselves to take a siesta in their cabin. Lydia must have dozed off, for she was roused from her nap by shouting from above.

The other bunk was empty. Without bothering to put on shoes, she ran from the cabin, calling Mattie's name, and raced up the ladder into the sunlight.

Nash grabbed her arm. "I tried to stop her!"

Lydia looked up to where Nash pointed and her stomach plummeted even as the ship rocked through a trough in the ocean. A small figure in pink clung to the rigging near the top of the mainmast.

Lydia's hand rose to her mouth, and she gasped in shock as someone raced past her, a blur at the edge of her eye. Faster than she thought possible, St. Armand flew up the rigging, barefoot, half-dressed. There was a small platform at the top of the mainsail, just before the tip of the mast pierced the sky. The captain stood there, his arm around Mattie. His white shirt shone in the sunlight, but Lydia could not see their faces.

No one on deck could hear the conversation between father and daughter, but they heard Mattie wail in dismay at something he said. He continued speaking to the child, then removed his arm from around her. To Lydia's horror St. Armand began to climb down, alone. Slowly. At one point he paused, waiting.

The ship's crew stood silent, all eyes on the pair above them, watching as Mattie cried out again, but after another remark from her captain, she too began to climb down, slowly. He matched her, staying below her, but he did not touch her again.

When his feet hit the deck he walked over to Lydia and stood in front of her, facing the mast, legs apart, hands clasped behind his back. Mattie made it to the deck, clinging to the mainmast.

"Climb again. All the way up."

Lydia's ears must be playing tricks on her. Surely that quiet, emotionless command could not have been the captain ordering his daughter into harm's way. The child looked at him, white-faced, tears streaking her cheeks. None of the crew said anything. He said nothing. Lydia wanted to speak, but dared not.

The moment stretched out, only the creak of the rigging and the snap of the canvas making noise in the clear sky. Then Mattie turned her back on them, put one bare foot on the mast and pulled herself up. Inch by inch, she made her way to the top. Her foot slipped once and a hoarse noise escaped from the man standing before Lydia. His hands were still clasped at his back, white with strain as they gripped each other, tension radiating from his entire body.

When Mattie was a small object at the top of the mast she

paused, then made her way down, slowly, but with more sureness than her first descent. Still, no one spoke.

Mattie made her way over to where her captain stood. Lydia'd inched forward and she could see his face. It was not the face of a doting papa, but a sea captain's face, the face of a man responsible for every life aboard his vessel.

"You are confined to your quarters for disobeying orders, Mathilde," he said in that quiet voice which nonetheless could be clearly heard by everyone on deck. "We will talk more of this later."

"Aye, Captain," Mattie whispered. Eyes down, she shuffled past the silent crew, none of whom spoke to her or offered a kind word. They knew the cost of a shipmate who disobeyed orders, and most of them had gone to sea at an age close to Mattie's. She would bear the consequences of her actions, captain's daughter or no.

"Back to work," Mr. Fuller called out, and the men turned to their tasks as Lydia watched St. Armand go below.

"I should have stopped her," Nash said.

"Knowing Mattie as I do, I am sure she waited until she knew no one was watching who would have stopped her. Do not blame yourself, Mr. Nash. It was Mattie's decision."

"Aye, miss, but it's no easy thing making that first trip up the mast. The lass has pluck. She is her father's daughter."

"Indeed, Mr. Nash. That is what concerns me."

Lydia went below and stood outside her cabin door, listening to the soft snuffling sounds of the crying child. She'd do. A glance across the passageway showed the door to the captain's cabin was closed. Lydia opened the door and walked in, straight over to the cabinet where he kept his spirits. She poured a hefty serving of rum.

"Here," she said.

Robert St. Armand looked out the stern window, his arms braced along the frame. He did not turn around.

"Get out."

She ignored him, set the glass down and seated herself, hands clasped in her lap.

He turned his head and looked over his shoulder, frowning.

"Why are you still here? Do you wish to gloat? Didn't today's events prove you right?"

"Prove me right? How?"

"Prove I am an unfit parent. Prove I should not have the responsibility of raising Mathilde."

He walked over to the glass she'd poured for him and drank, head tipped back, the solid column of his throat working as he sought relief in the rum. The captain's shirt had been hastily pulled over his head when he came above to check on the commotion. It was unfastened in the front and Lydia looked down at her hands, frowning.

"I cannot do this. I cannot be Mathilde's father. You will care for her. I will give you money, plenty of money, enough money to ensure you never want for anything. Just...just take care of Mattie."

"You are ridiculous."

He blinked, then looked at her as if she were some exotic species he'd never before encountered, and set his glass down.

"What did you say to me?"

"You heard me. You are ridiculous. Do you believe you are the first father, the first parent to feel unfit to raise a child? You are doing an adequate job with your daughter, do not make this into a Drury Lane drama."

Now his eyes narrowed until there was only a flash of blue and the firm mouth tightened. He leaned forward, hands braced on the table.

"You saw what happened today," he said through his teeth. "She could have fallen to the deck and died!"

"But she did not, did she? She needs to be taught, not deserted."

He looked at her for a long, drawn out period, as if this was the first time he was truly seeing her as a person. Good. He needed to learn she was a human being, a woman, not some kitten he could tease and annoy for his own entertainment. If he took her more seriously, he might leave her be.

She doubted it, but it was an encouraging thought.

"I would think I am the last person on this planet you want responsible for Mattie."

"I've seen worse. But how I feel is not the issue, is it, Captain? Mathilde is your daughter, you have accepted that, she has accepted her place in your life. The last thing she needs now, after her mother's death and the upheaval of not knowing where she would end up, the last thing she needs is to wonder if her father will discard her like yesterday's rubbish because she's become an inconvenience or a bother to him."

"That is not what I meant!"

"Perhaps not, but she will view it that way, I assure you. Children want, no, *must* know their place in the world. If she feels unsure of her place with you, she will not thrive."

He continued to look at her, assessing her words. She tried not to squirm under his gaze. It was easy, too easy, to dismiss him as an attractive rogue, but becoming curious about the layers of the attractive pirate would end badly for her, she knew that in her soul.

"She must be punished for disobeying my orders."

"Yes. What will you do?"

Those long lashes hid his gaze as he looked down at his hands, splayed before him on the tabletop.

"She doesn't flinch when I am around her."

"Why would she—"Lydia stopped. Some children flinched because they expected to be struck. "Will you beat her?"

"She is so small."

"Some would not hesitate to strike a child for such an offense, considering it appropriate chastisement."

"I would not strike a child." His looked up at her, his face drawn, the weight of his new responsibility bearing down on him. "A child should not look up and find a fist coming at hi —her." He looked over at his glass, but didn't drink more.

"I don't want her to hate me. I abandoned her, and her mother."

"That's not what Nanette said. You did not abandon her, and you did not know about Mattie. Nanette always spoke well of you, and you became a hero in Mattie's eyes, her brave pirate papa."

He flinched, but she continued.

"Do not prove her wrong by acting a coward now. Mattie will not hate you, even if you punish her. Children love their fathers and they know their fathers love them."

"Not all children. Not all fathers."

She could not argue that point and fell silent as he considered her words.

"I must treat Mattie just as I would any other youngster aboard ship who disobeys. I do not strike children, so I will think of an alternative."

He looked up at her a glimmer of a smile playing around his lips. "My girl is a brave one, isn't she? Not many would attempt climbing the rigging as she did, not at her age."

Lydia felt her own proud smile creeping out. "Mattie is a challenge, but that is what makes teaching her a delight. I am not a teacher who wants a pattern card of a little person, sitting quietly and never questioning or striving to do new things."

They sat looking at one another, each comfortable in his or her regard for the child, but then the mood flowed into something else, an acknowledgement that they were sitting together, alone, in his cabin, and they were not squabbling. Lydia wasn't wary and on guard with the captain as she normally would be.

She jumped to her feet and he straightened too, his eyes never leaving hers. The look in them was one she had not seen before, not from him, a look of regard and respect and something else she did not wish to contemplate, not now, not when they were on a ship in the middle of the ocean. In his cabin, a few steps from his bed.

"I will leave Mattie's punishment to you then, Captain. I am sure you will think of something appropriate."

He nodded, and as she turned to leave she heard him say, "Thank you, Miss Burke."

"For what?"

"Thank you for Mattie."

He said nothing more, and she just looked at him, then nodded and left to go check on the child. Mattie had cried herself to sleep in the cabin, a rag doll clutched to her tear-streaked face. Lydia smoothed the hair off of the child's forehead, and tucked her cover closer about her. So fragile, and so small, the bones in her body easily shattered, the dreams in her child's mind so easily crushed.

ROBERT TOLD Mr. Fuller to muster the crew and sent word below to the ladies. They arrived on deck, Mattie's face freshly washed and serious. She held her teacher's hand until they reached the solemn men arrayed in a row, as disciplined and straight as any crew in the navy. Robert stood at the end, feet apart, hands clasped behind his back. He looked down at the child and said, "Mathilde St. Armand. You will walk down this line and apologize to each of your mates for your disobedient acts. Then you will return to your bunk and spend the evening without supper."

"Aye, Cap'n," the child whispered.

She released Miss Burke's hand, and when she looked up at her, the governess nodded and took her place a step back from the crew.

Mattie's bare feet shuffled across the deck.

"I am sorry that I disobeyed orders, Mr. Nash. I am sorry I disobeyed orders, Mr. Conroy…"

Each pirate gave the child a nod after her apology and she moved down the line. Sails winked at her, but a frown from the mate had him toeing the line again. Finally, she reached the end of the long row of solemn men.

"I am sorry that I disobeyed orders, Mr. Fuller."

Then she stood in front of the ship's commander.

"I am sorry that I disobeyed orders, Captain. I will not climb again without permission."

She gulped in a noisy breath and looked up at him. "Do you still love me, Papa?" she asked quietly.

He crouched down on his heels so he could look her in the eye. "I will love you always and forever, Mathilde. That is a promise."

She threw her arms around his neck, sobbing into his shirt and he clutched her to him. There were suspicious sniffling noises from some of the pirates, and Norton apparently had something in his eye, but Mr. Fuller said, "All right, back to work, you lot!" and they dispersed to their tasks.

It was good they left, for Robert needed to get past the lump in his own throat. The fragile arms clasped around his neck held him as if he were a safe harbor from life's dangers. He hugged her to him and looked over her head. The governess stood quietly to the side, watching, her gray dress helping her blend into the weathered wood, the washed out sails of the ship. Quiet and obedient. If he did not know she kept a burning coal of passion hidden behind her demure gown he'd worry she was not the right teacher to have Mathilde under her care.

"Papa, will you read to me tonight?"

He kissed her atop her head. "Yes, Mathilde, I will read to you tonight. Now, go to your cabin."

The child walked off with her head raised higher, and Nash said, "We'll see you later then, lass," and a smile broke out on her face.

"Did I do the correct thing?" Robert asked the woman standing beside him. She looked...right, standing there, as if being at his side was where she belonged. He frowned, because his plans for the future did not include drab governesses, not for more than an evening or two in his bed. And even that seemed unlikely, not just because she'd screech like an owl if he suggested such a thing—though he was convinced it would do her even more good than loosening her tight hair—but because bedding proper ladies had consequences. You could not walk away from them without some kind of reaction completely out of proportion to a night or two of pleasure. They wanted commitment and false words and, heaven help us all, marriage.

"It appears you handled that well, Captain," Miss Burke answered his question. "Mattie needed to be disciplined, but she also needs to know she will be accepted by the crew. I believe based on their response and hers you did exactly the right thing."

She was Mattie's governess, and asking her opinion was prudent. It was not because *he* wanted her approval, but her words still lightened something in his chest.

"In that case I will excuse myself until this evening."

"I will stay with Mattie in the cabin, Captain—"

"No," he interrupted, an idea forming in his mind. "You will join me for our meal, as usual. Mattie does not need additional attention while she's confined to her quarters. This will give her more time to reflect."

"But—"

"Do not argue with my orders, Miss Burke. If I am responsible for ship's discipline then you must do your part by not undermining my efforts."

He favored her with a smile, his careful "I'm a figure of authority" smile, and she nodded at him, mulling over his order. It was reassuring to know he could still command small children and governesses without worrying too much about mutiny. On that cheering thought he went below to prepare for the evening.

CHAPTER 8

*M*attie was bored and restless when Lydia joined her later in the day, but was enduring her punishment with a martyred expression, and made a point of saying that she must bear up under her punishment as any of the men would. Lydia knew Mattie was secretly thrilled with herself. She'd climbed the mast—twice—in front of her shipmates and shown them she could do it. She'd been chastised for her transgressions just like the rest of the crew, though Lydia suspected their punishments took a harsher form than being sent to their hammocks without supper. Being sent to the hammocks without the evening grog might be considered severe by some aboard though.

Thinking of appropriate punishments for malefactors made her think again about her missing hairpins and caps. She just knew the captain was responsible, he'd all but admitted it. What would be an appropriate punishment for him? It was a childish act, performed by one who seemed to have all the self-control of a child when it came to satisfying his own urges, so perhaps a good spanking was in order!

Oh dear, she thought as she looked into her chest of clothing. An image of Captain St. Armand across her lap, sprawling there with his trousers down around his ankles, or worse, completely naked—there was no way she would be able to unthink that now. It was too…delicious. He would need a firm hand, of course, and stern warnings not to wiggle—

Lydia dropped the fichu in her hand and walked to the washbasin where she splashed some tepid water on her face and tried to bring her unruly imagination under control.

Control. That was it. If she could continue to maintain control, or at least the illusion of it, she would survive her encounters with the captain. If he thought he had the upper hand he would do more to force his will on her, bend her to his way of thinking, entice her into a world of sensuous pleasures that had no place in her life now. Not if she wanted to maintain her freedom and the life she'd built as Lydia Burke, governess, rather than—

"Miss Burke?"

Lydia scrubbed her face and turned to face her charge.

"Yes, Mattie?"

"Do you like my papa?"

Lydia's hand rose to her throat. "What do you mean, child?"

Mattie sat up on her bunk, her arms wrapped around her knees. Lydia didn't say anything about the unladylike position, because Mattie was looking at her intently. She may be young, but she was not as sheltered as many a girl her age.

"My papa is a handsome man and a successful pirate," Mattie said with pride. "Sometimes though, I think you don't like him. You argue with him a lot."

Lydia came over and sat beside the child. "Your father and I disagree on many things, Mattie, including his being a pirate. There is one thing we do agree on. We both want what is best for you. That's my mission as your governess, and your father's responsibility. If we sometimes argue about it, it is because we are both doing our best to do the right thing for you."

"I do not want to be a burden to Papa. I want to be a helpful crewmate."

"You are a helpful crewmate," Lydia said firmly. "You care for the animals and do your chores with a minimal amount of grumbling. Your improvement in your numbers will help you to be even more useful to your father. In addition, you have gotten others involved in learning and that is important."

"It is?"

"Yes. We must always strive to improve ourselves, and now some men who did not think they could learn have returned to the schoolroom. When Mr. Turnbull and Mr. Nash finish this voyage they will know more and be better prepared to serve aboard this vessel, or other vessels."

"Because of me?"

"You helped. You study with them and you make them feel that it is safe to try new things."

"So it is good to try new things?"

"Within reason," Lydia said sternly. "I do believe there will be more climbing in your future, as long as you have permission."

"I understand." Mattie nodded. "So if Mr. Conroy offers to teach me to spit farther, then I can learn as long as it doesn't interfere with my chores."

Lydia opened her mouth, then shut it. There were only so many things she could say "no" to in the course of a day. She changed dresses, retrieved her fichu and tucked it into the already modest neckline of her blue gown. For a few heartbeats she wished it were a brighter shade of blue, a sapphire blue like the captain's satin shirt, the one that flowed over his torso like liquid silk, the sheen catching the light and the eye.

But that would defeat the purpose of wearing drab colors to blend into the background. Sapphire satin was for pirates, not for governesses who did not wish to draw attention to themselves.

When she pinched her cheeks to put some color in them, she told herself it was just so the captain would not ask if she were pale. His personal questions had a tendency to take on new meanings and subtleties and she did not wish to spar with him. She told Mattie she'd see her later in the evening and walked over to the captain's cabin, the narrow passageway seeming a great distance though it was just steps away.

Her knock on the door was answered by a firm, "Enter," but when she stepped across the threshold she paused, arrested by the sight. The captain's cabin was dimly lit and empty but for its owner, clad in the same shirt that entered into her fevered thoughts. It was unfastened and he seemed not to be aware, or care, that his chest was on display, the bands of muscles rippling across tanned flesh.

"I will return when you are dressed, Captain, and when the others dining with us are here."

"I am as dressed as I need to be aboard my own ship, in my own cabin, and it will be just the two of us tonight, Miss Burke."

Without another word she turned to leave. Let him play his games with someone else.

"Stay."

She looked over her shoulder. "Are you ordering me to stay here alone with you? I can tell you in advance, this will not end well."

He looked puzzled. Clearly he was either unfamiliar with the thought of someone disobeying him, or with woman resisting his charms. Either way, she needed to be somewhere else, not alone with all that satin and flesh.

"Stay. Please." He sighed. "I will fasten my shirt and put on a coat if it makes you feel more at ease."

She couldn't uncover any innuendo or hidden meaning in his statement and reluctantly Lydia said, "If you will fasten your shirt I will stay, Captain St. Armand."

He did as promised, and Lydia seated herself. The food was already on the table, a sea pie featuring dubious meats, but enough onions and seasonings to make it tolerable, pickled beetroot, peas, and a treacle pudding at the end.

The captain served her before serving himself. He also poured her some of his excellent burgundy, no doubt purloined from another vessel. She took a sip, cautious because the wine was an improvement over the ship's drinking water at this point in the voyage, and she didn't want to quench her thirst with a beverage that could lead to bad decisions.

"Why are we dining alone tonight, Captain?"

"Is that a complaint?" he asked, putting some peas on her plate.

"Just a question."

"Mr. Fuller is busy and I thought this a good opportunity to get to know you better."

"Why?" she asked bluntly.

He paused and set down the dish, reaching for his wineglass in the silence. Above them she heard the sounds of a ship at sea, a vessel that was never completely quiet as wind moved it ever closer to its home.

A shiver raced down her back.

"Cold, Miss Burke?"

He didn't wait for her reply but fetched his jacket and, standing behind her, draped it over her shoulders, smoothing it down her arms. His scent enveloped her, the light air of sandalwood and citrus wrapping itself around her senses. He lingered at her back, then returned to his seat.

"Did you give Sails your clothing as I said?"

"Yes, Captain. He will have a jacket for me by the end of the week. I told him brown or black would be suitable if he has those materials."

"We will see," St. Armand said. "I trust Sails to make a wise choice for your jacket, and you should trust him as well. He is a busy crewman and you do not wish to burden him with additional requests, do you, Miss Burke?"

"Really, it is foolish—"

"Let me decide what obligations the men can assume. It is, after all, my responsibility, not yours. Now, tell me about Mattie's lessons. She seems to have an aptitude for numbers. Can you teach her geometry?"

The question startled Lydia because she'd thought when he invited her here tonight, with just the two of them and the low lantern light and the wine—she had not expected to discuss geometry.

"Yes, I can teach her the fundamentals of geometry. Why is that important?"

"Navigation skills, Miss Burke. Geometry is basic to learning how to navigate the oceans. I do not know where Mattie's future lies, but if she marries a seaman and wants to accompany him it will be a useful skill for her."

Lydia was struck speechless. Captain St. Armand so often seemed to present himself as a wastrel and a rogue that when he said something making sense it startled her. It was out of character, much as if he started reciting sermons.

"Do you know women who have been navigators, Captain?"

"I knew one, the daughter of a Boston whaler. She married a sea captain, accompanied him on his voyages to the Pacific Ocean and helped crew his ship. I always thought it handy for Captain Jerome. If a woman goes to sea with her husband she often is called upon to physic the men when they're ill, keep the log, and in Mrs. Jerome's situation, navigate."

"You intrigue me, sir. I do not expect such a practical attitude from—" she paused.

"You want to say, 'from a pirate.' Think of me rather as a merchant, nothing more, though I'm sometimes called upon to fight. Since I don't have a navy at my back I have to be prepared to defend myself."

"I imagine that there are other ships' captains who would disagree with that."

"Not publicly. Not if they value their good health. More wine?"

She shook her head, but what he'd said did raise an issue she hoped to discuss with him. "Now that you have the care of Mattie will it affect your plans when you arrive in England?"

He steepled his fingers and looked at her. His face was lightly shadowed by new growth on his jawline, the stubble making him look even more disreputable, but she also wondered how it would feel if she touched him there. Would it be rough against her skin, or would it add to the sensation if he were kissing her on her neck, his mouth moving down her throat—

Dear heavens, she was going to have to rein in these thoughts. Robert St. Armand was pretty to gaze upon, but he should have a sign around his neck that said, "Danger, sharks!" For that is what he reminded her of, a toothy predator swimming about, looking for vulnerability in its prey. She recalled an islander telling her that if one encountered a shark you could try and escape by rapping it on the snout. She did not want to explore that theory with Captain St. Armand.

"That is a question I have asked myself, and one of the things I wish to discuss with you. It is obvious to me there is something in England worrying you and you want to flee the country as soon as we land. Whatever it is you are fleeing from, I can help you, but you must tell me what it is. Did you murder someone?"

Lydia looked at him, then shook her head, a rueful smile on her face. "Only you would ask me so blithely if I murdered someone and offer to assist me. Are you not afraid if I murdered once I will do it again?"

His lips curled up in a lazy grin. "No, not now that I've begun to know you better, Miss Burke. There are some people who will kill others with little or no provocation, or just for the fun of it. Most people are not like that. You certainly are not. You might be capable of killing in self-defense, or in defense of someone else, but you do not strike me as the cold-blooded type."

"What about you, Captain? Would you describe yourself as a cold-blooded killer?"

His smile did not change, not by a fraction. "Do you care? After all, you have already established to your satisfaction that I am a pirate. What does it matter how I choose to dispose of my victims? If you need help returning to England I can be of more assistance to you than men without my particular skills."

"I do care, Captain, because you now have the keeping of an impressionable youngster. Children need to learn moral values from those they look up to. Just as Mattie climbed the mast today to show you she could do it, she might one day attempt other feats to win your approval."

"Mattie is not going to grow up to be a pirate, Miss Burke."

"I am guessing your mother never expected you to grow up to be a pirate."

He lost his smile. "We will not discuss my mother. My family is not your concern."

"It is my experience, Captain St. Armand, that how our families treat us has a great deal to do with how we treat our children, for good or for bad."

He leaned forward, resting his arm on the table. "In that case, Miss Burke, tell me more about yourself. How is it *your* parents didn't provide for you and you have to earn your way in the world? Why are you not protected from whatever is threatening you in England?"

Lydia stiffened. "My situation does not affect how Mattie will learn or be raised by *you*, sir. It is irrelevant."

"I disagree. Here, now, you are Mattie's governess. I have seen the quality of the care you offer her and I want to continue to have you work with her when we arrive in England, but you have made it clear that you do not intend to stay and I demand to know why."

Lydia gripped the arms of her chair. "You can demand all the answers you want, but I am not obligated to answer to you and you cannot make me tell you what you want to know. You kidnapped me. I did not hire on with you voluntarily. I owe you nothing, but I choose to take care of Mattie. That ends when we arrive in England as I do not intend to stay employed by you."

He smiled at her again and a primitive part of her brain screamed, "Shark!" but she did not think leaping across the table and hitting him in the nose was the right response. Not yet.

"Miss Burke, you are so naïve. I cannot *make* you answer me? I could do things to you that would have you babbling everything you know."

"If you torture me, how will you explain it to Mattie?"

He walked over to her, pulling her up from her chair, gently, not forcing her, and yet she rose to his touch as his coat slid off of her shoulders to pool on the deck.

"Torture? What an imagination you have. Who said

anything about torture?" he murmured. His hands slid up to cradle her face, his eyes on hers, and his breath whispered across her mouth. She licked her upper lip, tasting burgundy and spice. His gaze honed in on that movement before his own lips were on hers, lightly, warmly, teasing out the moisture her tongue left behind.

She knew she should move, swim to safety, do something to escape, but her legs wouldn't follow her brain's commands, and then her brain shut down all together as his mouth teased its way across hers, lightly touching on the corners before moving up her jawline to her ear. At her shiver of response his luscious lips moved back to hers, lightly kissing, coaxing, not attacking at all.

He ambushed her common sense as he brought other sensations to bear, sensations missing from her life for far too long. She moved closer to him, her hands resting on his shirt, on his shoulders, and he went still.

Did he think *her* a shark, moving through troubled waters to devour him? She almost smiled at the thought, but was distracted by his muscled chest covered in fabric as smooth as his smile, the feel of hard flesh beneath satin sending a shiver down her spine even as his firm lips coaxed her mouth open to delve deeper at her gasp of desire. Caressing the pirate awoke feelings long dormant, feelings having nothing to do with prudence but only with sensation, the touch of passion, of decisions enjoyed in the moment, but regretted later.

Not always regretted, a secret part of her mind whispered to her. *Seize the moment and the pleasure...*

How she wanted to, wanted to stop thinking and just feel, to experience again the explosion of pleasure that came from being with a man. The right man. This man, she knew, would touch her just so, and stroke her to completion. Nanette had not been shy in praising Captain St. Armand's bed skills, and the women in Madame Cornelia's brothel sought out his company as well. His own self esteem would be tied to bringing pleasure to his partner, not just seeking his own satisfaction. He would demand it.

"We can continue this in my bed, Lydia," he whispered in her ear, and that moment, when he used her given name, broke the spell. It was the height of intimacy, shaking her from the sensual fog enveloping her in a brief moment of madness. Her hands clenched on his chest, crushing fistfuls of fine fabric, reminding her of what she was now and where she was.

"No," she whispered, then cleared her throat and tried again, not looking up at his sculpted face. "No, Captain St. Armand. I—I don't know what came over me. I must leave, now."

She pushed at him but he didn't release her, holding her against him. He desired her, that much was obvious, and she feared he wouldn't listen to her, but after an endless minute he put his hand beneath her chin, forcing her head up so he could meet her eyes, his own heavy-lidded, promising sensual delights.

"I will let you leave, little hedgehog, but this conversation is not finished. We will talk, either aboard this ship or when we dock. You will not leave until I am satisfied with your answers."

"Are you threatening me?" she asked, her desire supplanted by outrage.

"I do not need to threaten, Miss Burke. I am merely stating facts so you can come to your own decision."

He released her and stepped back.

"It is time to go to the cabin and read to Mattie. You go, I will join you there."

Lydia did not want to give him the opportunity to change his mind about releasing her, and, after two fumbling attempts, wrenched his door open. She wouldn't look over her shoulder to see if he watched her, smiling that shark smile at her discomposure.

ROBERT WAS NOT SMILING. Kissing the governess was a mistake. She couldn't learn how touching her affected him. He'd started the game with the idea that she'd reveal some of her secrets and ideally reveal some of her delightful body to his gaze and touch, but when his mouth brushed across hers and those slim hands of hers moved up his chest it was all he could do to not pick her up and toss her on his bunk. Her hesitant touch inflamed him and he couldn't understand it. After his weeks at Madame Cornelia's he would have thought himself, if not wrung dry, then so sated he would not be tempted by a drab governess with shining hair and eyes flashing green fire. It wasn't as if he'd been at sea for months on end without ease, he'd just come from the finest brothel in the islands!

And yet there was something about Miss Burke—Lydia— that rocked his composure and his control when they touched. He'd seen her talking with Conroy and he'd been tempted to walk over and push Conroy away from her, maybe overboard, which was stupid. Conroy was a valuable crewman and she was just a governess whose caps annoyed him and whose scent drove him insane. It wasn't fine perfume or creams, but the smell of soap and a faint scent of lemons and a note of womanly musk weaving itself around her, pulling him in and making him do rash things.

Most of Robert's rash decisions over the years involved taking on foes too large to be easily defeated or prey too fast to chase, but those gambles largely paid off. When it came to women there was no question of rash decisions. On the contrary, his moves were well thought out, studied, plotted. A strategy bringing him hours of pleasure in beds from England to the United States and to the Caribbean. He didn't have to fight his way into the arms of lovely ladies, not when they were all too willing to fall into his, from duchesses to doxies.

Now though just the thought of the governess's chestnut hair spread across his pillow gave him a cockstand that needed to disappear before he went to read bedtime stories. Robert splashed water on his face, retrieved his copy of Captain Johnson and took some deep breaths, getting himself in order to face the ladies.

When he opened the door to the cabin there was a suspicious odor of cinnamon, and goat stew. He looked at the governess who said dryly, "I suspect elves—or pirates—brought this little malefactor supper when we weren't looking, Captain."

"Mattie? Did the men sneak food in to you? Who did it?"

Mattie crossed her arms over her skinny chest and said, "I will not peach on them, sir. I'm not a former."

"I believe you mean to say you're not an informer, Mattie," Miss Burke said.

"That is right. I am not an informer. You can keelhaul me, Captain. I won't tell!"

"Hmmmm..." her papa said. He would never tell Miss Burke this, but he was glad the men were supporting Mattie and that she wouldn't squeak on them. He did not desire a lickspittle of a child trying to curry his favor by telling tales.

"I will leave this go for now, miss. Shall we continue with our reading of the life of Anne Bonny?"

"Oh yes, Captain Papa! Anne Bonny would never tattle on the crew, would she?" Mattie sat up on her knees, her nightshirt tangled in the bedclothes.

"Under the covers with you, so you don't catch a chill, and then if Miss Burke will adjust the lantern we will read."

Mattie hurriedly climbed beneath the quilt, folding her hands atop the covers and looking like a curly topped cherub, a cherub wanting stories of mayhem and murder.

"Now, where were we—did we talk about Anne's special friend, Mary Read?"

Mattie shook her head, her eyes wide. "The other girl pirate, Papa?"

"Yes, and we'll read more of her later. But for now you need to know Mary and Anne were the best of friends. Anne was loyal, and as you say, would not peach on another pirate. More than that, when they were finally captured, she and Mary fought back to back against the seaman boarding their vessel. Anne was not the captain, but was the lover of 'Calico Jack' Rackam. We'll read more of Captain Rackam another night, but suffice it to say he came to a bad end, and it was largely of his own doing. Anne said of him on the day of his execution that, 'if he had fought like a man, he need not have been hanged like a dog.'"

The governess stirred when he said Calico Jack and Anne Bonny were lovers, but she did not interrupt. Mattie's eyes were wide as she took this all in.

"Pirates get hanged if they're caught, don't they? *Maman* said there was going to be a hanging in town, but we would not go."

She sat straight up in bed and grabbed Robert's arm. "Papa, the navy's not going to hang you, is it?"

"No one is going to hang your papa, Mattie. I am too smart and too wily to get caught by the navy. Haven't I stayed away from them all these years? That will not change now."

"Anne Bonny was caught, you said so, and she was a

smart pirate. Even smart pirates can get caught and hanged by the navy!"

"Listen—no, don't fuss, just hear me out, Mathilde. I am sailing to England and will make sure no one hangs me. You have my promise on that. Did I not say in St. Martin that you will live with me? That means I take care of you, no matter what. No one will keep me from doing that, not the navy, not storms, not sea monsters."

Mathilde giggled, her good mood restored. "There are no sea monsters, Papa. That's silly."

"And who has been at sea most of his life, miss? When it comes to sea monsters I am the expert. I will protect you from Leviathan and mermaids and krakens and everything else in the ocean, real or just possibly real."

"Will you protect Miss Burke too? Isn't she valuable to us?"

He looked at the dowdy little governess. As cargo, she did not have a lot to offer, though he imagined some Algerian bey might pay for an English governess. He wondered again what her full value would be if he stripped off those ugly garments, loosened her hair, coaxed her to his bed. If he were serious about protecting her, he'd leave her alone. On the other hand, putting her under his protection in England, now *that* had a certain appeal. He suspected he would not tire of her as quickly as his previous paramours and he longed to see what she would look like dressed for a night at the theater, gracing his arm. He answered the child without taking his eyes off the woman.

"Yes, Mathilde, I will protect Miss Burke also. You have my promise on that."

"Good," Mattie said. "Promises are important."

The governess shifted uneasily under his scrutiny.

"You have had a busy day, Mathilde, and if you want your

father to read to you it is time for quiet. Questions can come later."

"Yes, Miss Burke," the child yawned and snuggled deeper into her bunk, and judging by the eyes at half-mast he wouldn't be reading aloud for much longer. Sure enough, he'd moved on to the story of Captain Davis and saw the child's eyes were closed.

"Goodnight, poppet." He leaned over to kiss her on the forehead.

"G'night, Papa. I love you," she murmured, and Robert felt that ache in his chest again. He cleared his throat.

"And I love you, Mathilde."

He arose and looked over at Miss Burke, watching Mathilde, a look of longing on her face as she gazed at the sleepy girl. Did she wish for children and a home of her own? Surely she did not want to spend the rest of her life caring for other people's brats.

He did not want to leave her with a child, he was careful about that—most of the time—but after a liaison with him she'd be free to find herself some merchant or farmer to marry. That thought made him scowl and he was more abrupt than necessary when he said, "Our conversation earlier was interrupted, Miss Burke. I will have answers before the end of this voyage. As you heard, I promised Mattie I would take care of you, and it's important to keep a promise, isn't it?"

"You are not responsible for me, so your promise has no meaning," the governess whispered angrily.

"Shall we step outside to continue this discussion?"

"This discussion is finished, Captain. Good night!"

"No bedtime kiss?"

She strode across the deck, no easy thing to do in these close quarters, and opened the door to usher him out.

He paused in the doorway, looked over her shoulder at

the little girl sound asleep, then back at her. "You can tell me all you like that our conversations are finished, but I am not your charge, so I do not have to follow your orders. I made a promise to keep you safe, and I always keep my promises."

"My life is my own. I will make my own decisions and my own choices once I am free of your control."

"That's the sticking point, isn't it? You are under my control, and by extension, under my protection."

"A situation which shall be remedied when we are in England and I am booking passage back to the islands."

"So you insist, Miss Burke. Bear in mind that much can happen on a voyage across the Atlantic Ocean. Already your life has taken a different, and dare I say, more interesting turn than what awaited you on St. Thomas? You should be open to life's possibilities, that's all. You never know what the next day will bring."

"As long as it brings me out of the grasp of pirates and their ilk, I will seize those opportunities, Captain St. Armand."

"You're not being open-minded now, Miss Burke. You are not considering the advantages of spending more time in my company. And in Mattie's company too, of course."

"I've given long thought to the advantages of your daughter's company, sir," she said sweetly. "I will miss Mattie. You, I will be glad to see the back of."

"So you say. Good night, then. Tomorrow is another day."

CHAPTER 9

$\mathcal{T}$he following days were fair, but with winds convincing Lydia a substantial jacket of any design was fast becoming a necessity. She wrapped herself in her warmest shawl and was standing at the starboard rail with her arms clutched about her when a brisk voice said, "Miss Burke, put this on before you catch your death and are no use to me whatsoever."

Captain St. Armand loomed behind her holding out a wool coat, a more practical looking garment than most of what she'd seen him wear. It was cobalt blue, a deep, rich shade, its gold buttons gleaming in the sunlight. The scent of cedar clinging to it made her breathe deep of the fresh smell. She suspected it was the captain's own winter gear, brought out of storage.

"Here," he said, pulling the shawl off of her shoulders and before she could protest, putting the coat around her so she could get her arms in the sleeves. They were too long, of course, but she used the extra length to tuck her hands in, sighing at the warmth of the rich wool. He pulled the jacket closed and frowned down at her, his hands on the lapels, holding her in place. They were standing too close, there on the deck in the sunlight and the full view of the crew, but no one watched them. Was the crew used to their captain bringing women aboard? Or was it simply they'd come to accept her presence in their little wooden world, and didn't judge her by the same standards as the good people of the merchant class in the islands? As a governess she was always under scrutiny, for while the islanders might tolerate misbehavior amongst themselves they expected the upper servants to be above reproach, their behavior reflecting on their employers. Too often Lydia had to keep her opinions to herself, even when she heard the man of the house spouting total nonsense about the workings of Parliament or discussing the war with Napoleon, and later with the United States. They were all fine patriots on the surface, but every merchant she'd had dealings with was quite willing to trade with American and French privateers when the opportunity arose. Men like Robert St. Armand became rich during the war because there were outlets for their piratical activity, businessmen who cared only how their ledgers balanced at the end of the day.

Maybe she too shouldn't be so quick to judge the pirate. After all, those merchants had paid her modest wages with the proceeds from their dealings with scoundrels of every stripe. Living with Nanette was different, since Nanette made no bones about being anything other than a loyal daughter of France in exile. She'd been more honest than the customers of the whorehouse who paid her in silver, but wouldn't acknowledge her on the street.

"Why are you looking at me like that, Miss Burke?"

"How am I looking at you, Captain?"

"I'm not sure," he said, irritated. "You are looking at me—

it's not how you usually look when you're preparing to scold me over something I've done, or not done, or should be doing."

"Maybe I'm just grateful you're willing to give me your coat."

He cleared his throat. "Yes, well, Sails says he'll have your gear finished soon."

She stroked her hand down the sleeve of the coat she wore now, the wool soft and fine beneath her fingers, so different from the fabric purchased by those without funds to spend on golden buttons.

There was a time when she had clothing like this and took it for granted, as much a part of her life as regular meals and a comfortable bed at night. Hard living had a way of making one appreciate what one had, not what one lacked. She'd gotten that much out of her experiences.

What awaited her in England if she was discovered would make the hard life of a governess look like a walk in the park. No matter how much the captain's offer of protection lured her, she had to protect herself. Nothing could interfere with that, not Mattie, not Captain St. Armand, not people she hadn't thought about for many years.

"Have you been to America, Captain?"

"Yes. I have business associates in America, in New Orleans and Boston, and in Baltimore."

"Which of those cities would you pick if you were settling there?"

He cocked his head and looked at her. "You would go to the United States? That is unusual for a single woman. Most English women who settle there do so because of marriage."

Lydia shrugged and began walking, and he fell into step alongside her, his hands clasped behind his back. He was wearing a wool jacket too, not as substantial as hers, and he'd pulled up the collar against the wind. She smiled to herself because the captain was also rigged out with a fully fastened white shirt, waistcoat and cravat. While the waistcoat was a rich marigold shade embroidered with primroses, the cravat was a sober and respectable cloth tied neatly. Colder climes seem to have put an end to the more flamboyant costumes of the islands.

"I was led to understand in the islands that Americans place a premium on English governesses for their children. Since it is my occupation, and since I'm no longer in the islands, it makes sense for me to go where I have the best opportunities. Which of those cities would you recommend to me?"

"None of them. New Orleans and Boston have miserable climates, and New Orleans is rife with disease. In Boston you're less prone to keel over dead from yellowjack, but the weather is disgusting. Frigid, wet winters and stiflingly humid summers. You wouldn't like it."

"What about Baltimore?"

"It does have a more temperate climate," he acknowledged grudgingly. "But the summers are still infested with insects and disease. For your health's sake you are better off in England."

She stopped and looked at him. "Captain St. Armand, why are you so eager for me to be in England? Are you, yourself English? I suspected you might be French."

"My life is not important in your consideration, ma'am. However, I have contacts—legitimate contacts—in England who could assist you in finding a position there."

Lydia resumed walking. "With all due respect, I hardly think a reference from a notorious pirate will help me find employment."

He looked at her out of the corner of his eye. "I could

convince someone to take you on, Miss Burke. I can be most convincing."

"Don't you mean, 'most threatening'?"

He made a rude noise that would have earned Mattie a reprimand if she'd been caught doing that.

"I cannot fathom why people keep accusing me of making threats. I never threaten. I make suggestions, I smile, I put forward my bona fides—it seems to work quite well for me."

"Regardless, I have no intention of staying in England, as I have pointed out to you numerous times. If you won't assist my going to America, I will manage on my own."

"Is that how you ended up in the islands? Managing on your own?"

She walked beside him in silence as she thought. Offering pieces of the truth was better than obfuscating, less likely to trap her in a falsehood.

"I had letters of recommendation to families in the islands who friends thought would be interested in hiring a governess. They were right, and I did have employment until I lived with Nanette and Mathilde."

"I have to ask, how is it that you fell in with a woman of Nanette's background?"

"You couldn't possibly be judging her, could you?"

"Not at all," the pirate said. "Just curious."

"I'd often seen Nanette and Mathilde in the marketplace, and was struck by Nanette's *joie de vivre*." Lydia smiled in remembrance. "It was like having a butterfly hovering around, something lovely to look at who made you happy. One morning, a year or so back, she was indisposed and I helped her to her lodgings. She'd begun to experience symptoms of the disease that would carry her off."

"I should have been told," he said, frowning. "She should have contacted me."

Lydia kept her lips pressed together. He did not need to

hear comments on irresponsible men, not when he was so clearly feeling remorse at not being with the mother of his child when she needed him.

"We talked, Nanette and I, and found each other's company so congenial that I was open-minded when she offered me employment with her. It was an opportune offer, as I was looking for another family to hire me. And when I spent time with Mathilde, well, I knew that was where I needed to be."

He stopped and put his hand on her arm. "How can you leave Mathilde now?" he asked softly so the men wouldn't hear. "How can you leave after you've been with her through so much?"

Lydia looked away from him. Damn him for making her feel it all over again. He did not deserve to see her cry, and she would not, not in front of him.

"I knew, Captain, from the day I first saw her in the market, that Mathilde was not mine. She was Nanette's child, and yours. Nanette had faith if anything happened to her you would care for the child and it was her dying wish that Mathilde know her father. Now she is your responsibility, and I will go on with my life as I always knew I must."

"You could stay."

She turned back to him. "In what capacity, Captain? You have not explained to me what your plans are when you reach England."

He was the one who looked away now. "My plans are not your concern."

"On the contrary, your plans are very much my concern if you expect me to continue caring for Mathilde."

Whatever the captain was going to say was drowned out by a call from the lookout.

"A sail, Captain!"

"Mattie, fetch my spyglass," he called out, moving away

from Lydia, already moving toward the mast to climb for a better view.

Mattie scampered up from below with the captain's glass clutched in her fist, her bearing showing her pride at being given this important task.

St. Armand climbed and looked out at the ship following.

"Is it a prize, Papa?"

He came back down, frowning.

"Mr. Fuller, we're being chased. I believe that's a frigate on our tail. Make preparations for when they catch up with us."

"A frigate? You mean the navy?"

He looked at Lydia as if only then recalling she was there, and his face lit up.

"You can be useful to me, Miss Burke, you and Mattie. Take Mathilde below and dress her in her most girlish frock, something with plenty of furbelows and trim. Mathilde, you will gather one or two of your dolls—and your tea set, bring that up as well. Miss Burke, I want you to put on your most hideous governess outfit. Oh, and pin your hair tight under your ugly cap."

"I cannot do that, Captain," Lydia said through her teeth. "Some malefactor stole into my cabin and purloined my last cap and my hairpins!"

"Are you going to fight the navy, Papa?"

"Now, why would we do that, Mathilde? The navy is our friend."

"It is?" Mr. Fuller asked.

"It will be when they see we are a peaceful merchant ship, Mr. Fuller. Take some men to the hold and do what needs to be done while I prepare the appropriate documents. The navy has far too much time on its hands now that the war is finished, and there's nothing they'd like more than to round up pirates. That is why we're going to be sure not to give them any reason to suspect us of piratical tendencies."

"Aye, Captain," Fuller said, and ordered a team to go below with him and make preparations.

He tapped his spyglass against his hand while he thought. "Mathilde, when the frigate catches us, we will be on our best behavior. If you are asked questions about pirates, just tell them I'm your papa, captain of the *Prodigal Son*."

"We're not going to fly false colors, Papa?"

"Captain St. Armand! It is wrong of you to involve Mathilde in your deception!"

Both the child and her father looked at her in puzzlement.

"There is no deception here, Miss Burke. Am I not Mathilde's papa? Is she not the captain's daughter? The alternative is for the navy to believe we are pirates and arrest us all. You also."

"Me? I am not a pirate!"

"Can you be sure the navy will believe that? After all, there is precedent for women pirates as you well know. I can't be certain they would believe you, and you might find the experience of being accused and questioned unpleasant."

"But—" Lydia sputtered, then stopped. It was hard to argue with the man's logic.

"That is why we are going to be ourselves, but the least threatening 'ourselves' we can be. Miss Mathilde St. Armand rather than Marauding Mattie, Miss Lydia Burke, governess and not a notorious pirate—"

"What!"

"How do I know for certain what you did before I met you? And as for me, I will be who I have ever been—Captain Robert St. Armand, merchant. Now, go below, ladies. Being ourselves means dressing appropriately."

"Aye, Captain," Mattie said, and scooted below. St. Armand snapped his fingers.

"Ugly cap and pins. Right. I will locate them and bring them to you in your cabin."

"You will not get them back!"

He leaned in, smiling. "Would you care to wager on that, little governess?"

Instead, she turned on her heel and followed Mattie below.

CHAPTER 10

*L*ydia tugged her cap down another fraction of an inch. It felt odd to be wearing it again, which was strange because she'd worn them for so long in St. Martin. But wearing the cap was the right thing to do, even if Captain St. Armand treated it as a disguise, part of his japery to catch the Royal Navy off guard. He was speaking now with an earnest young naval officer looking around the ship's deck with a frown.

"But of course all these guns are needed, Lieutenant Finch. Now that we're no longer traveling in convoy with the navy, we have to defend ourselves. There are still malefactors on the water looking for merchant ships to rob."

"You refer to pirates, Captain?"

"Naturally. If anything, those rascals have become bolder since the end of the war."

"Yes, so we've heard," Lieutenant Finch said dryly, looking around at the *Prodigal Son's* crew. For their part they looked no more piratical than most sailors. Some of the men who normally festooned themselves with select pieces of booty were more sedately attired, taking their cue from the captain.

He'd rigged out himself as sober as a schoolmaster in an unadorned blue coat, a waistcoat with a subdued brown stripe and dark trousers. He even had boots on today.

A costume, she sneered to herself. Her attire was her own at least.

Lieutenant Finch came around to where Lydia was perched and stopped, then recovered himself.

"Your pardon, ma'am. I did not know this ship carried passengers."

"Lieutenant Finch, may I present Miss Lydia Burke, and my daughter, Mathilde."

Mathilde and Lydia rose and made their curtseys. Finch was still looking at Lydia as if trying to determine her place aboard the *Prodigal*. She had to admit that at the moment she looked about as little like a pirate as was possible, though Mattie may have trumped her. The child was decked out in a pink frock festooned with ruffles, her curly hair tamed by ribbons, a doll clutched under her arm and her thumb stuck in her mouth. The latter affectation was purely for dramatic effect, as Lydia well knew.

They'd been seated, per the captain's orders, at a table where they set a pretend tea party with some of Mathilde's dolls arrayed around them as guests. Lydia had to admit it was a disarming sight and Mathilde had entered the planned deception with enthusiasm—too much enthusiasm in Lydia's opinion.

For her own part, Lydia's hair was confined by pins and cap, her gray dress with its white collar and cuffs neatly buttoned and smoothed down. Captain St. Armand had taken a long look at her, sighed and said, "You'll do, Miss Burke, though it is a shame to hide your beauty under such drab feathers."

"Your Spanish coin will not buy my good favor, Captain… or anything else."

"Miss Burke, I never deal in false flattery. It is not necessary and if I did not know you better I would suspect you of fishing for compliments."

Her appearance had deflected the lieutenant's interest as he squatted down on his heels and gave Mattie a smile that lit up his rather nondescript face. Captain St. Armand had nothing to fear if he was competing with the naval officer for dance partners, but the young man's freckled countenance was open and encouraging.

"That is a pretty dolly you have there. What is her name?"

Lydia held her breath since just last night that doll had been re-christened "Bloody Anne Bonny" in honor of Mattie's new favorite pirate, but today Mathilde just popped her thumb out of her mouth and shyly whispered, "Her name is Annie."

"Annie, hmmm? I have a little sister named Annie. She likes playing with dollies also."

There was such a look of longing on Lieutenant Finch's face that Lydia was prompted to say, "Has it been a long time since you've seen your sister, Lieutenant?"

His face cleared and he smiled at Lydia.

"It shows, does it? Yes, Miss Burke, I have not seen my little sister in over a year. I don't even know if she still plays with dolls, or if she remembers me at all."

"The lady is Mathilde's governess," Captain St. Armand said. "I am certain she has duties to attend to with the child. We should retire to my cabin so I can show you our papers, Lieutenant."

Lydia looked at him in surprise, her brows lifted. She was doing all that he'd asked of her and then some, so he had no call to be brusque.

"Can Lieutenant Finch stay for tea, Papa? We have biscuits, but they are pretend biscuits."

If he was dismayed at his budding actress's attempt to

steal the scene he didn't show it, but only said, "Lieutenant Finch's captain will be expecting him to report back as soon as possible, poppet, so they can continue cruising."

"Your papa's correct, Mathilde," Finch said, tweaking the child's curls, which earned him a look from the poppet that had Lydia glad Mattie wasn't at knife practice. "My captain expects me back and we must do what our captains—and our papas—tell us to."

"Just so," St. Armand murmured.

"Goodbye, Lieutenant Finch," Mattie said, clutching Bloody Anne to her chest.

"I hope you have the opportunity to see your family soon, Lieutenant," Lydia said.

He gave her an intense look before smiling at her and saying, "I hope so also, Miss Burke."

The captain cleared his throat and Lieutenant Finch gave Mattie a small wave of his fingers and followed St. Armand below while his men stayed on deck, watching the crew. For their part the men went about their normal tasks, keeping an eye on the seamen from the *Epione*.

She and Mattie continued their tea party, which wasn't so different from other tea parties they'd enjoyed except that Mattie seemed primed to become Marauding Mattie should the need arise.

Turnbull and Nash paused to let the ladies know that they were still prepared to drink tea with them in exchange for lessons.

"Today would not be the best time for that, gentlemen," Lydia said. "We are all on edge and I doubt Mr. Fuller would release you from your duties."

"Not a chance," Nash said, looking at an *Epione* seaman standing at ease, but keeping a watchful eye on the ship. "We have to get this lot off and be safely away before Mr. Fuller will let any of us catch our breath."

To punctuate his statement the captain and Lieutenant Finch came up from below. St. Armand wore a relaxed smile, while Finch looked unhappy. His eyes rested on Lydia and she heard him say, "I need to speak with Miss Burke, Captain. If you'll excuse me?"

"I will accompany you."

"I'd rather you did not," Finch said, and while his voice was mild, his words made his boarding party come to alert stances. A ripple of tension ran through the *Prodigal's* crew, but St. Armand just said, "Of course, Lieutenant. My ship— and its passengers—are at your disposal."

Finch walked over to her and Lydia stood until he stopped before her and said, "May I speak with you? I won't take her far," he added for Mattie's benefit.

She carefully did not look at the captain, but inclined her head. "Of course, Lieutenant."

He motioned for her to step away from the tea set, then clasped his hands behind his back and said softly, "Miss Burke, I had the pleasure of examining the documents in Captain St. Armand's cabin. They are the neatest and most complete manifests I have ever seen."

He looked at her sidelong but she said nothing, so he continued, walking the deck with her by his side. "This is not my first voyage in these waters and one hears tales, tales of various ships and their captains, and which side of the law they sail on. When I see paperwork as pretty as that aboard this ship, it reminds me of those stories I have heard."

He stopped walking, and she did as well, looking up into his earnest face as he leaned in and said for her ears alone, "Are you on this vessel of your own will, Miss Burke—no, do not look over at the child, but answer my question, please. I can assure you no harm will come to you. This ship is well defended, but the navy is quite capable of handling one rogue pirate if it comes down to that."

Lydia's heart raced. She'd heard Finch say the *Epione* was bound for Jamaica, and it would be easy enough to return to the islands, or leave for America after the safe harbor of being rescued by the Royal Navy.

WHAT WAS that bastard saying to her? Robert couldn't read their lips from afar but he saw how the naval officer bent down to hear what the little governess had to say, how her face lifted up to his, but her stupid cap hid her expression from him. He was going to burn those rags as soon as he had them back in his possession, and he *would* have them back in his possession, if she didn't say something ridiculous, bringing hordes of sailors and marines attempting to board his vessel. That wouldn't happen, not while he had breath in his body.

Then his gaze fell on Mattie, who came next to Miss Burke and leaned against her side, thumb in her mouth, dolly clutched beneath her arm. The woman's head turned away from the officer, toward the child, and her hand rose to rest atop the girl's curls like a dove alighting on a slender branch.

The governess shook her head at something the lieutenant said, and Robert relaxed. He may not be able to read lips, but he was good at reading people, a skill taking him into many beds and out of many fights over the years. Miss Burke leaned away from the navy man now, holding Mattie closer to her side.

She wouldn't peach on them. She wouldn't do anything that might harm the child, even if it meant she had to stay aboard the *Prodigal* and continue on to England.

The lieutenant made his bow to Miss Burke and came back over to Captain St. Armand. Robert worked hard to keep a smile off his face. Today he wore his "sober merchant captain" expression, which did not include a smile. He'd practiced it for days like this.

Lieutenant Finch did not appear to be as susceptible to Robert's charms as most young ladies, and even a navy man or two, and put no effort into schooling his own expression.

"Everything *appears* to be in order, Captain."

Robert's inner devil, the one that over the years too often counseled actions with interesting consequences, prompted him to ask, "Did you expect otherwise, Lieutenant Finch?"

"Do not push me," Finch said softly. "You should be damned grateful your passage includes a lady and a little girl, for if there were not innocents aboard this hulk we might be having a very different discussion."

Robert generously let the "hulk" slur pass. He could afford to be generous.

"If you have no further business with us, we will set sail for England, Lieutenant."

Finch watched him for a few heartbeats longer, then turned on his heel to board his boat back to the *Epione*. The men watched it depart without jeering or cat-calling, as they too knew the value of acting prudently to stay out of the sights of the Royal Navy.

When the ships were a safe distance apart Robert told Mr. Fuller to give the men an extra ration of rum as a reward for their avoiding trouble, and the crew cheered their captain.

"And you, Marauding Mattie, get an extra portion of pudding, if your teacher approves. Your behavior today was everything I would expect from Captain St. Armand's daughter."

"What about Miss Burke, Papa? She was good today too, wasn't she?"

"Very good indeed," Robert said, smiling at the woman next to the child. She did not smile back. "Would you like extra pudding, Miss Burke?"

He had a thought then, heaven knows where it came from —probably from inside his breeches—a thought of him and Miss Burke sitting in his bed, naked, feeding each other bites of jam roly-poly, the sweet sliding off the spoon and into her mouth, or perhaps she'd use her fingers and then he could lick them clean.

And if he didn't stop thinking like that he was going to have a cockstand in front of a small and impressionable child.

"No, I do not want pudding, Captain St. Armand. If you're feeling grateful," she added quickly, "I want your assurance my cap will not go missing."

She was secure in her knowledge that she had the upper hand because there was no way he'd promise her in front of Mattie and then break his word by stealing the garments.

She was right, dammit, and his reaction showed, for her upturned lips blossomed into a full smile and it stopped him where he stood. When she turned that look upon him it made him think of her as she would look if he had the dressing of her, her skin aglow in satins and laces, amethysts around her neck making her malachite eyes look an even deeper green.

"Very well," he conceded. "You may keep your cap, Miss Burke, and no one will tamper with it aboard this ship. You have my word."

"My hairpins also!"

"You should have negotiated that sooner, Miss Burke. We're done here. Mr. Fuller!"

"Aye, Captain?" the older man said, trying not to grin at the governess's expression.

"Make sure the men know they are not to tamper with Miss Burke's cap. That's an order."

"Aye, aye, Captain."

"Mathilde, I am going below to freshen up. You may wish

to change your clothing into something more suited to your lessons."

"Am I climbing today, Papa?"

"Yes, I will take you aloft, Mattie, and you will show me what you've learned from Mr. Norton. Then we'll have knife practice."

It wasn't necessary to add this, but he was fond of the sound of the governess's teeth grinding against each other. It meant she was paying attention to him. In a cheerful mood, he turned to go down to his own cabin to change into more comfortable attire.

"Captain St. Armand."

He stopped and turned. They were alone now, Mattie having headed below, Mr. Fuller back at his duties.

"Yes?"

She stepped even closer, so no one else could hear. "If you intend to foist false papers on the authorities in the future, you might be wise to make sure they pass muster."

"Those papers are completely satisfactory, Miss Burke."

"Too satisfactory. Lieutenant Finch expected something not quite so perfect, and I imagine others might also catch that. It is like having banknotes too crisp and unused."

"That is excellent advice, and most interesting, because only someone who has familiarity with forgers and their craft might know that."

She went quite still, like a doe sensing danger nearby. "You can take my advice or not, Captain. Lieutenant Finch noticed the condition of your papers, and I felt it worth mentioning to you. For Mattie's sake. If you were hauled off in chains, what would become of her?"

"Believe it or not, I have given the question of Mattie's future some consideration. We will discuss this again in England. Before you leave to return to the islands, or

America or Timbuktu, or wherever you are off to after this voyage."

She continued to study him, then nodded. "That conversation would ease my mind before I leave, knowing provision is made for Mathilde's future. It is not an easy world for women who have to make their own way."

"As you know all too well?"

"Exactly right, Captain. If you will excuse me?"

She turned on her heel and went below, but he watched her go, considering everything she'd told him—or not told him. Someday he would uncover all of Miss Burke's secrets, he promised himself.

Later that night he was poring over the ship's papers, the ones he kept for the edification of the Royal Navy or other governmental bodies intent on interfering with his livelihood. He had to acknowledge that the little governess was correct. The papers were too perfect. He needed to fix them, and when he was next in London he would have a chat with his favorite forger, reminding Stockwell his artistic abilities were best kept for the paintings he forged. Documents required authenticity, not flourishes. He was confident Stockwell would take the message to heart because he enjoyed Robert's generous pay. He also enjoyed breathing.

THE CLOCK WAS STILL a few minutes shy of midnight when the crying from Mattie's bunk woke Lydia. She threw back the covers and pulled on her wrapper as the cabin door was flung open. Captain St. Armand stood there, a naked blade in his hand.

"What is it? What is wrong with Mattie?"

Lydia assessed the situation and made a quick decision.

"She is having a nightmare. Pick her up and hold her, Captain."

He reared back. "Me? She needs you. You are her governess!"

"She needs her father. You are the person she trusts now."

"I'm not ready," he said lamely.

Lydia said nothing to this but stepped back. He sheathed his knife and sat on the bed alongside the child, his hand on her shoulder.

"Mattie? Mattie? Wake up, poppet."

The child jerked awake, eyes blinking dazedly in the dim light entering the cabin from the passageway.

"Papa?"

She threw her arms around his neck, clinging to him.

"I was in prison, and the navy was going to hang you, and *Maman* was dead and I will never see her again." The child sobbed. "Don't leave me, Papa!" He held his child tightly in his arms and looked helplessly at Lydia over Mattie's head, but she was not about to give him assistance on this. Mattie was usually such a cheerful child one could forget it had been less than a year since her mother died. Lydia knew from her own life it was a pain that never completely fades.

St. Armand ran his hand down his daughter's sleep-tousled curls. "Mattie, I will never leave you!"

"You will leave me in England and go to sea and get yourself hanged!"

"Leave you in England? I would never go to sea without my best crewman, now would I? I will not sail without my Marauding Mattie by my side." He hugged her closer, rocking her in his arms. Lydia sat on her bunk, clutching her hands together as she watched the father soothe his child, and yearned for those safe times when she'd had someone who would hold her after a nightmare and assure her all would be well.

Those times were past, and she had only herself to look to for comfort in the night. She could do better for Mattie. She needed reassurance there was stability in her life, someone who would be there for her, because Lydia was leaving.

"Your mama loved you very much and sent you to me because she knew I would take care of you, Mathilde," he assured the child. "You've had a bad dream, but you have nothing to fear. I will not leave you."

"Is that a promise, Papa?"

"You know it is, Mattie. Didn't I say I will love you always and forever?"

He laid her back down and tucked the covers around her.

"Stay, Papa, please?"

"There is nothing here to frighten you, Mattie."

"I won't be frightened," the child protested. "But Miss Burke might get afraid during the night if she hears a noise. Please don't go!"

He looked over at Lydia, then back at the child.

"Miss Burke is as fierce and courageous as Anne Bonny or Mary Read, poppet. Didn't she travel all the way to the islands? And who else would take on the task of teaching Nash and Turnbull their numbers? I will be directly across the way if you need me, but I have confidence your governess will protect you."

Mattie looked skeptical, but yawned and said, "*Maman* used to sing to me when I had a nightmare. Will you sing to me?"

"Sing?"

"Yes, Papa."

He looked at Lydia, but she said nothing, so he cleared his throat and started singing "Haul Away Joe." His voice was not on a level with his amazing looks, but he could carry a tune, and soon the child's eyes were closed.

"She's asleep," he whispered, and stood.

"Hardly the most appropriate lullaby, Captain St. Armand."

"Trust me, it was the most inoffensive chantey I could recall on short notice."

She tilted her head and looked at him. "You think me as fierce and courageous as a lady pirate?"

"It's only the truth, Miss Burke. Goodnight."

CHAPTER 11

"*S*ee, now angle the knife so it skates along the bone instead of cutting straight down. Does more damage that way. Miss Burke, it is difficult to teach with you making those squawking noises."

"Captain St. Armand! Is this teaching of violence truly necessary?"

"It depends on whether you want some assurance that if Mattie ever gets into a fight she can walk away with her parts intact. Remember, child, there is no unfair fight. The only unfair fight is the one you lose. Run, hide, throw dirt in their eyes, kick them in the bollocks, bite, scratch, punch, claw their eyes out—whatever it takes to walk away alive, that's what you do."

"Aye, Captain."

Lydia must have made another disapproving noise because the pirate turned his attention on her.

"What do you know about defending yourself against attackers, Miss Burke? For example—here, take this."

He passed her his boot knife, taking up the wooden blade he used with Mattie.

"Now, face me and try to stab me."

"This is ridicul—" Lydia never finished the statement because St. Armand moved toward her with a stabbing motion and she fell back, coming up against the mainmast. He pulled up a fraction from where his "weapon" would have entered her belly.

"You see? You never know where violence will come from. It is always best to be ready for it. Mattie, what's the first rule of a fight?"

"Run away if you can."

"Excellent. There is no sense in standing there and allowing yourself to be injured or killed. But sometimes a fight is necessary. Miss Burke, if you saw someone attacking Mattie, what would you do?"

"I would try to stop them!"

"You see? That is your natural response, and it is a good one." He looked down at the child and ruffled her hair.

"Our lesson is finished for today, Mattie. I want to spend some time helping Miss Burke improve her skills. Practice with your blade in your left hand because we're going to work on that tomorrow."

Mattie looked disappointed her lessons were ended, but passed over her practice blade.

"Here, Miss Burke. It hurts if Papa raps you with this, but it will help you learn quicker."

"Thank you," Lydia said, gingerly taking the implement from her pupil.

He slipped his knife back into his boot. "Soon enough you ladies will be practicing with real blades, but you should be prepared to turn anything at hand—a book, a teapot, a parasol, a shoe—into a weapon."

"A shoe?"

"Not as effective as an axe if you throw it, but it could allow you a few more seconds to escape danger. And if you throw it with enough strength and aim you could put out an eye," he finished on an encouraging note. His eyes tracked Mattie as she went to the stern to talk to Turnbull.

"I have enemies. They won't hesitate to use Mattie to get to me. Until recently I never had to worry about anyone else being hurt because of who I am—the men know the risk and can take care of themselves. But now there's Mattie..."

"'He that hath wife and children hath given hostages to fortune...'"

"Yes. Bacon had the right of it, Miss Burke." He braced his shoulders and when he looked back at Lydia his face wore its usual charming expression. "You too should know how to defend yourself. I do not know—yet—what dark secrets you're hiding that make you so averse to returning to England, but I would wager some tricks to defend yourself might come in handy for you as well. So today we will have a lesson, and we will have a lesson every day, little hedgehog, until we make landfall. Who knows? Perhaps your next employer will appreciate the added skills you bring to your classroom?"

"The odds of me being hired by another pirate are rather slim, Captain St. Armand."

"Of course you think that, but what were the odds of being hired by even one...merchant captain...Miss Burke? The sea is a dangerous place, and additional training could come in handy for you."

Lydia knew there was no avoiding this and there was a small part of her cheering inside, the part of her who rebelled against pulling her hair into a tight bun and keeping her eyes down to play the role of a meek governess. More than most, Lydia knew being able to defend oneself from attackers was a useful skill indeed for a woman on her own.

"What do you want me to do?"

He smiled at her, pleased with her acquiescence.

"Just as with Mattie, we will start with the basics. Now, hold your knife like this—a good grip, blade edge down. You see how you can angle your wrist—here, let me show you."

Before Lydia could protest he stepped behind her, so close she felt him pressing up against her.

"Try to relax, Miss Burke. I'm not going to ravish you here up on deck in full sight of the crew. They would be jealous of my skills. I'd much rather ravish you in the privacy and comfort of my berth."

She attempted to pull away, but his arm was wrapped about her waist, holding her secure against him.

"You're correct," she gritted through her teeth. "Knowing how to knife fight might save me from unpleasant encounters with all manner of scoundrels."

"Exactly. Now then—what is that cologne you're wearing? You smell heavenly."

"Captain St. Armand! Release me at once! And I am not wearing cologne. I only use soap and water. Your soap."

"Is that so? It certainly smells different on you."

He leaned his head forward again, inhaling deeply. Lydia's gaze darted around frantically, but none of the men were watching them. Taking hold of her wrist, the one holding the wooden blade, he said, "Loosen your grip so I can reposition your fingers."

She followed his command blindly, too aware of how close he was, how she smelled his soap on him, and it *was* different, muskier, darker, making her breathe in his clean scent of salt and man along with the soap.

His warm hand moved over her nerveless fingers, stroking along the length of her hand, moving the wood until it was satisfactory to him, then he closed his hand around hers.

"You see? This grip will keep you from being sliced by your own weapon. You would be amazed how often that happens with people who just grab a knife and start flailing away with it."

She forced her focus back on what he was saying, what he was doing as he extended her arm in front of her, then moved it to the side. It was more comfortable holding the knife like this, but when he stepped back she was finally drew air into her lungs to the full.

He glided in front of her and watched her, his smirk doing nothing to improve her temper.

"I am glad you insisted I learn how to do this properly, Captain St. Armand. One never knows when one will have to defend oneself against ne'er-do-wells."

"So true. However," his face grew serious, "you would be at a disadvantage in a fight based on reach, strength and your lack of experience. What you have going for you is the element of surprise. An attacker might expect a tavern doxy to be armed with a knife, but he wouldn't expect it of a lady such as yourself. Surprise can be a powerful weapon and properly used can give you a chance to escape danger or stop it. The best knife-fighters depend on speed for success, so that is what we will work on today."

All of what he said was sensible, and Lydia forced her total attention on his words and actions, not on how he looked standing there in his open jacket, the laces of his shirt fluttering in the breeze, his hair disarranged so that a gleaming lock fell across his forehead. He hadn't shaved this morning, and his jaw was darkened by a shadow making him look even more piratical. She'd felt it against her neck when he leaned in earlier. That clash of textures against her skin, the abrasion of his stubble woke nerve endings long dormant, rousing memories of a man's body against hers, a man's hair-roughened limbs entwined with hers and how long it had been missing from her life.

Her body remembered those sensations, her instincts

drawing her into dangerous waters where she was poorly armed to defend herself against bad decisions.

"And once an attacker realizes you're armed, he may grab for your knife. Remember, a soft grip to throw, a tight grip to keep. Sometimes you will see people grip the weapon with the point down, to stab from overhead. Always a mistake, unless your goal is to make your victim burst out laughing. Look, I will show you."

He came and stood before her, his movements workman-like as he focused on the task at hand. He moved the blade in her hand so that it pointed down.

"Now, extend your arm and see where the shadow is on the deck."

She saw the plank where her knife's shadow ended, a tiny bit of tar marking the spot.

"Flip your knife over so that you're holding it as I showed you, then extend again. Your shadow is longer now, your reach better. It's also easier to disarm an opponent using the other grip. Switch again and try to stab me—and don't smile as you're doing it, even though I am sure the thought of running me through gives you great pleasure."

She switched to the point down grip and moved in to stab him, realizing what he was saying as soon as she stepped forward. She had to raise her arm high, which exposed all of her side and chest, and as she brought her arm down he easily blocked the move then grabbed her wrist, twisting until she was forced to drop the wooden knife.

It also brought her up against him.

"You see, Miss Burke?" he breathed, his lips nearly against hers, so close she could taste the scent of coffee. "Now you are defenseless and I could poke you with my…weapon with little resistance."

So she brought her knee up in a movement as old as women dealing with annoying men, a movement he'd been totally unprepared for. Her angle wasn't perfect so it was a glancing blow, but enough to make him curse and jump away from her.

"You're correct, Captain, that element of surprise is quite valuable when opponents aren't equally skilled."

He glared at her, his eyes cobalt slits, but then bowed his head and said, "A true hit. I made the elementary mistake of misjudging my opponent, and you were right to take advantage of my error. Let us continue."

It had been an entertaining morning, Lydia admitted to herself that afternoon as she strolled the deck. It was far too beautiful to stay below as Mattie napped and she wanted to savor her freedom, pretend there wasn't the possibility of disaster at the end of this voyage. At the very least she would not be able to enjoy this feeling of flying across the waves, the salt spray on her face making her lick her lips, savoring the special taste of the ocean, a memory to store for darker days. She had the impression of eyes on her and looked over to the stern where Captain St. Armand watched her, his face shadowed by the canvas straining above them. He exchanged a word with Conroy, then walked over to her and she watched him, watched the lithe grace of his body, the play of muscles beneath his breeches and his coat.

He took her arm, without asking permission, and began to walk around the deck with her. She did not think to protest, and frankly, did not wish to. She was honest enough to admit to herself that the pirate captain may be many things she could not approve of, but he was not boring.

Far from it. Every time she was in his vicinity it was as if she were awakening from a nap, her senses coming alive as they had not for a long, long time. She asked him questions about his ship as they walked. Not only was she curious, but one never knew when knowledge would come in handy. If she wanted to stay in the islands or live in a coastal community, knowing something of ships and sailing would help her teach her students information they needed in their own lives.

"Repairs are a substantial expense on this vessel, or any vessel of this size. Fortunately, many of the ships with which we do business have what—"

"A sail, Cap'n!"

The call from Norton distracted Lydia from any caustic remarks about stealing rope. Captain St. Armand dropped her arm without ceremony and went to where Norton pointed before directing the man aloft.

Mr. Fuller came alongside the *Prodigal Son's* commander.

"Looks to be the *Marianne,* Cap'n. "

"Last I heard the *Marianne* was in Havana, stocking up on rum for the Liverpool trade, Mr. Fuller. Easy pickings for us. Prepare for action, Mr. Fuller!"

Lydia could not stay silent. "Is this how you will teach your daughter? By robbing ships?"

St. Armand's entire body stiffened, and he did not turn and look at her. "It is a short walk to starboard and into the ocean, Miss Burke. If you do not wish to experience it, I suggest you keep your opinions to yourself."

"She's right."

Both Lydia and St. Armand looked at the mate, whose lugubrious face was turned to his commander. Fuller kept his voice low so the men would not overhear their discussion.

"We are closer to England and you know what is waiting for you at the end of this voyage. If you are taking the child with you, you must think of the future."

"Do you have any idea of the value of that ship's cargo of rum, Mr. Fuller?" St. Armand's eyes were narrowed and white lines of anger bracketed his unsmiling mouth. Both men appeared to forget Lydia stood there, hardly daring to breathe as she watched the argument.

"Yes. You must choose, Robert. Booty, or being the father you need to be. You cannot have both, not today."

Lydia jumped at his use of the captain's name, which brought St. Armand's anger to focus on her, and it felt like he was looking at her down the barrel of a rifle.

"Orders, Cap'n?" called the helmsman.

"Steady as she goes, Mr. Conroy. Mr. Fuller, you have the command."

Lydia's questions for Mr. Fuller were forgotten when a hard hand clamped down on her arm.

"Come with me."

"Captain—"

"Not another word, Mr. Fuller. You have said enough for one day."

He pulled Lydia behind him, allowing her down the companionway before he slid down after her, forgoing the shallow steps, pushing her into his cabin and slamming the door behind him.

"How dare you question my commands in front of the crew?"

Lydia's knees quaked as he paced before her like a panther eyeing an interloper in its territory. She had no weapons except her conviction that she was correct. She straightened her back and clasped her hands before her.

"I dare because I am the person you made responsible for teaching your daughter. A governess teaches values as well as arithmetic and geography. I would be failing in my task if I did not concern myself with her moral welfare."

"Her moral welfare? You are interfering with my ability to provide for her physical welfare! You do not have the right to tell me what to do."

"Yes, I do. I earned that right when you forced me aboard the *Prodigal* to care for Mathilde."

She did not mention Mr. Fuller backing her up. The way St. Armand looked she was not sure the captain wouldn't grab a pistol and shoot the mate, then grab another one to finish the job on her. She turned her back on him and started to pull the cabin door open to escape, but a hard hand shot out and slammed the door, so hard it quivered in its frame.

"You are unwise to turn your back on me, Miss Burke. I am not finished with you, not yet."

He was standing close, too close. Lydia refused to flinch, or move away from him. She looked straight ahead and his voice at her ear was light, pleasant, even.

It froze her blood.

"You are not wearing your cap today. Did you mean to court my favor? Not having to see that hideous rag on your head is only the beginning of what it will take to restore me to a good mood after your puling morality robbed me of a tidy cargo."

She swallowed and stood there knowing one could not display fear to a predator. There was no place to run, no place to hide from the pirate who stood so close the fabric of his coat brushed against her back. She arched away, but a hard arm clamped around her waist and pulled her up against him, his heat surrounding her, burning away the ice in her veins from her fear of him disposing of her over the side. It would be so easy for a governess who annoyed the captain to have an unfortunate accident.

What she didn't know was if she feared him as much as she feared her response to his toying with her, alone in his cabin, helpless in his floating world.

"If you were in my keeping I would dress you in satins and creamy silks so that the sight of you would not depress me. Perhaps you would be dressed in nothing at all."

He kept one arm around her while the other came off the door to trace along her trembling arm.

"We have been together on this ship for many days, Miss Burke. Many days and many nights when I could imagine you draped in pearls, adorned with gold, your long limbs entangled with mine. Do you share those thoughts? Do you ever think of how easily you could slip into my cabin in the dark?"

A warm finger traced the outline of her ear and followed the line of her artery down her throat to where her collar rose up, hiding the rest of her from his gaze. It was empty armor, for with one tug she'd be stripped and at his mercy. She quivered, eliciting a low chuckle from her captor.

"Scared, little governess? You don't need to be frightened, but you should be begging my forgiveness for your insolence. I can be magnanimous...given the right motivation. Can you motivate me?"

His lips brushed against her nape, just above her neckline, and the hairs stirred as a treacherous fragment of her mind whispered, *Oh yes, do that some more.*

"Do you want me to forgive you?" he whispered, placing a kiss along her jawline. "Do you want me?"

She moaned, a broken sound wrenched from deep within her.

"Do you want?"

She wanted. Her body knew her wants, her nipples hardening as his lips explored the small area of exposed flesh above her collar, her breath hitching as his teeth nipped softly at her earlobe. Liquid heat pooled between her legs.

She craved him. Even now, even with his threats, she wanted, wanted him in all the ways a woman can want a rough man, one who seized what he desired. She was so sure he would leave her wants satisfied, breaking down her careful façade of respectability.

And that was why she had to reject her body's needs and choose safety.

"Captain St. Armand," she said, her voice low, but thankfully, steady. "You can have an unwilling bed partner, or you can have a governess for your daughter. You cannot have both."

As soon as the words left her mouth she realized they echoed what Mr. Fuller said earlier about the choices St. Armand—Robert—had to make. She could not call the words back, nor did she wish to.

He stood behind her, still, and the moment dragged on an eternity.

"Unwilling?"

It was a dark whisper in her ear, then a chill at her back.

"Get out."

She blindly fumbled with the latch before managing to wrench the door open and escape to the small safety of her cabin and the child napping there.

Lydia tried not to think about him the rest of the afternoon, but it was impossible. She dug her cap out from the bottom of her trunk, secured her hair and tied the cap on. That pirate did not own her.

Her traitor mind conjured images of what it would be like to be owned by the pirate, to have her keeping in his care, to not have to worry, and hide, and scheme for her future. But she also knew the reality of such a life was not as Captain St. Armand said. Nanette was a rare exception, a woman whose protector set her up in comfort so she did not have to return to her former life, though it was really Nanette's hard work building on what she'd been given that assured her and Mattie's comfort. There were women who would have let the money run through their fingers like beads falling from a broken string,

When Mattie awoke, the day was stormy as the ship tossed in a fast-moving Atlantic squall. At suppertime, trays of cold meats, cheese and bread were brought to their cabin with instructions to stay below. Conroy assured them it was a minor blow and nothing to fret about, and his relaxed demeanor calmed Lydia. She was fortunate she and Mattie were both good sailors with strong stomachs, though she ate sparingly to not risk fate.

"Eat some bread now and save the rest for later, Mattie. If you keep a small amount of food in your stomach it is easier to handle the ship's motion."

"Did you ever get sick from the sea, Miss Burke?"

"Yes, on the voyage to the islands, but I found my 'sealegs' within a few days and now I tolerate the ocean well, but it's a good idea to plan ahead."

"Papa never gets seasick, but he says cats make him sneeze and that is why I cannot have a kitten. I do not get seasick and cats do not make me sneeze," she finished on a satisfied note.

The image of dangerous Captain St. Armand felled by a sneezing attack brought on by a soft, fluffy kitty tickled Lydia and she was smiling as the door to their cabin was rapped upon, followed by the captain himself entering a moment later.

He stopped in the doorway, looking at her intently, and the smile flowed off her face under his gaze.

"Papa!"

Mattie threw herself at her father and he scooped her up in his arms, careful of her head not hitting the deck above. The man was a mass of contradictions to Lydia. One moment he was preying on her, or on some hapless merchant ship, the next he was the doting father.

"Did Norton get a brace of pistols for spotting that ship, Papa?"

Lydia inhaled sharply, but St. Armand did not look at her.

"No, Mattie, he did not get a reward because that ship was not a prize."

"Too bad. Maybe the next ship will be a prize. Have you come to read to me?"

"Of course, Mattie. How could I sleep without a bedtime tale?"

She giggled at this silliness and Lydia stood, brushing down her skirts.

"I will leave you two to read—"

"No, stay, please! Tonight we are reading more about Anne Bonny!"

"Yes, stay," Captain St. Armand said, but when he said it, it sounded like a command. "You would like this tale, Miss Burke. Anne Bonny was a wild child who likely did not listen to her governess."

Lydia did not want to be anywhere near the captain, but she saw no way to politely extract herself, especially since Mattie was nodding at her father's words, her curls flopping about in silken corkscrews.

"Very well," she said, reseating herself and putting her hands in her lap. He sat on Mattie's bunk and picked up Captain Johnson's book.

"Her father was an attorney at law, but Anne was not one of his legitimate issue…"

"What does that mean, Papa?"

"It means Anne Bonny's papa was not married to her mama. He was married to another lady when Anne was born."

"So she is a bastard like me?"

Lydia gasped, and her hand covered her mouth.

"Where did you hear that, Mattie?" her father asked. He closed the book with his finger inside.

"The children in town. They used to say that about me, and I heard two ladies say it when *Maman* took me to church. Afterward, on the church steps *Maman*, said things to them that would have gotten my mouth washed out with soap!"

She did not appear upset at her illegitimate status, but Lydia knew children could be good at hiding their true feelings.

"Come sit on my lap, Mattie."

The little girl climbed into her father's lap and he put his arms around her. Lydia had the stray thought that Mattie's legs were growing and she would be a tall woman, taking after her lean papa. Watching the two of them together, so close, the rich dark hair and features so similar, she couldn't help but think pirate or no, Mattie was fortunate to have a father who cared for her so much.

"It is true your mama and I were not married, and in the eyes of the law, that means you are a bastard," he told the child calmly. "However, the law has nothing to do with how much I love you, for you are my own sweet Mattie."

"Did Anne Bonny's papa love her?"

"As I recall the tale, he did. Sit here next to me and I will find out."

He set her next to him and, reclaiming the book, flipped a few pages then smiled.

"See here, Mattie? It's a picture of Anne Bonny sitting on her papa's lap, just as you sat on mine. Yes, according to Captain Johnson, he 'had a great affection' for the child, but he dressed Anne as a little boy to fool his wife, who'd heard about the birth of a daughter that was her husband's child. He began living with Anne's mama and then took them to Carolina where he prospered."

"Was he a pirate in Carolina, like Blackbeard?"

"No, a merchant and a lawyer, though given those two professions, he may have had some of the pirate in him."

"I am wondering if this is the best bedtime reading for a child."

He looked down at Mattie. "Well, child? Is it a good bedtime story?"

She nodded vigorously. "Yes! I want to hear more about Anne and her pirate ways!"

"There you have it, Miss Burke. 'She was of fierce and courageous temper...and she was so robust that once, when a young fellow would have lain with her against her will, she beat him so, that he lay ill of it a considerable time.'"

"Captain St. Armand!"

"You are interrupting, again. If you cannot refrain we will never get this finished."

Lydia snapped her mouth shut, but really, what a story to tell a young girl! However, Mattie straightened her back and said, "It is good Anne knew how to fight, because her papa was not there to protect her."

"Exactly, Marauding Mattie. Even Miss Burke would agree a woman needs to know how to defend herself in a difficult situation. Swooning and waiting to be rescued is not a good way to deal with attacks."

They both looked at Lydia, who nodded, once, only a tad reluctantly.

"See? Here is a picture of Anne, with a pistol and dressed as a man. She looks strong, doesn't she?"

Lydia's curiosity grew the better of her and she rose to look at the picture too. The woodcut in Captain Johnson's book showed a robust young woman with long locks flowing beneath her hat, her outstretched hand firing a pistol as a ship loomed in the background. Her shirt was open, exposing her breasts, no doubt to ensure there was no confusion about her gender. Titillating the largely male reading audience and selling more copies was an additional benefit any good author and publisher would leap upon.

"What happened, Papa? How did she become a pirate?"

"Let us save the rest of the tale for tomorrow night, Mattie. I will tell you it starts out as these stories so often do. Anne Bonny ran off with a worthless man, marrying him against her wise father's wishes," he finished sternly.

The cabin was largely dark, so he did not see Lydia go still at his words.

"Come now, Mattie, it is time for you to get ready for bed. We had a busy day today and you must be worn out.

Mattie started to shake her head no, but her wide yawn punctuated Lydia's words and she smiled at the youngster. Captain St. Armand waited for the girl to get beneath the covers, then tucked her in and kissed her on the forehead.

"Good night, Marauding Mattie."

"Goodnight, Captain Papa."

He straightened and looked at Lydia. He seemed about to say something to her, but only bowed and left the cabin.

CHAPTER 12

$\mathcal{T}$he men kept watch for signs of friends or foes on the water, but the voyage continued smoothly, even as the ship's stores began to develop a sameness, less variety in their diet. Mattie fussed over some of the concoctions coming from the galley, but her papa backed Lydia when she said, "This is shipboard life, Mathilde. We will have fresh fruit again when the ship docks, but for now you will eat the same food as the rest of the crew."

"The men are having burgoo also?"

"Yes, and they know better than to complain."

"If the rest of the crew is eating this, then I will eat it," Mattie announced, and that was the end of that mutiny.

For her part Lydia had no fears about her place aboard the *Prodigal*, at least as far as the men were concerned. They treated her with respect, and they approved of her efforts to teach Mattie knowledge not involving edged weapons or thievery. Nash and Turnbull joined in the lessons later in the day, days that grew shorter as they moved into northern climes.

It was at the end of one of those lessons that Sails came

looking for her. He was older than the other sailors, with a deep scar pitting his cheek but nimble fingers and sinewy arms from years of wrestling canvas and hemp into shape.

"I have your jacket here, miss. Captain St. Armand said to bring it to you as it's blowin' up stiff in the next day or two."

He unwrapped a length of worn, but clean cotton in the late afternoon sun. Inside was a pelisse, longer than the jackets the men wore and bearing no resemblance to their utilitarian gear. It was sapphire silk brocade lined with the pink satin. Golden buttons rimmed with seed pearls fastened the front.

Lydia stared at it, speechless. It was a garment fit for a princess, not a governess. Sails pointed out the features.

"See, the brocade would have been scratchy up around your face and neck, so that's why the captain told me to use the sable pelt to line it for you."

"Sable?" she asked dumbly. There was fur on the jacket, rich, thick brown fur. The collar was deep to provide additional warmth and there were fur cuffs also. She put her hand out to stroke it, and it was kitten soft beneath her fingertips. She nearly moaned with delight at the sensation. It was soft as the captain's pillow and it made her think of how that pillow must feel against bare skin.

"We took those pelts off of a Russian who traded to us and saved himself a trip to England for his efforts."

"Mr. Sails, it is lovely, but—"

"If you reject it, you will make poor Sails feel miserable," said a low voice in her ear. "Look at how much effort he put into your jacket. That hideous cap, however, is completely wrong for this ensemble. You need a bonnet, Miss Burke, something in plush to set this garment off."

Lydia turned to look at him, but he was looking down at the fabric spread out for her view, the brocade glowing in the mellow light.

"The pink works well for a lining and if you had a fabric rose or two adorning your bonnet it would add to the appearance. But only if the roses are on the crown, far enough from your face not to make you look sallow."

He leaned over and swooped up the garment, and while Lydia stood as still and dumb as a fashion doll he took his wool jacket off of her and helped her slip her arms into the new pelisse, the satin sliding over the rough wool of her gray dress. Then he turned her toward him, raising the fur collar to frame her face.

"I approve, Sails. You've done a masterful job on Miss Burke's gear."

"Thank'ee, Captain. I'm glad of the chance to make something pretty for a change."

Lydia wanted to turn to thank Sails herself, but Captain St. Armand was still holding the fur collar and looking down at her. She could get lost in those eyes the same shade as the brocade surrounding her, eyes promising dangerous delights. Her excellent imagination kicked in and she envisioned him against a collection of furs, his lean body spread out for her gaze. Perhaps there would be fur cuffs of a different sort there. She'd seen such devices before and never imagined them in her life. Until now.

"What thoughts are you thinking, that have made your eyes go all black and brought a flush to your cheeks?" he said to her in a low voice.

She stepped back, and this time he didn't restrain her. Lydia cleared her throat and stroked the cuff of her pelisse.

"I am thinking that while this garment is more than lovely, it is too fine for a governess. If an employer saw me wearing something like this it would spark either jealousy or the thought that I am being overcompensated for my efforts. Indeed, a prudent woman would ask what I'd done to receive so spectacular a gift from Captain Robert St. Armand. But I suspect you knew that. You deliberately gave me a beautiful garment unsuitable for my life, and my position."

He looked amused by her concerns, which did not help. Soon she'd be back in the world where people looked at you and judged you shallowly, not on a floating world of men who judged you for your skills rather than your family, your demeanor, or most importantly, your past. Nash and Turnbull cheerfully talked about episodes from their past that would have sent them to New South Wales if not the gallows, but aboard the *Prodigal Son* they were valued crewmembers.

"If I did, I may have done it to remind you that there is a woman inside those rags, a woman who is every bit as entitled to wear pretty things as the crows employing her. You have made a deliberate decision to dress like a dowd. I do not have to support that decision. I will *not* support that decision, not while I have to look at you."

In some ways, Lydia fit right in with these miscreants, but it was a temporary haven. That issue was on her mind at supper that evening, when she asked which port they would be entering.

"Liverpool," St. Armand said, watching her. "There are merchants there ready to purchase my wares from the Indies."

Some of her tension left her. If he'd put in at Portsmouth it would be more difficult for her to quickly book passage back to the West Indies, or to America. Bristol and Liverpool were her best options for getting out of England quickly. She'd been thinking about the best way to accomplish this, and to her regret, it meant depending on him.

"I have a request, Captain. Can you arrange my passage to Boston? I would be happy to stay aboard the ship until such arrangements are made."

It was just the two of them at supper, as they were dining later than usual and Mattie had already been tucked in for the night. This hadn't been Lydia's plan, but Mr. Fuller had excused himself early to tend to some ship's business and they were alone. She sat closest to the door, but it was scant comfort. She had no reason to think he would pounce on her, but there was something in his eyes when he watched her that put her too much in mind of a cat eyeing a mouse-hole, waiting for its prey to make a misstep.

He sat back now and steepled his fingers, watching her.

"I have to say, almost every time you open your mouth you surprise me. Any person who'd been at sea for weeks would want to get off the ship, stretch her legs, eat better food, shop for items to be restocked. But not you. Why is that? No, don't fob me off, because I will tell you what will happen. You will try to deflect the conversation, or tell me a half-truth or obfuscate further, but it will not work. You have aroused my curiosity, a desire to poke at things to see what happens."

"I am a governess used to dealing with obnoxious little boys. Your *poking* is nothing new to me. You find it amusing to make me feel on edge, don't you, Captain St. Armand?"

"Yes. Yes, I do, Miss Burke. More wine?"

He leaned forward and poured wine into her glass, and into his. Lydia's hand twitched toward the ruby liquid, but she refrained. As tempting as it was to grab the lifeline of wine-soaked oblivion, she needed to keep her wits sharp. He did not refrain, but drank deep, his throat working as he took obvious delight in to the beverage. The man was one of the most sybaritic humans she'd ever met. He surrounded himself in luxurious fabrics, glittering metals and jewels, scented soaps, and an appetite for food and drink that would lead to gout if he weren't careful. It made his fascination with her all the more disturbing. She wasn't a raving beauty, her mirror told her that. She was attractive enough not to scare passersby and her shape was proportional to her height, but surely someone like St. Armand wanted a woman by his side and in his bed who would compliment his good looks? Someone with lusher hair, a more buxom figure, even straighter teeth?

She was only a temporary distraction. Once she was out of his sight, he'd be like the little boy she knew him to be inside. He'd look for another toy, another pretty bauble, bored by her and her dowdy exterior.

"Despite your behavior, Captain, I would like to know more about you. You are well spoken, and appear to have had a solid education. Your manners and speech tell me you are no common seaman, unless you are an extraordinarily gifted mimic. It makes me curious, and I suspect your story is far more interesting than mine."

Lydia knew men. The best way to hold their attention and make them think you were fascinating was to get them talking about themselves. He'd want a woman who acted as a mirror, reflecting his prettiness, his sense of self-importance, his rampant masculinity right back at him. In his universe, it was all about what made his life better, richer, more enjoyable.

He did not rise to her bait and only gave a small smile making her suspect he knew exactly what she was up to. There was one safe subject they both could agree on— Mattie's welfare.

"Do you have lodgings in Liverpool suitable for Mattie, Captain?"

The question seemed to surprise him, and he sat up straighter.

"I had not truly thought about that until this moment. There are lodgings where I usually stay, but to say they're inappropriate for Mattie would understate the issue."

"Lodgings like Madame Olifier's?" Lydia said dryly.

"Worse," he admitted. He frowned while thinking about it, the remainder of his wine untouched.

"You will need to stay aboard ship with Mattie, at least until I can secure appropriate lodgings for us. Then I need you to continue caring for her until I can make further provision for her. You will join us in those lodgings. I insist."

"At a house in Liverpool?"

"I will find someplace appropriate, you can be sure."

Lydia wanted to argue this plan, but thought it best to stay silent. If she stayed out of sight in town, she should be able to leave without additional difficulties, and her being with Mattie offered protective coloration as well.

CHAPTER 13

*L*ydia counted her small supply of coins, then counted again. There was no help for it, she was going to have to collect her wages from Captain St. Armand if she wanted to get out of England. She'd concocted elaborate schemes in her head to slip away from the *Prodigal Son* or wherever he stashed them in Liverpool, but she was realistic enough to know there was only one thing that would get her out of England. Without money a woman alone had no options worth considering. The sailors could work their passage across, but a governess was not a valuable commodity.

Mattie had gone ahead to breakfast, as familiar with the ship and its routine as any powder monkey aboard a man-o-war. The crew kept an eye on her and this voyage had been just the tonic the child needed after the devastating loss of her mother, and upheaval from the life she'd known in St. Martin. Children adapt to new circumstances, but their enthusiasm and spirit of adventure can be quashed by adults who don't understand that not all youngsters fit in the same mold. It was especially difficult for young ladies who had that adventurous spirit. The pluck and courage admired in a young boy too often elicited shrieks of dismay when a young girl exhibited the same behavior.

Lydia had to admit, somewhat grudgingly, that Captain St. Armand understood Mattie's adventurous spirit. He seemed to her to be an overgrown child himself much of the time, a naughty boy playing pirate, but with all too real consequences for others in his game. It did help him in his raising of Mattie though. The child was frustrated by an arithmetic problem during the previous day's lessons, but instead of throwing a tantrum, she'd looked down at the offending numerals and said, "Beets! Beets, Beets, Beets!"

"Beets?"

"Papa said it is not right for a young lady who is also the captain's daughter to go around calling people buggering sods, Miss Burke. He said it shows a lack of imagination. I should learn from Captain Lowther instead, whose men tried to outdo each other inventing new oaths."

Lydia cleared her throat. "I would hope a young lady could avoid oaths and bad language all together, Mathilde."

The child looked at her with a skeptical frown. "I don't know if that is possible, ma'am, but I can try to change what I say so I do not offend. Papa asked me what was the thing I hated most in the world, and it is beetroot. So now when I need to swear a mighty oath like Captain Lowther, I say 'Beets!'"

In his own way he was trying hard to give Mattie what she needed, but the child would never grow up to be a proper young lady at home in society if she continued to be raised by pirates. One could hope the captain would find a good woman, a stable woman who would raise Mattie with balance, helping her to navigate the rocky shoals of adolescence and womanhood.

In the meantime, Lydia would do her best. When she

joined the child, Mattie bounced in her chair with excitement at breakfast, because today was the day for her tea party. She'd worked hard on her multiplication tables, but Lydia was even more impressed by Nash and Turnbull. The two scalawags were the ones who'd reminded her, repeatedly, that a reward was owed them for their efforts.

"Never thought an old seadog like me could learn new things," Nash had said.

"You learned how to balance a belaying pin on your head, that's a handy trick," Turnbull pointed out.

"That didn't involve a whole lot of brainbox, did it? Naw, this numbers work is important. I ain't going to get cheated in the market if I can keep track of the coins when I'm ashore. I'm real grateful to you, Miss Burke."

His words brought a warm glow to Lydia's chest, the feeling any teacher gets when a student appreciates her efforts. Yes, they were murderous pirates, but she'd made a difference in their lives, a positive difference.

The cook assured Mattie there wouldn't be a single beet on the menu, but promised figgy dowdy, ratafia biscuits and other sweets. Mattie asked Lydia to wait in the cabin because she wanted to set up the tea party, and Lydia acquiesced, enjoying the opportunity to put up her feet and relax with a novel.

When Mattie returned to the cabin, she debated what would be the more appropriate attire for the planned event. The pink frock that had such a positive impact on the Royal Navy, or her finest pirate gear? After consultation with Lydia she went for pirate, so Turnbull and Nash wouldn't feel out of place.

"That is a thoughtful gesture, Mattie. As you settle into life in England, you'll meet people from other classes, other places. A true lady does her best to make people feel at ease, not attempt to impress them with her own wealth or status."

"That's not what a pirate would do," Mattie said skeptically.

"Do not be too certain of that, miss. I imagine if you ask Captain St. Armand about his dealings with people of other backgrounds in the islands, he will tell you a personable and friendly approach can be quite effective."

"Only if you have big guns behind you, Miss Burke."

That twitch began below Lydia's eye, the one signaling a headache if she didn't move on. Proper deportment for piratical offspring was *not* a subject she'd studied to prepare for a career as a governess. Nonetheless, Mattie's accomplishments, as well as those of the pirate students, needed to be rewarded so she put on a cheerful face and said, "Will I do for your tea party?"

Mattie looked at her critically, the frown on her tiny face so reminiscent of her father that Lydia's breath caught.

"You look very fine, Miss Burke, but your new jacket will make you look even finer."

"I bow to your fashion advice, Mathilde," Lydia said as she pulled her jacket from the trunk, unconsciously stroking the lush collar, the fur beneath her finger tips sending a shiver down her spine.

Clad in their finery the ladies went up on deck. Mattie asked Lydia to wait at the helm while she checked on the arrangements, then came running back to her.

"We're all ready. Wait until you see it!"

She grabbed Lydia's hand and tugged her along to the spot beneath the awning where they did their lessons, but the plain little table was covered with a white cloth, and Nash and Turnbull awaited them. Mattie's china doll sat there as well, along with a rag doll with button eyes christened "Mary Read." It was a perfect day for a tea party at sea, the skies a crisp blue and the breeze just cool enough to warrant the fine jackets the ladies wore. Much of the crew was on deck, wanting to enjoy every bit of sunshine they could before they docked in England. Some of the men good-naturedly joked about Nash and Turnbull being the teacher's special pets, but Turnbull made comments about their ancestries and proclivities for relations with barnyard animals that sent them off laughing to their tasks, and left Lydia hoping she wouldn't have to explain it to Mathilde later.

If the child asked, she'd let her father clarify matters. There were times when passing off responsibility was a pleasure.

Mattie held her clean hands out for her governess's inspection, then demanded the pirates allow theirs to be examined, and pronounced them clean enough.

"Wait, Miss Burke, we cannot start without papa!"

She looked over her shoulder and a smile lit her face.

"Just look! Isn't my papa the handsomest captain ever?"

St. Armand ducked beneath the awning to join them as the men rose to their feet in the captain's presence. In honor of the party he was especially resplendent today, wearing a scarlet jacket encrusted with enough gold braid that it would stand by itself if he removed it. The shirt beneath it was open at the neck, the deeply tanned skin looking especially good against the white linen.

At a word from him the men took their seats, but before he sat Mattie said, "Papa, everyone here learned our multiplication tables to be invited to this party. Do you know your tables?"

"Of course I do."

"Then you must recite them, Papa, up through the twelves."

"Must I?" he said, raising a brow and looking around at the rest of the party.

Nash and Turnbull looked at each other, then reluctantly

DARLENE MARSHALL

agreed, and the little girl nodded vigorously, and Lydia said nothing.

So he shrugged, took a breath and started, "Two times two is four, two times three is six…"

Everything went swimmingly until "…eight times seven is fifty-seven, eight times eight is sixty-four…"

Turnbull's weathered skin went ashen and Nash sucked in his breath.

"Beggin' your pardon, Cap'n, but that ain't correct."

St. Armand stopped reciting and looked at Nash in surprise. "What did you say?"

"By Neptune's massive, wet"—Turnbull whispered at Nash, but paused and looked at Mattie—"trident, you're in for a keelhauling now, matey!"

"Naw, the Cap'n treats the crew fair," Nash said stoutly. "Numbers has to be accurate. The sprat knows that. We can't steer a shipmate wrong by letting a mistake go by, can we?"

There was a flag of color in the captain's cheekbones. To be corrected and embarrassed this way, in front of his child, in front of his crew, would make many men lose their tempers and Lydia held her breath. He looked at Mattie, then looked at Nash through narrowed eyes.

"Men who correct me, Mr. Nash, in public, had better be right. One might go so far as to say their lives depend on their being right. Now, are you absolutely sure about this?"

He smiled at the pirate at this last question and if anything, Turnbull went grayer at seeing those teeth bared.

"Aye, Cap'n," Nash said firmly. "Numbers don't lie. Multiplication is multiplication. If I multiply eight times seven, it's always fifty-six. Always. It ain't fifty-seven, and I know that because I memorized the tables, and because… Mattie, what's the other reason?"

"Because eight is an even number."

154

"That's right, because eight is an even number. Meaning no disrespect, Cap'n. It just is."

St. Armand stared him down, but Nash crossed his arms and didn't flinch, and Lydia was impressed. She knew enough about the goings on aboard the *Prodigal Son* to know he could easily arrange for something fatal, or at the very least, painful to happen to Nash for correcting him.

"Miss Burke, can this lot recite their tables without a mistake?"

All eyes turned to Lydia, who cleared her throat and said, "They can now, Captain."

"But it took practice!" Turnbull said.

"Yeah, if it ain't something you use every day, it takes a while to think through the right ones," Nash said. "Anyone could make a mistake."

"It's like knife fighting, Papa," Mattie said, and everyone looked at the child, brushing back some of her rag doll's yarn hair, tossed about by the sea breeze. "You use knife fighting more than you use your multiplication tables, so you're quicker at it."

Nash and Turnbull were nodding so vigorously Lydia feared their heads would bob off.

"That's right, Cap'n," Turnbull said heartily. "Everyone knows you're the man you want at your back in a dark alley when there's mayhem about, but your multiplication tables, well, that's just for special occasions!"

Captain St. Armand's eyes narrowed with a focus on Turnbull now. "How badly do you want that cup of tea, Turnbull?" he bit out.

Lydia leaned over, close enough to him to feel the heat coming off of his bronzed neck. "There are biscuits with currents also, Captain."

He jumped, as if startled out of the moment, then turned his head to look at her, then looked back at Mattie and the men, one watching with curiosity, the crew watching with a healthy dose of fear. He took a deep breath, then let it out.

"Thank you, Turnbull, for your endorsement of my skills." He looked at Mattie. "Not letting your shipmates down is important, Mattie, and yes, I can do my multiplication tables correctly. Will you all allow me to attempt again?"

There was more head bobbing, and this time he breezed through all the way up to twelve times twelve without making an error. Nash and Turnbull only offered a sigh of relief, and with her own sigh Lydia reached for the teapot to pour.

It was a tight squeeze, five people at a small table, but they managed. Nash and Turnbull kept an eye on each other, and there was some not-so-subtle elbow nudging when Turnbull slurped his tea.

Captain St. Armand had excellent table manners, which made Lydia curious, again, about the man's background. Based on his speech, his deportment, his manners (when he chose to use them) and his bearing she had to believe he'd been at least a gentleman's son. Perhaps, like Anne Bonny, he was baseborn and someone had invested in his care, just as Nanette had provided for Mathilde. It was a mystery she itched to solve, but that would require extended and personal conversation with the pirate, not a prudent idea.

It was difficult enough sitting next to him now, so close his leg pressed up against hers. Any farther movement to the side would have put her off her seat and flat on the deck, so she inched her leg away as best she could.

It was a useless gesture when he put his hand on her thigh, just above her knee.

Lydia froze. If she said anything it would disrupt Mattie's special day, the day for which she'd worked so long, not to mention how it would spoil the pleasure of her other students. They were discussing with Mattie the pastries and biscuits one found for sale in the bake shops in England, the treats they looked forward to enjoying when they returned to their homeland. Turnbull and Nash beamed in the glow of accomplishment, of knowing they'd earned a privilege denied to their shipmates because of their hard work and effort.

Lydia too would have basked in their glow if not for the fingers now stroking her leg. She put her hand down to pinch him, but the pirate anticipated the attack and grabbed her right hand in his left. He leaned in close to her ear while the others were discussing the merits of treacle dowdy and said, "Put your hand back up on the table. You don't want to upset Mattie, do you?"

"You are upsetting me!" she hissed at him under her breath.

"Don't care," he said with a grin.

"Papa, did you say something?"

"I was just explaining to Miss Burke the merits of some of my favorite treats, Mattie."

"You like sweets too, Papa?"

"For my palate, too much sweetness is cloying. I like treats with more bite to them."

"Like lemon tarts?"

"Exactly. The astringency of the lemons means you have to work a little more to enjoy it. It's not as obvious as something covered in sugar."

A perfectly innocuous conversation, had his hand not resumed stroking her, just above her knee, soft brushes back and forth that she could feel through the layers of skirts and undergarments as if she'd been completely bare before him. She clenched her legs together, trapping his hand between them.

A tactical error. He curled his hand into a fist and lightly rocked it back and forth, minute movements that nonetheless fired the nerves in her sensitive inner thighs, raising images of him between her legs, pressing them open with his muscled hips, how he would feel on top of her, her flesh to his flesh, sweat-slicked and yearning to open wider.

She had to bring a halt to this, now.

"If you do not remove your hand," she leaned over and whispered in his ear, "I will have a clumsy accident with my cup of hot tea spilling into your lap."

He paused, then with a small sigh of regret removed his hand and used it to pick up his own teacup, acknowledging her outflanking maneuver.

The rest of the tea party passed mercifully mayhem free, and they let the child carry the conversation. She was justly proud of her skills in mathematics and also her role as a member of the *Prodigal Son's* crew.

"Miss Burke, Mr. Fuller says I am to assist him on the dog watch tonight."

"Do you watch for dogs while you're doing that?"

Mattie giggled and the pirates grinned. "You would be a very silly pirate! The dog watch is in the evening, before my bedtime."

"I must disagree with you, Mattie. I believe Miss Burke has the makings of a perfectly adequate pirate."

The four others at table looked at their captain.

"I dunno, Cap'n," Turnbull said. "Miss Burke's a first rate teacher, but I ain't seen her swing a cutlass yet."

Mattie nodded.

"That's true, Miss Burke. How can you be a pirate if you cannot attack your enemies?"

"There's more to being a pirate than being good with weapons, Mattie," her father said. "Especially if you want to captain your own crew. For example, a successful pirate has to know how to strategize and plan, both for battle and for dealing with the booty afterward."

The other pirates nodded sagely at this.

"Your learning mathematics is one way you can advance yourself, Mattie, but your governess does have other skills."

"I do?" Even Lydia found this intriguing. She'd imagined herself in many situations over the years, not all of them to her taste, but she'd never imagined herself a pirate.

"Absolutely, Miss Burke. You command respect from those around you, you plan for various eventualities, you are willing to be flexible to meet your own ends."

"I am?"

"Certainly. There are some governesses who, if they found themselves kidna—er, employed by pirates, or even honest but unexpectedly handsome sea merchants, would be hysterical, or swoony, or unwilling to adapt to their changed circumstances. You have taken everything on this voyage in stride—to a point—and maintained your equilibrium. I salute you."

He raised his teacup, and Nash said, "To our teacher, Miss Burke!"

"Hear, hear!" Turnbull said, raising his own cup, and Mattie followed suit in her own toast.

Lydia knew she shouldn't be glowing in the pirate's praise, but it was hard not to. So often her skills were unappreciated by her employers. *She'd* been unappreciated by them. To be validated this way, to be told of her worth as a person—she blinked rapidly to clear her eyes.

"Thank you for those kind words. Even though I have no plans to become a pirate, I will always be grateful for the opportunity to share what skills I do have with the crew of the *Prodigal Son*. All the crew," she added, not looking at St. Armand, but at Mathilde, whose face lit with a smile, the gaps where her baby teeth were being replaced yet another reminder of how much she'd come to care for this child and how it would tear her heart out to leave her.

But leave her she must, for there was no future for her as a governess in England, maybe no future at all if the wrong people learned of her return.

At the end of their party the captain called over a crewman who went below, returning with Potter, the cook, who took their praise for his efforts with a small bow showing the top of his gleaming pate, his face florid from his work boiling the crew's victuals.

"It was my pleasure, Cap'n, miss. I know how hard Mattie and this lot worked to get to this day. 'Struth, if you'd told me that these two bast—sailors would be able to learn some new figuring, I wouldn't have believed it. Just goes to show you."

Nash looked down at his plate, all modest, while Turnbull grinned, displaying a smile missing some teeth of his own.

"We just needed the right reason to learn more, and the right teacher," Turnbull said.

"All I know is I'm going to keep careful count when I'm playing cards with you two, because it's going to be a lot harder to hoodwink you in the future," Potter said with a sigh.

Nash's face darkened at this revelation that perhaps he'd been taken advantage of and before their party ended in bloodshed, Lydia stood and said brightly, "Well! That was a most delightful afternoon, gentlemen. Mattie, will you help me clear this area so the men can return to their tasks. Perhaps a nap this afternoon will help prepare you for your turn on watch tonight?"

"An excellent suggestion," the captain said, rising to his own feet. "Nash, Turnbull, you have impressed me with your skills today. I hope to see them at work the next time we take a—next time we load new cargo aboard."

Potter retrieved his dishes and the leftover food while Mattie gathered up her dolls and yawned.

"You hold your dolls, Mattie, and I will carry you below."

"You don't need to carry me, Papa. I'm a big girl," but when he gathered her up into his arms she didn't argue, but placed her head on his broad shoulder.

"Can you carry me below without dropping me, Papa?"

"I have carried casks much heavier than you, my dear, without breaking them open. Once I carried a pig, and he was also heavier, and did not smell nearly as pleasant. But he was quite tasty," he finished with a pretend bite at her ear.

He looked over at Lydia then, and his face changed as he looked at her.

"Is anything the matter, Miss Burke?"

Lydia had to swallow around the lump in her throat. "I enjoy seeing a father and daughter smiling together, that is all."

He watched her for another heartbeat or two, as if parsing her words. "Marauding Mattie is my best girl, aren't you? I want to stay on her good side so that she treats me fair when we're dividing up the booty."

Mattie giggled. "You're the captain, Papa. You're in charge of dividing the booty."

"So I am!" he said cheerfully as they moved to go below. "Well then, I have nothing to fear, do I?"

THE LESSONS CONTINUED as the ship made its way to England and the crew showed its anticipation like a hound scenting supper, watching the eastern horizon, each hoping for the first glimpse of land, the men straining forward as if that would get them to their goal faster.

The stories also continued at bedtime, and Lydia had to admit she was caught up in Captain Johnson's stories of blood, gore and courage.

"So Mary Read's mother, described here as 'young and

airy, met with an accident, which has often happened to women who are young and do not take a great deal of care; which was, she soon proved to be with child again.'"

"Was my mother young and airy, Papa?"

Captain St. Armand put his finger in the book to mark his place and looked at his daughter. "Your mother was a delightful lady, and I believe 'young and airy' is an excellent description of her."

"Did you fall in love?"

He hesitated, then nodded. "I loved your mother Nanette as one loves the best of friends. She was someone I turned to for friendship, and for laughter, and we shared that."

"And hugs, Papa? *Maman* was good at hugging," she finished, a catch in her voice.

"Yes, Mattie, your mama was good at hugging," he said gently.

"I am glad, Papa, that you and *Maman* were in love and that you were friends. It is good to have friends. Turnbull and Nash are my friends and my mates, and Conroy also. Are you and Miss Burke friends?"

"Mattie, why don't you let your father continue reading so we don't have to cut your story short at bedtime?"

They looked at Lydia, who'd been sitting quietly on her bunk, listening to Captain St. Armand's deep voice carry her away to far off times and lands. It was best to do that, not to disillusion Mathilde about the relationship between her and the pirate.

"As you say, Miss Burke. Where was I? Oh, yes...so Mary Read was raised as a boy and went into service as a footman..."

He continued with Mary Read's amazing adventures, every bit as fantastical as Anne Bonny's. Read had been a footman, ran off from that post and joined a man-of-war, then carried arms in Flanders in a regiment of foot, as a cadet. While serving in Flanders, she fell in love with a Flemish soldier, according to Johnson, and after marrying him—a move that made Lydia want to cheer for the girl's conventional behavior—began living openly as a woman.

"But then, her husband died and Mary resumed life as a man, shipping out to the West Indies, and she fell in with pirates."

"Is that how she met Anne Bonny?"

"Yes, Mathilde. She also took another husband. Johnson says Mary fell in love again, and 'her young man being made of flesh and blood, he responded in kind and they plighted their troth to one another. She would not name him during her trial for he had been acquitted, not wishing to be a pirate.'"

"Oh, now this is interesting. It says Mary's husband had an enemy, another pirate who intended to do him harm. They quarreled, and Mary's unnamed husband was to fight a duel with the man. Instead, Mary—whom everyone else thought was a man—challenged her husband's enemy herself and fought a duel, killing him two hours before her lover was supposed to fight a duel with the man himself. Now, that's a woman who has your back protected! Johnson praises Mary, saying she was honorable in her own fashion, true to her husbands, modest, brave. All admirable qualities. It's unusual for Johnson to say anything good about pirates, so we can agree that Mary Read was an exceptional woman."

"But what about Anne and Mary?"

"We'll read more about them another time, Maurading Mattie. Now it's time for my goodnight hug."

He set the book aside and leaned down, and two little arms snaked around his neck, squeezing him tight before his daughter smacked a kiss on his cheek. He returned the favor, and then tucked her under the covers.

"Good night, Mathilde."

"Good night, Papa. Good night, Miss Burke," the child said, already halfway to sleep.

Lydia rose to her own feet, looking down at the deceptively angelic face above the coverlet, eyes closed, eyelashes fanning out against her skin. Mattie was browned from her time up on deck, her complexion an inheritance from the Caribbean and a legacy of her African great-grandmother. Life would be difficult enough for Mattie in England as a pirate's bastard, looking like an island child made it that much harder. She had to have some faith Mattie's father would take care of her and see to her welfare and protection.

She hoped St. Armand would marry, for the child needed mothering. But she sighed to herself, knowing there would be women aplenty attracted to the pirate's looks and money, but a good woman willing to take on his bastard child—that would be a rare creature indeed.

CHAPTER 14

"Is it always this cold?"

Lydia bent down and picked the child up in her arms with an "oof." "Mattie, I believe you've grown a foot and added a stone of muscle aboard ship!"

Mattie giggled, but snuggled in closer to her governess to warm up. Lydia couldn't say for certain, but Mattie seemed tall for her age and the constant activity aboard the *Prodigal Son* had added sinewy strength to her body.

Their arrival in Liverpool was marked by a gray mizzle dampening the air and their clothes. It was only autumn, but Lydia'd forgotten, after years in the sunshine and warmth of the West Indies, how unpleasant the weather could be.

"It is often damp and raining here, but the weather can turn sunny quickly. You'll enjoy the summers when the days are long, and perhaps this winter you'll see your first snowfall."

"Do people hide inside when it snows?"

"Oh no, especially not the children! There are snowball fights, and sleds, and making snow angels and skating. And when you're all done, you rush inside for a hot drink and cakes in front of a lovely fire," she said, her memories of much better times in her life rising to the surface. Lydia cleared her throat and brought her mind back to the present. "It's an adjustment, but you'll find much to do here that's fun and new."

The house Captain St. Armand located for them was not far from the docks, but far enough that they'd be spared the noise of carousing sailors and their women. It was modest, the furnishings shabby, but clean and comfortable. Mattie's room was papered with a cheerful blue-flowered print and adjoined another, matching room, which Conroy told her would be her quarters.

"We'll get the rest of your gear out of the hold tomorrow, miss," he said, swinging her trunk down to the faded carpet.

"That would be wonderful, Mr. Conroy," Lydia said gratefully. "At the moment though, I'm still adjusting to a floor that doesn't shift beneath my feet."

"You're one of the *Prodigals* now," he said with a wink. "You'll always have a bit of the ocean in you."

"That will be all, Conroy."

They both turned toward the doorway. St. Armand stood there, unsmiling, hands behind his back. Conroy hurried out of his captain's way, and he watched him, then turned back to Lydia.

"Is he bothering you?"

"No," Lydia said, somewhat puzzled by his demeanor.

"We are ashore now, and the easy ways of shipboard life are not appropriate here."

Lydia could only stare at him, then threw her hands into the air. "You are unbelievable, Captain St. Armand! For weeks aboard ship you acted like...like a mischievous adolescent, stealing my hairpins and caps, teasing me, making inappropriate remarks, and now you preach to *me* of propriety? Unbelievable."

"I'm still the captain," he said, a line between his brows.

"Oh, I beg to differ," Lydia said with a sharp smile of her own. "You are the captain aboard the *Prodigal Son*. You are not in charge of my life, not anymore, not on dry land. I will have the wages you promised me so I can move on. I am in England now," she brazened out, "no longer at your mercy as commander of your vessel."

In response he kicked the door shut behind him, enclosing the two of them in the room, a room that seemed much smaller with both of them in it and the bed behind her.

"For such an intelligent woman you say amazingly foolish things."

He advanced toward her and even though she wanted to take a stand she could feel her feet moving her backward until she hit the wall, but he continued until he was directly in front of her, one hand propped alongside her head.

She heard noises from below, street noises, voices, but all of that faded as her eyes tracked his hand, moving into her line of sight, hovering over her chest. She drew in a sharp breath, but he did not touch her. Not there. Instead she felt his warm fingers sliding along the line of her jaw, stroking back toward her ear, and her eyelids fluttered even as she fought the feelings his touch roused in her. He framed her jaw with his long fingers and angled his head, stopping at the very edge of her mouth, not swooping at her as she'd expect from him. Was he waiting for her to say no?

It was an empty question a heartbeat later as his lips brushed against hers, thoughts of "no" receding into the recesses of her mind. Every time he touched her it was so wrong, but like so many choices in her past, "wrong" was not as important as "right now."

His lips continued their gentle glide, and she leaned forward, away from the wall, closer to danger. That was all the signal he needed to deepen the kiss, moving both hands up into her hair, cushioning her head from the hard plaster, blocking out any noises from the street. She heard only the blood rushing thorough her, her involuntary moan as her lips opened beneath his and her hands reached up to grasp his shoulders.

He started to pull back from the kiss but she put her own hand behind his head and he stilled at her movement, caught by surprise at her response.

She'd be surprised by her response later. Right now she just wanted to feel, to escape her worries for a few moments and only dwell in the present, in the sensations of his mouth, his tongue gliding against hers, his small noise of surprise at her fervent acceptance of his attentions. She deepened the kiss, until a noise from below pulled her back into the present.

Back to sanity.

She opened her eyes when his hands moved on, away from her, no longer touching her.

Instead of the triumphant gleam she'd expect to see in his eyes, he looked bemused, almost unsure of himself as he backed away from her.

He cleared his throat, watching her, observing her. She knew her color was high, her breathing rapid, and his eyes lowered to where her breasts peaked against her garments, swollen and sensitive from her passion.

Lydia fell back on her rising anger, moving her passion in a different direction. He would get nothing more from her, no explanations or entreaties. She was no longer a young girl swayed by a charming rogue's ways, she was a woman with a future.

A future, and a past.

"Give me back my cap."

He looked down, appearing surprised at the object he clutched.

"Miss Burke…" he stopped, holding the cap. He ran his free hand across his face, as if wiping a slate of jumbled thoughts clean. When he looked up again he wore his usual insouciant expression, which enflamed her even more.

"Give me my cap, you…you…"

"Ah ah, do not use language that you'll later regret, a nice lady like yourself."

The anger was good. The clean flame of it burned away the darker emotions that roiled through her.

"You broke your word! You promised me you wouldn't take my caps!"

"I promised you I would not take your caps aboard ship. As you so imprudently pointed out, we are no longer aboard the *Prodigal*, so that promise no longer stands. This is only a small demonstration of how far my reach extends, aboard ship or on dry land. You have only yourself to blame for this predicament," he ended unnecessarily and gloatingly.

That was outside of enough! She moved toward him as he dangled her cap above her head, his long arms keeping it out of her grasp, and she stopped herself from using her fist to try and break his nose for him again, stopped before she was close enough for him to grab her. She had the satisfaction of seeing his eyes widen in momentary alarm at her belligerent stance.

"Your lessons have not advanced to the point where that would be a wise move, unless you want to find yourself in my arms again?" he finished with a look tempting her to punch him anyway.

But she refrained. Just as she had learned some measure of prudence in her deportment, she could keep from murdering the pirate for just a few more days.

Lydia drew herself up to her full height, grasped the bridge of her nose with her thumb and forefinger and drew in a deep breath, a mistake as his scent was still in her nostrils, his citrus soap on her hands.

"You will not ruin my day, Captain St. Armand. You no longer have any say in my wardrobe. Pay me! Pay me what I am owed and we will both move on with our lives."

"You said you would stay here until I found another governess."

"No. I did not say that. Do not try and manipulate my words. We had a bargain, I expect you to honor it."

His smile faded as he studied her, no doubt expecting his silence would prompt another outburst.

Not likely. He knew too much about her already, information damaging to her. The last quarter hour under the sway of his kisses had shown him that, even if he knew nothing else about her.

"Nothing is going to happen tonight, Miss Burke. I cannot access the funds that quickly—no, let me amend that. I *will* not get the money tonight. I have other plans. That is what I came to tell you before you started smothering me with kisses."

"Wha—"

He ignored her spluttering outrage and continued, "Mattie, Mr. Fuller and I are dining tonight with Mrs. Riley, the widow of Jeremiah, one of my former crewmen. She has young children Mattie's age and I thought Mattie would enjoy spending time with other youngsters before we move on. You are welcome to join us."

He'd done it again. He'd managed to surprise her. She would have expected the notorious Robert St. Armand to head for the nearest whorehouse and drink and wench his way through the evening while she stayed in the house with Mathilde.

This changed everything and her mind raced to keep up.

"No, thank you, Captain. That is a thoughtful offer, but I

think I will stay in. It's been a long time since I had a quiet evening just to relax with a book."

"I do not think I like finding myself taking second place to a book."

"That's because you generally spend time with women who would rather discuss fashion and admire your form rather than ones who are literate."

He acknowledged this and bowed, turning to leave.

"My cap?"

He paused, turning back to her. Then he lifted the cap to his nose and *inhaled,* a rather prosaic act causing heat to flare in her again. He stuffed the cap in his jacket pocket.

"*My* cap, Miss Burke. Enjoy your evening."

CHAPTER 15

*L*ydia hurried along the dark street, head down, clutching her shawl around her. The secondhand clothing dealer had been reluctant to pay what Lydia demanded for her brocade coat, but the fur collar and cuffs finally sealed the bargain. It was a loss, but a necessary one, much as she was missing the garment now for its warmth. There was a deeper coldness at the act of giving up the item Sails sewed for her, the coat Robert St. Armand designed for her to complement her and make her attractive, even if it was just for a few weeks aboard a pirate vessel.

It was better this way. Now she wouldn't have to explain where she obtained such a fine garment. Now she had money, or did have, before she used all her remaining funds to purchase a ticket on one of the new packets making the Liverpool to New York run. It amazed her to think she could board the ship at a set time rather than wait around for the captain to decide to sail, but it also made her quick escape possible.

The house was dark when Lydia let herself back in to grab what she could carry and head to the docks. She would find someplace to hide away from prying eyes until she boarded the ship. She'd done it before. But she must write Mattie a letter first, a letter she hoped would help explain why Lydia had to leave. She couldn't tell the child the truth, but she could try to assure her that she loved her, even if Mathilde only felt the pain of abandonment once again. Maybe she'd forgive Lydia some day. The child had suffered so much loss already and heaven only knew what would come of her living with a pirate. Lydia couldn't damage her spirit further by leaving without saying goodbye, even if it was only in a letter.

St. Armand did not keep servants overnight, not trusting his safety to anyone but his own crew, not wishing to leave himself vulnerable. Not trusting people was something she understood and the empty hall echoed with her steps on the creaking stairs.

Lydia lit a lamp and sat at the small desk, a sheet of foolscap before her as she tried to put into words what was in her heart. The scratching of the quill was amplified in the silence.

"Leaving a note? Seems rather inadequate, don't you think?"

Odd that on hearing the cool voice come out of the darkness her first thought would be, *Oh, now this dress is inkstained and ruined.*

It was unlikely she'd survive until dawn to worry about it. She stayed still, staring down at the black ink spilling across the desk. He was behind her, between her and the door, and she knew she'd not escape him. She didn't know why she feared he would kill her. Maybe it was their being alone together, ashore in an empty house without witnesses. Maybe disaster and retribution was what she'd come to expect as her due.

Maybe it was simply because of who he was. She'd heard

him quote Blackbeard once: "Damn them, if I did not now and then kill one of them, they would forget who I am!"

Captain St. Armand had a reputation to maintain, after all.

Lydia cleared her throat, pleased her voice emerged at all.

"Where is Mathilde?" she asked without turning to face him.

He came over to the desk, behind her, trapping her with his body. He righted the inkwell and moved the stained paper aside, putting his hands on the desk next to hers.

"Do you care where Mathilde is? You are leaving her, after all. You say so, right here, 'Dear Mathilde, I am so very sorry I cannot say this to you in person...' and the rest has been blotted, but I think we both know what it would have said."

Lydia looked down at the paper. "This is not proof that I am leaving her."

"The ticket to New York you purchased on the Blackball packet is proof enough."

He put his hand on her arm and pulled her out of her chair, turning her to face him. Not forcefully, but more in the nature of assistance. Perhaps he suspected her knees wouldn't support her. He'd be correct.

She was not dead yet, though. "Remove your hands from my person."

"Miss Burke, have you not realized over the past weeks you seldom get what you want, while I almost always get what I want? And what I want right now are answers," he finished in a pleasant tone. "I want to know what you are running from, or to. I want to know what it is you fear. Most of all, I want to know, to my complete satisfaction, that you are not a danger to me or my daughter."

"How can you accuse me of plotting to endanger you or Mathilde? You kidnapped me off the *Clementine*!"

"I do not know how you ended up with Nanette Lestrange. I only know what you told me. You could have been sent to find me, to connect with me through Mathilde."

"You are insane!"

"I am cautious and prudent, at least where the safety of my daughter is concerned. You may recall I let a valuable prize slip through my fingers because of you. I did not demand compensation then—much—but I am demanding answers now."

He said all this in a gentle voice soft as lamb's wool, finishing on a smile showing too many teeth. He was a predator and if she ran he would chase her down and consume her, of that she had no doubt. She was his natural prey.

She sagged in his grasp and his hand tightened on her arm.

"I am so tired," she said, looking down at her worn shoes. "Just kill me, or ravish me, or throw me out the window onto the street below. I don't care anymore."

He put his hand beneath her chin and tilted it up, studying her face in the lamplight. Then he sighed, releasing her.

"Sit. Do not move until I return, otherwise I will do at least one of those things to you." He paused as he turned for the door. "Maybe two."

She sat, numb, the sounds from the street below trickling in. She did wonder where Mattie was, but Mattie's father was responsible for her now, so it was no longer her concern.

Saying it to herself and believing it were two different things.

It was odd. Just sitting here, waiting for St. Armand's return, her mind feeling rather distant and detached from it all. Was this how condemned prisoners felt before an execution?

"Here," her captor said, returning with a glass he pushed into her hand. "Drink. I cannot torture you or do anything else exciting with you looking as pasty as wet flour."

She wrapped both of her hands around the glass, the odor of strong rum tickling her nose. She'd never especially cared for rum, but right now it seemed like the perfect solution to her life's problems. However, the glass was removed from her grasp before she could drain it.

"Your passing out and drooling on the floor is not in my plans either, Miss Burke. Stay there."

He left again, returning with another chair. He sat across from her, resting his elbows on the chair arms, steepling his fingers as he did so often when he was thinking.

"Why are you running out on us?"

Lydia took a deep breath and let it out, pulling together the frayed strands of her courage. Then she looked the pirate in the eye.

"I have a life that has nothing to do with you. I wish to resume that life. I am not obligated to share my life with you. I am your employee and I wish to resign my position. Immediately."

He said nothing to this, but watched her, two lines furrowing between his brows.

"You must have seen something in town today, something or someone that makes you want to run. What is it? Tell me, and I will deal with it for you."

It was tempting, so very, very tempting, to put herself and her problems in this man's bloodstained, but capable hands. That was not the answer though. She'd learned life's lessons about depending on a man to fix her problems and she would not travel down that road again.

"I am your daughter's governess, Captain St. Armand. If my efforts are not satisfactory, discharge me from my duties."

He sighed and tilted his head back, looking up at the ceiling. "Oh, Lydia Burke—if that's your real name—you are so much more than my daughter's governess at this point. Why are you pretending otherwise?"

"I am not pretending, Captain—"

"You may call me Robert when it's just the two of us. Or 'my darling.'"

"I am not pretending, *Captain*. I am resigning my position."

"No, you are not. I will not accept your resignation. Not yet."

"You cannot keep me prisoner here!"

"I am not going to keep you prisoner, I am going to help you, but you have to tell me what your problem is. Is someone trying to hurt you? You know I can resolve that issue for you quickly, and ensure the body is never found."

"Hiding inconvenient corpses is something you excel at, of that I am quite certain!" She wanted to tell him. She longed to unburden herself. Only Nanette had known of Lydia's past and she certainly was not going to condemn her. She looked down at her hands, twisting together in her lap.

"I made a…mistake. When I was younger, I made a mistake. I was foolish and headstrong, and my mistake has been my burden to bear, and I need to leave England to avoid —to avoid complications in my life. That is all you need to know."

"Did you kill someone?"

She shook her head.

"Did you bear a child and abandon it?"

She looked up at that, then shook her head again. He was watching her, an open expression on his face. She suspected she could have committed almost any hanging or moral offense and he would not condemn her, but she still could not bring herself to discuss her life.

"Then what is it? See here," he started, then paused. "Are you hungry?"

"What? Hungry?"

"I'm a bit peckish. Chasing you around this evening caused me to miss my meal, so I suggest we continue this conversation in the kitchen. I've decided not to kill you—for tonight, anyway—so you may as well eat a good meal."

As soon as he said it, Lydia realized she *was* hungry, and stood. "My stomach was tied in knots and I have not eaten all day, Captain."

He opened the door for her and she paused in the doorway, so close she could see the individual lashes on his eyes. He was looking at her with some amusement on his face, which grew when she said, "It's odd that suddenly I'm hungry after sitting here talking to you."

"I am famous for stimulating all sorts of appetites in beautiful women."

Whatever the reason was, her appetite had returned. Her life was still perched on the edge of disaster, and she had no caps, but she had Captain St. Armand on her side. There may be more morally upright knights out there prepared to defend a lady, but she'd take piratical cunning and skill over morality any day in a fight like this.

The house was shabby, but the food was excellent and welcome after shipboard rations. The men had stocked the kitchen with lamb scouse and loaves of fresh bread and butter, apple tarts, rich cream, Cheshire cheese.

"Some sailors come ashore and drink their way through their pay, but many come ashore and *eat* their way through fresh victuals. If you ask a man what he misses most aboard ship, the answer may surprise you. Landlubbers think it's wine and women, but more often, it's a loaf of yeasty bread with fresh butter churned that morning."

He paused from cutting a wedge of cheese. He was looking at her uncovered hair, and her hand reached up self-consciously.

"The candlelight on your hair is one of those sights that could make a man long for life ashore," he said quietly, almost to himself. Then he looked down at the knife in his hand, shook his head and said, "Would you fetch some apples from the pantry, please?"

This polite request, rather than an order or command, made her pause, but she turned and fetched the apples, saliva pooling in her mouth at the idea of biting into something crisp and tart, not desiccated and wormy.

They sat and did justice to the meal, and afterward she brewed tea for herself. He drank the rum, but it did not impair him. He talked about his dissolute ways, but when she thought about it objectively there were planters in the islands for whom she'd worked who had worried her more with their overindulgence in liquor. St. Armand always seemed prepared to fight, or scheme, or care for his daughter.

Look at him now, sitting across from her at table, dressed almost soberly. His navy blue kerseymere coat and buckskin breeches made him appear the same as most well set up men around town. He could have been wearing a monk's robes though and he'd look raffish to her eye. It wasn't just the diamond winking at his ear, it was how he carried himself. The man didn't have an ounce of humility, but that self-assurance gave him a strength that could pull others in his wake.

"Aren't you tired of running from whatever it is that drove you from England?"

She fiddled with her tea cup, organizing her thoughts. "Of course I'm tired of it. At least in America or the islands I have a chance to start fresh, make a future for myself."

"I want to tell you something." He clasped his hands before him on the table and held her gaze. "It does not matter what you have done in the past. We all have pasts. Yours is no worse than other members of the ship's crew. We move on, and just like Anne and Mary, you have the opportunity to reinvent yourself."

"I am not a member of your crew, Captain."

"Are you not? You worked aboard the *Prodigal*, earned your pay and your victuals. Had we taken a prize, I'd be discussing your share with you. A small share. I believe a governess may rank somewhere above a ship's boy."

His words should not warm her but she could not help feeling comforted. To belong somewhere after so long, even if it was amidst a crew of pirates and reprobates with a scoundrel captaining them—it was welcome. Her life had been so solitary since she'd left England, only Mattie and Nanette had offered true companionship. It was not the same as having a man interested in her, not at all the same as having this man interested in her.

She had to be honest with herself. Not since her clandestine meetings with Edwin had she experienced this excitement at a man's attention. Robert St. Armand lured her into dangerous waters, but the thrill of it made her feel more alive than she'd felt in years.

"You do have other options, if you want to stay in England. I can think of at least two."

"Options?"

He lounged back in his chair, looking at her. "Sign on as Mattie's governess. Our original agreement only applied aboard ship—"

"If you recall, there was no agreement, only a kidnapping."

He waved away this inconsequential detail. "All in the

past. As I was saying, sign on to the crew, as Mattie's governess. She needs you, you need a position, a position with more security than throwing yourself at America in the hopes someone will hire you on and treat you with dignity. My men respect you as they do any shipmate—you earned your place aboard the *Prodigal*, and we don't abandon crew."

"You're not alarmed at the idea of a woman such as myself, a woman with some dark secret in her background being responsible for Mathilde's moral education?"

"Have you *met* the men crewing my ship? No, you are the perfect woman to teach Mattie. You understand my headstrong lass and let us be realistic—finding another governess who fits in with the crew would not be a simple task."

She shouldn't feel warmed by his words, but how could she not? After being on the run for so long, tossed about like a piece of driftwood, she was ready to embrace the idea of belonging, of having a place.

"I have misjudged you, Captain. You are not the complete scoundrel you make yourself out to be. You are only a partial scoundrel."

"Do not make that mistake, Miss Burke. I would—and have—sliced a man's throat with a smile on my face, then sat down to eat a hearty supper celebrating an excellent and productive day. You realize I now know enough to cause my own complications in your life."

"You wouldn't do that."

"That sounds better if you don't phrase it as a question."

"I know you now, Captain St. Armand. You wouldn't harm me or Mattie."

"I would not harm Mattie."

"And you would not harm me."

Silence stretched between them as he considered that statement.

"There are many types of harm a woman can experience."

"Oh, I did not say you were not a scoundrel, I only said you are not a complete scoundrel."

Consideration of his ridiculous offer tempted her, but she'd known scoundrels of all stripes, and had learned from her encounters with dangerous men. She shook her head.

"I appreciate the offer, Captain, but I cannot accept. Much as I love Mattie, and want to stay with her, I have no future here. In America I have a chance at making myself more than a servant, someone dependent on her employers for her future and quite frankly, for keeping me alive. Thank you, but no."

"What would you do in America if you weren't a governess?"

"I realize you find little value in respectability, but I would like to lead a quiet, normal life. Perhaps I'll marry. I could keep books for a shopkeeper, be an asset in a marriage."

"You could do far better than that."

"Could I?"

"Yes. You could marry me."

The silence in the kitchen was so enveloping that she heard crickets outside.

"Did you just ask me to marry you?"

"I would not phrase it quite that way, but I did mention marriage, and you, and I was included in that sentence also."

"An hour ago you were threatening to throw me out the window! Or ravish me!"

"Must you dwell in the past so much? Let us focus on the issue at hand, please."

"For the love of heaven, why would I want to marry you?"

He looked startled. Startled, and perhaps hurt? It was difficult to read his face as she reeled from his announcement.

"Shouldn't you be asking yourself why I'd want to marry you?"

"Certainly not! Where else are you going to get someone to care for your child for no wages! Not to mention the other benefits you'd get from marrying me."

He blinked his eyes as if what she said made no sense to him at all. Typical man. If he married he gained a bed partner, cook, nursemaid…and what did she get from the bargain? A pirate who sometimes evidenced all the self-control and maturity of a five-year-old. Not a fair bargain at all.

Bollocks, said a small evil voice in her head. *You would get* Robert St. Armand. *In your bed, between your legs, in all the ways you've only imagined over the dry, dry years.*

She shut down that voice and continued, "I just said I want a quiet, respectable life. If I decide to remarry, I don't want a dashing pirate, I want a husband! A husband who will be home at night, who will help me raise children with proper values, who will show his love not by robbing ships, but by fixing the roof when it leaks. Someone who won't mind, or at least will say he doesn't mind, if I put cold feet on him at night to warm them up."

"Is that what husbands are good for? No wonder so many married women sought my company."

"You see? That is exactly the sort of thing to which I refer!"

He looked ready to argue his suitability with her, but instead shrugged his wide shoulders.

"Then take the other option. Sign on as crew aboard the *Prodigal*. I will double your salary—"

"The salary I've yet to see appear."

"The new position is double what I offered you before, and you would be crew, and have a share in any future action."

"Are you shipping back out to sea? With Mattie?"

"Did I not mention that part of the offer? No, your salary would be doubled as Mattie's governess because you would be accompanying us on our most dangerous journey yet. I am going home."

CHAPTER 16

"You have a home?"

"Everyone comes from somewhere, Miss Burke."

"I understand, but—" she stopped speaking and looked down at her teacup, puzzled. Robert let her mull over his offer. He would find a way to keep her with him—for Mattie, of course—of that he had no doubt. He had certainly surprised her when he offered her marriage.

He'd surprised himself. He was sure he hadn't meant to say those words, but they still spilled out of his mouth, almost of their own volition. It was a sensible offer on his part. Mattie needed a mother, and much as he didn't want to dwell on it, he needed a wife. If he was serious about returning home, having a lady beside him would help. Miss Burke—Lydia—was still every inch a lady, no matter what secrets she tucked away in the busy brain beneath her hideous caps.

He'd set his sights on his prize and he intended to have it —her—even if it involved standing before witnesses and a vicar. Lydia had crawled into his consciousness even if she hadn't climbed into his bed yet.

If he was asked what she brought that made her the one, he'd be hard pressed to say. He'd been with women more beautiful, and younger, and richer, but there was something about Lydia that kept him engaged when others would have bored him by now, sending him off to seek the next shiny bauble. He was not sure *why* it was her he wanted, but he wanted her, of that he was sure. He'd spent a lifetime gratifying his desires and knew he could not rest until he had her where he wanted her.

Regardless, if he was going to succeed with his plans, he needed a wife and she'd do quite nicely. Most other women would have run screaming into the night at the thought of marriage to him, but Lydia sneered at his offer and reminded him *she* was a prize, and oddly enough, he liked that about her. She knew her own worth.

"What do you say, Miss Burke? Do you accept my offer to stay on as Mattie's governess? Or my offer of marriage, your choice."

She sniffed dismissively. "I will take the governess position, Captain St. Armand. Less work and I can leave when I choose."

"In that case, you can tear up that letter you were writing to Mattie and we will discuss the arrangements for travel in the morning." He eyed her dubiously. "If you travel with me, I must insist you allow me to clothe you. Those sacks you wear…" He shuddered. "I realize we're in Liverpool, and not London, but I can find you a seamstress who will at least make you look human."

"I will pay for my own garments, Captain, out of the wages you assure me are forthcoming."

"As you wish."

He stood and started to gather up the dishes to leave for

the servants in the morning, watching Lydia out of the corner of his eye. She was pleating the cloth next to her plate, nervously, and occasionally glancing at him. Perhaps she was already regretting not taking him up on his marriage proposal?

"I need to sell back my passage if I can—"

"Already done. You will find your coat in the parlor as well."

She stopped and narrowed her eyes at him. "You assumed a great deal, Captain St. Armand."

"As I've said, I get what I want, Miss Burke. Your best option is to see your wishes align with my wants."

She looked as if she would respond to this provocation, but clamped her lips into a narrow line. "We will talk more in the morning, Captain St. Armand. There is one thing…"

"Yes?"

"If I am going clothes shopping I will need to bathe. I saw a bathing room upstairs."

"It was one of the reasons I rented this house. You need me to scrub your back for you?"

"I need you to carry hot water upstairs. Nothing else."

"Don't you tire of leading such a dull and circumscribed life?" He came over to her and leaned down, one hand on the table. She appeared to give his question serious considera-tion. He was pleased to see the color was back in her face, and the fire in her eyes. They were impressive eyes, he had to admit. Full of life, so clearly showing her emotions, flashing emerald as she sparred with him.

"No," she said, shaking her head, "I do not tire of my humdrum life, Captain St. Armand. As a matter of fact, I find it quite soothing."

"A bowl of broth is soothing, Miss Burke. It is not a feast to remember. Just think of all the wonderful things one could have instead. You could be licking an ice off of a spoon at Gunter's on a steamy, humid day. You could be gnawing on a tender chop, getting all the succulent meat inside you."

Oh yes, now the color was back in her face!

"This is a foolish conversation." She stood, but he did get out of her way. Instead, he moved in, and in farther, because she was backing up from the table, and him, and he knew she wasn't aware she was retreating to the wall until it came up against her back.

"Perhaps that is what you need in your humdrum life, Lydia. Something foolish. Something more solid and substantial than broth. Something hotter than an ice. Firmer than lamb."

He had his hand next to her head on the wall and leaned in. In fact, he leaned in so far that he knew she could feel something hot, solid and substantial against her leg. And it wasn't a lamb chop.

She put her hand on his chest and pushed, but it was a half-hearted effort.

"Stop doing this. You are so annoying!"

"True, but I have other qualities."

"Name one, other than loving Mattie."

"I am exceedingly handsome."

"That's not a quality, that's an accident of birth, a happenstance!"

"I am an extraordinarily gifted lover."

"So you say. I have no evidence of it."

He watched her eyes widen as she realized what she'd said, the door she'd opened. A better man might have ignored the provocation, but they already knew he wasn't such an individual.

He put his mouth next to her ear. "I have sailed to the Orient. I know sixty different points on your body, my dear little governess, where I can bring you to screaming fulfillment using only my mouth and my tongue."

He leaned back to gauge her reaction to that! It was almost all he could have desired.

Her eyes widened and her hand fluttered up to her throat. She slowly licked her lips, the tip of her own tongue darting out wetly. He hardened further at the sight and he schooled his face so his triumph would not show. He had her now.

"Really?" she asked throatily. "You can count to sixty?"

"Damnation! *You* are the most annoying person I have ever met!" he snapped as he pulled her into his arms.

He never lost his temper with women. Never. There were too many other things to do with them that were much more fun than fighting with them. This woman though, she made him do things that made him question his sanity.

Like now. Here he was, kissing her, his arms banding her and keeping her from fleeing to safety as his mouth ravaged hers. He would have expected her kisses to be tart, as astringent as the tongue she used to insult him, but she was sweet as a flavored ice melting in his mouth, her lips soft beneath his, her hands in his hair pulling him tighter to her.

Wait, a tiny, still functioning part of his brain spoke up. *She's not fighting you.*

Excellent! said the rest of his senses and he let her cling to him as his hands left her back to roam lower, down to the wonderfully full hips disguised by her shapeless garments. Dressing the little hedgehog in more flattering attire was something he would insist upon when they visited the dressmaker.

When he pulled his head back, ending the kiss, her eyes were closed and her rapid breathing made her chest rise and fall beneath her dull, ink-stained dress. Her eyes fluttered open and she raised a hand to touch her lips.

"I am not going to apologize for kissing you," he said softly, all his anger banished by other feelings. All he wanted to do was scoop her into his arms and carry her up to his bed, and spend the rest of the night uncovering the rest of her secrets.

"I would not expect an apology from you, but I will not change my answer to 'yes.'" she said, her voice low and strained. "I will be your governess, but not your whore."

"Not that," he said, one hand reaching up to brush back a curl fallen across her forehead. "A lover, Lydia. You want me, you cannot deny it. We would be good together. It would be fun."

"Oh, there's a good reason to climb into your bed," she snapped. "Fun!"

"Lovemaking should be fun."

"Yes, but I expect more, Captain St. Armand. I demand more. And I know too well that when the fun is over, there are still consequences. Sometimes permanent consequences, as Nanette—and now you—have discovered."

"I cannot regret Mattie coming into my life."

"No, nor can I," she sighed, "but I do not intend to add to the complications we're already experiencing."

"No one would have to know."

"That is the most naïve thing I have ever heard you say, Captain St. Armand."

He couldn't argue with that. Those traveling with them would twig to it soon enough and Lydia—Miss Burke—was correct too that there were enough complications in his life that he didn't need to be piling another on.

But she was such a *delightful* complication! He only hoped she'd regret stopping him as much as he regretted stopping.

"I will bring water up for your bath." He sighed, stepping back. "We stay here while arrangements are made for our journey. This will allow you—and Mattie too if she needs it—time to replenish your wardrobes.

"You and Mattie are not to leave the house without an

escort. One of the men will accompany you as you run errands."

"Where are we going on this journey?"

"I am not going to tell you. Not tonight. If I have to put up with some frustration this evening, then it will not kill you to be frustrated as well. Now, let me see to that bath."

LYDIA SANK below the surface of the fragrant hot water, letting some of the day's stress and much of the salt from her voyage soak out of her pores. If she wasn't careful she'd fall asleep in here. It wasn't just the water, filled with sandalwood oil soothing her senses, lulling her. It was the relief that she wouldn't be running again.

It would be so easy to fall into Captain St. Armand's strong arms and say, "Yes! Take care of me!"

It was a temporary reprieve, at best. She'd let a man take care of her. Now she was older, wiser, more experienced in the world and she knew she could only depend on herself. If she was going to align herself with a man again, it would be a man upon whom she could depend for more than bedsport and fending off attackers. She'd meant what she said earlier.

The sad part was, she no longer believed she could have it all. There were men like Robert St. Armand, handsome and entertaining wastrels good for a fling, but not someone you could see yourself with for a lifetime. The idea should have made her snicker, but instead it made her sad—and a little angry. There was goodness in the man, she'd seen it often enough in his dealings with Mattie, and even with his crew. He was not totally irresponsible. She had to be honest with herself. He displayed a great deal of responsibility, if she looked at him dispassionately. But she couldn't do that. Passion and the pirate went together like bread and butter.

She just couldn't trust him, not for a lifetime. He'd set off to sea, find another ship waiting to be robbed and fall back on his old habits. He was a pirate, after all. She'd accompany him to this mysterious home, see Mattie settled, then figure out what she was going to do with her life. And she'd make damn sure she was paid her wages!

If her problems intruded into her life she'd have the buffer of Captain St. Armand, and her shipmates. She smiled to herself at that thought. She'd earned her place among the banditti of the *Prodigal Son,* brandishing a slate instead of a cutlass, a pencil clutched in her teeth in lieu of a dirk.

Lydia popped her head out of the water and finished scrubbing her scalp. Grabbing the pitcher of fresh water thoughtfully left by her host to rinse off, she washed away the remains of the long sea voyage.

"If you stay in there much longer you'll grow gills," said a voice outside the door.

"I will be out shortly, Capt—"

The door opened and he walked in and she shrieked as she covered her breasts and tried to lower herself farther into the narrow tub. This only caused her knees to pop up and it was inevitable that he would get an eyeful.

"Did you just yell for assistance? I could have sworn I heard you say, 'Help! I'm drowning!'"

"Get out!" she yelled.

"No, that wasn't it."

The dastard removed the folded towel and sat on the wooden stool at the foot of the tub, looking as nonchalant as if he'd joined her for tea. He propped his elbow on his knee, put his chin upon his hand and studied her as she fumed and tried to cover herself. A brief list of her options ran through her mind, none of them good, but she tried anyway to grab at her towel, even though this fully exposed her breasts to him.

He moved quickly for such a lazy looking beast, scooting

backward and holding her towel over his head, out of her reach.

"Give me the damned towel!"

"Such language, Miss Burke! Be reasonable. If I give you this towel you'll just use it cover those delectable breasts."

He again looked like a little boy who'd just been given a shiny new toy to play with.

"Stop looking at my bosom, you...you...sharkbait!"

He grinned widely at this.

"I knew life aboard the *Prodigal* would expand your vocabulary."

"Scrub! Landlubber!"

"Better, but we'll work on it. In the meantime, what is it you want?"

She crossed her arms over her chest, which made him sigh with regret. "Give me the towel. You said you would not bother me."

"Not bother you? I am sure I never said any such foolish thing. I am not forcing you to do anything, am I? I am not even touching you, though if you would like me to demonstrate Oriental skills one through twelve, just say the word."

"Give. Me. The. Towel. Now!"

"You're no fun," he grumbled, but rose and looked down at her, then took one step back, his long legs making it a large step back. He shook the towel out and held it in front of him, just as she would if she were bathing Mattie.

"Here is your towel."

She was so angry she expected the bath water to start boiling.

"You are not going to hand it to me, are you?"

He just grinned.

"Very well."

Lydia wrapped her dignity around herself since she had no other garment and unhurriedly stood, the water sluicing off of her back into the tub. She didn't pose, but she made no attempt to hide herself either. She kept her eyes on his face as she carefully stepped out of the tub and walked toward him, slowly enough that she saw the gratifying change on his expression from playful to pole-axed.

Plucking the towel from his nerveless fingers, she wrapped it about herself and knotted it in front.

"The water's nearly cold, Captain St. Armand. You might find it useful to cool yourself down this evening. Good night."

Lydia turned and, with her dignity and towel wrapped about her, went back to her bedroom. She prudently placed a chair up against the door before climbing into her bed, which while it was cold and lonely, would not be complicated by a pirate invasion.

CHAPTER 17

*M*attie returned the next morning with jam on her face and nonstop chatter about her new friends at Mrs. Riley's including Jane, who had a rag doll with a lace trimmed skirt. The doll wasn't as special as her own Mary Read, but it made a good captive when they were playing pirates.

"They wouldn't believe me when I said my papa was the best pirate ever, so he'll have to go over there later and run one of them through so they *know,*" she finished with a gleam in her eye.

Robert St. Armand walked in on this last part of the conversation as Lydia wiped Mattie's face and his eyebrows rose.

"I told you we needed a governess, Miss Burke. Someone has to rein in Marauding Mattie."

"You could say, 'We don't run people through to make a point, Mathilde.'"

"Too late for that, my reputation precedes me. No, this is a task for Mattie's governess."

He helped himself to fresh coffee giving Jenny, the maid

of all work, a smile which nearly caused a catastrophe with the kippers she was placing on the sideboard. Lydia was pleased with the cook and staff hired by Fuller on behalf of the household. They were pleasant enough and went about their work without asking questions about the household. They knew St. Armand by reputation, if not by personal acquaintance

A great deal of wrist protruded from the sleeve of Mattie's dress as she reached for her glass.

"It appears our shopping expedition comes at an opportune time. Yon sprat is fast moving up from minnow to whale size," he said, which elicited a giggle from the girl with the milk moustache. "You both will need more heavy weather gear and winter clothes now that we're back in this dreary climate. I've sent a message to the seamstress, and she'll see you and Mattie this afternoon. Tomorrow we will look into new shoes and boots."

"Will you come with us, Papa? I would like a blue satin shirt like the one you have."

"I would be delighted to accompany two ladies while they shop for clothes. I will wait until I visit London to see my own bootmaker, but we can get you started on your wardrobes here. You two are lovely enough that you don't need London's finest tailors to make you look as good as I do. Was that inelegant noise a snort, Miss Burke?"

"Was it the eyerolling that gave me away, Captain?" Lydia knew sarcasm would only get her so far and changed the topic. "Mattie, you and I need to resume our lessons while we're here in Liverpool—how long will we be here, Captain? And where are we going after?"

Mattie too looked interested at this discussion.

"While you're in lessons this morning I will take care of business so we can get under way. We will be traveling as soon as we're able to leave and I've already sent Fuller ahead to make arrangements for us."

Lydia was cheered by this because she knew that no matter what one could say about Robert St. Armand's morals —and one could say a great deal, over hours and hours of discussion—he did love his creature comforts. If she traveled with him she could hope for better inns, better food and well-sprung coaches, a far cry from her life over the years since she left her girlhood home.

"Where are we going, Papa?"

It was asked quietly. The child had such a sunny disposition it was easy to forget she was a girl who'd lost everything within a short span—her home, her friends, and most of all, her mother.

She'd almost lost Lydia too. While her future remained uncertain, Lydia could at least be glad he'd stopped her from hurting Mattie.

"We are going to my home, Mattie, and it will be your home too."

"I liked being aboard ship with you, Papa, where you are the captain. It won't be the same here. On land."

"No, but I will still be the captain after a fashion, child. I will always take care of you, Mathilde, no matter where we make our home, on land or at sea," he finished gravely.

The child's shoulders had been hunched, as if to ward off this latest tempest in her life, and she relaxed now, picking up her milk to finish it.

Some of the tension drained out of her own shoulders. St. Armand still watched his daughter and the look on his face made Lydia think that having a pirate to protect you from life's blows was not the worst fate for a small, motherless child.

The morning's lessons included division and history, with an emphasis on the land where Mattie would grow up.

"Are you from Liverpool, Miss Burke?"

"No, Mattie, I lived in London before I came to the islands," Lydia said as she sidestepped the question.

"What is London like?"

"Big and noisy, child. You could take the marketplace on St. Martin and fit it into a tiny corner of London. But there are museums and theaters and shops and Astley's Circus and the Tower—all sorts of things to do. You'd never grow bored in London."

"I hope papa takes us there!"

"Perhaps he will, but he says for now we're going to his home."

"Where is it? Can you show me in the atlas?"

Lydia realized that while they'd discussed this upcoming trip to his home, it was always in an oblique fashion and she still had no real answers. Northumberland? Norfolk? Devon? His speech was cultured but betrayed no regional accent, and he'd never let a clue drop. She suspected he'd lived somewhere near the coast since he'd went to sea, but in an island nation that covered a lot of miles.

"You'll have to ask your father for the location of his home, Mathilde."

"I did ask him. He said it's a surprise."

Lydia suspected he wasn't telling just to annoy her. He was so childish sometimes.

On the other hand, it was the times when he acted like anything but a mischievous child that she feared the consequences. She could handle a naughty little boy. Handling a naughty muscular pirate was a very different situation. Even now, when she thought herself far past the point of being able to blush, just thinking the words "naughty muscular pirate" made heat rise in her face as she cursed the vivid imagination that had gotten her into trouble in the past.

"Then I'm sure we'll find out soon enough, Mattie. Now,

back to London... Do you remember the year of the Great Fire?"

Their escort to the dress shop, Conroy, collected them late in the morning and they enjoyed a chilly but bright day as they walked along, Mattie holding tight to Lydia's hand and chattering like a parrot as she pointed to the tall buildings and ships in the harbor. Mattie could identify many of the types of ships by their rigging, but made sure Lydia understood there was no finer vessel afloat than the *Prodigal Son.*

"I will agree with you, Mattie. It's the finest vessel I've ever sailed on."

Lydia observed Conroy as they walked the streets, nodding occasionally to acquaintances, but keeping his hand near the knife at his belt. The sailors they passed on the street looked at her and Mattie curiously, but made no attempt to approach them and Lydia appreciated again how while being with Robert St. Armand and his crew could ruin a woman's reputation, the *Prodigal Son's* reputation ensured she was treated respectfully.

Mrs. Culver's dress shop was tucked away on a quiet street before the docks, flanked by an apothecary and a bakery whose aromas elicited a promise of a side trip after Mattie was outfitted, but not before.

She started to fuss, but Conroy said, "Rigging first, miss. Your task is to be sure you're shipshape for the captain," earning him a grateful look from the governess, and a frown from Mattie's father observing them from the doorway.

He excused Conroy from his escort duties, taking Lydia's arm and muttering that next time he'd send Sails.

"Here are the lovely ladies I promised you, Mrs. Culver, ready to be outfitted. I'm giving you carte blanche to take good care of them and have their clothing to us by the end of the week."

Mrs. Culver was a lady comfortably past youth, her own clothing fashionable, crafted of fine fabric to complement her matronly figure. Lydia had feared a pirate's seamstress would have her looking like a blowsier Anne Bonny, but she could see Mrs. Culver would take appropriate care of her.

"I don't anticipate a problem so long as you understand, Captain, I will need to bring in extra girls to sew these frocks in time."

"I am paying for my own garments, *as you know*, Captain St. Armand, but since you are in a hurry to depart I am not unwilling to allow you to pay the extra for the additional seamstresses," Lydia said looking at Mrs. Culver, deliberately not looking at the man standing too close to her side.

"We can deal with the details later, Miss Burke, but I need to get measurements and begin work as quickly as possible. I do have some readymade garments here that the captain thought might help until the rest of your clothes are finished. He explained about the terrible accident at sea where your chests were damaged and you had to wear castoffs from other passengers," Mrs. Culver said with an admirably wooden expression.

Lydia was about to admonish the captain for telling tales, but felt a tug on her hand.

"Look, Miss Burke! It's blue like Papa's shirt. Please, Papa, may I have a dress made from that?"

"That velvet would make a charming winter dress for you, Mattie. I have an idea. Let's use it to make a gown for Miss Burke, and Mrs. Culver will make a dress for you too. Wouldn't Miss Burke look lovely in that shade of blue?"

"Oh yes, and then she and I would match because I would wear it also! Say yes, Miss Burke, please!"

Two pair of blue eyes turned in her direction, one pleading, the other amused because he knew he'd forced her hand.

"You must occasionally let me win an argument, without

the use of weapons or brute force. Even you must acknowledge the sapphire velvet would look good on you. You would shine like a jewel."

Did he really see her that way? She knew he desired her, but she also knew when a man's cock was thinking for him it was sufficient to have a glimpse of bosom and bottom to get him thinking a woman beautiful, or at least beddable.

"As Mattie's governess it is more appropriate that my gowns not draw attention to me, Captain."

"As your employer, it is more appropriate that your gowns do not make me lose my appetite. I must insist that if you are going to get new clothes that they do not offend my eye."

Lydia would have argued further, but Mrs. Culver spoke up first.

"Perhaps this would be more to the lady's taste? Sally, fetch the new silk, the one that arrived last week."

The seamstress who'd been hovering in the background returned shortly with a bolt of silk. She unrolled it on her table and an involuntary smile curled up Lydia's mouth.

The silk was a rich willow green, not as bold as the sapphire blue, but more color than a young girl would wear. The soft shade glowed in the light coming through the window.

"Mrs. Culver, you have an excellent eye," Captain St. Armand said as Lydia fingered the fabric. It slipped through her hand like cool water.

"I would fashion it with a net overskirt, repeating that at the shoulders, some cord trimming and you would look most appropriate, ma'am."

Lydia knew she should say no to such a colorful and eye-catching gown, but the rebellious girl inside her rose up and said, "Yes, that sounds perfect."

The dresses were more elaborately decorated than when

she'd left England, with additions of ruffles and furbelows, and the skirts were widening out, more triangular in design than in the past. She sighed over the illustrations of hats, fetchingly decorated and beruffled. It would be hard to wear a plain cap after seeing what was available to a lady with the wherewithal to spend on fine clothing. She'd be lying to herself if she didn't admit she was tempted by St. Armand's offer to outfit her, but she knew at the end of the day it was better if she took care of herself, watching her coins for her future.

The ladies continued to pick out dresses and garments through midday, with the help of their escort, who appeared to be enjoying outfitting them as much as they were enjoying it. Lydia's wardrobe was warm, modest and with Mrs. Culver occasionally siding with her against St. Armand, appropriate. Mattie's clothing was cut to allow her the freedom of movement both her father and governess insisted upon. Lydia realized she was smiling at the pirate, and he returned the smile without any discernible hidden messages. It was just two people who cared about a little girl.

It was dangerous, relaxing her guard that way and Lydia was glad she had one plain bonnet left, one hiding a good portion of her face from view. Walking beside St. Armand as they left the shop drew all eyes, the men because of the pirate's well-known reputation in the port city, the women because of the pirate's well-known reputation with women everywhere. Lydia tried to keep her head down, but Mattie's chatter and interest in everything around them drew her out. Mattie wore her same outgrown frock, but Mrs. Culver had a few day dresses that had not been picked up by clients who left Liverpool suddenly. When one sailed at the whim of the ship's captain and the wind, it could mean a hurried departure, but with a few quick alterations Lydia now wore a warmer wool gown of deep russet beneath the pelisse fashioned for her by Sails. Mattie too wore her pink coat, and Mrs. Culver had solemnly assured her she looked like a pirate queen in it, a comment which went far in making her willing to stand still for fittings and pinnings.

They were nearly to their lodgings when a light voice rang out, "Look, it's Captain St. Armand! Yoo-hoo, Captain!"

Lydia looked up and spied a lady across the street from them gaily waving a parasol while a scowling gentleman tugged at her arm. She ignored him and continued waving.

It was impossible to ignore *her*. She wore pink from head to toe, sporting a round dress trimmed with three rows of white satin rouleaus, with a deep rose pelisse of *gros de Naples,* and a large brimmed bonnet of the same shade as the pelisse, lined with white satin. It was ornamented with a full bouquet of flowers and Lydia sighed with envy. Having just spent the morning poring over Mrs. Culver's designs, she knew the lady was dressed in the first state of fashion and would never be caught out on the street wearing an ugly cap.

"This is...unexpected," St. Armand muttered, and he seemed unsure for a moment whether he should return the greeting.

The lady decided for him by pulling her escort across the street behind her.

"Captain St. Armand! I thought it was you, even though you have your shirt on, I said to Alexander, 'Look, it's Captain St. Armand!'" She leaned in, her cornflower-blue eyes wide and added, "Then he said something rude about you I shall *not* repeat."

Before either gentleman could respond to this, the lady, whom Lydia could now see was ridiculously lovely as well as fashionable, turned to her and said, "Did Captain St. Armand kidnap you? He really needs to stop doing that. Oh, and Pompom had puppies, Captain! Pompom didn't have puppies, he's a boy so that would be impossible, but his wife

Coquette had puppies so now Pompom's a papa. And is this your little girl? She looks just like you. Is she a pirate too?"

She paused to take more breath and continue speaking, but the scowling gentleman said frostily, "Daphne, I am certain St. Armand and his guests are on their way somewhere and we are keeping them."

Lydia hoped someone would step up and explain what was happening, but Mattie heard the lady ask if she was a pirate and practically glowed with excitement.

"I am Mathilde St. Armand, but the other pirates call me Marauding Mattie!"

The lady—Daphne—clapped her hands in delight. "You have a pirate name! How wonderful!" She smiled at Lydia and said, "Are you a pirate also Miss—?"

St. Armand sighed, saying, "I suppose I must do introductions."

"It's really not necessary," the gruff man said with a barely discernible Scottish accent.

"Miss Burke, I would like to introduce you to Miss Daphne Farnham and Mr. Alexander Murray. Miss Farnham, Murray, my daughter, Mathilde St. Armand and her governess, Miss Lydia Burke."

Murray gave Lydia a bow, then peered keenly into her face, but there was no judgment in his eyes for her, just for the man beside her. Mattie dropped a curtsy that did her governess proud, and the smiling pink lady said, "Captain St. Armand, I am Mrs. Murray now—not pretending, really married this time. I have an idea," she said, taking Lydia's hand in hers. "Dine with us this evening and we will get to know each other better. Marauding Mattie can join us—we will be informal, and she can meet Pompom and Coquette and the puppies."

"Puppies! Papa, they have puppies! You said I could have a puppy, you promised!"

Now he appeared slightly panicked and ready to find an excuse to decline, but it was so clearly evident Mr. Murray did not want his company at supper that Lydia knew he'd be unable to resist tweaking the dour gentleman.

"It would be our pleasure, Mrs. Murray."

Daphne Murray clapped her pink gloved hands together in delight again.

"Excellent! We will see you this evening then."

Her husband sighed, but echoed his wife's invitation and they walked off after giving the direction to their house, Daphne still chattering away, her arm tucked into the crook of his.

"I truly did not expect to see Murray or Miss Farnham again," St. Armand said.

"Captain St. Armand, if the only way you can get female companionship is to purchase it or kidnap women, you should work on your technique."

He raised his brows at her, and as two young women passed them he offered them his "dashing pirate rogue" smile that had one nearly walking into a lamp post.

"My technique is satisfactory as ever, Miss Burke. Come, Mattie. If we're going out this evening we will need to get our knife practice in early."

"Do you anticipate having to fight your way out of supper?"

"Mattie, what did I teach you about socializing with strangers?"

"Be courteous to all you meet, but have a plan to kill them," the child said skipping along and holding his hand. "Can I get a puppy first?"

"Captain St. Armand! You cannot teach the child such awful things, especially now that we are back in England!"

Mattie was singing a chantey to herself and didn't over-hear her father when he leaned down and whispered in

Lydia's ear, "I love it when you use your stern governess voice on me, Miss Burke. It makes me feel like a naughty boy in need of discipline."

Provoking man! He only said these outrageous things to make her lose her temper, and too often he was successful. She should know better by now, because he was correct, she'd dealt with little boys before.

Ah, but Robert St. Armand was anything but a little boy, despite his behavior. He outshone all the other men on the street and he knew it. Even now, dressed more sedately than when aboard the *Prodigal Son*, he drew eyes with his lean grace, his dimpled smile. She felt like a crow alongside a peacock.

It was probably better this way. After all, she didn't want to draw attention, she kept telling herself that.

When they were at their house and Mattie went into the back garden with her father to practice knifeplay, Lydia took out the only dress she owned suitable for evening wear and frowned at it. It was the beige silk, so washed out and faded it made her nearly invisible when she wore it. She had an idea on how to make it more appropriate for an evening dining with the Murrays, and reached into her bag for the green ribbons she'd purchased from Mrs. Culver with the idea of using them on her bonnet.

"WHAT A PRETTY DRESS, MISS BURKE!"

Mattie looked approvingly at Lydia's modified gown, the little critic every inch the daughter of a French *modiste* and a flamboyant pirate. Mattie wore the pink gown last seen aboard the *Prodigal Son* in their ruse with the navy, insisting on the pink because the puppies would like it. It was a close fit, showing even showing more wrist than when she'd worn it aboard ship. The child's new gowns wouldn't be arriving a minute too soon.

"Thank you, Mathilde. Now," Lydia said briskly, "I know I needn't remind you the lady and gentleman with whom we're dining this evening are *not* pirates, and you must be on your best behavior. Dining with adults is a privilege and I know you want to make your papa proud of you."

"Yes, ma'am."

Satisfied at least one member of the St. Armand family could be counted on for proper deportment, Lydia turned back to her dressing table, and fastened a small cameo set in gold around her neck, a present from her godmama when she was a girl. She'd hidden it when she realized the odds of her jewelry being reclaimed from the London pawn shops were slim.

It had been a long time since Lydia attended a supper as a guest and not a governess, and she too was pleased with the adjustments made to her old gown. The pomona green ribbon was wide enough to edge the sleeves and create a border at the newly lowered neckline. Another band of green encircled her beneath her breasts, the ends trailing down in a long line. She'd finished with a small garland of twisted ribbon entwined in a coronet of braids, a freshly trimmed fringe of hair around her face softening its lines. It might not be up to the standards of Mrs. Culver's shop or Mrs. Murray's London dressmakers, but it did well for an evening dining out with—friends? What was the relationship between the Murrays and St. Armand?

The two ladies held hands as they descended the stairs where Jenny the maid waited with their coats. St. Armand looked up from the papers he'd been reading and smiled at Mattie.

The expression on his face froze as he looked at Lydia, almost puzzled. When she reached the bottom of the stair he took her gloved hand in his and bowed over it, and there was no smirking or sarcasm in his gaze when he said, "You look lovely."

No effusive compliments, no flowery phrases, but the way the words were said sent a touch of color through her face and she wondered again who Robert St. Armand was when he wasn't pillaging shipping on the high seas—and what her life would have been had she encountered him when she was "young and airy."

"Too kind, Captain, but our escort this evening is also deserving of a compliment. Wouldn't you agree, Mattie?"

"I hoped you would wear your red coat with the gold braid," Mattie said repressively. "The puppies would like it, I am sure."

"Alas, Mattie, the puppies will have to take me as I am. I am guessing they are intelligent little beasts and will be able to smell my wonderfulness, even if they can't see it in my clothing."

Mattie thought about this seriously before she nodded. "You do look good, Papa."

He did look good, of course. His black evening clothes were superbly tailored and needed no gold braid to set them off. The white shirt against his tanned skin highlighted his masculine appeal while his overlong hair and the cabochon ruby in his earlobe gave the hint of raffish appeal one would expect from the notorious sea rover.

The journey to the Murrays house was not overlong, but they took the carriage hired for in-town use. When they arrived St. Armand pronounced himself surprised at the modest but well-kept property.

"Before she was Mrs. Murray, Miss Farnham was an heiress of note," he explained as he helped Mattie and Lydia down. "It makes me wonder if she was cut off for marrying a lowly surgeon," he said with satisfaction, but when he saw Lydia's face he amended his statement.

"It's not that I want to see Mrs. Murray suffer, or be estranged from her family, it's the idea of Murray triumphant that I cannot—it is complicated..." he trailed off finally as the door opened and they were ushered inside.

Their hostess was there to greet them, and seemed so genuinely pleased to have them as guests that Lydia couldn't help but warm to her.

"And look, here is Alexander with our biggest surprise yet!" She giggled. "James wasn't a surprise to us, after all I grew him, but he may be a surprise to you, Captain St. Armand."

Murray stepped into the room with a baby in his arms, the infant's red curls a brighter shade than his father's blend of russet and silver. The baby looked up at them sleepily, then yawned widely, stuck his finger in his mouth and put his head back on the sturdy shoulder supporting him. A white bichon trotted in at his heels, but after sniffing at their shoes he returned to his master's side.

"That is not a puppy, it's a baby," Mattie said disapprovingly.

"What a clever girl you are!" Daphne Murray said. "The puppies are in the scullery with their mother. When Prentice is finished with your wraps he will take you to the kitchen to meet them, if that meets with your approval, Miss Burke."

Lydia nodded and Mathilde did a fair job of repressing her excitement until the footman returned. The sleepy infant was handed to a nurse, Murray soberly greeting them while ignoring the damp patch of baby drool on his coat. He was dressed well enough, but looked slightly disheveled next to the pirate, who seemed well aware of the contrast they made.

They adjourned to a cozy parlor where a cheerful fire took the chill out of the room. Lydia was struck by how perfectly decorated the space was, just the right combination of luxury and comfort. A row of seashells sat atop the mantel, glowing in the firelight, and the soothing blues and grays of the room were highlighted by colorful touches here and there. Sherry was served and genteel conversation occurred, at least among the ladies.

"So, Murray, kill anyone lately?"

"Odd, I was about to ask you the same thing, St. Armand."

"You are both being silly," Daphne Murray scolded them. "I expect better behavior from you gentleman during supper. Captain St. Armand is a pirate, but you have good manners, most of the time, Alexander."

"One moment," St. Armand said, affronted. "I have excellent manners. Miss Burke will agree with that, won't you?"

All eyes turned to Lydia, and Murray had an eyebrow cocked and a sardonic expression on his face, while Mrs. Murray smiled encouragingly.

Lydia cleared her throat. "Captain St. Armand is capable of great courtesy and deportment. Mathilde could not ask for a more loving or caring father."

"You see, Alexander, I told you the captain wouldn't attack anyone tonight. He will be on his best behavior," Daphne Murray said, patting her husband on the arm. He looked skeptical, but St. Armand watched Lydia, and the look in his eyes surprised her. It was as if he had not expected her to come to his defense, or praise him in any fashion.

"Thank you," he said, with as much true sincerity as she'd ever heard from him. "Your good opinion of me as a father means a great deal to me."

"I only speak the truth, Captain. Sometimes your manners with others leave something to be desired, but with Mathilde you are always the father she needs."

"What of you, Miss Burke?" he leaned over and said for her ears alone. "What is it you need from me?"

Lydia could not answer that question, not here in front of other people, not now. Her life was twisting about like a kite in shifting winds, and she still did not know if she would soar, or if she would crash to the ground.

They moved into the dining room and Lydia was about to ask for Mathilde when Mattie rushed in and said, "The cook said if I had your permission, Papa and Miss Burke, I could eat in the kitchen and she said the delicious custard was made by you, Mrs. Murray, and if I stayed in the kitchen I could watch the puppies eat with their mama. Oh, they are so beautiful, Papa! They are like little white clouds and they're laughing and playing, please let me eat with them!"

Lydia looked at her hostess, who said, "If I were a little girl I would want to eat in the kitchen with puppies also. I have no objection, if Mattie has your permission."

Permission was granted, and with a swift thank-you the child ran back to her play, leaving the adults to their meal. It was probably better this way, Lydia thought. She did not know yet what the history was with the Murrays and Captain St. Armand, but she wasn't surprised there was a beautiful woman, and animosity from her husband, and St. Armand acting naughty. It probably was better Mattie not be there, in case they were forced to beat a hasty retreat at swordspoint.

"This is so much fun! I have not had supper with pirates in ages."

"Pirates, Mrs. Murray? I assure you, I am a merchant captain, nothing more," St. Armand said with a wink, and Daphne Murray giggled, and Murray frowned, and Lydia saw the evening moving in a disastrous direction if something wasn't done.

"I am almost afraid to ask, but how do you all know each other?"

Murray spoke up first. "Daphne and I were castaway and Captain St. Armand rescued us and brought us to England."

Lydia waited for more, but St. Armand just sat there, looking as if butter wouldn't melt in his mouth. "I was surprised to see you in Liverpool, Murray. I was led to believe you'd open a surgery in London."

"We are here because Alexander and I are learning about my father's shipping, Captain. Someday I'll inherit it and we need to know more, so we are spending time working for my father."

"This is a temporary sojourn," Murray said, waving off a servant who offered him more wine. Lydia did not mind a touch more in her glass, as Mrs. Murray set an excellent table and managed her household well. She was dressed plainly, in a simple striped muslin the same blue as her stunning eyes, trimmed in modest pink rosettes with a matching satin bandeau in her golden curls. She wore no jewelry other than her wedding ring, and Lydia knew after seeing the fashionable outfit worn earlier that Daphne was being kind, so as to not embarrass her guest.

Captain St. Armand carried on a perfectly normal conversation over supper about shipping and the future of the industry as the men debated which markets would be expanding and what goods would be valued now that the wars were over. Murray solicited his wife's opinion, which seemed to surprise St. Armand, but Lydia had seen while Daphne Murray acted silly, she wasn't stupid. It was good her husband recognized this, because in Lydia's experience as a governess, oftentimes men failed to realize their wives could do more than pop out heirs.

They dined on poached turbot and a good English roast beef with pudding, fresh beans in a bechamel sauce, and Mrs. Murray's custard, which was indeed excellent. It was the style of English supper Lydia'd missed most in the islands, and the Murray's cook did it justice.

Rather than adjourn separately, the men to their port and the women to await them, they all trouped into the kitchen. The pups were in the scullery and Mattie sat amidst them on the floor as they frolicked about her looking like animated snowballs. Their mother watched them closely, but Daphne came over and hummed to her, scratching her behind her ear, and the dog relaxed. Coquette's coloring was more varied than Pompom's, as she sported dark tan ears, a pattern carried over onto some of the pups.

Most of them left Mattie to mock-fight amongst themselves, but one, the smallest of the litter, ran at Mattie, pounced on her gown, then jumped off. He hunkered down on his chest with his bottom in the air, tail wagging as he yipped in joyful play.

Mattie scooped the little clown up and covered him in kisses as he squirmed in her hands and tried to lick and bite at her chin. She looked up at them then, her blue eyes wide over the dog's head.

"Oh look, Papa! Look, Miss Burke! It is our puppy!"

Lydia leaned over and said in St. Armand's ear, "*I* am not going to tell her she can't have that puppy."

He scratched his own chin. "I should have known if we took Mattie to see puppies we would end up with one," he turned to their hostess. "May I purchase a pup—that one, if he's available—for Mattie? Is he weaned?"

Daphne tapped her finger against her lush mouth as she thought. "I will give you the pup, Captain, but he's just started eating regular food. Can you get him at the end of the week? That way he won't be separated from Coquette too abruptly."

"That should be acceptable, Mrs. Murray. And thank you."

He went over to where Mattie sat and squatted down on

his heels, listening intently as Mattie explained all about the puppies. Lydia watched fondly, but was startled by a light tap on her shoulder.

"May I have a word, Miss Burke?"

She followed Murray out into the kitchen, where he looked at her out of grave hazel eyes.

"Miss Burke, are you being held against your will? Do you need assistance? We can offer you safety here—St. Armand is not the only one with friends who carry knives."

Lydia was deeply touched this man would put himself, and possibly his family, at risk for a stranger. But she answered truthfully when she said, "I am with Captain St. Armand of my own will, Mr. Murray. Mattie needs me, and I will stay with them as her governess."

He studied her without speaking, hands clasped behind his back. Finally, he said, "As you wish, ma'am. No doubt you are a civilizing influence on the child. If you—or Mattie—ever require assistance, you may call upon me."

"Thank you, Mr. Murray, but my place, for now, is with the St. Armand family."

He looked back over his shoulder to where the father and daughter sat on the floor, their dark curls close together. "The child seems healthy and is clearly St. Armand's offspring. She has no mother?"

"No, her mother Nanette lived on St. Martin but she became ill and died, and that is how I became Mattie's governess," Lydia said, more or less truthfully as they returned to the scullery. There was enough animosity between the men, she did not need to add fuel to those flames.

Mattie was making crooning noises to the little pup as her father talked to her, "And we will bring one of your old shifts, Mattie, and rub it all over Coquette, then put it in the puppy's bed at our house. It will calm him and he'll sleep better at night, because it will smell like his mother, but also like you."

"You have owned puppies, Captain?" Lydia asked.

"I had a terrier once. Samson."

He turned back to the dog, poking a finger under its chin and the pup jumped and fell over in delight at the new toy.

"What will you call him, Mattie?"

"See the brown patch around his eye, Papa? He looks like a pirate dog. I will call him…" she thought about it, then grinned. "Jolly Roger! Or just Jolly because he is such a jolly little darling."

"An excellent name for this ferocious creature, Marauding Mattie."

Lydia said to their hosts, "It has been a long day and it might be best if we end it now before someone gets cranky and unreasonable."

"I'm being quite well behaved."

"I meant Mathilde, Captain."

St. Armand fluidly rose to his feet and they thanked their hosts and promised to return for Jolly Roger. Daphne and Alexander Murray stood close to one another, her hand resting lightly on his arm and Lydia sighed, remembering what it was like to be close to another human being that way, not the closeness of a teacher and pupil, as she had with Mattie, but the closeness of adults who found companionship together, sharing life's events, having someone to turn to at the end of the day, someone who knew you and cared about you.

Mattie perked up when she washed for bed. When St. Armand stepped in to kiss her goodnight, she said, "What about my story, Papa?"

He returned with his copy of *Captain Johnson* and arranged himself on her bed while Lydia took the chair. She didn't want to admit it to the two pirates, but she also was captivated by the tales of long ago miscreants and their adventures.

"As you know, Mattie, Edward Teach, or Blackbeard, was a commodore of pirates, commanding other captains beneath him. He was not a good man at all, but he was a very successful pirate, so successful that the governor of Virginia Colony offered a huge bounty on his head—one hundred pounds!"

Mattie's eyes grew large as her father gave her an edited version of Blackbeard's life, but even so she was frowning at the end.

"'Here was an end of that courageous brute, who might have passed in the world for a hero had he been employed in a good cause; his destruction...was entirely owing to the conduct and bravery of Lieutenant Maynard and his men.'"

"Blackbeard did not treat his crew well, Papa. You are the better captain. I am glad Lieutenant Maynard stopped him."

He closed the book and looked at Lydia. "You seem pensive, Miss Burke. Did you not like it that Blackbeard received his just deserts?"

Lydia looked at the father and daughter together, and thought on Murray's offer to rescue her from pirates. "'Who might have passed in the world for a hero had he been employed in a good cause...' It makes me think, Captain St. Armand, of what could have become of brave and bold people like Edward Teach and Anne Bonny and Mary Read if they had not become pirates."

"No doubt their lives would have been duller."

"No doubt, but I imagine their families would have been happier."

He raised his brows at this statement. "Consider this—they may have been fleeing from a worse situation when they went to sea. Not all families—"

He stopped and looked down at his daughter, who'd

dropped off to sleep during their conversation. "We're done here, Miss Burke."

THEY LEFT the room and she paused, looking down the hallway to her dark and empty room. Robert raised his candle to peer into her face.

"Is there something wrong?"

"No. Yes." She straightened her shoulders and spoke brusquely. "Yes. I have a request, Captain St. Armand. I would like to be held."

"I beg your pardon?"

"You heard me," she said, her rich voice low, and hushed, but she kept her eyes on his face. "I wish to be held. Not ravished, not kissed senseless, not exposed to fur pillows and exotic Oriental techniques, simply…held. Are you capable of that?"

She swallowed and he knew she'd been pushed far beyond what any reasonable woman could be expected to tolerate. There were fractures in the safe life she'd constructed for herself, fractures he'd caused. The evening spent in the company of a dull and respectable married couple no doubt reminded her of what was missing from her own life. Most of that could not be put at his doorstep, but as he'd reminded her more than once, she was a member of a pirate crew, for good, but also for ill. She may not have chosen a life of danger like Anne Bonny, but she was none-theless cast adrift.

He did not regret what he'd done and he knew the day was not yet over—he could still do things for Lydia Burke she could not begin to imagine, but for now he could give her what she wished for.

He set down his candle, and the book. Wordlessly he

opened his arms and she hesitated, then walked into them. As he enclosed her in his embrace her body lost its stiffness and she rested there, in his arms, silent. She was not motionless. She trembled, as slightly as a fern brushed by the passing of a sparrow. After a moment as long as a lifetime of regrets she pulled back, but his arms tightened about her, offering safety and she sighed and rested her head on his shoulder.

He did not know how long they stood like that, just holding one another and listening to their heartbeats, but she stepped out of his embrace and he released her, reluctantly.

She smoothed down her skirts.

"Thank you," she said as mildly as if he'd passed her the butter at table, not as if his entire world was now realigned on its foundation. Being desired was not new to him. All his life women desired him for his looks, for his charm, for his dangerous ways. The idea of being desired for comfort, that was new.

Any caring man could offer comfort. A clerk in a counting house. A parson. A farmer. A surgeon. You did not have to be a beautiful and dangerous pirate to offer comfort. An ugly man, a scarred man, a blind man could offer comfort to another human being.

Was he worthy of this regard? If he did not have his looks, and his wealth, and his skill at bedsport, what could he offer a woman? What could he offer this woman?

"Now I have a request to make of you."

"What?"

She knew his answer when his lips touched hers, a soft kiss, at first, not demanding, but a seeking kiss, a kiss to learn who she was, what she wanted—no, a kiss to learn who *he* was, what *he* wanted. It was something he'd never considered, never had to consider, but he needed to know, now, that he still had value, this new man who comforted little girls with nightmares and big ones who wanted to be held.

What he wanted now was not what he wanted two months ago. He feared what he wanted now would rock his vessel in ways he could not imagine, put him in waters he could not navigate, not without Lydia Burke at his side. She was so beautiful tonight in her simple gown, but the lowered neckline exposed more of her creamy skin to his gaze and the candlelight gleaming on her rich hair had him vowing to burn any ugly caps remaining in her possession, no matter what promises he'd made.

It terrified him to feel this way about the prickly governess. He'd worried that he could not be Mattie's father, not the father she needed, and Lydia reassured him and helped him understand that yes, he could be that father. But could he be the man Lydia needed? Could she ever come to see him beyond his pretty face and his smooth ways, and value him?

There would be no definitive answers until they reached their destination and she saw him for who he really was. In the meantime, he would protect her from that which threatened her safety, and he would do his best to give her what emotional support he was capable of giving her, because he did not know if he was capable of being the man she needed.

CHAPTER 18

*M*attie's repeated questions of when they'd get her puppy drove all to distraction, but they finally secured the animal and said farewell to the Murrays. Mrs. Murray praised Lydia's new Coburg cap of blue velvet lined with white satin as being an excellent and fashionable match with her sapphire brocade pelisse.

The headgear was the last item to be delivered and there were finally enough dresses, boots and bonnets for Captain St. Armand to pronounce them ready to move on.

"Now will you tell me where we are going?"

He looked up from where he and Mattie were stretched out on the floor playing with Jolly, who kept jumping out of the basket Mattie prepared for him to sleep in while they traveled. The pup had done a good job of chewing through the basket rim until Norton gave the dog some rawhide to teethe upon. He tugged at it, then chased it when Mattie threw it across the floor for him to fetch.

St. Armand leaned up on one elbow and gave her his "I'm such a mischievous scamp" smile. She resisted the urge to kick him while he was down.

"You will find out where we're going soon enough. I will tell you I do not expect to be on the road for more than a few days, weather permitting."

Lydia paused and did some geographic calculations in her head. She still suspected they would be near the coast, but ruled out too distant locales such as Cornwall, Portsmouth and most importantly, London.

She was also glad of the new wardrobes for her and for Mattie. One forgot how dank and chill England could be in autumn, and they weren't even into the heart of winter yet. The substantial woolens replacing her St. Martin gowns were welcome, and Mattie looked every inch the young lady in her new gear.

There had been some arguing initially about Mattie's shipboard trousers being replaced by gowns, but Lydia assured her girls could still run and play and climb trees, even in dresses.

"Did you do all of that when you were a girl?"

"Indeed I did, Mattie. I would not let my wardrobe hold me back, and you will find other girls and boys will enjoy having you play with them, even if you are in a skirt."

"Will they call me names because I am a bastard?" the child asked all too matter-of-factly as she bit into her toasted bread at breakfast. Her father looked up from his own meal, frowning.

"If they do that, you should tell me, Mathilde and I will deal with—you disagree, Miss Burke?"

Lydia'd folded her linen and put it on the table. "Mathilde will learn to deal with other children, Captain, it is part of life. She did in St. Martin, she will in England if you will be making your home ashore. Just don't go around stabbing people, Mattie," Lydia added with a pointed look and the child's father didn't gainsay her.

Now Mattie gathered up her dog and her doll, which

she'd been careful to keep away from the pup's teeth, and her father picked up the basket in one hand and rested the other on the child's head.

Norton looked proud and capable in his new coachman's suit, seated atop the traveling coach with Conroy beside him, and he gave Mattie a wink when she scrambled in. After checking out everything in the coach the pup settled down into his basket and sighed, worn-out and ready to sleep. Mattie though kept her gaze on the countryside as they rolled along, asking questions about the trees, the crops, pointing out cattle and sheep, and waving at people they passed. Lydia used the opportunity to teach the child about her new home, and knew from the placement of the sun they were heading southeast.

She'd forgotten how autumn in England had its own fragrance of smoke with a hint of apple, crisp air heralding the coming of winter, and she breathed deep. Like it or not, it was the smell of home.

St. Armand faced away from the horses and read, having no difficulty with a moving coach after a lifetime aboard a shifting deck. The paint and varnish still smelled fresh, and they traveled in warm comfort thanks to the hot bricks and their new clothes. The puppy left his basket to curl up beside Mattie and Lydia and share their heat. Mattie finally stretched out on the seat and put her head on Lydia's lap to join the puppy in sleep, and Lydia looked up to see St. Armand watching her, watching her hand resting atop the girl's shoulder to steady her against bumps in the road.

"You are attached to Mattie."

There was no sense in denying it. "Yes, I am, Captain. I will miss being her governess."

He frowned at her. "Why would that occur? We worked out your agreement to stay."

"For now, but I cannot stay forever. What if you marry,

Captain? Your wife will not want a governess who is part of the *Prodigal Son's* pirate crew."

"If I marry, my wife will have to accept my crew as well. Nash, Turnbull, Fuller—they're already at our destination. Norton and Conroy are here with us. Sails will join us soon." He looked down at the sleeping child. "And then there's Marauding Mattie…"

Lydia didn't realize her hand tightened protectively on the child until she murmured in her sleep. Would a step-mother love Robert St. Armand's bastard? She bit her lip and gazed out the window at the village they were entering as the sun cast a golden afternoon glow over the countryside.

"You could—" Whatever he was starting to say was cut short when Norton pulled up on the horses, and Conroy jumped down and opened the carriage door.

The inn yard was bathed in light and a few fallen leaves, looking prosperous and tidy. The innkeeper himself rushed out to greet the new arrivals.

"Lord and Lady Huntley! How wonderful to have you stay with us. Your man Fuller has made all of the arrangements, and we have two chambers and a private parlor, as you requested."

Lydia froze at the innkeeper's words.

"Who are Lord and Lady Huntley?" she whispered to the man beside her. The rogue didn't even twitch as he took her by the arm and said, "We are, of course. And this is our little girl, Mathilde. Right, Mattie?"

"That's what you said, Papa, and I remembered," the littlest rogue fibbed. "I can play along."

"Captain—"

Lydia wasn't sure what she could say at this point that wouldn't make the situation worse, but it was like being in a bad farce. Not only was she traveling with pirates, she traveled with pirates pretending to be part of the aristocracy and who knows what other bouncers they were telling people. Not to mention she'd been introduced as "Lady Huntley," and she did not think the role was that of St. Armand's mother.

She also knew from her association with the piratical crew surrounding them that if she made a fuss and the situation turned bad, cutlasses and guns were liable to appear. It would give the people of the county something to talk about for years, but it would not end well. She clamped her mouth shut, took Mattie by the hand and followed the lead pirate into the inn.

"Everything is as you requested, m'lord. The girl will bring hot water to your rooms and we can serve your supper in an hour if that is satisfactory."

"Papa, I need to take Jolly out for his walk."

"We'll all go, Mattie."

Good. Outside she could have her say and not worry about revealing themselves to the entire inn.

The little family group headed outside with Jolly on his leash, and as soon as they were out of earshot of the inn yard, Lydia rounded on him.

"Lord and Lady Huntley? Are you insane?" she hissed. "You can't go around impersonating a member of the peerage!"

"I find I get better service if innkeepers think I'm a peer. You saw how we were welcomed. Would you rather we announce ourselves as 'the pirate captain St. Armand and the crew of the *Prodigal Son*'? Which, I might point out, includes you and Marauding Mattie here."

"And Jolly Roger," Mattie piped up. "He's part of the crew as well."

The newest crew member had taken care of business and was now sniffing around a pile of autumn leaves and acorns, jumping back and barking when a puff of wind blew the leaves up in the air around him. Mattie took the rawhide and threw it, and Jolly yipped and raced after, fetching it back to his mistress to throw again, which she did, running with the dog and stretching her legs after the long carriage ride.

"Captain St. Armand—"

He looked back at Lydia and shook his head. "No, *Lady Huntley*, for this ruse to work you must immerse yourself in the role—please, address me as Huntley or even better, Robert, or *my darling*."

"This is ridiculous! I cannot participate in this fraud!"

"Of course you can, you're well on your way to being a pirate." He glanced over to make sure Mattie was out of hearing range. "Don't you ever think about what your life would be like if you lived with fewer boundaries, scoffing at society's rules and restrictions rather than being crushed beneath them?"

"You know nothing of my life, and please do not change the subject."

"I know more than you suspect," he said, stepping closer and taking her by the elbows. He looked into her eyes, and there was no laughter in his face, none of the naughtiness he usually inflicted on her. Instead he looked solemn as he said, "Tell me what has you so afraid. I will take care of you, Lydia. I can protect you. I can keep you safe."

"By pretending to be something we are not? Dressing up as lords and ladies and telling whoppers to innkeepers does not make it real! We must be who we are, and right now I am your daughter's governess. That is all."

"I can offer you more than that."

His words must have distracted her because without realizing it they were standing even closer.

"Why do we continue to discuss this?"

"Because you are a woman of great passion, Lydia Burke, no matter that you keep it under caps and pinned up, and garbed in sackcloth. I know it, and you know it, and there is no reason we cannot appreciate what we have to offer each other."

"Passion, Captain? For every night of passion there is a morning after when the cold light reveals truths we'd rather not face. No doubt you think yourself an excellent lover. It's not enough."

"'An excellent lover'? I am flattered, but that is something you should verify for yourself, Mis-Lady Huntley."

"Stop that!" she hissed. "The child is returning, and we should return as well. The sooner we can end this ruse and get back on the road tomorrow, the better."

"But what if someone is watching us, Lydia? Shouldn't we demonstrate our affection to add verisimilitude to our roles?"

Before she could protest his lips were on hers, and her traitorous body and mind remembered the kisses they'd shared, and how he stoked within her the fires she kept banked, coals that would flare up and consume her if she wasn't careful.

But oh, she was tired of the word careful and wanted to fan those flames as he was now, and she pushed aside governess Lydia for a heartbeat, an interlude of letting rebel Lydia come out to play because that Lydia knew how to have fun, and seize life, and not worry about the morrow.

She was the one to pull away and step back from his embrace. Rebel Lydia had thrown aside respectability, and ended up hounded and running. She could not allow herself to be foolish enough to make that mistake twice in a lifetime, no matter how delicious his kisses were, how much they made her ache with longing.

"Do not say that was a mistake. It felt like anything but a mistake to me."

"Exactly why I need to do the thinking for both of us.

One person here needs to be the responsible adult. I cannot rely on you to make the correct choice, so I must."

"Are you so certain it is the correct choice, Lydia?" he said softly. His hands still held her arms, not pinioning her or restraining her, but offering strength and comfort. It was nearly as dangerous as the passion between them, that comfort. It was a false harbor.

"Enough, Captain. We should return to the inn."

"No, it is not enough. But it will have to do for now."

He released her and turned away, but she stopped him with a hand on his arm.

"You secured two rooms. I will sleep with Mattie in hers."

The corner of his mouth quirked up. "That was what I always intended. You might try to sneak into my bed during the night, but I'm willing to risk it. Attach your pup to his leash, Mattie, we are going inside."

Mattie called the dog to her and he tripped over his own paws running, then wagged his tail, proud of himself for making the child laugh. She scooped Jolly up and kissed him, while he reciprocated by licking her all over her face. Lydia almost said something, then shrugged. Children had been kissing dogs—and vice versa—for millennia. Mattie would survive the experience.

Captain St. Armand stooped and picked up his beaver hat from where it fell to the ground during their embrace and brushed it off before reseating it atop his curls. The air grew cooler with the fading sunset and they were glad to return to a hot supper and warm beds.

The bedtime story that night would have been another pirate tale, but Mattie requested a pirate story with a dog, and since there wasn't one in Johnson's book, she settled for a brief re-telling of the tale of Captain Calico Jack, but grumbled that it would have been better with a dog in it.

After kissing his daughter goodnight and reminding her

Jolly was to sleep in his basket, he invited Lydia to join him in the private parlor for a brandy, or tea, or something else that would fill the time until the adults were ready to turn in.

"I am not interested in drinking ale in the public room or joining in their dice games," he said. "We have a busy day tomorrow."

Lydia was so stunned by this mature and adult statement that she nearly said something, but was afraid she'd spoil the moment and said, "Tea sounds lovely, Captain."

He returned from making arrangements and an apple-cheeked serving girl appeared shortly with a tray, her face becoming even rosier at St. Armand's smile as he took it from her. Lydia poured them each a cup and inhaled the fragrant brew. A quiet cup of tea was one of the pleasures she'd enjoyed in the islands as a reminder of home and England. She fixed his the way he liked it, with extra sugar, and passed him the plate of shortbread.

He set the plate down after taking two pieces and said ruefully, "I fear I have been supplanted by a mongrel in that child's affections."

"I, for one, cannot regret this new development, Captain. Owning a dog will teach Mattie responsibility and add to her maturity. Being a pirate does not prepare a young lady to enter society and function there."

"Are you so certain? As Mattie's father I believe knowing how do defend herself against attackers puts her on a better footing with her future peers. There are sharks in society just as in the waters of the Caribbean, and I already fear I will not always been there to defend her against so-called gentlemen who will see an attractive woman and—"

He stopped, and she looked at him in sympathy. Being a father was no easy thing, especially father to a lovely young woman. Her own father had been loving, but too often exasperated by her behavior before—

That too was a path she had no desire to tread, and she steered the conversation into small talk, probing St. Armand for answers about their destination that he easily parried. After yawning a time or two she excused herself for bed, knowing they had an early start.

He made no moves to seduce or kiss her, and she assured herself she did not regret this as she climbed into her lonely bed. The dog's basket was near the door and after poking his head up to investigate he huddled back down under Mattie's old shift.

Lydia wasn't certain what woke her during the night, but she could hear a voice outside her door. Mattie was sound asleep, a small mound beneath her covers, and Lydia slipped out of bed and put her ear to the door to listen.

"And you must be very quiet so we do not wake anyone. Shhhh! Stop kissing me!"

That apple-cheeked serving girl must have returned to his room and offered more than shortbread. That libertine! St. Armand brought a woman to his rooms, here, a few feet from where his daughter lay sleeping!

Lydia didn't want to think about what it meant to her to hear him speaking in that low, affectionate tone to another woman. She was only Mattie's governess, after all, that is what she kept insisting to Mattie's father when he turned his sparkling eyes in her direction and used his "Wouldn't you love to invite me into your bedchamber?" look on her.

She carefully opened the door a crack, grateful the innkeeper kept the hinges oiled. In the darkened passage she saw him at the top of the stairway.

And he was alone.

No, not alone. There was a tiny "yip" from inside his shirt.

"Now, see here, Master Jolly, you cannot be disturbing the ladies. They're not the sort who are interested in a good romp in the dark with a handsome fellow—no, stop kissing my chin, I am not interested in romping with you either. A quick stop outdoors and then back to your basket with you, m'boy."

He moved down the stairs, still talking to the dog. After a while, Lydia heard his firm footsteps as he returned with the puppy, and she closed her eyes, expecting he would sneak the dog back into his basket. But the steps continued past her door into St. Armand's own room, and soon it was quiet again in the inn.

Lydia waited and waited for Jolly to be returned, and eventually her curiosity had the better of her. She arose and padded over to the connecting door between their rooms, opening it a notch. All was silent in St. Armand's bedchamber and she tiptoed in.

He was fast asleep, his arm cradled around a furry white ball snoring up against his shoulder.

Lydia's heart turned over with a thump.

That was it, she might as well strike her colors and surrender. The pirate boarded her heart and took it captive in the night, armed not with a pistol, but with a puppy. She had no more defenses against Robert St. Armand. Yes, he was a lying scoundrel, and she hoped fervently if there was a genuine Lord Huntley he never learned of their ruse, but he was the scoundrel who'd awakened Lydia's soul, and her passions. He was the pirate who took care of little girls and puppy dogs, and also a governess who often wished she too had a strong shoulder she could rest her head upon, someone not to take charge of her life, but to share her burdens with her. How wonderful it would be if there was a person she could turn to in the middle of the night for comfort and cuddling.

He was nude under the covers. He'd mentioned often enough in her hearing that he slept without a stitch of clothing. Her gaze traveled down the long length of him, the lithe frame and smooth muscles, the scars that made her want to lean closer and run her fingers over them.

She'd kiss his chin. And other parts of him as well.

Lydia eased back into her dark room and her narrow bed and nearly burst out weeping, angry at herself.

How could she love Robert St. Armand? It was ridiculous. She'd already been disastrously in love with one feckless male. Was she that stupid? That weak?

She ran these arguments through her mind, but like lawn bowls they were knocked asunder by what she'd observed. St. Armand—Robert—was not a feckless boy. He took action, caring for his men aboard ship, seeing to their comfort— heaven knows she'd seen ship's captains in the islands who cared only about profit, and not whether their crew had decent food and foul weather gear.

Robert cared for Mathilde. Robert loved Mathilde, but he understood you showed love to a child by being a proper parent, one who ensured she was adequately fed and housed and shod and who assured the girl her papa loved her and would not desert her. He'd taken on the responsibility of the child and never looked back.

Robert cared for Lydia. He was a scoundrel and a sea thief, but he'd never forced himself on her. He lured her, he enticed her, he intrigued her, but he did not use his brute strength to get his way. He did not have to. His kisses were dangerous weapons wielded by an expert. She did not know if he exaggerated his supposed repertoire of sexual skills, but she suspected not. Yes, men did like to brag about their supposed prowess in the boudoir, but based on snippets of conversation with Nanette—who of all women Lydia knew was the expert on men and their skills—he'd been more than her protector and financial support, he'd also been a welcome lover.

For the first time since the notorious Captain Robert St. Armand kidnapped her, Lydia began to nurture a tiny seed of possibility inside her chest. That rebel girl was battering at Lydia's restrictive walls, demanding to be released again. Maybe, just maybe, there could be a future for her with the captain.

Provided they weren't hauled off to the magistrate for impersonating members of the peerage and defrauding innkeepers.

CHAPTER 19

"You are dwelling on this deception business far too much. I am paying well for staying here. Now, finish your bacon so we can get on the road again."

He picked up a well-polished spoon and paused, distracted by his own reflection.

"You are like a magpie, Captain. Stop admiring yourself in bright, shiny objects and tell me where we are going!" she snapped.

He smiled inwardly. Every time he flustered the little hedgehog into becoming all prickly he wanted to swoop her into his arms and cover her with kisses until she melted. It was enjoyable and helped distract him from thoughts of what lay at the end of the journey.

He put the spoon down abruptly.

"You are so demanding, Lady Huntley," he said as the door to the private parlor opened, but it was only Mattie returning with Jolly from his walk. The fresh air added pink to the child's cheeks and he opened his arms to hug her, inhaling the fragrance of the crisp morning and little girl.

Jolly sniffed all around the carpet as Mattie climbed onto Robert's lap, telling him of the horses she'd seen, the chickens who'd scurried away when Jolly barked at them, and how she had helped Norton with the harnesses for their carriage. Mattie casually munched on some bacon off of Robert's plate, and Robert didn't say anything when he saw Lydia slip a tiny piece to Jolly beneath the table.

For all her prickly outside, the governess had a soft center, a fondness for little girls, and puppies, and maybe, possibly, even a pirate. He had plans for the governess, but much would depend on what they found at journey's end. Conroy came to tell them the horses were ready, so he gathered up the ladies, accepted the innkeeper's bowing thanks for the patronage of Lord and Lady Huntley, ignored Miss Burke's frown and put them in the carriage.

The muscles in his neck tightened as the miles rolled away beneath the carriage wheels, the landscape becoming familiar. The nearer they drew to their destination, the more he recognized. That elm, he'd climbed it as a lad. The old sycamores and oaks along the lane. Even the cattle looked the same as the ones he'd seen more than twenty years past.

He startled when Lydia put her hand over his. She looked at him with concern in her eyes, shaded by her bonnet but still reflecting the light of dusk coming through the windows.

His hands were clenched on his thighs, so tightly fisted they ached when he moved them to open his fingers and stretch them. Mattie slept on the seat and didn't hear her governess ask him if there was anything the matter.

"What could be the matter? The prodigal son is returning home."

He knew he was smiling, but had no description for this smile, because what he felt was something he hadn't experienced in years, a mixture of anxiety and nausea and wanting to hunch his shoulders and appear small and unnoticeable.

She looked ready to say something, but Norton pulled up on the horses, bringing the carriage to a stop.

"It's Mr. Fuller, Cap'n. He's waiting for you."

Fuller rode up on a horse that looked nearly as battered and grizzled as the first mate. Robert jumped down and twisted his neck back and forth, working out the kinks from sitting, and from the tension.

"Stay here," he said, walking out of earshot to Fuller before the governess could argue with him.

"Did you find him there?"

"Aye, Captain. He's in residence with his mates." Fuller glanced at the governess, talking to a yawning Mattie, who'd poked her head from the carriage. "Are you certain this is how you want to play it out?"

"A fast strike is an effective tactic against an unprepared foe, Mr. Fuller. It's time to hoist the black flag and make our presence known."

"Aye, Captain," Fuller said with a nod. "The others are in place, and we'll be ready for action."

"Ride beside us then, Mr. Fuller."

He climbed back into the carriage. Mattie started to say something, but Miss Burke whispered in the girl's ear and she quieted, watching her father with large eyes.

Robert knew his fingers were drumming on his thigh, but he couldn't seem to stop them as the carriage jostled into an open drive overgrown with neglected hawthorn, the road narrow and pitted.

"Is this your home, Captain St. Armand?"

The governess frowned, looking out at the dilapidated condition of the property they rode into.

"I lived here."

"That is not what I asked."

He didn't have to respond to that because the carriage lurched to a stop.

"Come down, Miss Burke, Mattie. I want you close by me."

"What about Jolly?" the child asked.

"He'll stay in the carriage."

"Jolly won't like that, Papa."

"Do as I say!" he snapped. The governess and his daughter looked at him with wide eyes, and he took a deep breath. "I am not angry with you, Mathilde. Leave the dog. We'll fetch him later."

"Yes, Papa," the girl said in a small voice and Robert mentally punched himself for taking his nerves out on the child. He was better than that. He had to be, because he swore Mattie would not grow up as he did. He smiled at her, but it fell short of the mark and she clung to her governess for reassurance.

He almost offered his arm, but thought better of it. He wanted both hands free and could more easily step in front of the woman and child this way.

The Tudor manor was much as he remembered, and the sandstone facing looked warm in the afternoon light. It was deceptive. His memories of the house were of it being cold, dark, always a step away from dangerous for a boy no one wanted.

At least it had been well-maintained then, but it was neglected and dirty now, and his lips curled up at the corners to see what had become of it. At one time there were flowerbeds at the entrance, now there were only weeds and untrimmed shrubs.

Robert thought about banging on the door, but it opened on its own. An old man in a worn suit of black clothes waited there, clinging to the oak, and while his smile missed a few teeth, it animated his face.

"Master Robert! Fuller said it was you coming, but I had to see with my own eyes."

"Braxton," he said, striding over to the elderly butler and clasping his hand in both of his. "Finding you here is more than I dared hope for."

"I knew you would come home someday, Master Robert —I mean—"

His words were cut off by raucous laughter from the interior of the house. Robert looked down the darkened hall and his hand moved down to his coat pocket pulled askew by the comforting weight of a pistol. Strapping on a cutlass would no doubt have alarmed the ladies, not to mention ruined the line of his coat, but he'd never cross this threshold unarmed.

"Would you care to announce me, Braxton?"

"It would give me the greatest pleasure. This is your child, Master Robert?"

"My daughter, Mathilde St. Armand, and Miss Burke, her governess," he told the butler.

"Welcome to Huntley, Miss Burke, Miss Mathilde," the butler said with a bow.

"Captain—"

"Not now, Miss Burke. All your questions will be answered in time, I assure you."

"Captain, Mattie may enjoy a visit to the kitchen while you...talk," Fuller said.

"I could get Jolly a bone," Mattie said. "Then he won't be sad about being in the carriage."

A young, wide-eyed footman peered around the corner and Braxton motioned him over.

"That's a good idea. Why don't you ladies go to the kitchens, and see if something can be found for you to eat? For Jolly also," he added, looking at his daughter and giving her a wink.

At Braxton's order the footman nodded, never taking his

eyes off of Fuller and Robert, then led the women into the house.

Mattie's good humor was restored as she went with her governess, asking her a hundred questions the poor lady was not prepared to answer. She appeared dazed by the latest turn of events, but Robert knew she was up to the task ahead and he would deal with her later. For now, Lydia and Mattie were out of harm's way.

Fuller and Conroy accompanied him inside, and they paused outside the closed doors of the great hall. Drunken laughter and the sound of breaking glass drifted out as Braxton opened the door, and Robert stepped into a scene of debauchery and destruction. It did not have the same cachet when he was not at the center of the debauch. It also did not have the same cachet when it was his money being wasted, but his entrance had exactly the effect he'd desired.

The butler straightened as best he could and in a voice no longer quavering said, "Robert St. Armand Huntley." Then he bowed in Robert's direction and added, loudly enough for the others in the room to hear every word, "Welcome home, Lord Huntley. You've been missed."

The men in the room gaped at him like fish hauled out of the ocean. The one at the head of the table started to rise, wobbling on his feet.

"It's the Frenchwoman's bastard!"

Robert almost smiled at this. He and Mathilde had more in common than Miss Burke imagined. His boot heels rang on the stones of the floor, part of the original hall. Huntley was a hodgepodge of additions over the years and this room was one of his least favorites. Cold, drafty, but impressive as hell as he walked past the now silent crowd, watching him as if they were at a London play.

He intended to give them their money's worth, well

aware of the figure he presented, especially compared to the sot at whose side he now stood.

"Well, Lionel? No welcome for the prodigal son? I see you already slaughtered a fatted calf or two. My calves, I might add."

"But…you can't be here. You're dead! I'm the baron!"

"No, I am not and no, you are not. Get out of my chair. And my house."

His cousin blinked blearily at him. Lionel's neckcloth hung loose and his shirt was open and wine-stained. Lines of dissipation were already forming on his face, though he was three years younger than St. Armand. He had the true Huntley coloring, thinning blonde hair and hazel eyes, but softer eyes than the late baron. The cousins had not known one another well as children. Uncle Alfred was a weasel unable to hide his resentment that he was the spare, not the heir, and Robert's father enjoyed pointing out that with his three sons—even one of questionable provenance—Alfred would never be baron.

The junior weasel was doomed to disappointment as well.

Lionel pushed himself to his feet as his drinking cronies muttered to themselves uncertainly.

"Here now, Huntley, you can't let this man stroll in here and throw us out!"

Robert looked at his cousin, not bothering to glance at the other man.

"Tell him, Cousin Lionel."

Lionel floundered for something to say, but Braxton spoke up first.

"I have served in this household for longer than you… gentlemen…have been alive. This man"—he pointed dramatically at Robert—"this man is the heir to Huntley. The baron is Robert St. Armand Huntley, not Lionel Huntley."

"I will fight this!" Lionel blustered.

"You are welcome to try, *Mr. Huntley*, as long as you use your own funds and do it elsewhere. You may wish to stop first at the office of my solicitor in London. He tells me he assured you I was still alive and that you were not the inheritor of Huntley, or the title. This is the last time I'm going to say this... Leave. Immediately. Or my crew will be happy to help you leave. All of you," he said raising his voice at the end to be sure they heard.

There was more muttering, but Conroy and Fuller, joined now by Norton, looked prepared to handle a bunch of drunken town louts with ease.

"My clothes...my possessions..."

"Will be sent along after you give us your direction, cuz. If you wish to leave with your skin intact and not leaking blood, you will not worry about that."

Robert's demands finally penetrated through the drink fogging Lionel's brain, for he moved away from his chair and waved at it with a shaky hand.

"So, all my father wished for has come to naught, *cousin*."

Robert shrugged and walked over to the chair, seating himself, and propping his feet on the table. It was already a mess, so he wasn't concerned about making it worse, and his pose sent its own message to the inebriates beginning to gather their gear together, still muttering amongst themselves.

"Many predicted I would come to a bad end and not inherit Huntley, Lionel. My father. Your father. You. The only important thing is, I'm still alive and I intend to remain that way. I have a great deal of practice at staying alive and ensuring that those who would wish otherwise—well, let's just say most no longer concern me."

"I heard you were a pirate," Lionel sneered, and Robert had to give him points for not cowering in fear. "I also heard you were hanged by the navy."

"Really? I cannot imagine how those rumors start," Robert said, reaching for a glass. He thought better of it when he saw its condition, and took a wine bottle in hand, drinking directly from it. It was an excellent vintage, a burgundy. Thank heavens Lionel hadn't drunk his way through the cellars yet, because that was one expense Robert hadn't factored in for his return to Huntley. He had a feeling he would need all the alcohol in the house before he was finished here.

His men hustled the drunks out the door, and blessed silence descended when they were gone. He looked around the hall. There was the crack in the ceiling between the center timbers, the one he'd thought looked like a dragon when he was a little boy. There was still a gouge in the paneling near the door where his father had thrown a silver platter at Nicholas. It was a room full of memories.

Robert sighed and ran his fingers through his hair. Life was much more complicated now that he was back on land. He'd known it wouldn't be easy. There was damage, but it was fixable, he hoped. If his drink-sodden cousin hadn't spent down all the funds, it could be restored to its former glory.

Huntley could be a home. A home for Mattie, and maybe, for the first time in many, many years, a home for Robert.

He looked longingly at the wine bottle as the footman in too-small livery poked his head in, looking around the empty room until his eyes settled on Robert.

"Is there anything you need, m'lord? I'm William, sir. Mr. Braxton sent me."

Word had gone belowstairs quickly. Robert counted on Braxton's assistance to make the change as smooth as possible, but he knew it would take time. In the interim, change could begin.

"Yes, William, you may begin clearing this away. Open some windows too, and air this out."

Odd, how the miasma of a good debauch would once have been exactly what he wanted to bring his mind to a happier place. Clearly, whether Miss Burke realized it or not, Robert had changed.

"Do you need something to eat or drink, my lord?" William asked.

"No, I'll go to the kitchens, and yes, I know the way," he said, pushing himself to his feet. William warily watched him and Robert wondered what stories were already circulating downstairs and buzzing off to town. He stopped first at the front where Lionel and his cronies were being stuffed into their carriages or hoisted onto their horses. They protested, but were not about to argue with the well-armed pirates assisting them on their way. Fuller had brought the other crewmen from the inn in Ashwyn where they'd been established, getting the lay of the land in advance of Robert's arrival. Since Fuller had everything under control here, Robert went to hunt down the rest of his crew.

Mattie and Lydia were seated at a well-scrubbed table in the kitchen. This room at least was clean and well maintained, and Mrs. Farmer and her helpers stopped their work to greet the master of the house.

Mattie had a large mug of milk and a plate of chicken and potatoes and was making inroads into the grub while the governess sipped a cup of tea. Jolly was eating from a plate on the floor. The dog looked up to acknowledge Robert's presence, but then went back to his meal.

"That looks good, Mattie. May I join you?"

"Oh no, m'lord, you cannot eat here in the kitchen!" the cook said in horrified tones.

"I have eaten in far worse places, Mrs. Farmer. Your kitchen is warm and inviting and the prettiest ladies in the house are here. Why would I want to eat elsewhere? Miss Burke, I can hear your eyes rolling."

Mattie giggled. "That's silly, Papa, you cannot hear Miss Burke's eyes rolling!"

"Your father has a way with words," she said tartly. "But *as long as he tells me the truth* we deal well together."

She skewered him with that last statement, and he knew there would be a reckoning soon, but for now, he was hungry. His appetite had been off this morning, an unusual occurrence. Normally before a battle he ate well, and after a battle he'd wipe the gore off his cutlass and sit down with a will to celebrate ending the day alive once again.

Returning to Huntley changed it all. He could not let memories overwhelm him. He had a task ahead that would take all of his concentration.

What to do about the governess was one of those tasks, albeit one that could be most pleasant if he played his cards right. For some reason though, with Lydia Burke, he was more prone to annoying her than charming her. He glanced at the kitchen maid who placed a white dish in front of him heaped with chicken pieces in a brown gravy, potatoes, fresh bread and beans from the kitchen garden. Mrs. Farmer was new since he'd been away, but as he dug into the plain fare he knew one thing on the estate would not need to be replaced or changed. Provided she wasn't robbing the household accounts, she was well worth keeping.

"Did you brew this excellent ale, Mrs. Farmer?"

"No, milord, it comes from the village. They don't like it upstairs, but it's good enough for folks who don't have London ways." She sniffed. "Begging you pardon—I didn't mean you—"

"I am quite content with good home brew. It is one of the things I missed most on my travels, so please keep ordering it. My men enjoy it as well."

He finished by giving her a smile that had the red-faced cook dimpling and fluttering her plump hands at her helpers. He glanced at the governess, but she calmly sipped tea and ignored him.

"When you are finished, Braxton will show you the nursery. See if you can get it usable for Mattie to sleep tonight."

"What is a nursery, Papa?"

"It is a place where children have their rooms, Mattie. Miss Burke, whatever you need, tell Braxton."

She looked at him steadily, then looked around the kitchen. The servants were listening to this conversation with interest, as he intended. He wanted to establish Miss Burke's authority as second to his own, and she understood this. Her role at Huntley needed to leave no question she was there as governess, not pirate doxy. Housing Mattie in the nursery also clarified for the staff *her* place in his life.

"Don't you want to see the nursery, to assess its condition, Captain?"

He hesitated but Mattie spoke up.

"Please come with us, Papa. You said a good captain always makes sure the crew's quarters are shipshape."

"Aye, Mattie, I did say that. Well then."

He rose and the ladies followed, Mattie thanking the cook for feeding her and Jolly.

"I'll keep a bowl of fresh water here for the pup, Miss Mattie, don't you worry."

The carved staircase was as he remembered, though his perspective was off as he climbed. He'd been far smaller when he last trod these worn steps. Some of the portraits were missing from the walls, others were splattered with unknown substances. There was a damp patch over the front entranceway where a leak had gotten through to the plaster and he made note of all of the depredations Huntley had suffered.

Once he thought he'd never walk this hallway again, and was glad of it. Now, as he trod the worn runner, there were remembrances of bad times, but others too, like the time he balanced along the rail overlooking the hall below, nearly giving poor Braxton a heart seizure.

The nursery was not as bad as he'd feared. It needed a good airing, but most of it was covered with dust cloths and he and the governess removed them carefully, taking them out of the room to the hallway so they wouldn't make a mess.

Mattie exclaimed with glee over the toys. There was a rocking horse, missing one glass eye, a battalion of tin soldiers he remembered well, a battered desk and chair sized for a youngster, wooden balls and cricket gear.

He heard Braxton's faltering step in the hall and turned.

"It has not been used in a long, long time, m'lord. I will fetch bedding and coal for the fire."

"Braxton, where are the maidservants? They should be doing this."

The old man sighed. "We couldn't keep maids, m'lord. The late baron—none of the girls from the village would work here. It wasn't safe. The ones in the kitchen return home each night."

"What about footmen?"

"There's only William. The others left when their wages weren't paid."

The governess looked up at that, but Mattie distracted her with a request to help rescue a wooden puppet from Jolly, who'd thought it was for him to chew on.

"I'll get Paget up here to help get your quarters ready, Mattie. Miss Burke will put you to bed tonight."

"No story, Papa?"

He hesitated, but shook his head. "I will have to owe you two stories on the morrow, poppet. Right now I'm needed elsewhere."

The child looked troubled, but she nodded. "I understand. You're the captain. That has to come first."

He opened his mouth to explain to her that she would always come first, but it wasn't the time or place for that conversation. The child understood that a vessel—even if it was landlocked Huntley Manor—needed to be cared for even if the needs of its crew had to wait.

"Speaking of wages, *Lord Huntley*…"

"Not now. Come to the study, later, after Mattie's asleep."

The governess did not look happy about this, but didn't argue with him. He gave her a smile that only earned him a scowl in return, then he kissed and hugged Mattie good night. Robert wanted to retire to his room with a bottle of brandy, but knew he'd never sleep. Too many memories, too many unanswered question, and an interview with an irate employee awaited him.

That last problem kept his smile in place.

CHAPTER 20

*R*obert adjusted himself in the chair, a massive leather throne that had been his father's seat of power for so many years. It was disorienting to see the study from this angle. As a lad he'd stood on *that* spot on the Axminster carpet, a rosette he'd seen all too often, his eyes cast down as his faults were enumerated for him. The listing of those faults usually culminated in a whipping as he gripped the edge of the desk where he now sat as master.

He would burn the desk. It was time to replace it with something more to his taste. This chair also. It would make a lovely bonfire.

Until then he was going to savor the moment, and to celebrate, he pulled a cheroot out of its case, took the lamp and lit it, leaning back, putting his boots on his father's desk, and blowing smoke rings up at the Greek gods decorating the ceiling.

Right on cue, the door slammed open. He grinned to himself but didn't rise from his chair. It was a calculated move to enhance the fireworks about to erupt. He didn't analyze why annoying lovely Lydia entertained him so much. It was sufficient to enjoy the moment.

"You! You are...you... Aargh! Stand up when a lady is addressing you, you mannerless blackguard!"

He peered at her. Was that steam coming out of the governess's ears? No, only the smoke from his cheroot, which he reluctantly put out for later.

"I have a better idea. Why don't you sit down, and then we can both relax."

"Relax? Relax! I am not relaxed, Captain St. Armand or Lord Huntley or whoever you are today! You lied to me all along about your identity!"

He folded his hands on his stomach, knowing he looked nonchalant and at ease. Truly, it was a wonder she didn't go up in flames like a misfired rocket. Her hands were clenched and he would wager she was sorry now she hadn't taken him up on his offers of weapons practice.

"I never lied."

"What? How can you say that?"

"At the inn when you accused me of perpetrating a fraud, I only said telling people I was a peer earned me better accommodations. You jumped to conclusions. Will you please sit down so I do not have to resurrect my fading memories of being taught proper behavior?"

She sat ungracefully, almost collapsing into the chair in front of the desk, a poorly upholstered seat which he knew to be purposely uncomfortable. He'd burn that one on the bonfire as well.

"I came in here to tender my resignation," she said, gripping her hands together. "I want my wages and I want a letter of recommendation. I will stay to get Mattie settled, but then I want to *leave*."

Now he came around the desk and sat on the edge. She didn't move.

"You don't want to leave, Lydia," he said gently. "You want to hear the whole story, unvarnished, and you want to stay and see what happens next."

She opened her mouth, then closed it. He knew he was correct.

"You should not address me in such a familiar manner, Capta—Lord Huntley," she finished lamely.

"Please, continue calling me Captain. The men address me so, and you are part of the crew, aren't you?"

"We are not aboard ship now, Captain. We are in the countryside."

He shrugged. "It's a different command, but I'll adjust, as will the crew. I need you, Miss Burke," he said seriously. "As you can see, this house is sorely neglected. I have no idea how badly the rest of the estate has been damaged and I can't take time to get the house in order. I need your help with that while I tend to the estate. I need your help with Mattie. It is important to me that she adjusts well to life here, and you are vital to her continued development. I will be occupied with sorting things out, reviewing the books—"

He stopped abruptly, looking down at his hands as a memory passed through his mind, then he took a deep breath.

"I never expected to inherit. I was not supposed to inherit."

"What happened?"

"People died. Come, I want to show you something."

He stood and offered her his hand, and didn't release it when she was on her feet in front of him. Her hand was soft, but strong, capable, and he longed to feel her hands on his body as she learned all the things that brought him pleasure. He suspected the real pleasure in his bed would come from him learning what pleased her. Her affection was hard won, but worth so much, so genuine and real, not the paid affection of whores pleased that they had a client who didn't beat them, but the pleasure of a strong woman who knew her mind, knew the best and the worst a man could offer her. He wanted to offer her his best. Whatever he'd learned in his travels and voyages, he wanted to share with her. All of that was only a prelude to making a life with Lydia by his side.

But it was too early to share those feelings with her. She was still skittish, unsure of her footing on a shifting deck. In addition, she had secrets and until her past was dealt with, one could not move forward. It would take time.

Of course, if he continued to find excuses not to give her her wages it would be that much more difficult for her to pack her bags and leave.

She removed her hand from his when they exited the study, not comfortable showing affection in a household where she was an upper servant. He would be certain to establish her place here without question, one way or another.

He led her up the stairs past the master's quarters, the rooms that had been his father's, and into the lady's suite. As he thought, it had remained unoccupied, uncleaned, but largely undisturbed. The cheery wallpaper covered in twining spring vines and golden flowers showed a water stain at the corner of the ceiling, but otherwise it was much as he remembered it. He lit the candles around the room, their wicks sputtering as the dust of years of neglect burned away.

Lydia stepped in front of the massive framed portrait over the empty fireplace, staring at it in silence as the dust motes stirred in the dry air.

"Mattie looks just like her—or will."

The painting showed a tall, muscular man wearing the clothing of thirty years past, a country squire in his element. He had washed-out blonde hair, hazel eyes and a ruddy complexion. In one hand was a riding crop, the other was placed on the shoulder of the adolescent standing beside him and cradling a fowling piece, a brace of ducks at his feet.

The artist had talent. The two men, clearly father and son by their build and resemblance, looked like self-satisfied slabs of Saxon beef, as English as ale and kippers.

There was another, younger youth flanking a seated woman. He was a faded version of his father and older brother, like a watercolor left in the rain. The lad was pale and slender, with long fingers cradling a flute. He looked away from the artist into the distance.

Robert inhaled and for a fleeting moment thought he'd caught a whiff of French perfume, a fragrance as delicate and ephemeral as the lady in the portrait.

The seated woman was a study in melancholy, but she was immediately recognizable. Her familiar sharp cheek-bones, the ebon locks clustered around her face—it was an adult version of Mathilde St. Armand, but with haunted azure eyes rather than Mattie's laughing ones.

The bareheaded baby on her lap waved a rattle. One could imagine him waving a cutlass in a similar fashion years later.

"My mother insisted, I'm told, that I not be posed in a cap despite my father's orders. You can see how little I resembled him and he did not want anyone to speculate on a cuckoo in his nest. *Maman* was firm, one of the few times she stood up to him. My hatred of ugly caps goes back a long way," he finished with a humorless smile.

"I would like to hear your story," she said, still looking at the portrait.

"Will you like me better if I have a sad tale to tell? If I ran off to sea because of my tragic childhood, rather than because it's where the money was?"

"Tell me, and I will decide for myself."

"Very well, but I warn you, it's the stuff of bad melodrama."

He clasped his hands behind his back and looked up at the portrait. There they all were, a family far from happy.

"My father's roots go deep in this land and in fairness to him, he was a good steward of the legacy left him as Huntley. He avoided London, preferring manly activities, hunting and sport, tending to his crops. His sons were one of those crops, but in this he suffered disappointment.

"That is Ralph, the eldest next to him. Ralph was exactly what father wanted—a son who drank hard, wenched hard, was a bruising rider, and essentially was a copy of his sire. Except for one key difference... Ralph was like an oak that looks attractive and whole at a glance, but when you get closer, you see the rot at its core.

"Nicholas..." his voice softened as he looked at his second brother, the musician. "Nick was...a disappointment. Father had Nick's life planned for him. He would take a commission in the army and bring honor to the family in battle."

He saw her head turn toward him as she asked dryly, "Never tell me that as the third son you were destined for the Church."

He almost smiled at the idea of him standing in a pulpit and preaching on proper living.

"Things changed, so we'll never know."

The smile faded from his face.

"Nick hated bloodshed. Father took him hunting and Nick sobbed when he shot a rabbit. Ralph laughed at him, called him girlish and weak. Nick kept telling Father he did not want to go into the army, he wanted to compose music. Naturally, Father responded by beating Nick. It was his response to any rebellion by us—a fist or the strap or a caning. Ralph took to leaving dead animals in Nick's bed, in his room, in his wardrobe, laughing when Nick would cry."

"Animals?"

"Squirrels. A rabbit. My terrier, Samson."

"Dear heavens. Did you tell your father?"

"I tried, one last time. He caned me for being a talebearer. It all ended the day Ralph discovered Nick and a footman locked in an embrace in the stables. He told Father, who beat the footman with his fists until the man was half dead. Ralph held Nick, his arm twisted behind his back, forcing him to watch. I tried to help Nick, but Ralph laid me out with a blow that nearly shattered my jaw."

"How old were you?"

"I was ten. Ralph was twenty-five."

"Where was your mother?"

"My mother? She'd died the year previous, but had been ailing for years. Father never let her forget that his last son looked nothing like him, and too much like a dancing master who'd traveled through the area the year before I was born. You see, mother was my father's second wife. On one of his infrequent trips to London he met Juliette St. Armand, daughter of French émigrés. Juliette's face was her fortune, and my father wanted a second wife, one to bear him more strapping sons. After birthing me she began taking laudanum for her pains, for headaches, for escape. Eventually she took too much and her escape was permanent."

She made a noise, but he didn't look at her, instead swallowing the bile that rose at what he'd say next.

"I was angry with my father, angry with Ralph, angry with Nicholas weeping in his room. I took a pony cart and helped the beaten man get away to a house in the village where he could recover. When I returned to the stables to put up the pony I heard a strange noise in the rafters, a creaking sound. It was almost like the sound the rigging makes when the wind is just so, and you know a storm is brewing before midnight."

He was lost in his own memories now, in the nightmare. He'd walked the pony into the stable, exhausted from the day's events, his face aching and swollen. The noise hadn't registered with him until the pony nickered and danced nervously, shying from the shadows moving on the stall.

That was when Robert heard the creaking and looked up. Nicholas swayed there, at the end of a rope, his unseeing eyes following the shadow of his body in the lamplight.

"They told me afterward it was my screaming that brought people running to the stables. Of course father tried to hush it up, but too many people knew what happened and Nicholas was buried in unconsecrated ground."

Until her soft hand brushed at his cheek he hadn't known there were tears on his face. She made soothing noises, offering comfort, a comfort he had not received on that nightmare evening when his father yelled orders at the servants and Ralph just stood there, an expression almost of satisfaction on his face.

He pulled Lydia into his arms and held her, his face buried in her fragrant hair, her warmth bringing him back.

"I left after they buried Nick and I've never returned."

"But where did you go? You were only a child!"

"Not much older than Mattie. I hadn't realized it until now." He cleared his throat and since she did not seem inclined to push him away, he continued holding her, finding comfort in her embrace. Was this why she'd asked to be held —"just held"—that night? For the comfort of knowing you're not alone, that even in your darkest memories there might be someone, somewhere, who could bring you back to the light and warmth? It disturbed his notions of what he wanted from Miss Burke, why he wanted Lydia with him, why he was willing to tell her all of this.

"I started following the canal, knowing it eventually would take me to the sea. The first night I slept under a hedgerow and nearly froze to death. But by my second day I saw a man limping along, and I recognized him."

"The footman?"

"Yes. He was on his way to Liverpool, where he planned to take ship and leave England. He didn't want me tagging along with him, but he wasn't in a position to push me away, and he soon realized a young, pretty boy begging farmwives for food was more likely to get something than if he'd asked."

"Did your father look for you?"

"I don't know. I don't care. I was done with that life. My home now was on the oceans and it was a life that suited me."

"What about the footman?"

"Life aboard ship suited Mr. Fuller as well."

"Ah. That explains much," she murmured, then was silent, thinking it over.

"What happened to Ralph?"

He sighed, and she grasped him tighter, which helped him continue.

"I had contacts with people who kept me apprised of the situation here. I did not return when my father died. He'd made it clear through his solicitor in London that he was not interested in having me return and left money with his man to encourage me to stay away."

"Did you take it?"

He pulled his head back and looked at her. "Do I strike you as the sort of person who would leave free money on the table? Of course I took it. Some of the finest taverns and brothels in the islands grew richer on my patrimony."

She made no comment to this, but asked, "And what happened to your eldest brother?"

"Fortunately for the people of Ashwyn, Ralph did not survive my father's death for long. While he was alive, father could keep the worst of Ralph's excesses in check. Once he was gone—you heard about the difficulties keeping maids here. I have no doubt we'll hear further tales of depredation that can be laid at my late brother's feet. He died after falling off of his horse in a drunken stupor and drowning in a ditch. I received word in the islands that I was now Huntley and you know the rest, Miss Burke."

He stopped talking because he was increasingly aware of the woman he held, her soft, comforting curves nestling against him, her warmth seeping into places in his bones he hadn't realized needed warming until this moment. He put his fingers beneath her chin and tilted her face up so he could look into her eyes. They were clear, and aware, and expectant.

He was the one who was nervous as his lips hovered above hers for a breath, and she was the one who sighed and closed the brief gap between them, looping her arms around his neck, drawing his head down to hers as she opened her mouth to him.

He took his time, letting her warmth flow into him like the noonday sun after a stormy night, relishing the feel of the rightness of her body close to his, only thin layers of clothing separating them. She made a needy sound he felt as much as heard and he slanted his mouth against hers, drawing out the mingled sweetness and tartness of her kisses, of her essence. He knew now why he'd had to bring her here, why he'd shown her the portrait, why he'd told her the story. She was the one who would bring the light into his gloom, her, and Mattie, and the puppy, and even the weak winter sunshine of England.

It was why he'd left the tropics, why he'd finally returned to this place, why he was tentatively ready to call it home without the tinge of sarcasm discoloring what this land was to him, what it could be to him in the future.

Huntley could be his home again. Whether or not his father's suspicions were correct, he was the baron now and he felt that obligation, the need to see to the estate and the village and the land just as he'd always seen to his ship and its crew. He could not do it alone. He needed his hearty crew, rascals all, including their lovely, luscious—dare one hope for lusty?—governess.

Ah yes, that was the cue he'd been hoping for. She moaned, and her mouth opened farther as he slanted his lips across hers, caressing her, slipping his tongue inside to deepen the kiss, to get all the sweetness he could from her mouth, from her soul. She tightened her arms around his neck, pulling him closer, her hands fisting in his hair as he moved down to embrace one soft, full breast, the nipple peaked in anticipation as his sensitive fingertips learned every inch of her form.

When the kiss ended, as all kisses do, he looked down into her face, her gaze dreamy, her lips moist and inviting, and he took a chance, every bit as risky as facing down a well-armed frigate.

"Stay here, Lydia. I need you."

"I cannot—I cannot make any promises to you. There's too much I—"

He put his finger over her lips. "Stay with me tonight."

FOUR WORDS. Not words of love, or words of commitment, but words flowing deep into her, moistening her parched core, bringing a hope of renewal, a yearning for something more than mere survival and existence, one day following another at the beck and call of people who did not value her.

The pirate valued her. He showed her in his insistence that she was a member of his rag-tag crew, in protecting her, in allowing her to love and care for his most precious treasure, Mattie.

She knew she was a good governess, but there were times she suspected she'd be an even better pirate. Pirates Anne and Mary lived lives that were short, but they were full lives. They took what they wanted, wrenching their happiness from danger and despair, living lives of color and passion.

She could only lie to herself so many times. Inside, she was still that girl willing to risk it all for love and excitement. Color was returning to her life, to her heart. Bright colors, bold colors, the colors of passion. The sapphire blue of glowing eyes, the burnished ebony of thick hair, a fine form kissed golden by the sun and chiseled with muscle and sinew to make a woman's pulse race.

She'd had passion in her life and reveled in it. With Robert St. Armand there would be passion, of that there was no doubt, but she'd have more. It was time to take the leap, to embrace what life offered her once again, to let the lush blooms inside her heart burst out in bold colors and make a statement that Lydia was here, she was alive, and she could not be ignored.

So it took little effort now to look into those eyes darkened to onyx ringed with blue fire, to reach up and caress the face she knew now was more than just a pretty façade, to see his long lashes flutter down as he turned his head to place a soft kiss in the center of her palm.

Tomorrow would bring...tomorrow. That's all anyone knew. Not whether the day would be for good or for evil. She owed it to herself to have tonight for her own well-being, to have her own needs satisfied.

She also knew, whatever tomorrow brought, she would not face it alone. She was a *Prodigal*, part of a pirate crew that took care of one another, starting with a badly beaten man and an emotionally beaten child bolstering each other as they escaped to freedom on the seas. She'd seen army and navy veterans discarded in Liverpool like so much trash now that the war was over and they were no longer needed, but pirates took care of their own.

And tonight she suspected Robert St. Armand—for that is how she would always think of her pirate captain—needed her. She understood better now the pain in his eyes when he talked of home, how important it was to him to create a real home for Mattie, and for himself.

Maybe, just maybe, she could be a part of that home too. It was a great deal to hope for, and she suspected she'd still have to leave rather than face her own past mistakes, but tonight could be hers. Tonight could be theirs.

He brought his eyes back to hers, still holding her hand. "Yes."

One simple word that could change a life.

He scooped her into his arms and she looped her hands around his neck. He looked around the room in its disarray and said, "Not here."

She understood. Too many ghosts would crowd into their bed in this room.

"Your room," she said, and he nodded, still carrying her as he walked the short distance to his quarters. Paget and William the footman had cleaned in here, removing evidence of his cousin and preparing the space for the house's true master. Robert kicked the door shut behind him and gently put her on the wide bed, saying nothing more, but turning to light the lamp.

She must have made a noise because he turned back to her with a wicked twist to his lips and said, "I have been dreaming about what you look like underneath those garments, Miss Burke. I will not be denied this opportunity."

She propped herself up on an elbow. "I seem to recall you had an eyeful when I was bathing."

"A glimpse! A mere taste of what the feast would be."

He returned and loomed over her until she lay back

against the pillow.

"Tonight I intend to feast my fill, little hedgehog."

He stepped back and began removing his clothing, starting with untying the cravat at his neck.

"Here is your revenge. You will see me naked while you are still clothed, so we will be square on this."

"You are hardly acting like this is a hardship for you, Captain, disrobing before me."

He paused, the two ends of the long cloth grasped in each hand, his collar undone. He let the silk sift through his fingers before discarding it on the floor.

"That is because I know what a magnificent sight I am in the nude, Miss Burke. And soon, you will know too."

That noise emerging from her couldn't possibly have been a snicker, but really, the man was ridiculous!

Ridiculous, and beyond handsome. She wouldn't say it, at least not at the moment when he seemed inflated enough. He continued with his boots, seating himself on the wooden chair to pull them off, not hurrying, but letting her get her fill as he unfastened his breeches, slowly, button by button, knowing that she watched.

Lydia never before appreciated the beauty of a man undressing, particularly this man who knew how to dress—and undress—with a skill rivaling that of a professional courtesan. Each garment removed was handled deliberately, her eyes following his hands as he grasped the hem of his shirt to pull it over his head.

At the end, when his smallclothes were laid neatly atop the breeches and shirt, he stood straight, hands by his sides.

He was without a doubt the most beautiful man she'd ever seen, far more beautiful than any engraving or statue she'd ogled. She'd shared her bed with men who were more muscular, but there was nothing lacking in the pirate. He walked back to her, his fencer's form lithe and supple, muscles moving in a smooth dance of their own beneath his skin, no excess flesh marring the ripples across his hard belly. When he saw the appreciation evident on her face he gave her a smile that said, "Yes, I am one devilishly handsome specimen and I know it," then turned so she could appreciate the view from all sides.

And it was a view worth appreciating. The muscles of his chest were mirrored by the anatomy of his back, and he raised his arms and folded them behind his head, flexing so she could see the lean flesh tighten and move in concert. Deep dimples on his bottom were echoed by the indentation in his face when he looked over his shoulder and grinned extravagantly at her.

"Never tell me you practiced that maneuver in front of a mirror!"

"I am used to a certain amount of appreciation, even awe when I disrobe—please don't giggle, it ruins the moment."

"Then you must restore me to my mood, Captain St. Armand," Lydia said.

He grinned wider, untying his hair where he'd restrained it at his neck and he turned back to her. He ran his fingers through the curls to loosen them and they clustered around his bronzed face, making him look like the kind of mischievous angel who would have been chucked out of heaven for tying the others' wings together.

A line of dark hair arrowed down from his chest, spreading to frame his anatomy, his cock dark with his desire, heavy and full as it stood before him. Her tongue darted out to lick lips gone dry at the thought of having all that flesh, all of his strength, in her arms. She longed to be free of her own restraints and sat up, undoing the fastenings of her garments.

"Let me. Please."

He silently came to her and stilled her fingers as he sat

beside her, removing her clothing. He did not rush. She would have expected him to be the sort who ripped wrapping off of gifts, but instead he focused on delicately undoing every knot, pausing as each garment fell away, revealing more of her. Goose flesh ran over her arms when he pushed the folds of her dress apart and studied her chemise and corset clad form.

"You deserve silks and satins, Lydia. The finest, softest linen, but none of that would make you more beautiful to me than you are at this moment."

He undid the rest, and she placed her hands on his wide chest, so warm, so full of life.

"Robert," was all she said, and at his name on her lips he stopped, and closed his eyes, and when he opened them they were nearly black with heat. He took her shoulders and brushed his lips across hers, caressing them, learning them, gliding his tongue across the seam where they were shut until she opened for him, allowing him entry, and his tongue glided inside as his hands moved up to frame her face.

She put her hands on his shoulders and felt the tension vibrating through him, the sweat beading at his neck. He did not rush his exploration of her mouth but acted as if that alone was the most important thing he would accomplish that evening, as if kisses alone could bring him complete satisfaction. His hands roamed down her, leaving pleasure behind as he caressed her with those skilled fingers, taking his time, punctuating it with kisses.

It warmed her and nourished her soul, those kisses, each cherishing movement across her mouth, against her tongue, across the tiny gap in her teeth feeding the flames bursting into life in her heart. When he put his head down and sucked on her breasts, laving the tips with his tongue, she could only make inarticulate sounds of need, sounds he interpreted correctly and encouraged with further loving by his mouth.

He was skillful, as promised, but it wasn't a mechanical skill —she could offer herself that with her own hand. It was a skill born of experience, but also awareness of whom he was loving, of her as a person. The events leading to this night, to her finally being in his arms, gave their lovemaking a tenderness she'd never anticipated. She'd promised to stay with him until he was home, and now he was, and she was in bed with him, doing what she once swore she would not do—entangle herself with another unsuitable man.

It was not a fair comparison. Edwin never took the time to know her needs so well, to put her pleasure so far above his. Sometimes she climaxed during their lovemaking, sometimes she simply enjoyed the closeness and the time together, but when Edwin finished he'd roll over and go to sleep, while she'd lay beside him, fists clenched in frustration as she wondered what she'd done wrong, why she couldn't find her release.

She was older now, and knew from the life she'd led that she was entitled to satisfaction. Clearly, Captain St. Armand had learned the same lesson.

Or perhaps it was because Robert was one of those rare men who truly appreciated women and their needs. He certainly understood what she was needing, sometimes intuiting it, as he did when he stroked her neck and felt how her pulse raced, or by asking if she liked being touched with two fingers *there* or perhaps she enjoyed it more when he stroked her *here.* He was aptly named a prodigal, for he gave lavishly, freely, holding nothing back as he pleasured her with his hands, his mouth, his body. She panted in his arms as his mouth moved across her shoulder, little bites exciting her nerves, making her back arch.

However, she had not completely lost her mind in sensation.

"Wait—Robert—do you have a French letter?"

He pulled his head back and looked at her, eyebrows raised. "You are a well-educated governess."

She was glad he'd lit the candles, because the expression on his face was priceless, and she smiled gently at him, raising her hand to stroke the back of her fingers down his tanned cheek.

"I want this, but what I do not want is to find myself with a case of the pox or in a situation like Nanette's."

"We will deal with this, my dear, but tonight"—he put his finger over her lips, hushing whatever she would have said —"put your trust in me. I am clean, and I will not leave my seed inside you."

His disheveled hair fell across his forehead as he brought his mouth down to a sensitive point on her neck.

"Trust me," he murmured again.

Oddly enough, she did trust him. In this bed, in her arms, she trusted him. He was not any other man, he was Robert St. Armand Huntley, her pirate, and a glimmer of hope began to grow in her chest that perhaps she could have a future here. Wasn't it one of the reasons she'd said yes tonight? Not just for the pleasure, but because she'd finally allowed herself to believe in the possibility of a full life, a life of satisfaction and love?

She knew now she loved Robert, and tonight she could show him some of that love. Clearly he cared for her, and for now, just for tonight, it was enough. He was holding himself back, she could feel the tightness in his frame, and when she moved her hand down between their bodies she felt how hard he was, how ready, and her stroking grasp made him swear a mighty oath.

"Lydia—"

She opened her thighs and he took those long fingers, the hand that had proven itself capable of not just harm and destruction, but also of cradling those in need of protection, and delicately ran his knuckles over her, spreading moisture, preparing her.

"I need you, Robert. Now."

The finesse vanished as he yanked the bedding back, his arms braced alongside her shoulders and she knew a moment's trepidation as he loomed over her, his eyes glittering with lust and heat. She also knew a moment of feminine triumph that this beautiful man was in her bed, with her.

He entered her as carefully as a thief sneaking into a jewelry store in the dark, watching her face in the candlelight, pausing at her gasp.

"Too much?"

"Not enough," she gasped, "but let me—" She raised her legs, allowing him to go deeper and her purr of satisfaction was reflected in his own guttural sound as he pushed fully inside her. There was discomfort, because it had been a long, long time for her, and the strain on his face, his eyes shut in concentration warmed her as he gave her body time to adjust, to relearn what it needed.

Then his eyes opened and the tenderness within them flowed into her much as he began flowing into her like a surging tide, his movements controlled, at first, calibrated, at first. She could see from the strain on his face this was more than either of them could have anticipated, could have prepared for.

Her passion climbed in concert with his thrusts, but she realized the moment before he swore and pulled out that he was not as much in control of himself as he'd wish and he held her hard against him as he spilled his seed onto her belly, as promised.

She sighed, but he put his finger across her lips.

"No, we are not done yet."

"But—"

"Shhh…trust me," he said again, punctuating it with a kiss while he moved his hand down. She felt herself tense, but he only said, "shhhh" again and she closed her eyes when he touched the overly sensitive junction of her thighs, stroking her, so lightly at first, little touches like flower petals tapping at her, then growing in intensity as her excitement ramped up again until she was gripping his upper arms with passion and the feelings mounted in her belly, exploding outward with her cry of release.

He had his arm beneath her, holding her as she relaxed back onto the bed, boneless and replete with satisfaction. When she opened her eyes and could speak again she was surprised to see not triumph in his expression, but tenderness.

"Next time," he whispered to her, "we will complete our journey together."

Next time…

"Oh no, you cannot pull back into your shell now, Lydia," he said, tapping her lightly on her nose. "I can see your thoughts written on your face. No regrets, no chastising yourself, not tonight."

She inhaled the scent of their lovemaking, a reminder of the past as much as memento of tonight's passion, and it brought her comfort, but also concern.

"Robert—there are things about me—"

"Your next words are going to be, 'things you do not know…' No doubt you have a delightfully gothic tale you will share with me at some point," he said with a chuckle. "But it will not be tonight."

He rolled over and put his hands beneath his head, a look of complete satisfaction on his face as he gazed up at the ceiling.

"This room could use some naked cupids frolicking on the ceiling, don't you think?"

CHAPTER 21

*J*ust before the stars faded, Lydia slipped out of Robert's bed and returned to her own. They'd taken a huge risk last night, gambling Mattie wouldn't awaken and come searching for her governess, gambling no servant or pirate would see her sneaking out of his room, gambling Lydia wouldn't find herself in the same position as Nanette, giving Mattie a sibling.

But as Lydia rose from her bed and stretched, feeling unfamiliar soreness in her limbs and in more personal parts, she could only summon a tiny amount of regret for her choice of the night before. It opened a door, reawakening the girl—no, the woman—within her. She'd locked that woman away, hiding her under ugly caps and dowdy clothing, but she was still a part of Lydia, she still *was* Lydia, the Lydia who'd turned her back on society's strictures, paid for it, but also earned memories and knowledge of a life lived with passion and purpose, not just existing and hiding and nibbling at crusts thrown her way.

It took a pirate to bring those memories back, and to give her new ones.

She confessed to herself a burning curiosity about Huntley Manor, wondering what she would find in the light of day. And that raised another issue. How long did she intend to stay? Would she ever get her wages, and, if she did, was she still anxious to leave as quickly as possible? There was a part of her—the wild child, piratical *Prodigal Son* part of her—that favored hunting down her enemy and dispatching him silently and permanently, but it was only a daydream. As long as she felt threatened in England, it was best for her, for Robert, for Mattie if she slipped from their lives. Lord Huntley needed to marry someone who wouldn't be a further embarrassment to him, a wife bringing a sterling reputation to her marriage, if not additional property and wealth. Rich lords only married milkmaids or governesses in silly tales for impressionable and vapid readers. In the world as it truly was, wealth, status, land and societal connections were what mattered.

She chewed her lip, examining her wardrobe. The best course of action would be to continue as she had, wearing dowdy and washed-out gowns. A shudder ran over her frame at the thought, and she reached instead for a new gown, Pomona green with lace at the collar that she was sure she had not authorized as an additional expense. *Someone* had sneaked behind her back to countermand her orders to the seamstress, but she could not work up much anger over it as the fine fabric slid over her arms, soft as lamb's wool.

She tucked her hair beneath a new cap from the seamstress, because too much change would get people talking and speculating, a complication she did not need.

Wandering the halls of Huntley brought her to the sound of voices and a room with an air of neglect, but admitting a cheerful amount of sunshine. It was much cozier than the formal hall, and Mattie and her father were already at table. Robert rose to his feet at her entrance, giving her a wink as they both recalled her entrance into the study the night before.

Pleased that she offered no telltale blush Lydia ignored that and filled her plate while one of the kitchen girls brought in fresh coffee, and she inhaled the aroma gratefully. Tea was all well and good in the evening, but she'd joined the pirates in an appreciation for a heartier brew to start her day. As Mattie and her father were still talking, Lydia took in her surroundings.

The room was papered with a faded yellow silk and the draperies showed some moth damage and might not be salvageable. Most importantly, the windows were in need of a good scrubbing as were the baseboards and the carpet.

She shook herself mentally. St. Armand asked for her help, but it was too easy to see herself slipping into the role of mistress of the manor. She needed to finish her conversation with him about her duties, in the light of day, without distractions.

On the other hand, she could easily envision herself spread across that wide and sturdy desk of his, being distracted. Or perhaps he'd sit in that heavy chair and she would straddle him, holding on to the back of the chair as she raised and lowered herself onto his thick...

"Miss Burke?"

THE GOVERNESS JUMPED in her seat, yanked out of whatever fantasy had put that dreamy, distracted expression on her face. Naturally, he suspected he was at the center of that fantasy, and would quiz her later on exactly what she'd contemplated.

Last night proved a delight in so many unexpected ways.

Lydia was a lusty bed partner, clearly a woman of passion and experience.

It was her experience that concerned him. He was not concerned with being Lydia's first lover, but he intended to be her last. When he had more information, uncovered her secrets, he'd be better prepared to ensure that happened. Binding her to Huntley, and to him, would be a good first step.

"Have you created a schedule for Mattie yet?"

Lydia looked at the child, who tried to speak around a mouth full of food until her governess put a halt to that breach of manners with a stern look.

"I have, Captain. Now that we're on land again, our lessons will resume. I also want opportunities to take Mathilde to church and into the village. Surely there are other children in the area, and it would be good for her to spend time with them. You enjoyed visiting in Liverpool, didn't you?" she ended with a question to her young charge.

"Yes, ma'am. But Papa," she said, turning to her father, "I also want to continue my lessons with you."

It pleased him that the child wanted to spend time with him. He'd come to value their sessions together, time for the two of them alone without distractions. Mattie had a sharp and inquisitive mind and sometimes her questions stumped him, but her trust in him warmed a place he'd never realized was still cold and aching, the void left in a little boy's heart by a father who despised him and tried to make him feel worthless.

"Yes, our lessons will resume this afternoon. I will have targets placed behind the stable, and"—he drew out the tension, enjoying the anticipation on her face—"we will add pistols to our sessions."

He heard rather than saw the governess suck in breath to berate him and preempted her tirade.

"Miss Burke, powder is less expensive than a human life. This is why we have shipboard drills, over and over again. This is why one practices with knife, sword and pistols until you don't even have to think about the weapon, it's simply an extension of your hand. Oftentimes the difference between the quick and the dead is that moment of hesitation."

She closed her mouth with a snap of her teeth, and he knew the discussion wasn't finished. It did not signify. Multiplication tables were her area of expertise, staying alive was his. He would do everything in his power to keep Mattie safe and that included teaching her to defend herself.

"In the meantime," he said, rising from the table, "I need to meet with Mr. Fuller. One of the first improvements I intend to make to Huntley is to the plumbing, which is positively medieval. If I am to live here it should at least be as comfortable as my ship. I want a proper bathing room, hot water, and a Bramah closet."

"Is this our home now, Papa? Forever?"

"Yes, poppet. This is our safe harbor, and our home."

Robert didn't think about the truth of the words until after he'd said them. He did not know he would miss Huntley until he was here again, walking these corridors, inhaling the scents of his childhood, obscured by dust and decay, but still there. He needed to make Huntley a safe harbor for Mattie, and if things worked out as he planned, for Lydia Burke as well.

Issues still remained to be resolved and Horace Fuller found him later in his study, ready to tear out his hair, or even better, hang someone from the yardarm.

"I thought I was the pirate! I'm being robbed by my own employees."

Fuller poured himself a dram of rum and brought one for his captain as well before seating himself in front of the desk. Robert drank, then settled back in his chair, rubbing his eyes.

The estate books were a disaster and he feared he'd have to dip into his own capital to keep the manor afloat, something he had not wanted to do. It irked him that his ill-gotten but hard-won silver would prop up the place he'd loathed for so many years.

However, he had the child to think about. And his tenants. And the merchants in the village who depended on Huntley for business.

He stood, but waved Fuller back into his seat.

"Stay there. I need to move about before I grab my cutlass and begin solving these problems like Alexander did with the Gordian knot."

"It's as you said, Captain. Your brother's steward could teach you a thing or two about robbery."

"What did you find?"

"Neglect and theft, but little rot and if your tenants follow your lead, it's not a disaster. Your father left the estate in good condition, but your brother and your cousin took money out without putting any back in. The cold summer a couple years past didn't help. You need new roofs for some of the cottages, better harvesting and crops to replenish the soil, new drains—it's manageable. This is a productive property, Captain, with proper management, and this house is still sturdy."

Robert sighed and turned away from the view out the window, leaning against his desk with his arms crossed.

"You knew you'd be coming back, even before Mattie showed up," Fuller said.

"What I planned, Mr. Fuller, was to return to piss on Ralph's grave, take everything of value that wasn't nailed down, and leave again for sea as quickly as possible."

"This is me you're talking to, remember? I was the one you sent to gather information."

"The only benefit I received from reading about your

damned mangel wurzels in those agricultural journals was an ability to fall asleep faster."

Fuller leaned back in his chair and crossed his ankles, lacing his gnarled fingers across his stomach. Those hands were blackened by tar that would never come out, ground into his skin from his life working alongside Robert over the years, then guarding his back when he seized command of the *Prodigal Son*. The two knew enough about each other to get them hanged together, but he was the one person Robert trusted to be honest with him—though he hoped to add another person to that short list soon.

"More turnips means more cattle, more cattle means more money. You are Huntley," Fuller said, unnecessarily. "No matter what you or your father believed, you belong here. You can do far better than Ralph, and you know you would do better than Nicholas. You have the gift of command, Captain."

"Then let us talk about something more entertaining, Mr. Fuller. How quickly can you bring me John Heath's head on a pike?"

"I have good news for you there. We caught him sneaking away with Lionel Huntley's set."

"Do you need help hiding the body?"

"No. We convinced the steward to show us where he hid the booty, explained to him that crime doesn't pay—unless you're part of the crew—and sent him limping down the road. He won't bother you again, and he'll think twice about robbing anyone else."

Robert frowned. "What's the good of being lord of the manor if you can't display a malefactor's head on a pike as a lesson to the villagers?"

"Welcome back to civilization, my lord."

～

LYDIA MET with Mrs. Farmer and Braxton to organize the refurbishment of Huntley for Robert and Mattie. She would do her best to put the house to rights, but she would not presume she would be staying. She couldn't do that, no matter how lured she was by her time in Robert St. Armand's arms. It would be impossible to hide her love for him, especially if they were together in bed, and she knew he intended to join her there as often as she'd allow. Why wouldn't he? He was a man, she'd shown herself available, and while she could tell herself that this was what she wanted—because it was true—she also knew only one of them would bear society's censure if word leaked out. And word always leaked out. Servants washed the sheets, they knew when a bed had been used by more than one person. They were not deaf and dumb statues, they could see a lingering glance, a forbidden touch of hands, people standing closer than they should.

In the meantime the butler and the cook treated her with respect. Servants had an unerring knack for determining someone's status within a hierarchy, and Lydia's place had been firmly established at the top, for now. Braxton dispatched William to the local village to get the word out that Huntley was hiring and it was safe to work in the manor again. He seemed genuinely pleased to have Lydia's acceptance of responsibility as housekeeper, if not as lady of the house.

"But Miss Burke," the cook asked, "beggin' your pardon, but we've all heard stories about Lord Huntley before he came home, that he was a—well, you know. Those men of his are a rough-looking lot!"

Lydia smiled to herself as she thought about how once she would once have lumped the crew together as "murderous pirates" before she learned that Nash and Turnbull thirsted for knowledge, that Sails was talented at making ladies' garments, that Paget played the flute like a concert-master's dream.

"Lord Huntley's men are firmly under his command, Mrs. Farmer, and I can assure you after crossing the Atlantic with them that they will not press unwanted attentions on anyone working here. However," she added dryly, "you might want to keep a close eye on the girls, because I know these gentlemen can spin yarns capable of swaying the most respectable of women."

The home farm was producing well and Lydia was especially pleased by the dairy cows, their milk a welcome addition to Mattie's meals. In the summer she would introduce the child to ice cream, a treat Lydia'd missed in the island.

She hurried off to the child's lessons. Huntley needed a firm hand and a great deal of cleaning to be brought back into shape, but her first responsibility was as Mathilde's governess. The child was in the nursery with her father, playing jackstraws on the rug while Jolly watched them from his bed as he chewed on a piece of rope.

"Miss Burke, there are wonderful things in here! Papa says when he was little he used to play with these, but now I can play with them."

"I am pleased you are happy with your new quarters, Mathilde, but if your father will excuse us it is time for lessons."

"Where are Mr. Nash and Mr. Turnbull, Papa? We are studying division now and they said they wanted to learn also."

Lydia'd been wondering the same thing. Some of the men left the crew to ship out with other vessels, one or two left to rejoin families in England, but she hadn't heard from her two other favorite pupils.

"They will be here soon, Mathilde. I gave them a task to

perform first, and you know for the men it's duty before lessons."

"Until then, Mattie, we need to resume our lessons," Lydia said.

"I will rejoin you at luncheon, ladies." He picked up Mattie's hand and blew a noisy kiss into her palm, which made her giggle. But when he picked up Lydia's hand, the rogue *licked* her, which brought heat to her cheekbones.

"Away with you, Captain. We have numbers to conquer!"

Mattie giggled again at Lydia's command and after the handsome distraction left, the remainder of the morning was spent productively. A cheerful fire took the chill from the room while the gloomy skies kept Mattie from whining about being outside, though Lydia planned nature lessons for a better day.

With the materials in the nursery and Lydia's own supplies there was plenty to keep them busy until a growl from Mattie's stomach signaled it was time for a break. After luncheon Lydia thought longingly of a brief nap while Mattie and her father were occupied, but there were new girls in the kitchen who'd come for work, and there was work aplenty for all. Lydia even commandeered one of the younger girls, Sally, to be a nursery-maid and free up the governess for other duties.

A knock at Lydia's door late that afternoon as she dressed for supper showed Robert in the doorway, looking much more Lord Huntley than Captain St. Armand. He wore an informal frock coat in claret superfine, a modest neckcloth and waistcoat of dull gold. His "country squire" appearance did not fool her—the gold loop in his ear was a giveaway that the man still had piratical aspirations.

"We will all dine together when it's only family, as we did aboard ship, Miss Burke. We'll keep country hours so Mattie can join us."

This was phrased as an order, but there was a thread of longing beneath it only one who knew him would hear. The lonely little boy had a family again in this place that haunted him—a bastard daughter, a governess whose background would not stand up to scrutiny, a first mate who'd paid for loving another man, a puppy who confused leather gloves with appropriate chew toys.

Once upon a time she could not imagine herself close friends with a retired prostitute or consorting with pirates. That Lydia no longer existed. The one who was here now was glad of her place in this strange little society of outcasts and criminals.

"As you say, Captain. I will be downstairs shortly."

"One other thing—if you wear an ugly cap, you will not get dessert. One must have standards, even here in the country."

He took himself off before she could come up with an appropriate rejoinder, and what annoyed her most was two minutes after she closed her door she thought of at least four witty and cutting *bon mots* she could have flung at Captain St. Armand!

They ate in the smaller room, the one where breakfast was served, and the room looked much improved.

"You have been busy, Miss Burke. I can see it, and Braxton is most pleased to have the house restored," St. Armand said.

"My plan, Captain, is to clean Huntley room by room, starting with those areas used daily, then most often, then finally, the public spaces."

"We have furniture in the attic if you need additional pieces. Braxton will know what's there."

"What did you do today, Papa?"

"Today, Marauding Mattie, I talked with Mr. Fuller about crops and tomorrow or the next day I will ride out to the tenant farms, if the weather permits. Can you take a break from lessons to accompany me one day soon? I want to show you both more of Huntley, and this way Mattie will meet some of the young people in the area and their families."

"Is there no village school, Captain?"

"I do not believe there is, but we can learn more by making rounds of the farms, and then going into Ashwyn. Of course, organizing a school for the local children would be the natural task of Lady Huntley. My father's first wife, I'm told, was quite involved with that endeavor."

Lydia compressed her lips into a thin line. There would eventually be a Lady Huntley. Lydia's job was to focus on Mattie, her charge, and leave those responsibilities to whoever would take up the duties of the baron's wife.

"I will talk with Mrs. Farmer about making baskets to take with us as we visit. She might be able to make some biscuits, and I'm certain I saw enough jars of preserves that we could take that as well."

She looked over at Mattie, who was listening intently. "Just as a captain is responsible for his crew, the lord of the manor is responsible for his tenants, Mattie. It is a relation-ship of give-and-take, and when you are a grown lady you will have responsibilities to your husband's dependents as well."

Mattie shook her head firmly. "I will not marry, Miss Burke. I will be a pirate captain. Then no one will be able to tell me what to do!"

Lydia looked at St. Armand in exasperation, but he just raised his brows and said, "You have many years, Mathilde, before you have to concern yourself with either marriage or piracy. For now, practice your mathematics and your knife fighting and you will better prepare yourself for both."

"Captain St. Armand!"

"Look, here's William with dessert, a syllabub, if I am not mistaken."

Lydia excused herself after supper to spend time with Mattie in the nursery on needlework and they were they were joined at bedtime by the captain, his copy of *Captain Johnson* tucked under his arm.

"Hurrah! Tonight you will read the rest of Mary Read and Anne Bonny's story, Papa?"

"That is my plan, Mathilde. I seem to recall there are books in the nursery also."

"Books about little children who are always polite and do their lessons and never fight," Mattie sniffed disdainfully.

"Yes, I recall that as well," St. Armand said. "Who wouldn't choose pirates instead?"

Lydia stayed silent because she too would rather hear about pirates. She'd been thinking too much over the past hour about St. Armand, and what the coming night would bring when Mattie slept.

Mattie settled herself under her covers, and her father sat on the bed beside her while Lydia took up her mending again. Soon she too was caught up in the tale of the lady buccaneers.

"'While Mary Read sometimes claimed she abhorred the life of a pirate, men who sailed with her said under oath that no person amongst them were more resolute, or ready to board or undertake anything that was hazardous, as she and Anne Bonny. Particularly at the time they were attacked and taken, when they came to close quarters, none kept the deck except Mary Read and Anne Bonny... Mary Read, called to those under deck to come up and fight like men, and finding that they did not stir, fired her arms down the hold amongst them, killing one and wounding others.'"

Lydia sighed and put her hands in her lap, looking at her

young charge's reaction to this most inappropriate tale. Of course Mattie's eyes were wide in her face as she took this in.

"'This much is certain, that she did not want bravery,'" Mattie's papa continued. "And then...hmmmm...in this section Captain Johnson explains how Anne took a liking to Mary, thinking her a young man, but once Anne realized Mary was another woman they became fast friends. Anne, you will recall, was the paramour of Calico Jack Rackam."

"Perhaps this is a good point to *stop?*"

"Oh no, ma'am! Please, Papa, read some more about Mary Read!"

"Very well, Mattie. I told you about Mary's husband, for whom she fought a duel. Tomorrow I will finish Johnson's tale of Mary's final battle alongside Anne Bonny when they were captured. For the end of Mary's tale though, we have this... She testified that her young husband was an honest man and had no inclination to be a pirate, and Johnson says she was not a woman who was wanton or behaved badly with men. The court might have had compassion for Mary Read, but she was done in by the testimony of Rackam. Do not be sad, child," he said gently, "for it was a long time ago, and the story of that brave girl lives on. Now it is time for you to say good night."

"Good night, Papa," the girl whispered as he leaned down to kiss her forehead, "I love you."

"I love you too, poppet."

When Lydia rose to leave, Mattie said in a small voice, "May I have a kiss from you also, Miss Burke?"

"Of course," Lydia said, and leaned down to place her own kiss on Mattie's soft cheek. As she straightened up she brushed a wisp of hair off of Mattie's forehead.

"I love you, Miss Burke," the little girl said drowsily, but Lydia had no reply that could move past the lump in her throat.

When she stepped out of the nursery Robert was leaning against the wall, waiting for her. She'd been unsure of how the night would proceed, but the look in his eyes warmed her, and worried her. Last night brought her to full awareness again of what it meant to be a vibrant, passionate woman, but there were so many risks involved in continuing along that path.

Oh, but she longed to be like Mary Read, whose passion for her lover was "no less violent than his," according to Captain Johnson. If Mary fought a duel for her man, what lengths would Lydia go to for hers? Would she cross the threshold into his room, and spend the night in his arms, forgetting her problems, or at least some of them, for a few blissful hours?

She raised her eyes to his. Fire burned there, fire for her.

"Will you come to my room tonight?"

The words came out of her mouth before her thoughts were clear. "Yes. At midnight, after the house is asleep."

"I will look for you then and curse the hours that must pass before," he said, running the back of his fingers down her cheek. "For now though, I must excuse myself to work further on those bedamned account books." He sighed. "Life was easier as a pirate, I must say."

Lydia occupied herself with her own mending as the hour grew late, but the day's events caught up with her and she fell sound asleep sitting up in front of the fire. She went downstairs and the door to Robert's study was closed, but indistinct voices drifted out.

"Braxton, do you know who is in the study with Lord Huntley?"

The butler was making his rounds, checking the windows and doors.

"It is two sailors, ma'am. They were ushered directly in and food sent for them."

"Two sailors? One tall, dark-skinned, the other short, red-haired and missing fingers on his left hand?"

"Exactly. They appear to have been expected."

"Turnbull and Nash," Lydia murmured to herself. Mattie would be pleased her shipmates were returned, but she wondered what was so urgent the men met with Robert now, so late in the evening.

The hour grew late, the door to Robert's study remained closed and she prepared for bed, her braid of hair falling across her shoulder over her plain wrapper. After checking on Mattie one last time Lydia took her candle and entered her own room, sighing at the thought of her empty bed.

"Who is Thomas Wilson and why is he interested in your whereabouts?"

Lydia shrieked and nearly dropped her candle. She spun around, and made out the form of the man sitting in the dark, waiting for her. Then his question registered with her.

"Who—what?"

He sighed.

"You heard me, Lydia. Put down that candle. You are shaking so hard you might drop it. Now, once again, who is Thomas Wilson?"

She put down the candle, for she was indeed shaking, and clasping her hands pulled herself together.

"Not—not here, not now, Captain. We might wake Mattie with our talking."

He rose to his feet. "It will be now, but we can adjourn to my room if it makes you more comfortable."

Going to his room would not make her more comfortable, but it gave her some time to collect her thoughts.

They made the short journey to the master's rooms in silence, and once there he pulled out a chair and motioned her to sit. After examining her wordlessly he walked to a table and poured some rum into a glass. She wondered if she looked as pale as she felt, for he brought her the glass.

"Drink."

She did, and while it burned as it went down, it helped, but he took it away after one swallow and set it aside.

"I intend, my dear Lydia, to get to the bottom of this once and for all, tonight, and to determine if you are a threat to me, my crew, and most importantly, to Mathilde. The longer you delay, the shorter my temper grows."

She'd thought them long past the point where the pirate might dispose of her if he found her inconvenient or annoying or a danger. Clearly, she'd been premature in feeling herself safe from harm.

Lydia took a breath and looked down at her hands. She stopped her fingers from their nervous twining, spreading them wide on her lap, forcing them to stillness.

He took another chair and sat, arms crossed over his chest. The room was softly lit by the fire, and candles, a haven against the cold night.

"My story? It is not as exciting as Mary Read or Anne Bonny's tale, but there *is* a man involved."

"There always is, Lydia," he said with surprising gentleness. "Just start from the beginning."

"The beginning—I suppose my story begins as so many do, with a foolish, headstrong girl who thought herself special. Not like the other girls. No, for her everything had to be...more. She wasn't content to sit at lessons all day, she had to run and be in motion. She wasn't content to wear washed-out white and pastels, she wanted to dress in reds and purples and gold. She wanted to be shiny, and glittery, and let her voice be loud, and her feet pound the ground and her brushstrokes be bold and outside the lines of what was appropriate for girls to draw."

A smile tugged up the corners of his mouth. "I think I would like this girl."

"No doubt," she said tartly, "because rogues like you are attracted to the girls most likely to get into trouble."

His smile broadened at this and slouched back in his chair, his long legs stretched out before him, ankles crossed, hands clasped on his lap as he settled in to hear her tale.

"Her behavior did not improve when her parents died and she was sent to live with relatives who had strict notions of how girls should comport themselves. Naturally, she also thought herself wiser than all the adults around her, and knew them to be nothing but dried-out old sticks who'd never lived, and could not possibly understand how deeply she felt about everything. She was a great one for fervid drama and florid verse."

He frowned at this. "Is this what I have to look forward to in ten years or so?"

"If so, it will only be what you deserve, Captain St. Armand."

He waved his hand in the air to have her continue.

"So, this girl grew up and was the despair of the relatives raising the orphan—"

"What happened to her parents?"

"Do you want me to continue, or not?"

He raised a finger in the air to have her pause, took the rum and drank it.

"That is my rum," she scowled.

"You will receive more if it's warranted. Continue."

Lydia shifted in her seat and forced her shoulders to relax. "Where were we?"

"This interesting girl was the despair of all who knew her."

"Ah. Yes. Her parents died in a boating accident and she was told—repeatedly—how fortunate she was that her aunt and uncle took her in, considering how little money was left from her parents for her upbringing."

"Were they cruel to her?"

"Not in the way you might think. She wasn't beaten, but she knew they saw her as a burden, a test of their Christian charity. They made that clear to her. There were those who didn't object to this girl and her bold ways. She was popular with the young gentlemen who knew she was always up for a bit of fun, a 'good 'un' as they would say, a girl who wanted find out for herself what all the fuss was about, a girl who would sneak behind the bushes to try a cheroot—or a kiss."

She looked down at her hands, remembering, not totally with regrets. He didn't say anything, but she saw him shift in his seat, so she took a breath and continued.

"Then one evening at an assembly, she met a man. He wasn't like the boys in her village who talked big but had never done anything with their lives. This man was a naval lieutenant who'd had adventures and been places and done things, exciting things."

"Wasn't this girl warned about sailors and their ways?"

"Of course she was. But why would this obstinate chit listen to that when she'd never listened to any other good advice? So she began spending time with the lieutenant, Edwin Carstairs, who was on half-pay. When her family warned her he had a reputation as a hothead and a braggart she did not listen to them. When they forbade her from seeing him, she sneaked out of the house to meet him at night in the woods. When Edwin asked her to run off with him, she said yes, because it sounded romantic and adventurous and it would get her away from all the censorious eyes constantly watching her."

This time when she paused, and looked at the glass of rum in his hands, he passed it to her. When she was done drinking he stepped out and returned with a second glass. He didn't tell her to stay put. He didn't need to. Both she and he realized this was story she needed to tell, a story he needed to hear.

If nothing else, she thought wryly, it was an excellent cautionary tale for a man with a young daughter.

"She packed a valise, taking her book of poems, because what could be more necessary to life and love than that, and the few coins she'd saved and her small pieces of jewelry—a gold locket, a strand of pearls, a cameo brooch. Pieces suitable for a young lady."

"He was disappointed by her lack of money and jewels, wasn't he?"

"You speak from experience?"

He shook his head. "No, but I have an idea of how the minds of men like Carstairs work."

"Of course you do. Our lovebirds traveled to London and it was all quite exciting and romantic, staying in questionable inns, giving him her possessions because when you were in love you share everything, don't you?"

"Did he abandon her in London?"

"Do you want to hear the rest of the tale?"

"My apologies. Please, go on."

"No, Edwin did not abandon her. He really did want her, and was glad of her company and her love, and the feeling was mutual. But he was without funds of his own. He was owed prize money but it was not forthcoming. He'd spent the small bequest from his late father, he had no prospects except his hope of another ship. When they arrived in London he took her to Wapping, to an inexpensive house where he knew people, people who would not condemn a young couple who were in love, but without the benefit of the church sanctioning it. He didn't have the funds for a special license, she could not marry without her guardians' permission, but they did not care for they had each other."

"It must have been horrid for her."

"She loved it," Lydia corrected him with a smile of remembrance. "Every day was a new adventure. While her beau wrote letters to contacts who he hoped would secure him a berth on another vessel, she spent the day playing house, chatting with the other women in the building, learning how to shop in the marketplace without getting robbed—by the merchants or the pickpockets—writing bad poetry until she could no longer afford ink. It did not feel tragic at all. In the evenings they joined his friends at a nearby tavern, a mixed crew of all sorts. There were vicars and whores, gentlemen and rat-catchers, and a political assortment of deists, utopians, abolitionists, Spenceans, Paineites—if someone had thought of a way to upset the usual workings of government and society, he'd be found there. It was all quite educational for a young lady of gentle birth."

They *had* been heady times. Talking—really, arguing—late into the night about the rights of man, and the rights of women as well, drinking cheap ale, sharing what little they had with others who had less. At night when it was cold she and Edwin had each other's warmth and she felt satisfied. In some ways they were the best days of her life.

"In every Eden there's a tempting serpent, isn't there?" Lydia sighed. "We debated Bentham and were fond of his ideas of 'sinister interest' keeping the common man from reaching his full potential. Of course, once you accept such ideas it's easier to take a step into a more Jacobin attitude— am I boring you?"

"Not at all. Had I known I could spend evenings debating political reform and philosophy with you I might have focused less on your quite attractive bosom. Unlikely, but one never knows. Continue, please. You haven't gotten yet to the good part, the part where you no longer have this man in your life and you're in the islands, and how Thomas Wilson enters into it."

Lydia shrugged her shoulders. "What does it matter, Captain? You know now that once I ran off I threw away whatever chance I had at respectability here in England, and as so many others have done, I want to make a new life for myself elsewhere. I still do."

"Where people don't know you. Yes, I understand, but there is the issue of that man who was not your husband."

She looked down at her hands. It still pained her, when she thought about it. Did she regret what she'd done? Sometimes, but in her heart she still believed it was the only choice she could make.

"One day, my uncle showed up in London. Word had reached him of where I was, and what I was doing. He's a wealthy man, Uncle Frederick, and he approached Edwin when I was at market."

Lydia could never forget that day. When she returned Edwin was gone from their lodgings, along with his few possessions. Her dour uncle waited for her there. He explained how Edwin took the money offered him to leave her. Uncle Frederick would take Lydia home, and if she lived a repentant life, in time people might overlook her sins and her shame.

"I refused his offer. I was so angry. Angry at Edwin, at my uncle, at the world, at my parents for dying and leaving me alone, but most of all, I was angry at the thought of losing my freedom again."

"You did not stay in touch with Carstairs?"

"No. I heard from someone in London that Edwin died of illness when he was sent to America toward the end of the war. It saddened me that he was dead, but to be honest, I was not interested in hearing anything more from him after he took money to abandon me."

"Brava, Lydia."

She looked up at the pirate. There was no amusement on his face at her missteps and bad decisions. Instead the glow in his eyes was tender. He understood. Of all the people she'd met over her life, she knew that whether he'd kill her or keep her, Robert understood her choices.

"After my rejection of his offer, Uncle Frederick said if that was my choice, there would be no more communication among us. He would tell people I'd died—it would be better for his family."

"What?"

She nodded. "My uncle is—well, he's a man of consequence and rigid morals. I had to think about my cousins, I was told, what my disgraceful ways would mean to them, how it could hurt their chances at finding husbands."

He swore under his breath. "You must have been terrified, once you realized you were on your own."

"Yes. It was frightening, of course, and while I had our new friends around me, I also knew that I needed to find a way to support myself."

She stopped talking and looked down again, her lips clamped together because she really, truly did not want to say more. Robert leaned forward, his fingers under her chin as he eased her face up so he could look into her eyes.

"Whatever you have to say, I can hear it. You need not fear telling me," he said in a gentle voice.

She swallowed. "It's not what you're thinking."

He raised his brows at that. "Then enlighten me, Miss Burke."

Oh, he'd be enlightened all right. Lydia sucked in a deep breath and stood, walking to the window. She looked over her shoulder at him. He'd stood when she did, and leaned over with his hands on the chair back, watching her.

She stared at the window, her dark reflection looking

back at her, the shadow of her inquisitor behind her. There was no moon tonight, a good night for doing things one didn't wish to have revealed. She touched the glass, but didn't turn around.

"I am being blackmailed. As long as I stayed away from England, I was out of reach of my enemy. Now that I'm here, word will get to him and everything I've worked so hard to build in the past few years could be snatched away from me."

"Blackmailed?"

At his tone she turned back to him.

"Why are you smiling?"

"Generally, one is blackmailed over acts illegal or immoral. Neither of those things would especially bother me, but it makes your story so much more *interesting* than the usual story of a young woman's ruination. What *could* you have done that is so terrible?"

She wanted to tell him without looking at him, but she fancied herself braver than that. She took a breath, and turned.

"Some of that reckless girl's new friends were publishers of pamphlets, political pamphlets. I mentioned the Spenceans and other radicals with whom she consorted. She began to earn coin writing for them."

"Writing radical pamphlets?"

"Sometimes," she prevaricated, "but that wasn't all she wrote."

"Lydia, getting information from you is like trying to pry pearls from oysters. Who was the publisher of this seditious trash?"

She glared at him. Who was a pirate to call what she wrote trash?

"The publisher was William Drysdale of Drysdale Press."

His brow furrowed as he thought. "Drysdale Press...that name is familiar," he paused, then a delighted grin crept over his expressive mouth, curling it up the corners. His face lit like a boy who'd just been handed a piece of warm gingerbread.

"My dear Miss Burke! My *darling* Miss Burke!" He wagged a finger at her like a scolding nursemaid. "You have been a naughty, naughty girl, haven't you, Lydia!"

"I have no idea what you are referring to," she muttered, looking past him at the blank wall.

"There are only two types of publications that emerge from Drysdale Press. I know this because I like to read one of the two. Drysdale Press publishes treasonous tripe"—he paused dramatically, then waved his hand with a flourish —"and entertainment for lonely gentlemen!"

"Are you quite finished being amused at my expense?"

"Finished? I've hardly begun, my dear, dear governess!"

He capered over and putting his hand on the window frame leaned in. His mercurial disposition, one moment threatening, the next gleeful, nearly caused nausea with the rocking of his back-and-forth moods.

"Tell me your entire story, I must insist," he said in a low voice. "You interested me before, but now you *fascinate* me."

She felt heat rising in her face, though she stoutly told herself she had no need to apologize to the likes of Captain Robert St. Armand or Lord Robert Huntley or anyone else.

"I needed to pay the landlord and it was what the publisher was buying."

He stepped back, his hands clasped behind his back. "Rather like my trade, wouldn't you say? I needed money and there were all these ships on the water, just begging to be raided."

"My writing entertaining stories is nothing like robbing people, Captain St. Armand!"

"Entertaining stories? Is that what the Society for the Suppression of Vice is calling it these days? I know I would have remembered stories written by Miss Lydia Burke, so what was your *nom de plume*?"

She mumbled something and he cocked his head at her.

"Louder, please, I didn't quite catch that."

She sighed. "I wrote under the name Randy Scribe. Not very original, but it made a point."

Now his smile threatened to split his face. "You wrote the book about the gardener, the vicar, Lady Buxom, and what the milkmaids saw?"

"You read that?"

"Read it? It was my favorite! If there hadn't been a war on and ships to pillage I would not have left my berth for a week!" He bounced on his toes, all thoughts of murdering her gone. She hoped. Perhaps like Scheherazade, her story-telling abilities would keep her alive for now. However, there were still other issues to deal with, so she returned to her chair and sat, resigned, as he enjoyed the moment at her expense.

"Wait! There were drawings! Did you illustrate your own stories?"

"No, I have no artistic talent of that sort. Others supplied the illustrations."

"Pity." He sighed. "I liked looking at the pictures."

"Are you quite done enjoying my discomfort? If you recall, you threatened to kill me and I would like to know if we have moved beyond that."

"Never assume someone's not going to kill you, you'll live longer. I'm ready to hear the rest of your story, Miss Burke— or should I say, *Randy*?"

"If you do, I'm liable to throw that cup of rum at you, Captain."

He just grinned again. "Wasn't Randy Scribe the author of *Birching the Barrister*? I'm sure someone with such a fertile imagination can find a better way to punish me than by throwing things. How *did* you gain the skills to become a writer of such renown?"

"Our little group of malcontents enjoyed sharing books frowned upon by the church and Crown—*The Memoirs of A Woman of Pleasure*, *The Frisky Songster*, tracts on the philosophy of birch discipline, that sort of thing. After reading these salacious works I knew I could write them as well as most of the people being published, if not better. The combination of morality, political philosophy, the rights of women, and entertainment intrigued me. Most importantly, it was what the publisher was buying. The more I wrote, the more I could pay the rent and purchase food."

"A very practical attitude. I approve."

"You may laugh, but it was my association with Drysdale and his publications which forced me to flee England. There was an underling at the publishing house, an odious little man. Thomas Wilson. He was popular with the writers and hangers-on because he was willing to buy them drink in the tavern where we'd congregate."

"The tavern where you talked radicalism."

"Exactly. He was a government plant, brought in to keep notes on the Spencean Society and others in our group. Wilson's value to his masters increased with our supposed illegal activities, so the more they drank and talked treason, the more he had to offer. Since he worked for Drysdale, he naturally knew about my writing. Wilson felt my status as Edwin's paramour and my writing gave him license to take liberties with me."

"Did he assault you?"

The question was asked softly, but with an undercurrent that chilled her. "Not successfully. He did corner me in the offices, but I'd learned a trick or two from the women in the marketplace. He did not take rejection well."

Lydia leaned forward. "Wilson used his connections at the

Home Office to discover my background. He threatened to publish articles highlighting my salacious career, my involvement with radicals, my living with Edwin without benefit of clergy. There was also the issue of my companions. He could make a case to his superiors I was involved in seditious activities. Now that I'm returned—remember, Peterloo is still much on peoples' minds, and the government is watching to see who stirs up trouble, or is perceived as stirring up trouble. Arrest and exposure of my activities would bring attention to my family, the family that told everyone I was dead. I'd made my choice to reject them, they do not need to suffer further because of my actions. I understand that and I accept it, even if I do not like it."

"Bollocks."

She raised an eyebrow at the obscenity.

"I will not apologize. If your family cared about you, they would stand behind you."

"Actions have consequences, Captain. Isn't that what we're teaching Mathilde? If one acts in such a fashion as to being shame on one's family, there is a consequence. I will not do that to them, not to make my own life more comfortable."

"Do you think I could ever abandon Mattie? Even when I was looking for someone to care for her in St. Martin, it was because I wanted to do the right thing for her. Your having to run and hide from this worm is not a consequence you should be forced to bear alone. We prodigals must stick together because who else will stand by us?"

"I seem to recall the Bible story having a different outcome and message."

He waved away that point. "You understand what I am trying to say. You, me, Mattie, we are all of us frowned upon by society for our behavior, or simply for what we are. We're outcasts. When the enemy is preparing a broadside you have only your own cunning and your shipmates beside you. Knowing those other outcasts stand with you gives you the courage to fight, and win gold and booty."

Lydia looked at the man standing before her who combined some of the best and worst of human nature. He loved his daughter and was a good commander, but he was also a pirate and a reprobate. His deeds were not written on his face, it glowed with good health, showing none of the signs of his riotous life—yet—but she knew him. If he continued on his life's path it would only be a matter of time before disease or disaster caught up with Robert.

She'd never believed a good woman could change a bad man, but a flawed man could change himself into a person a flawed woman could stand beside. It was a fragile candle flame of hope inside her chest after the emotional turmoil of finally telling him her whole story, but he'd been correct about one thing. It was time he knew it all. Whether that made a positive difference in her future remained to be seen.

"Your philosophy of life and mine are not aligned. I hope for more than a good fight and ill-gotten gains."

"Then I think you've put your finger on exactly what your problem is, Miss Burke."

"No. My goal is to be a better person than I was in my youth. I am an adult now, I have put away childish things. And you, Robert, you like to paint yourself as only a pirate, but you are much more than that. You were not the prodigal son. You did not take your patrimony and spend it wastefully until you had nothing. You built your own fortune. Granted, it was a fortune built on piracy, but it was your own hard work, nonetheless—I cannot believe I am saying this," she muttered. "Regardless, your ship is not aptly named. Yes, your crew may be free spending with their booty, but... I cannot believe I am defending all of you!"

"All of *us*, don't you mean?"

"Yes, me also, because I too threw away my life of safety and security to live passionately, if not profligately."

"There is nothing wrong with living life passionately, Lydia. It is the only life we have, so why not take advantage of fine fabrics, furs, good food and drink? Leave the righteous crusts and thin broth of sanctity to those who will nibble on such fare and judge themselves, and others, in their gray, colorless manner."

He began to pace around the room, hands clasped behind his back. His focus had shifted from her as a threat to him onto a different plane. "Now that I'm home, I could become that prodigal son, Lydia. I could spend down the remaining monies in this estate, ruining it even further. Huntley's almost there already, thanks to my brother and my cousin. With just a slight push it could all topple into dust. That is what I intended with this return."

"Then what?"

"How do you mean?"

"So you ruin the estate further, throwing even more people out of employment, not bringing your custom to the local merchants, not holding up your end of your ancestors' bargain. For that's what it was initially, was it not? The baron protected the people and in return they supported him. *That* is your patrimony. Not the beatings and ill-feeling of your father and brother, but the agreement between lord and land, your responsibility to your people. You are Huntley. Not your father, not your brother, not your cousin. You."

"And what of you in this plan, Lydia?"

She took a deep breath. "I agreed to see you to your home, and care for Mathilde. I have done so. But my problems remain, Captain, and I still must leave so you can move on with reclaiming your legacy."

"Do you want to leave?"

"You know I do not, especially now. But you and I both

know that part of your responsibility is to marry and father your own children, because otherwise your cousin will inherit the estate."

"I could easily eliminate him…"

"Not a good solution, Captain."

"I don't know why you say that when accidents are so common. I could see a fool like Lionel accidentally falling on a knife."

She felt that twinge behind her eye signaling a headache if she didn't steer the conversation in a different direction.

She stood, and her feet moved her toward his bed, where she could grasp hold of the post at the end. She looked down on the old bed, carved long in the past, and she'd wager it had been slept in by Lords Huntley going back generations. Robert had replaced the bedding, but kept the furniture. Was that a conscious decision on his part? A link to the men whose name he bore, whether or not he believed himself the heir by blood? She knew what she had to do if he was going to truly take on the baron's role.

"I would embarrass you if I stayed."

He laughed aloud at this, and she turned and looked over her shoulder. He was close behind her, and put his hands on her shoulders.

"My darling Lydia, I am a pirate—or so people say—and you think you would be an embarrassment to me?"

She turned to look in his eyes. "You're handsome, titled, rich, from a good family, sometimes you display a modicum of wit—hostesses will poison each other for the opportunity to invite you to their soirees, and mothers of marriageable daughters will find ways to thrust their offspring into your path. You must marry, and marry well. Your past will be overcome by your obvious assets, not nearly the barrier you would think. To be fully accepted into society though, your wife must be above reproach."

She smiled, but she knew it was a fractured smile because it reflected the truth, as unpleasant as it was.

"It's different for a woman. I did spend my currency prodigally, my currency being that of other young women—my reputation."

His hand rose and cupped her cheek, and her eyelashes fluttered down at the tenderness of his touch. It was something she craved, something she'd tasted during those brief moments when he held her to comfort her, and when he loved her in his bed.

"If you marry me, you will be Lady Huntley. That is all anyone needs to know," he said softly.

"Please, Robert, do not do this to me—not tonight. There is too much happening."

He sighed and stepped away, and she gripped the post for support until she was sure she would not weep, or collapse onto his bed, a far too tempting option. Instead, she returned to her chair and sat while he replenished their rum.

"Let us return to our original problem then. Is Wilson the only person threatening you?"

"To the best of my knowledge he's working alone. He's greedy and would not want to share with anyone else. I'm living under constant threat as long as I am in England, because I don't know where Wilson is and I could be spotted or recognized by someone who knew me or who knows my family."

"As it happens, I know where Wilson is. He's in London."

"Nash and Turnbull," Lydia whispered.

"Yes. I knew you were fleeing from something or someone, and my men—those two in particular—are good at ferreting out information in unsavory settings. I told them to spend money freely and to drop your name into conversation."

"You had no right to interfere with my life that way!"

"I had every right. My daughter is in your keeping. I would not risk her well-being. I would not risk *your* well-being. Information—knowledge—is power. I'm not only a successful man because of my skills at sea, but because I know information is itself a currency and I gather as much as possible when planning my business opportunities. The men learned Wilson spent a great amount of his time and coin a few years back asking about a woman named Burke. He seemed to think you'd gone to ground in London."

"I could have stayed in the islands, as I wished! I would have been safe if you had not kidnapped me!"

He shrugged. "I will not apologize. I am glad I took you, Lydia. You belong with me. Stop worrying about Wilson. When he contacts you I will deal with him."

"Wait—when he contacts me? How can you be certain he will?"

"Because Turnbull told him you're here."

"What?"

"Do not screech, you will wake the household."

She didn't realize she was on her feet, fists clenched, until she saw Robert eyeing her warily. Good. He should be afraid. How *dare* he throw her into harm's way when she'd worked so hard to hide from Wilson.

"Be reasonable, Lydia. You cannot spend your life running, looking over your shoulder in fear of this worm. He will come here. I will take care of him. It is simple."

Hope flared in Lydia's breast. How wonderfully easy it would be to put her head on Robert's broad shoulder and let him put her under his protection, solve all her problems.

She couldn't do that. She'd put her fate in the hands of a man once, and when he abandoned her she ended running away, threatened with ruin and possible imprisonment.

"I cannot let you deal with Wilson for me, Captain St—Robert. It is my problem, not yours."

"Come here."

She didn't move, so he stepped closer to her. The only sounds in the quiet night were the call of an owl hunting its prey. She knew how that poor little mouse felt, worried about being consumed by something so large and fierce. Robert grasped her arms, holding her in place.

"Lydia Burke. I have two things to say to you. You are brave and resourceful and you've done a marvelous job taking care of yourself these past years, even if you had to hide your beauty behind such a drab front. That is thing number one. Thing number two is, you are an idiot. You are a governess, but I am a pirate. I do not attempt to teach higher mathematics or write stories, you should not attempt to stop me from doing what I do best—removing unpleasant people."

"Idiot? How dare—"

She would have finished that screed but he shut her up by pulling her against him and kissing her. He used some diabolical technique learned in his travels to the Orient because her brain ceased functioning under the assault of his lush mouth. As far as her newly roused passions were concerned, the only idea that made sense right now was adjourning to his bed and exploring his skills in depth, doing further thoughtless and foolish and passionate things with him simply because they made her feel so alive.

His lips were his weapon as he overcame her resistance and her scruples. His soft lips, moving across her own, coaxing her mouth open, prompting her to lean into his embrace, a broken moan escaping from her.

It was all too much, the tension of the night, the highs and lows of their interaction, this too visceral reminder of what life was when it was full of excitement and color. Once she'd led a life where she was warmed by the passion of people arguing late into the night, the passion of sharing her bed with a man who wanted her, at least for a while, and now that she was wanted again and it made her feel—everything.

More than that, in Robert's embrace, in his kisses, she felt things she'd never felt before. A wholeness from sharing this experience with him, not because he could ravage her senses with his skills, but because it was Robert, her Robert, the man who loved puppies and had tea parties with little girls and could take men destined for the gallows and give them another chance, a chance to be a part of a crew of shipmates who watched each others' backs. She was a *Prodigal* and that warmed her, but Robert's kisses inflamed her, caught her up in a tide of feeling.

When they broke apart both were breathing heavily and she looked up into his eyes, then felt her own narrow. She saw triumph in his gaze. He thought he could keep her here with his body, with his kisses, with his handsome face. She was still put out with him for sitting in the dark again, waiting to scare the life out of her. And for calling her an idiot. And for—well, for being the notorious Captain St. Armand and Lord Huntley and such an outright rascal. Tonight he would learn that he could not always get his way. She knew things, Lydia did. Even if she hadn't done everything she'd written as Randy Scribe, she'd done enough and knew enough to teach the pirate a lesson or two.

"Trust is so very important in a relationship, Robert," she said softly. "You want me to trust you, to let you take over all my problems and fix them for me, correct?"

"Why are you looking at me like that?"

"Do I make you nervous?"

She ran her finger down the front of his open shirt, feeling the robust flesh against her hand. Oh yes, skin this firm would respond nicely to what she was contemplating.

"Do not be ridiculous," he scoffed. "What could you possibly have in mind that would make me nervous?"

She thought of the objects deep in the bottom of the case where she kept her most personal possessions, used on those evenings when she sought self-gratification. After all, there weren't always pirates around when you needed them. Most of those implements were more exotic than this evening called for, but at some point it might be amusing to pull them out and give him an experience he'd not soon forget. In the meantime there were other things she could do.

She smiled at that thought, leaving his embrace and walking over to his chest of drawers, to the top one where she knew he kept his cravats. Lovely cloth, linen and silk, finely made, some stiff with starch, others comfortably pliable. They were exactly what she needed.

She turned back to him and ran one of the lengths of silk through her fingers and his eyes followed her motions, darkening as his breath caught. He was, after all, an experienced man with a certain reputation in the brothels of St. Martin, she'd heard that for herself.

"You want me to restrain you," he said huskily.

"You forget, Captain St. Armand. *I* am the governess here."

"Oh? Oh!" he said, licking his lips nervously. "I don't know if that is such a—"

"Silence."

He shut his mouth so quickly at her quiet command that she heard his teeth click. But he didn't run, he didn't come over and take the cloth from her and turn the tables, he only stood there looking slightly ill at ease.

Slightly ill at ease, but with a noticeable tenting of the fabric in his breeches.

Lydia leisurely walked to the armchair, turned it around and seated herself, sprawling in a way that would have earned a reprimand from her own governess, but it suited her mood. Tonight she felt like a queen, a barbarian queen with serving boys at her beck and call. Or like Anne Bonny, picking the most strapping and handsomest of the pirates to service her.

"Tonight you will serve me, in all ways, Captain, as a demonstration of trust. If I am pleased with your service, you will be rewarded. Otherwise, there may be…punishments. And I warn you, I can be an exacting and strict mistress. I have long felt your unruly ways would benefit from some discipline. From a firm hand."

She continued running the silk through her hands while she spoke, and at the end snapped the section of cloth taut between her fists. His eyes widened, but he made no move toward her, nor made a move to stop her. He cleared his throat.

"I am not unfamiliar with these games, Lydia—"

"Miss Burke, or Madam, to you."

"Miss Burke," he continued, "but I am the one in charge when I play."

"Then tonight will be an opportunity for you to try something different, won't it?" Rising from her seat, she strolled over to him, walking around him in a circle, standing behind him. She draped the white silk across his shoulder, gliding it up across his chest as she spoke softly in his ear.

"Think about it, Captain—tonight you are not in command. You are not responsible. You do not have to decide anything. All you have to do," she said, running her fingernail up his neck, a move that brought a twitch and a shiver, "is feel. All you have to do, is give in to your desires, and obey."

She savored the moment, the tang of the light sheen of moisture rising on his warm neck, the heartbeat she saw accelerating in his neck. She debated tying the cloth around his eyes, but thought it would be more satisfying for him to see her, to know exactly who was toying with him. She walked back to her chair, her face set in stern lines as she took her seat and steepled her hands in front of her, a gesture mirroring one he'd used many times.

"As I was saying, I am in charge. You will remove all your clothing, fold it—neatly—and place it on the floor at your feet. Silently," she added with an upraised finger when he opened his mouth. That lovely mouth was set in mutinous lines, but she wasn't quelled by his frown. He was clearly much more engaged with her commands than he let on. There were certain things a man could hide, but a gratifyingly large cockstand wasn't on that list.

He took his time, and she enjoyed the show. When he finished she rose again, walked over and looked at the pile of clothing. He'd disobeyed her command. Rather than fold the shirt and breeches, he'd dropped them on the floor.

"Tsk. You are greatly in need of correction. I will deal with your insolence. For now, lie down on your bed, hands over your head. Higher."

His eyes were on her as she gathered more cravats, and when she leaned over his prone form he inhaled, and she knew what that meant to a sensualist like Robert Huntley. All his senses would be engaged. Hers were as well, hearing his breathing deepen, seeing the drops of liquid pearling at the tip of his cock, scenting the unique musk of an aroused male, feeling the heat of his skin beneath her fingertips. She lashed his wrists and ankles to the bedposts with his silken neckclothes, and if her knots weren't shipshape, they were sufficiently well done to keep him in place.

Lydia surveyed her handiwork, then undid her hair, running her fingers through it to loosen it, let it fall forward as he watched intently. Finally she untied the plain wrapper she wore and let it drop to the carpet. Beneath she wore only her stockings, held up by cunning garters Nanette crafted for her.

They were red satin with lush black roses bearing prominent thorns, the black silk stabbing through the red material in embroidered spikes. She wore these garters on those occasions when she wanted to feel like the woman she'd once been.

It was time Randy Scribe came out to play.

His eyes widened.

"How long have you been wearing those?"

"Do you like them? I save them for special occasions. I wore them when I met you at Madame Olifiers's house. I wore them tonight anticipating your coming to my bed. You didn't come to my bed, Captain. You kept me waiting, which was so very wrong of you."

He could only nod, and ran his tongue over his lips.

"If you're a good boy, I'll let you untie these garters. With your teeth."

She leaned down and put her mouth lightly on his, just touching him, pulling back when he strained to kiss her deeper. He swore in frustration.

"No," she placed her finger across his lips. "If you speak out of turn I will have to gag you, and I have plans for this lovely mouth."

She finished by running her finger over his lips, and his tongue darted out to lick it, sending a frisson of anticipation down her back. Such a naughty boy! It had been forever since she'd engaged in these sorts of games, and she felt her own heightened arousal at the thought of having this large, muscled pirate under her hand.

"Hand" gave her an idea. Lydia went to his chests and rummaged until she found his new gloves. Lovely things, soft calfskin, beautifully tanned. She examined them in his full view, running them through her fingers, then taking one and snapping it against the palm of her hand, smiling a satisfied little smile when his eyes grew large. He was learning who was in charge tonight, and it wasn't the notorious Captain St. Armand.

"For the love of God, Lydia—"

"Tsk. I did warn you, didn't I?"

She leaned over him again, the sweat-sheened face as he strained at the ties gratifying her.

"Open," she said, tapping his mouth.

He only frowned, keeping his lips tight like a little boy unwilling to take his medicine, but there was nothing little about this naughty pirate. She lightly tapped him across the face with the glove, not a hard slap, but hard enough to make her point.

"Open."

He grudgingly opened his mouth and she slipped the edge of the glove in, knowing as he tasted the clean leather it would remind him of a bridled horse, a stallion kept firmly under the hand of his knowing mistress.

"If you release that glove before I tell you to, I will whip you with it."

She didn't wait to see his reaction but turned around to retrieve the other item she wanted—yes, there it was. She walked across the room, slowly enough that he could get a full view of her from behind, then leaned over at the waist, legs straight, and picked up the fur pillow from where he'd carelessly tossed it. She turned back to him and taking the rich sable held it to her chest, embracing the sensual caress of the silken hairs, easing it across her flesh, over the nipples standing erect, eager for a firmer touch, down across her belly, his eyes never leaving her hands as she fondled herself with his pillow. She walked back to the bed, holding it against her belly, then took the fur and mimicked her actions on his body, enjoying how he bowed up at the center, pulling at his silken ropes. She set it aside for later and settled herself atop him, straddling his muscled thighs.

He made a noise behind his glove. His body spoke for what he was feeling, and as she adjusted herself against his shaft she gave herself, and him, a moment to savor the sensation, their bodies slick with desire, hot with anticipation. He throbbed against her and she slid herself on his straining length, the warmth and strength of him captive beneath her as stimulating as she'd fantasized.

"Now, my naughty pirate, let's discuss the price to be paid for all those caps of mine disappearing…"

CHAPTER 22

*A*t breakfast Mattie chattered away because Turnbull and Nash were back, and they'd join in her lessons, if Miss Burke permitted.

"How can I refuse to teach two of my best pupils?" Lydia smiled at the child. After breakfast Mattie took Jolly out for exercise and to take care of his needs, and Lydia enjoyed a second cup of coffee. Robert was gone that morning, off early with Fuller riding outlying areas of the estate to let his tenants meet the new lord and see for themselves that he wasn't Ralph or Cousin Lionel.

She was stirring in a spoon of sugar when the door to the breakfast room opened.

"Ah. Just the men I want to see."

Nash froze, his hand on the doorknob.

"We can come back later, ma'am. Don't mean to disturb your meal or nothing."

"Come in, Mr. Nash. Mr. Turnbull also. Close the door."

Reluctantly, the two entered, Turnbull yanking his cap from his mostly bald head. They stood like schoolboys expecting a scolding and she let them suffer. She knew the effectiveness of silence and waited until Nash blurted out, "We had to report everything to the captain, Miss Burke!"

Turnbull nodded rather frantically. "That's right. Captain gave us orders, he did, and we had to follow them."

Lydia toyed with letting them suffer longer, but it wasn't their fault. "I am not angry with you gentlemen," she said. "I know you were under orders. In fact, I suppose I should thank you."

They looked at each other, then back at her. Today they were dressed more as seamen from Liverpool than pirates ravaging the Caribbean, but they were still festooned with gold earrings and likely had a weapon or two tucked away.

"Thank us?"

"Yes, Mr. Turnbull. Please, have a seat."

The men sat, and poured themselves coffee, eyeing the freshly polished silver on the table with a professional appreciation for its value.

"Captain's doing all right for himself here," Nash said with approval.

"Remember, he ain't the captain now, he's Lord Huntley," Turnbull said. "Who would have guessed it, our own Captain St. Armand a baron?

"See, Miss Burke, this is why we went poking around in London. Captain says he wants to drop anchor here, settle down with Mattie, and with you."

Lydia paused from the act of refilling her own cup. "With me? He said that?"

"Not in those exact words, no, miss," Nash clarified. "What he said was, he needed to know what you were hiding from, and if you were facing a hempen jig, we should get the scuttlebutt to make sure that don't happen. People who make the captain's neck twitch tend to disappear, and it's clear to all of us that he cares about your neck too."

"Yeah," Turnbull added from the sideboard, where he was

filling a plate with the sausages and steak left from breakfast. "I dunno what you did to annoy that poxy dog Wilson, but getting him to accidentally fall off a pier wouldn't make me shed a tear. Word around the docks is he peaches on his mates, and that ain't right."

Braxton entered the room as Turnbull seated himself, and the butler pokered up at this democratic assembly, but didn't say anything. Lydia knew there would be unavoidable questions and comments downstairs. Part of the problem with St. Armand reestablishing himself in England with his crew at hand was that his pirates were not servants nor were they sailors serving before the mast. They prided themselves on their independence, and while they'd follow a strong captain, he too could have an accidental fall off a pier if the crew wasn't happy with him.

Nash and Turnbull dropped unsubtle hints as they ate that they wanted to know what Miss Burke was hiding, but she had no intention of sharing that information. It was bad enough Robert knew her secret.

"Are you planning on staying here?"

"Not for long, miss." Nash looked around him. "They do things different in the country than aboard ship. They let chooks run around underfoot instead of keeping them in their proper place like we do at sea. Ain't natural. And hearing birds singing in the morning? Gives me the colly-wobbles, it does."

Turnbull stuffed a buttered roll into his pocket and rose. "Me and Nash are old seadogs, ma'am. We can't hardly walk without a deck rolling beneath our feet. Captain has some tasks for us here, and we'll see what he intends with the ship and then decide. He's holding our money for us, says we can come back anytime and he'll find us a berth here."

Lydia knew if she left Huntley she would miss not only Mattie and Robert in her life, but she would also miss the crew of the *Prodigal*. Where else could she have a friendship with men like Turnbull and Nash, who treated her as a mate and looked out for her?

There were worse things in life than having pirates watch your back and keep you from harm's way.

ROBERT DISMOUNTED, carefully, wincing at the sudden reminder of the previous evening's entertainment. It had been a night of unexpected delights and he looked forward to turning the tables on the little governess at a future date. He had plenty of cravats.

He paused at the entranceway once again struck by the activity, the feeling of weight dissipating from Huntley. Maidservants scrubbed down the front hall, a pair of gardeners were cutting back the dead growth from the shrubs in the front, and he found Lydia in the study, examining a globe with Mattie. Dark circles bloomed under Lydia's eyes and Robert felt an unusual pang in his chest. It took him a moment to remember what that feeling was, and then it struck him.

It was guilt.

"Miss Burke, you are working too hard."

She raised her brows at this abrupt greeting. "Good day to you also, Lord Huntley."

"Papa, we are studying geography," Mattie said. "I can see on the globe where I was born, and where we are now. Do you know why it is colder here than in the islands?"

"Because God wants England to suffer?"

"*Ahem.*"

"I believe Miss Burke is trying to convey to me her disapproval of that answer."

"Indeed, Captain. Mattie knows why England is colder than the islands, don't you, Mattie?"

"We are farther north, Papa, and the farther away you go from this line here—"

"The equator," he said, but at the governess's scowl realized he should have let Mattie answer.

"Yes, Papa, the equator. The farther you go, the colder it gets. And right here, at Greenwich, that's where we measure all of east and west from. But you knew that."

"Indeed I did, child, measuring latitude and longitude is a sailor's life. We'll talk more about that later, but for now it's time for luncheon. Run along and wash, Mattie. I'd like a word with Miss Burke first."

When the child was gone, Robert stepped up to Lydia and put his hand beneath her chin, frowning at the fatigue he saw.

"You will hire a housekeeper, Lydia, before you work yourself to a nub. It is too much, trying to oversee the house and care for Mattie. I did not bring you here to slave away at getting Huntley in shape. That is what servants are for. The locals will be glad of the employment."

"Is it bad?"

"If Huntley were a ship, the captain would deserve being marooned by his own crew for mismanagement, theft, dereliction of duty... I received an education today, Lydia, on what happens when you only take money out of property and do not put any into growth and maintenance."

He stepped away from her and ran a finger over the globe, giving it a gentle spin on its stand. "Ships are in constant need of work and repair. Careening and scraping the hull, replacing rotted wood, mending the sails. If you don't care for your vessel, it becomes a death trap. At the very least, it won't serve you as it should. I suppose an estate is much the same, isn't it? No wonder so many boys dream of running away to sea, though of course, they're just replacing one set of tasks with another. Ah well, at least there's booty to be had at sea."

Lydia did not add that it had been his intention at one time to do the same thing as his brother and cousin—take what he could from Huntley and turn his back on the estate without another glance. Now, having seen the condition of the cottages, the hope in the eyes of the farmers who talked with him about what the land could do with proper seed and equipment, he felt that unknown feeling in his chest again.

The guilt was tempered by something else, a drive to succeed. He prided himself on reaching his goals, whether it was having the best wardrobe of any sea rover in the Caribbean (hardly a contest, given the competition), being the most favored patron at the most notorious brothel in the islands (ditto), or simply being alive each night with his limbs intact and the ability to fight another day—Robert thrived on success. Transferring his goals from shipboard to land management was not as much of a wrenching experience as he'd feared.

The hardest part would be not being able to deal out summary punishment to malefactors. As he'd learned today in his ride around the land, one couldn't simply maroon or flog people who didn't do as they should, who didn't evidence good self-preservation skills when confronted with Captain St. Armand. He'd already had a discussion with Cyrus Pilling, whose ramshackle dwelling and slovenly yard did not bother Robert nearly as much as the bruises on Mrs. Pilling's face. He took Pilling for a stroll and explained to him that if he wanted to continue in good health he'd keep his fists to himself. Robert made a mental note to mention it to Lydia. She could check on Mrs. Pilling more easily than he could. Sometimes women shared confidences about such things.

It was what Lydia would do if she were Lady Huntley.

And she would be Lady Huntley, he simply had not figured out the best way to make that a reality. One *could* carry off a bride and hold her captive until she said yes to his charms—he knew from experience that didn't always end well, but it was an option.

He could dangle Mattie as a lure, but that too wasn't enough. He wanted Lydia to stay because she wanted to stay with *him*. He was puzzled, naturally, as to why she did not fall into his arms without argument as so many others had done. He knew he wasn't losing his touch. Her cries of fulfillment in his arms last night, the way she gasped out his name when he used his mouth to bring her body arching off the mattress in delight, it told its own tale. The responses from the farmwives he'd met today satisfied him that his smiles still had the same effect on the female population they'd always had. It was just that one, nagging, annoying, prickly governess with her knowing jade eyes and her hair capturing sunlight in its strands and reflecting it like an autumn sunset, her delightfully long legs that wrapped around a man just so —she was the only woman he could not be sure of. His luscious, lovely, lickerish Lydia, who, whether she wanted to acknowledge it or not, was born for a pirate's life and to share a pirate's bed.

Now he needed to guarantee *he* was the pirate in her life.

Eliminating Thomas Wilson would be an excellent first step in making that happen, but he needed to woo Lydia, not just present bodies at her feet like a cat bringing its mistress a mouse.

"Do you want a hug?" he asked abruptly, turning away from the globe spinning like his thoughts.

Lydia paused from where she gathered books on the desk and stared at him. "A what?"

"A hug. An embrace."

She watched him, puzzled. It was not a difficult question, but suddenly the answer mattered a great deal. "Yes, Robert. I would like that very much."

She spoke softly, but it was as if a band constricting his chest loosened. She wanted a hug. From him. He opened his arms and she stepped into his embrace and he clasped her to him, feeling the tenseness in her body, and then the relaxation of her muscles as she sighed, and rested her head on his shoulder.

He knew his shoulders were broad. He'd admired his form enough in mirrors to understand the value of such things in swinging a cutlass or making a coat fit well, but now he was glad his shoulders were broad so she could lean on him. He could hold her and they could stand there together in the silent room, listening to each other's breathing and heartbeats.

But a pirate always wants more, doesn't he? That's why they seek more gold, more jewels, more riches, more wine.

This pirate did not want more women. He wanted the one who trusted him to hold her, to let him kiss her atop the hair that smelled of lemons, to place his fingers alongside the warm skin of her cheek and angle her face off of his shoulder so he could brush his lips across hers, coaxing her, lulling her, sneaking past the starchy barricade of her reticence to explore her mouth, to taste the passion she kept hidden but for him.

"Lovely," he murmured against those soft lips. "My lovely Lydia."

He eased her back against the desk, running his hand up her leg and raising her skirt but she moved her hand across his mouth when he would have resumed his exploration with his tongue.

"The open windows—the door—anyone could walk in."

"Marry me, Lydia."

She stiffened, then pushed against him.

Numbskull! He beat himself mentally. If he boarded ships as blindly as he just blurted out his command, he would have been skewered, shot or hanged long ago. It was strategy as well as skill which carried the day.

She pushed harder and he sighed and stepped back, adjusting his clothing because it was clear he wasn't going to get relief for his throbbing member any other way.

Lydia brushed down her skirts, then patted her hair.

"It is still pinned. No one will suspect anything."

She stopped and looked at him.

"We cannot make this situation worse, Robert—"

"Yes, yes, I know. I am good enough to sneak into your bed at night when the house is asleep, but not good enough to marry."

"What? That is insane!"

"Is it? Then what is your resistance, Lydia? Why do you keep pushing me away?"

"I will not be bullied into marrying anyone. I am tired of men pushing me around and telling me what to do! I will make up my own mind about what I want, and when I want it, and that reminds me—where are my wages? You promised —repeatedly—to pay me what I am owed and I am tired of asking for what is mine!"

She glared at him and he gritted his teeth to keep from saying what he feared. If he gave Lydia her wages she could leave him, go away, hide and begin her life anew. One did not make a successful career of piracy by letting others possess the weather gage.

He had to come up with a way to keep her here without her feeling bullied or pressured to stay. He had to find a way to convince her to stay because she wanted to be with him more than she wanted anything else.

Fortunately, there was a scratch at the door.

"Enter."

"Luncheon is served, m'lord."

"Thank you, William."

She gathered up her papers, a move that did not allow him to take her arm, and brushed past him and out the door behind the footman.

"Let us say there are two hundred and forty-two barrels of rum in a cave, and seven pirates. How do you divide the rum so each crewman gets his—or her—fair share?"

"If you slice one bugger open, it's only six, and that's easier to divide into an even number."

"Mr. Nash, you can't slice a shipmate open," Mattie scolded him. "Miss Burke's right, we need to figure out how to divide with odd pirates."

"Some of 'em are odder than others." Turnbull snickered, elbowing Nash. "Remember Gunner Goose?"

"Gentlemen, we need to concentrate. Mr. Nash, take your slate and show us how you would divide the rum among the actual number of pirates."

Nash hunched over his slate, the child-sized chairs in the schoolroom looking even sillier with the taller Turnbull perched atop it, and Lydia made a note to herself to have more adult seating brought in.

"There! It's thirty-four barrels for each pirate, with a remainder of four. Swive me, that's a good haul!"

Lydia rubbed the throbbing bit between her eyes. "If you would, share with the rest of the students how you did your work. Without oaths, if you please."

"I used my multiplication," Nash said proudly. "Because I could recite my tables I could look at it and know that seven, the...the..."

"Divisor," Mattie whispered.

"Right, the divisor. Seven times three is twenty-one and seven times four is twenty-eight, and since the first two digits in the"—he furrowed his brow in thought—"the dividend is twenty-four, that's bigger than twenty-one and smaller than twenty-eight, so it must be three first in the quotient."

"Hurrah!" Mattie said, clapping her hands.

"After that it was easy," Nash preened. "When you subtract down, twenty-one from twenty-four, you get three, you bring down the two for thirty-two, and seven goes into thirty-two four times. You write the four up top in the quotient and the answer is thirty-four with a remainder of four barrels!"

"That is correct, Mr. Nash. Well done!"

"Thank you, Miss Burke."

"Teacher's pet," Turnbull muttered under his breath.

"Sod off, ye beet lovin' bugger."

"Gentlemen! Remember you are in the classroom, not aboard the *Prodigal.*"

"Yes, Miss Burke," her errant pupils said in unison. A knock at the door interrupted the intricacies of long division, as Sally entered and asked if she and Mattie could join the master in the parlor. They had visitors.

"Do you know who it is, Sally?"

"It is Mr. Castle, the vicar over at All Saints, and his wife and they have their little girl with them."

Mattie looked intrigued at the idea of visitors. It would be her first encounter with the locals and she was no longer just a rough-and-tumble crew member of the *Prodigal Son.* Learning to navigate the rocky shoals of society was a task Mattie faced as she grew older. Robert knew this when they took the child from St. Martin to England, and all they could do now was stand by her if there were difficulties as she adjusted.

"Very well, Sally. Please tell Lord Huntley we will be down shortly, and if he has not already ordered tea, ask Mrs. Farmer to prepare a tray."

"Yes, miss."

"Mattie, wash your face and hands. Gentlemen, we are done for now. Here are some problems for you to work on tonight, and we will go over the answers tomorrow."

She passed them each a sheet of foolscap with problems in division, and reminded them that while they could assist one another, it did not mean copying answers.

LYDIA ENTERED the parlor holding Mattie's hand. The two of them looked so right together that it made Robert's heart stutter. He could not envision any other mother for Mattie. Nanette knew what she was doing putting Mattie in Lydia's care, and Robert sent a silent prayer of thanks to the dead prostitute who'd given him this most wonderful gift.

Robert and Mr. Castle rose to their feet to greet the ladies, and Robert did the introductions. He'd been suspicious when Braxton announced the visitors, but Martin Castle and his wife Susanna, a round woman with a substantial bosom Robert couldn't help but admire, appeared to be pleasant, ordinary people.

It was rather refreshing to socialize without worrying overmuch over about whether your visitors would attempt to kill you.

Their daughter Nell was quiet and sat patiently as the adults conversed while waiting for the others. Nell was flaxen haired and pink like her mother, and looked to be close to Mattie's age, but smaller. Given that the vicar was a good head shorter than Robert it was to be expected.

Mrs. Castle seemed fascinated by the earring Robert wore, and he couldn't resist giving her a wink when he caught her peeking, causing her to rosily flush. What was the fun of being a pirate if you couldn't brighten up the afternoon of a country lass, even if it went no further than a wink?

Now Mattie greeted their adult guests and walked straight over to Nell.

"I am Mattie St. Armand. Do you want to play pirates?"

Nell's eyes grew big as blue saucers and she nodded eagerly. "Oh yes, please! I want to be a pirate ever so much!"

"I'll be Anne and you can be Mary. Jolly—he's my puppy —was digging in the garden this morning—it might be buried treasure!"

"Mattie, Nell needs to ask permission of her parents before going off with you," Lydia corrected the child gently.

"Playing pirates sounds like a perfect idea," the vicar said with a smile. "There are many sunny afternoons, Miss Burke, when I'm sitting in the study wishing I was off playing pirate instead."

Susanna Castle reminded the girls not to go far, and had a hug from her daughter before the two skipped off to plot mayhem, passing Braxton and the maid with cakes and tea sent up from the kitchen.

Robert motioned the butler over. "Tell Paget to secure the weapons locker, Braxton. I would hate for the small pirates to become carried away with their adventures."

"Yes, m'lord."

Braxton was in his element, setting out the gleaming silver service for tea. He had a new spring in his step as Huntley was restored to a semblance of its former glory. If there were still moth-eaten draperies in need of refurbishment, at least the tables were dust free and freshly waxed, the windows sparkling in the autumn sunlight. Robert relaxed against his chair, watching Lydia pour from where she sat at the tea table. She was every inch the lady, far better than he could have ever hoped for with his dissolute ways. He could have won a bride with his looks, his social graces, his title and, of course, his money. That was never in question. He could not have hoped to win a woman like Lydia though, someone who would stand toe-to-toe with him and tell him when he was full of bilge-water.

Taking his role as lord of the manor no longer filled him with dismay or displeasure. He would always leave a part of himself on the water, but he'd brought home from his island adventures two of the greatest treasures he could imagine, a daughter of his heart, if not his name, and a woman whom he hoped would take his name and his heart for herself. When you added that to his already bountiful blessings—his amazing good looks, his *savoir faire*, his skill with his blade and the disposal of most of his enemies, he had much to be thankful for. He'd lived his life prodigally, but his welcome back to his home was all he could have hoped for.

He realized the vicar had been speaking while he ruminated and brought his attention back to the man.

"Yes, Mr. Castle, you can expect to see me at church this Sunday."

There was a rattle of china from across the carpet as the governess righted her fumbled teacup, fortunately empty yet.

"You startled me, Captain."

"That's right, you were a sea captain until recently, were you not, Lord Huntley?"

"I've been at sea for most of my life, trading here and there, but when word reached me of my brother's passing I knew I had to return to Huntley and take up my responsibilities."

Lydia still looked as if she expected a bolt of lightning to shoot down from heaven and fry him where he sat, so he ignored her and focused on his visitors. The vicar looked pleased at his intention to come to church. With his livelihood tied to the manor and its lord it meant a great deal to have the baron sitting in the family pew.

"It will be good for the village to have you join us, my lord. The past years since your father's passing have been difficult. The economic situation and the bad harvests have affected all of us, and the situation here at Huntley—" His voice trailed off but the frown on his placid face filled in the rest.

"Miss Burke, do you have family in this area?"

"No, I have lived in the West Indies for some years now."

She neglected to add where her family was, but the Castles said nothing and the talk turned to the village, its needs, and Robert asked about some of his tenants and gathered information on their situations. He could see Lydia warmed to the Castles and he asked them to supper, with Nell, in two days' time. Lydia sent him a look of approval and his chest expanded at her glance. It was the most prosaic of actions, inviting the vicar and his family to dine, but like a hug, it was one of those things that a man could do to demonstrate that he wasn't the worst candidate for marriage to cross her bow.

The girls bounced in, grimy and grinning from their piratical adventures, a furry white bundle weaving in and out and yipping in excitement. A promise of cakes after clean hands were presented sent them scurrying. Mrs. Castle looked at Robert, and she wouldn't have been human if her eyes hadn't darted to Lydia, but Mattie's heritage was written on her skin.

"Your daughter does not share your name, my lord?

THE PIRATE'S SECRET BABY

Forgive me, but it will be bound to come up in conversation in the village."

"Mathilde was born in the islands," Robert said easily. "Her mother died, so my daughter came to England with me." *And that's all anyone needs to know* was the unspoken remainder of that sentence.

"She seems to have found a fellow pirate with our daughter," Susanna Castle said easily. "If you bring her into town, Nell will introduce Mattie to the other youngsters. We have a village school, ma'am, and I teach the young children there. Perhaps you could visit sometime and speak about life in the islands?"

"I would be delighted to," Lydia said as the girls ran in, marginally cleaner, but enough to pass muster and get cakes to take up to the nursery. When Joan entered with more hot water for tea, Mr. Castle rose and said, "I am loathe to end such a pleasant afternoon, but I have other calls to make before sunset."

"You are welcome to leave Nell with us so the girls can continue playing," Lydia offered, but Mrs. Castle shook her head.

"I am afraid not, not today, but if you bring Mattie to the vicarage tomorrow I know Nell would like to show off some of her dolls. She's been learning to sew their clothes."

"Oh dear," Lydia said, "I'm afraid our sewing lessons are sometimes neglected for more physical activities, but Mattie is learning."

"She is young yet, and full of energy," Martin Castle said. "I would have preferred climbing trees to studying Latin at her age, so I cannot blame her. In fact, I'd still rather climb trees—or play pirate—than write prosy sermons, but now I don't have that freedom. Let the children be children is my motto. Their innocent state does not last long."

Robert wondered how the good reverend would feel

about the innocence of children if he saw Mattie's glee when she threw her knife square into the target's "heart." Lydia said that Mattie would be thrilled to visit, and if Mrs. Castle was good enough to watch the girls it would give her a chance to take care of some errands in the village.

"I will accompany you."

It came out more as a command than he'd intended, but he was firm on this point. After what he'd learned from Turnbull and Nash about Wilson, he wasn't about to let Lydia too far out of his reach until the threat was eliminated.

Lydia raised her brows at his tone, but said she'd be delighted to have his company.

"I have an idea," Susanna Castle said with look of pure innocence on her round face. "We could have an assembly in Ashwyn! It would be an opportunity for you to meet more of the people and it has been forever since we have had entertainment."

"You must forgive my wife," the vicar said with an indulgent chuckle. "She does love to dance, and the assembly rooms have been little used in the past years."

Robert knew he was expected to help fund the assembly rooms, especially if the village was in economic straits due to poor harvests and bad management. When he saw Lydia's face light up at the idea of dancing, and her animated discussion with her new friend, it was no hardship at all to say yes.

The ladies chatted together in the entryway while waiting for the gig to be brought around. It was misting again, and when Nell came down she was bundled into a coat with a scarf around her neck. She petted Jolly and listened to Mattie explain how she received the dog, and the two fathers watched fondly as the girls talked.

"It is good for Mattie to have friends her own age," Robert said. "I did not know how well she would settle here, but she and Nell seem to have found common ground."

"It is good for all of us to have you settled here, my lord. The land needs a steward who will preserve and care for it. When that happens, everyone prospers. Our proximity to the T&M makes us an area primed for growth, but the people still look to the local leaders for direction. One hears tales..." The vicar's voice trailed as he turned to Robert with a smile and said, "Your success as a sea captain precedes you, my lord. A little excitement in the village is a healthy tonic now and again. Just not too much excitement."

"I will do my best not to show up at church with a brace of pistols in my hands and a dagger clamped in my teeth," Robert said.

"The little boys will be sorely disappointed," Castle said as he put on his hat and helped his family into the cart.

"I will see you tomorrow, Nell!" Mattie called.

"Bring your cutlass, Mattie!"

"No," said four adult voices simultaneously, then with a laugh, Castle started his placid horse down the drive to their next visit.

Robert looked at Lydia and Mattie waving goodbye, *just like a family.* He liked that. It made a spot in his chest feel warm and safe, as if he was back in the parlor in front of the fire, not standing in a cold mizzle.

"Mattie, if you're not too worn out from playing, we still have time for knife practice."

"Out in the elements?"

"One must be prepared for all weather, Miss Burke. Danger does not always present itself in front of a cozy fire. However, even pirates might enjoy some hot drinks when they return."

"And ginger biscuits!" Mattie piped up.

"I will see to it," Lydia said. She no longer winced or made disapproving noises when they had weapons practice. Either the governess was becoming more piratical, or she'd resigned herself to accepting this as an appropriate father and daughter activity, which reminded Robert of something else he needed to do now that he was at Huntley.

"Do you ride, Miss Burke?"

"Of course, my lord. I was raised in the country."

"I need to get Mattie on horseback. If you did not order a riding habit in Liverpool, we need to have one made for you."

"My father taught me to ride," Lydia said with a soft smile of remembrance. "It is one of my favorite memories, the time we spent together."

"Mine also," Robert said in surprise. He'd forgotten those times with his father, good times. Alfred Huntley used to berate Ralph for being harsh with the horses, Nicholas for being skittish, but Robert he praised for his skilled hands on the reins. Riding brought father and son together, a period where they could forget Robert bore little resemblance to the rest of the Huntleys.

His childhood hadn't always consisted of canings in his father's study. He had land to roam, and Nicholas, and sometimes, the regard of his stern father. Would the late Lord Huntley be pleased to see Robert sitting in his seat? Robert knew what *would* have pleased his father—to see the estate properly managed again, its people cared for, a legacy restored for the next generation.

He looked at the woman walking beside him, her soft chestnut hair gleaming in the lamplight.

"Thank you," he said, the words popping out before he'd thought about them.

"For what?"

"For everything. For helping to make Huntley a home again. For taking such good care of Mattie."

He wanted to say more, but she watched him, evaluating his words, looking for hidden meanings, traps for unwary governesses. He wasn't certain himself what he meant. All he knew was that returning to Huntley, something he'd dreaded, had become a far different experience from what he'd feared and it was all due to the woman by his side.

Without Lydia, Huntley was simply a cold, worn pile of stones. With Lydia, it was a home. He had to ensure she would stay here, forever, with him and Mattie and their motley crew of pirates and puppies.

She left him to return to the nursery, and he watched her ascend the stairs, admiring her bottom, of course, but also thinking. The most successful and long-lived pirates don't get that way simply by being faster with a blade, one needed strategy as well.

It was time for Robert to hone his strategy beyond using his amazing handsomeness, bed skills and charm to win the lady. It still surprised him when he considered it, but that was no longer enough. Probably better that way. He wouldn't want her in his bed and his life only because he was so wonderfully attractive. After all, even the most accomplished of rakes and pirates eventually grow old and find themselves sucking in their guts or examining their thinning hair in the looking glass each morning. He needed to bind Lydia to his side for all time using more permanent methods.

Of course, his amazing handsomeness, bed skills and charm wouldn't hurt in the campaign and he'd enjoy his gifts while he still had them. He flashed the maidservant at the door a smile that had her dropping her feather duster.

Yes, it was good to know one still had all of one's skills.

CHAPTER 23

*R*obert didn't realize how smoothly he'd been steered until they entered their fifth shop on High Street. Mattie was enjoying herself with Nell, and so far he and Lydia had been to the draper's (pins), the grocer (tea), the tavern (ale for the manor), apothecary (headache powders) and now they were standing in front of the blacksmith's.

"You need an iron hinge?"

"You see it right here on my list, my lord: 'hinge for kitchen door.' Mrs. Farmer mentioned it to Braxton, and since I was coming to Ashwyn, I offered to drop by the blacksmith and let him know."

"Miss Burke, I know how to spot a ruse when it's in front of me. You intend to visit every shop in the village, don't you?"

"No," she said for his ears alone, "I intend for *Lord Huntley* to visit every shop in the village. Now, let's take care of that hinge."

So Robert followed her into the smithy, where they heard the clang of metal from the back. A young woman with a babe on her hip came out to the front of the shop and her eyes grew large at the sight of her visitors.

"My Lord Huntley!" she said and bobbled an awkward curtsey that made the babe crow and wave a fist in the air, clutching a pewter ring he then shoved in his mouth and began gnawing.

Robert removed his hat. "How did you know who I was, Mrs…?"

"Rostron, sir. Janet Rostron. There's my husband, George," she said with a toss of her head to the back, and she smiled, bringing the freckles on her nose and cheeks into prominence.

"And who else would you be, sir? A fine and handsome gentleman, newly arrived in our village. I also had tea with Mrs. Castle this morning," she added. "You must be Miss Burke."

"I am indeed," Lydia said. "That is a handsome boy you have there."

"Little George," Mrs. Rostron said with an indulgent glance at the drooling baby. "He's going to be big as his da someday."

Big George emerged from the back of the smithy, ducking so he wouldn't smack his head against the lintel. If the child was on his way to becoming large as his father, he had a ways to go. The massive smith looked capable of molding a hinge with his fingers alone.

Robert offered his hand and the blacksmith took it, and Robert appreciated having his hand back uncrushed.

"You have calluses, my lord," the blacksmith rumbled. "Not what I expect from the gentry."

"I was a sea captain long before I came into my title. Being Huntley is a new position for me as well."

"This is Miss Burke, Lord Huntley's governess," Mrs.

Rostron said, jouncing the baby on her hip. "There is a little girl?"

"My daughter," Robert said crisply, but neither Rostron appeared interested in Mathilde's origins.

"I hear there is to be an assembly soon." Janet grinned. "Mr. Clegg heard it from Mary who works at the vicarage. That would be the Mary who's sister to your Martha at the manor."

"For such a quiet spot, word travels fast."

"You are adding excitement to Ashwyn," Lydia said. "It's to be expected."

"I live to add excitement to peoples' lives."

Rostron said he'd come out to Huntley to have a look at the hinge, and Lydia said she'd have a list for him of other repairs for which they'd need his skilled services.

As they exited the smithy Robert turned to her and said, "You have a skill with people, Miss Burke."

"You do also, Captain."

"I certainly have enough charm to get my way most of the time—really, must you make that snorting noise?"

"I cannot help it."

"As I was saying, I can charm, but you are good at—" He thought about it, trying to phrase it properly. "You are good at people. I am always looking out for my own advantage, or my own safety, but you are skilled at understanding people in a different way. You are skilled at making people comfortable and at ease."

"What a lovely compliment," she said, a glow in her moss-green eyes lighting an answering glow in his chest, in the region of his heart. They returned to the vicarage to collect Mattie, and Mrs. Castle gave them the particulars of the upcoming assembly.

"There is much excitement among the younger set, and

the older folk said they remember well when Huntley was the site of a festival each wakes week, my lord."

"I shall make it a goal for Huntley to once again host a festival next year, Mrs. Castle."

Mattie and Nell came running down the steps and while Nell still wore a pinafore, she had an eye patch and a wooden sword, as did Mattie.

"Look, Papa! Nell's papa had these packed away. He said he'd been saving them for when Nell has a little brother, but we explained how silly that was when there are two girls who could play with them now and he agreed. Then we tied up a doll and held her for ransom and we wanted to dress Nell's cat Snowball as a pirate, but Snowball ran off to the kitchen."

"Cats have a strong instinct for self-preservation," he said.

Lydia confirmed plans for the Castles to come to supper and they headed back to Huntley.

It was one of those perfect autumn days helping Robert see there were some attractions to living in England. The crisp air and the colors of the landscape were a change from the languid humidity and heat of the islands, heat that brought fevers raging through populations in that unhealthy climate. It was better for Mattie to be here, and each day he felt as if he was shedding a shell that formed around him when he turned his back on his native land. As a youth he only longed to be away, but as a man, as a father and a landholder, he saw his life here with a new eye, one that appreciated a life where excitement came in the form of village dances, not at the end of a blade.

It was a better life for Mattie, for him, and by all that was holy, he'd make it a better life for Lydia Burke as well.

Their carriage was well maintained, as Ralph had no doubt wanted to travel in style and comfort. The horses too were good stock and as they traveled the short distance back to the manor he breathed deep of the scents of a familiar place, a place he never knew he'd longed for until he returned.

He glanced at the woman at his side, the child snuggled against her for warmth. She looked at him from beneath her attractive cottage bonnet of lavender sarcenet, headgear finally enhancing her attractiveness rather than disguising it, and she smiled at him. It looked like a smile saying nothing more than, "I am glad I am here beside you at this moment," and he knew that might be the most important smile he'd ever seen.

LYDIA AND MATTIE were already dressed for church and eating breakfast when Robert joined them the next morning.

"Papa, I have not been to church in ever so long. Will it be like St. Martin with Father Jacques?"

"You will find some things familiar, some things different, child. I confess that I have not been to church in so long much of it will be new to me as well. We can learn together."

"I suspect it will gratify Mr. Castle—as well as the Almighty—to have you in All Saints, my lord. In these villages it means a great deal to have the baron in his pew at Sunday worship."

"No matter what he's been up to on Saturday night, Miss Burke?"

She blushed again and it fascinated him. It was as if she was able to leave all of that starchy governessing behind once she entered the bedroom, and don it again when she was out in public. The parts of Miss Lydia Burke made for a fascinating whole, one he intended to explore further, for many more years. He knew what he wanted, and he'd never let obstacles keep him from his goals. There were many ways he

THE PIRATE'S SECRET BABY

could ensure she was spliced to his side and accompanying her and Mattie to church would help in that campaign.

She'd have to make up her mind soon. Last night all their delightful play caused him to forget himself and spend inside her. He had no need to prove his virility—proof was sitting beside him with strawberry jam smeared on her rosy little cheeks—but the idea of Lydia carrying his babe, her belly rounding and her already lush bosom becoming fuller was an image that struck him as highly desirable. She would not be happy though if she felt forced to marry, not an independent soul like her. Lydia Burke was not the kind of woman who could be carried off like a treasure chest.

No, he would have to make changes in his life. Be Huntley, not St. Armand. Toddling off to church was an excellent first step.

He'd dressed for church, not to make a piratical statement, and was pleased with himself. Sober tobacco brown coat, conservative cream striped waistcoat, the smallest of plain gold rings through his ear. It was a good disguise and he saw some of the older ladies, who everyone knew were the real power brokers in any small village, nod in approval as they entered All Saints.

The Reverend Mr. Castle, as predicted, was pleased to see Lord Huntley in his pew. After worship he made a point of introducing Robert to people he hadn't yet met and Robert could tell from their looks that his reputation preceded him despite the protective coloration he'd donned for the Sabbath.

He watched his daughter with concern. Mattie seemed completely unaware her status as the bastard child of an island mother and a pirate caused some of the townsfolk to look askance at her. Based on the looks the governess turned back on these individuals he knew if Lydia had a basilisk's power they'd be stone statues now.

The children didn't care. The boys in particular seemed fascinated by Mattie's chatter about life aboard ship, and no wonder.

"Mattie, I don't recall anyone getting devoured by sharks on our voyage to England. I'm certain I would have remembered such a thing."

"Maybe not on this voyage, Miss Burke, but I am sure *someone* has been eaten by sharks, maybe even tossed over the side by Mr. Turnbull and Mr. Na—"

"Ladies, I believe it is time for us to return home," Robert said, coming to the aid, once again, of the beleaguered governess. She flashed him a grateful look, a gesture that did not go unnoticed by the ladies. Lydia's reputation was already at risk in his household. Steering her to a safe harbor was becoming more imperative with each day they dwelled here.

The church service seemed to be the signal people had been awaiting to pay calls at Huntley. Some of it was curiosity about the manor, some was motivated by curiosity about Robert. Fortunately for him, he was away most afternoons following up on the improvements to the estate. Fuller accompanied him on these rounds, and after a week Robert formalized the situation by offering his friend the position of steward, which the older man accepted.

"Mind you, you could probably do better with someone with more experience in land management," Fuller said.

"Perhaps, but it wouldn't be someone I trust as much as I trust you. Being mate of the *Prodigal Son* prepared you for management. Much of the rest of it you'll learn as you go on —we both will."

Robert looked out the library window to where Lydia and Mattie sat together in an overgrown flower garden, coats and scarves on against the November air, but warmed by the steady sunshine. They were examining a red leaf together, and Lydia gestured with her hand to a copse of trees nearby.

He turned away from the nature lesson to see Fuller's lined eyes watching him.

"Neither one of us ever expected this, did we?"

"No, Horace, we did not."

Robert walked to the decanter on the table, pouring them both a tot of rum. Brandy might be the gentleman's drink, but the burn of rum brought back memories of fair winds and following seas. He raised his glass.

"To us then. Two prodigals who survived to return home and resume our places."

"We've done better than that," Horace Fuller said, downing his drink. "We've prospered. Much of what I have I owe to you, Captain. You had a knack for knowing which strikes would be rich hauls, and which ones could end with us standing before the hangman. At that time I wouldn't have traded it, not for all the safety and security of a life in Lancashire.

"So. When will you and Miss Burke marry?"

"Is it that obvious?"

"Only to anyone with eyes. The crew will make you walk the plank if you don't take that woman as your bride. There are few women who'd put up with you—and them—and Mattie as well."

The dog had been sleeping in the sun, but when Mattie stood Jolly began romping around her until she threw his rawhide toy so he could chase it and fetch it back.

"I worry about Mattie," Robert said to his oldest friend. "We know life in an English village is difficult for people who are different."

"Another reason for you to wed the governess as quickly as possible. Raising Mattie in a well-established and soon-to-be respectable household will surely benefit her."

Robert nodded silently as he took another drink, then set his glass aside. He smiled to himself as he thought about how he'd never again run up charges for liquor as he had at Madame Olifiers. He didn't regret that last debauch, though he truly wished he could recall details of his night with the "twins," but he also knew he wasn't that person anymore. Captain St. Armand had been superseded by a baron who held the lives of dependents in his hands—his females, his household, his community. That person could not afford to drink himself into a stupor.

Huntley took on more of a shine each day, and the staff turned to Lydia without question as mistress of the house. It was a position the vicar unsubtly mentioned when he stood next to Robert in the assembly rooms over the tavern.

"Do you enjoy being at All Saints, Mr. Castle, or are you ready to move on to a living elsewhere?"

The clergyman smiled without rancor, an unusual response to one of Robert's threats. He must be losing his touch in this bucolic setting.

"I would not be the shepherd All Saints needs if I didn't raise a rather obvious issue, my lord. I like Miss Burke. More importantly, Susannah likes the lady, and I will get no peace from my wife if she suspects her friend is not being treated with all due respect. Then of course I worry for you, my lord, since you too are a member of my flock."

The lady in question—the pirate's lady, not the vicar's—was being squired through a vigorous country-dance by Mr. Clegg, a diminutive soul who nonetheless showed great skill on the dance floor and was much in demand by the ladies. Everyone in the village who could move was at the assembly. The musicians were also locals, and what they lacked in skill they made up for in enthusiasm. No one seemed to mind a dropped note or a missed beat, they were having too much fun. The older ladies sat together and gossiped, and he suspected the newest residents of the town were the focus of much of it. No doubt they were rehashing every rumor about his parents, Nicholas, Ralph, and for all he knew, the Huntleys going back to the Conquest. Some of them looked ancient enough to have been on shore to greet the Normans.

When they'd entered the assembly rooms, there was a gratifying sigh from all the ladies present as Robert stood in the entranceway and Mr. Clegg, serving as the master of ceremonies, announced them.

His evening wear bore little similarity in either cut or fabric to that worn by the other gentlemen. The breeches were silk, as was his black evening coat, so closely tailored Sails was needed to wedge him into it. The waistcoat of gold embroidered satin glowed against the crisp white cambric shirt, and his neckcloth was tied in a fashion that he knew the younger men would be attempting at home later. He wore a gaudy emerald studded order pinned to his chest, another gift from the grateful Mexican revolutionaries, and a filigreed gold ring with smaller emeralds in his ear. The jewelry was set off by his hair newly styled *ala* Brutus. Hiring Sails as his valet was a brilliant move, as the man was a wizard with a blade, whether cutting canvas, disemboweling foes or trimming Robert's hair.

Robert drew all eyes with his piratical splendor, but he only had eyes for the woman on his arm.

She wore her new willow-green silk, which while not as dramatic as his attire was charmingly becoming. The soft color set off her creamy skin and made her hair catch highlights of russet and gold in its chestnut depths. The gown was trimmed with silver cord under the bodice, and silver flowers and cord lavished the hem, drawing eyes to her neat ankles and dancing slippers with silver ribbons. She looked like a woodland sprite. Lydia would not let him deck her in any of the jewels he had on hand, but wore her grandmother's cameo on a silver chain. Her hair was dressed in plaits coiled at the back of her head, and a satin fillet trimmed with the green ribbons purchased in Liverpool was twisted through the shining braids.

How had he ever thought her drab? Her beauty shone, not in flamboyant parrot fashion as his did, but in a dove-like softness that might have looked muted in the tropics, but was perfectly suited to Huntley.

Mattie passed approval on her father and her governess before they left for the evening. Nell was spending the night with her at Huntley, making up for any disappointment over the girls not attending the revels in town. Recent developments brought a quiet word from Robert to Sails, who'd keep watch over the ladies, and he expected Fuller would check on them as well. Mrs. Farmer also agreed to watch over the youngsters, declaring that her corns would never allow her to dance and if she were going to sit, she'd just as soon do it in front of a warm fire at Huntley having a pleasant coze with that nice Mr. Sails.

Nash and Turnbull may have been ready to set to sea again, but some of the others were content to make a home at Huntley for now. Norton took on the coachman's position, and also looked after the stables with the assistance of a weedy boy from Ashwyn who was grateful for the chance to work with the horses and help out his widowed mother. Conroy was accruing a following amongst the village lasses, and Robert hoped he wouldn't be called on to deal with any angry fathers in the near future. He'd also have a talk with Conroy to determine what the young man intended to do with himself if he stayed.

When he'd mentioned this to Lydia she looked at him with approval, it being more evidence of his entry into life as lord of the manor.

"My crew is my crew," he'd responded, "on land or on sea."

"Then you are different from many sea captains I knew in the islands who'd cut their men loose with no concern about their welfare. You have difficulty seeing yourself here, but you were born to this role, Robert Huntley."

Now that lady was being escorted back to his side, her cheeks pink and glowing from her dancing.

"I believe the next dance is ours, my lord."

"I have been counting the minutes until this time, Miss Burke."

She cocked an eyebrow at his florid response, but took his hand without further comment. They stepped out onto the floor as the musicians started to play something in waltz-time, not perfectly, but well enough that they could waltz without suffering too much.

"Have I told you yet tonight how beautiful you are?"

She looked up at him warmly as he clasped her in his arms, her trim waist feeling exactly right beneath his gloved hand, her eyes shining up at him in the candlelight. She did not need jewels, not with those glowing emerald eyes, that pearly smile, the soft coral blush in her cheeks.

Even so he could envision her draped in ropes of pearls—and nothing else—and hoped to see that vision for himself someday. Soon. There was a conversation they needed to have, one that could change everything, but she'd been so excited about the assembly, her and Mrs. Castle plotting together with some of the ladies of the village, that he'd put it off, unwilling to do anything that would affect her enjoyment.

That was his mission in life now, not to be the best pirate, or the most favored client of a brothel in the Caribbean, but to be the man who'd keep Lydia Burke safe, who'd always be there for her, to protect and guard her from life's turmoil.

～

LYDIA COULD NOT REMEMBER an evening when she'd so enjoyed herself. Perhaps she never had, because while she'd known men who were handsome, or capable, or excellent dancers, she'd never known Robert Huntley. Now though, she knew him, and she knew there was no other man who'd ever be able to give her what Robert could.

Tonight he drew all the ladies' eyes to him, but his eyes were only for her. The way he looked at her now, the deep regard she saw in his heated glance warmed her to her core. Joan had helped her prepare for the evening and showed the makings of a lady's maid. She was cunning with hair and Lydia acknowledged there were times when having a servant to assist one was a wonderful asset. When she'd come down the steps and found Robert waiting for her the look on her face told her even more than her looking glass that she was attractive. His regard was a heady and potent wine, especially now when he looked down at her, her gloved hand clasped in his as he skillfully twirled her across the floor. If there were other dancers she did not see them, only Robert filled her senses, the warmth of his lithe body next to hers, the heat in his eyes and the way his mouth made her want to stop moving, reach up, and pull him down for a passionate kiss.

His pupils darkened as some of what she was thinking was reflected in her face.

"My clothing is closely tailored, Lydia. If you keep looking at me like that, I will never get off the dance floor without embarrassing someone."

"Yourself?"

"Please. I am justifiably proud of my cockstands, not embarrassed by them. I would not wish to be responsible for giving Mrs. Baker a heart seizure."

Lydia glanced to the side. The old lady was fanning

herself quite vigorously as she watched them and gossiped with the woman at her side, and Lydia moved in Robert's arms a few inches away, mourning the loss of their close bodies but knowing it was for the greater good.

So she enjoyed the waltz, her favorite dance, though she'd never enjoyed it as she did now in the arms of her pirate. He danced as he did all things, with skill, flair and purpose, but the set look on his face, the determination, made her forget she was a governess and he a lord, that once she'd been rejected by everyone dear to her. What mattered now was that she mattered to this man, *she* was the prize the pirate coveted, and in his arms she felt safe, and loved.

The music stopped, eventually, as it always does, and if she'd remained in his arms any longer she would be kissing him and *that* would give the good people of Ashwyn something to discuss. Instead, she allowed him to lead her off the floor to where her next partner awaited her, and where Turnbull awaited him.

Lydia tried to follow their movements but the men stepped outside, and when they returned Robert was alone and did not look like anything of importance had been discussed. If anything, he looked pleased with himself so she relaxed through the steps of the quadrille and thought nothing more of it.

By the time the evening ended everyone was looking a little less formal, the young men had clearly found a way to augment the punch, and the general consensus was the Ashwyn assembly had been a rousing success. A few brave souls unsubtly mentioned the wonderful harvest balls hosted at Huntley and the wakes week holiday, and their lord assured all he'd keep it in mind as the seasons moved through the year.

In general the townsfolk had a new air of purpose. Lydia'd overhead discussions of mill building and canal-shipping, and with judicious investments and skilled management the area would revive with Robert's input. It gave her a glow, to know her pirate was the man the people looked to and depended upon. He had been born to this role, no matter what he thought, and she was glad she had played a part in bringing him home.

Seeing him here tonight in his element was another reminder that her presence could cost him and be a distraction if they wed. She owed him, and Mattie, more than that. He would move on with his life if she left him. Eventually, she would find peace for herself, though she knew there would always be a pirate-sized hole in her heart that no other man would be able to fill. Making difficult choices was not easy, but she'd learned the hard way to make those choices that had the best outcome for her and for the people she cared about. Leaving would be the most difficult thing she'd ever done, but if there was an ocean separating them, it would be easier.

The ride back was silent and after handing the horses off to the sleepy lad in the stables, Robert took Lydia's arm and escorted her in. Braxton had waited up for them, insisting it was his responsibility to lock up at night, and they didn't argue with the old man whose pride was an almost tangible thing now that Huntley was undergoing restoration.

Lydia checked on the sleeping Mattie and Nell and dismissed Joan for the night after she helped her out of her lovely frock. The green silk glowed in the soft firelight, a reminder of springtime to come, and as she pulled pins from her hair she thought about where life might find her when the seasons turned.

The hairpins were carefully placed in a dish on the mantel. Keeping track of her hairpins and caps was still an issue as both had a tendency to wander off. She'd found one of her plain cloth caps in Jolly's bed two nights ago and it was unlikely the dog pulled open the wardrobe and fetched it himself.

On the other hand, there was a sheer lawn nightrail in place of the cap in her wardrobe, a sleeveless and cunningly embroidered garment fit for a courtesan. She had just dropped that nightrail over her head when Robert entered the room, closing the door and leaning against it, arms crossed over his chest. He was dressed in his robe, the open neck drawing her eyes to the column of this throat and down to a glimpse of his muscled chest. He never wore a nightshirt to bed, and knowing all of Robert Huntley was on display beneath the brocade of his robe made her lick her lips, a movement bringing a smile to his own lips, a smile that made her breasts feel fuller, her nipples tight and sensitive. She could feel that smile in her belly, as if his lips were there, tracing their way down to her core.

She picked up a cloth and wet it in the still warm water left by the maid, wringing it out, then running the cloth over her neck and her arms as she watched her lover in her mirror.

She wanted to tell him how she felt about the evening, how it would be a memory she'd hold in her heart forever, even as she feared she'd soon be on the run again, seeking a safe haven far from all she held dear. She didn't want to use her words to show how much she cared, she had better methods at her disposal.

He came over to her, picked up her wrapper and put it about her, tying it at her waist.

"I will wait for you in my room."

She sighed, hating sneaking around in the middle of the night, and he kissed her on the forehead and said, "Soon this will not be an issue, Lydia. You will see."

She started to say something, but he put his finger across her lips.

"Do not ruin the magic of this evening, my dear hedge-hog. Pretend, just for now, that there are no barriers between us, that we are free to love one another as we wish. And trust me."

He smiled at her expression. "I know. Generally when I say 'trust me,' it's good to also have a weapon at hand. Tonight we will simply be Robert and Lydia, two lovers. Two friends."

She only nodded at this, saying nothing more. Tonight they would continue the magic, the joy of being together as lovers, and as friends. If she could not have everything, she could have this.

CHAPTER 24

*L*ydia received a summons the next afternoon and she smoothed her hair and looked in the mirror to be certain she was presentable before she joined her employer in his library.

She looked more than presentable, she had to acknowledge, she looked better than she'd looked in years—if ever. Her eyes had a glow to them, the slight lines of tension tightening her face were eased, her new frocks flattered her and made her look like the lady she would have been had she not run off with Edwin.

But had she not run off with Edwin, she never would have met Nanette Lestrange and Mathilde. She never would have met Captain Robert St. Armand the pirate, who changed before her eyes into Lord Robert St. Armand Huntley of Huntley Manor.

She'd like to think that if her path had crossed Robert Huntley's there still would have been an attraction between them, but she could not be sure of that. She was attracted to the pirate before she was attracted to the lord, and she suspected part of his attraction to her initially was the mystery she presented, the Englishwoman in the islands who had no good explanation for how she ended up so far from home.

"Come," Robert said at the knock on his library door. He looked up from the notes on his desk, and ushered Lydia to a chair, then he came around and sat on the edge of the desk, watching her.

"I am meeting tonight with Thomas Wilson," he said without preamble.

Lydia gasped and covered her mouth with her hand. "Wilson is here? I must leave—"

"Calm down, Lydia," he said, looking as if he'd just announced it would rain in the morning. "You are not going anywhere. I will meet Wilson, I will settle this, and tomorrow it will no longer be a problem."

"What? How can you say that? Are you going to kill him?"

"Would you mind?"

Lydia knew her hesitation was wrong, but she *had* been living aboard a pirate ship for weeks and some of their attitudes were bound to infect her. She felt compelled to add, rather lamely, "It can cause problems, willy-nilly disposing of people, Captain."

He just smiled, a look that said while they weren't in the middle of the Atlantic ocean, willy-nilly disposing of unpleasant people still was not a problem for him.

"Where are you meeting him?"

"At the tavern. He sent a note last night to Lord Huntley, informing me he has information and it is in my best interest to meet with him. As you know, Miss Burke, I always do what is in my own best interests."

"This isn't amusing," she snapped. "The man is dangerous."

Robert leaned forward, put his fingers under her chin and tilted it up. "Lydia, *I* am dangerous. Wilson is an annoyance. Stop fretting. I said I would take care of Wilson, and I will."

"I want to be there," Lydia said abruptly.

He leaned back and crossed his arms over his chest. He looked about to deny her this, but then asked, "Why?"

"Because, it is my problem. If I cannot stop Wilson myself, I at least need to see with my own eyes how you deal with it."

"The evening could end unpleasantly."

"Again, it is still ultimately my responsibility, Captain— my lord. Do you think I would stay here idly, wringing my hands while you ride off to fight my battles?"

"What I think, my dear Lydia, is that you have been infected with some of the spirit of Anne Bonny and Mary Read yourself."

She was about to deny any connection between herself and those lady malefactors, but she could not. They were women who'd refused to stand idly by, wringing their hands while their men fought for them. Had not Mary Read fought a duel to save her lover? Hadn't Anne Bonny beaten the man who attempted to take liberties with her? Lydia was, after all, one of the crew of the *Prodigal Son*. She practically owed it to the spirits of Anne and Mary to be at the meeting with Wilson.

"I will accompany you tonight, Captain. Sally will watch over Mattie while we're out."

Lydia stood, wondering what one wore to meet with one's blackmailer. She almost wished she had a wardrobe like Anne and Mary—much better for intimidating people.

"One other thing… You will not be in the room when I meet with Wilson. You can hear what we have to say from the parlor." He held up a hand when she started to protest. "I have plans, and having you in the room will interfere with those plans. If you accompany me, I will insist on this. If you intend to be one of my crew tonight, you will follow my commands. Even Mattie knows what happens to crew who disobey orders. You don't want to be sent to bed without your supper, do you?"

Lydia said nothing to this, but as she had her hand on the door to leave she suddenly stopped and turned around.

"You knew this last night, didn't you? When Turnbull came to the assembly—" she drew herself up to her full height and pointed an accusing finger at him. "You made love to me last night without saying a word, you scoundrel!"

He leaned back in his chair and had the audacity to grin at her. "When a stunningly attractive woman enters my room wearing nothing beneath her robe but a sheer garment showing off her luscious form, all the ability to think pours out of my brain. I'm certain I meant to say something, but then I was distracted."

"You are an…an annoying beet!"

"A direct hit, Miss Burke. Close the door behind you so I may lick my wounds in private."

CHAPTER 25

he Knight's Head was enjoying steady business when the traveler entered and paused to scan the room. There were clusters of drinkers near the welcoming heat from the blackened fireplace, and Johnny Gibson gave him a cheery nod and said, "Evenin', sir! Good night to be out of the wind."

The stranger's own smile sat firmly in place. He knew the tavern keeper would see a nondescript individual, clothes slightly worn but clean, thinning brown hair sprinkled with gray when he removed his hat, a face that was friendly without being obsequious.

Thomas Wilson worked hard to cultivate that image. It helped him in his tasks for the Home Office, the tasks the government knew of.

It also helped him in his supplemental profession, the one the government did not know of. Collecting payments for information he gathered was all well and good, but there were individuals who were much more generous than his overseers in London were, individuals who'd pay well—and often—to keep information about their personal and political peccadilloes hidden.

He was confident Lord Huntley would either pay to keep his "governess," if that was indeed the whore's job, or he would throw her out. And if that happened, Thomas would be waiting for her. They had unfinished business, he and Lydia Burke, and he could be satisfied with a pound of flesh in lieu of payment, though if he played his cards right, he might get both—sweet Lydia and Huntley's money. The night ahead proved most promising, but he only took ale, nothing stronger, because he didn't want to get bosky when there was money at stake.

"I am meeting someone," he said, pushing a coin across to the tavern keeper. "I do not wish to be disturbed. Do you have a private parlor?"

"Afraid it's not available," Gibson said, pocketing the money before Wilson could take it back. "If you take that table"—he gestured with his rag to a shadowy corner near the parlor—"you'll have some privacy. Not as much warmth there, but good for quiet conversation."

Wilson grunted. It would have to do. He wanted to slip out of Ashwyn without anyone remembering him, so he settled at the corner table and sipped his ale while taking stock of the room. There were a few rough-looking types, but most were what you'd expect to find in a village of this size—farmers, merchants, craftsmen. Four sat at a table playing cards, a handful gathered at the dartboard, one older man with graying hair sat reading.

Wilson stretched his legs out and settling in, contemplated the wonderful things he'd do with the baron's blunt. Travel would be pleasant. He could visit France, where English silver was especially welcome now that the war was ended. Italy was warm, and one heard stories of how talented the doxies were in the Roman brothels.

A flurry at the door caught his attention, and someone entered who could only be Huntley. The man's clothes were better quality than the other patrons, but to the London man the poor fit and lack of style had "bumpkin" stitched into the fabric.

As he made his way to the table, Huntley exchanged greetings with a few of the patrons and Wilson rose to his feet. Huntley shook hands with a quizzical smile on his face, then sat.

"Mr. Wilson, I confess I am full of curiosity as to the news you said you had of Miss Burke, my daughter's governess."

Thomas settled back comfortably. He was in his element now. Having hooked his fish, it was time to reel him in.

"...And so, my lord, that's the full story as I know it," he said in low, confidential tones. "Your governess was the light o' love of a man who was not her husband, and bad enough as that was, her involvement with radicals could follow her here. One hears things in London," he said hesitantly, "isolated as you are here in the country you may not be aware of how seriously the government takes these activities."

"My dear Wilson! I am so pleased you have contacted me. My Mathilde is a delicate and impressionable child. One shudders to think what would happen to her if she's exposed to anything less than the best influences."

"In that case, perhaps I can help you with your problem, my lord. I can persuade Miss Burke to leave with me and then you won't need to deal with this unpleasantness. I have connections, contacts. I can ensure her whereabouts aren't discovered and no one knows of your having kept her under your roof."

"Miss Burke would go with you?"

"Indeed, sir. I hesitate to mention this, but she and I had dealings when she was living in the city. She pursued me most vigorously, but I was not about to tie myself to a woman of that stamp. I have no doubt she continues to have enough fondness for me that she'll accompany me. Unfortunately, I do not have sufficient funds to undertake her travel expenses. In addition, I'm afraid it cut into my meager resources to travel all the way up here to meet you and there are people who want to know where she's been hiding herself. They may offer me financial incentives to share information, and I would hate to bring your name into the conversation. I know you have to think of your reputation, and of course, the reputation of your daughter."

"I see," said Huntley, frowning. "You would like a payment to stay quiet?"

"I would term it a gift of appreciation, my lord."

Wilson looked around the tavern, satisfied with how he'd presented his case to this rustic flat. The room was emptier than when he'd sat. The cardplayers were still at the table, as was the older man with his book, but the others had left. In fact, the tavern keeper himself was leaving, with a nod to one of the card players.

A chill ran down Wilson's spine. Something wasn't right.

He looked at the baron, who sat, calmly watching. Wilson start to rise from his chair, but two hands on his shoulders shoved him back down.

He glanced up and behind him. The older man stood there, looking at Huntley.

"Thank you, Mr. Fuller. Now the fun begins."

Fuller moved to a chair at Thomas's back and sat, and Thomas could feel his eyes boring into the back of his head as he watched him. He ran a finger around his suddenly too tight collar.

"Fun?"

"Why, yes, Wilson. I've enjoyed your tale this evening. Most entertaining. I especially enjoyed the part where you suggested I show my appreciation in the form of a monetary gift, because that's something I understand quite well. However, I did not come here to allow you to bleed me of my gold, and I certainly cannot allow you to abscond with my governess."

He sat back and gazed at Thomas almost benevolently, but a wild glance around the room showed the others seated there were not looking benevolent at all.

"Why then?" he croaked.

"Do you think you found me by chance, Wilson, or through your own skills? You are not that intelligent. You were directed here, much as a steer is led to the slaughter-house. You may recall my men over there, the ones who stood you a round in London."

He pointed out two of the darts players. One was a tall, bald mulatto, the other ginger-haired and missing two fingers on his left hand. Thomas remembered them. They were sailors off a ship newly arrived from the Caribbean.

"*The Prodigal Son*," he whispered in rising horror. "You are the pirate St. Armand."

"Nonsense," the pirate said, with a smile out of Thomas's nightmares. "I am Huntley, everyone knows that. Gibson knows it, which is why he was willing to give me the use of his establishment this evening."

"You can't try anything," Thomas protested. "There's someone in the private parlor."

"Indeed there is, and I imagine that person has been listening to our conversation tonight with great interest."

He raised his voice at the end of this and to Thomas's dismay, Lydia Burke stepped out. She was more mature than the apprehensive girl who'd fled his grasp, and she did not look cowed or scared now. Rather, she looked ready to injure him again and he hunched over, protecting his gonads.

"Since I'm Huntley and not this St. Armand fellow, I understand I must challenge you to a duel for insulting this lady. If I were a pirate, I would just dispose of you, but I'm willing to give you a fighting chance."

"You do not need to battle this man on my behalf," Lydia Burke said, scowling.

"I must have *some* reason. Sails, why am I challenging this bilge rat to a duel?"

"His waistcoat's ugly, Cap'n—I mean my lord. Ugly enough to make birds fall from the trees dead with horror."

"There you have it, Wilson. I cannot allow you to walk around slaughtering innocent larks. You will meet me tomorrow morning, at dawn, for your insults to the lady, and on behalf of the birdies. It does not matter whether you choose swords or pistols," he said, waving his hand negligently. "I have a great deal of experience dispatching faster, smarter, and stronger men than you. This is what will happen... If you bring swords I will first disable your arms, then slice low across your belly. With your arms injured you will find it difficult to tuck your guts back in, trust me on this. If you bring pistols I will blow your balls off. That is not always a fatal wound. You may survive, whether you want to or not. If you bring clubs, I will club you until your brains spatter my boots. Then I will sit down and eat a hearty breakfast. I love mornings that start that way."

Thomas wiped his damp palms on his lap. He realized two things. One was that something went terribly wrong with his plans. The other was he was in imminent danger of pissing himself, but he hadn't gotten this far in his career by caving in to the first sign of trouble.

"You cannot threaten me in front of all these witnesses, whoever you are, Huntley or St. Armand. I don't have to duel with you. I have friends in London, powerful friends, they'll take care of you and that strumpet."

There was a stirring from the men in the room but Huntley held a hand up and they settled themselves.

"I said before you are not as clever as you think you are, and you just proved it by threatening me and insulting Miss Burke, again. You're correct, you do not have to show up for a duel. You should know, though, men who threaten *me* tend to have odd accidents."

"Accidents?"

"One ready to testify against me fell on a knife and disemboweled himself. Another had an unfortunate episode where his bedsheets became tangled around his neck. Then there was the poor sod who walked off a sea cliff after managing to tie his hands behind his back. I still don't know how he did it. All of your so-called witnesses?" He gestured to the room so quiet now Thomas heard the soft scrape of a knife being dragged across a stone to hone its edge. He did not look around to see who was doing this, but kept his eyes on the man in front of him, still talking in the same soft tones.

"These men are quite fond of our governess. *Their* intention is not to let you leave alive this evening. I'm prepared to offer you an alternative."

"Alternative?" he croaked

"Life—of a sort."

He nodded and rough hands grabbed Thomas, yanking his arms behind his back and securing his wrists. When he started yelling for help, they shoved a dirty rag in his mouth.

"That's better," Huntley said, standing and leaning close to Thomas. He was no longer smiling.

"Since you don't wish to duel, you will take a sea voyage, Wilson. If I ever hear a whisper, a word, a rumor that your carcass is back in England, you will wish I finished this tonight. If that's clear to you, bob your head. If you need further clarification, these gentlemen will be happy to help you understand your choices."

Visions of Italy and gold coins were blown away like a

freezing gale, Thomas's mind twisting even as he tried to twist his hands out of their bindings, but he'd been secured with sailors' knots tied by experts.

"I'll take that as an affirmative," Huntley said. "Haul him away, boys, with my respects to Captain Boylston. Poor man, he loses so many of his crew to death and disease, I'm sure he'll appreciate the offer of a replacement."

The last thing Thomas saw as he was yanked out of the warmth and light of the Knight's Head tavern was Lydia Burke, standing in Huntley's embrace.

CHAPTER 26

"*I* suppose I should say thank you, but I wish I could have dealt with Wilson myself."

She tried to step back, but he hooked his arm around her waist and wouldn't release her. It was as good as a declaration in front of Fuller and the other crewmen in the tavern, but she didn't resist when he rested his chin atop her head and held her close.

"Sometimes, Miss Burke, there are situations where only a pirate will do. I am happy we could be of service to you tonight."

"I know—" she started, then sighed. "England is a land of laws, Robert. If you make your home here, then piratical ways will not do."

"What was your alternative? He was neither a thief nor a murderer, not the kind that a court would convict. A man can be transported for poaching to feed his family, but scum like Wilson escape punishment for their misdeeds. Do not scold, little governess."

Lydia let out a deep breath, the tension of the evening draining out of her. It was more than that. She'd been on the run for so long, always looking over her shoulder, always prepared to flee—who would have suspected it would be a pirate who'd offer her a safe haven, shelter from life's storms?

She'd thought herself done with rogues and rakes when Edwin deserted her, but Robert showed her there could be substance beneath a pirate's leer. As she leaned against him amidst the conversation and laughter of her friends and shipmates she acknowledged a truth about herself she'd rejected for such a long time.

She liked bad boys. She always would.

This time she'd latched onto a man who was deadly, conniving and cunning, yes, but who was willing to be all of that for her, and for Mattie, and for his crew, and maybe, with a little direction and some new outlets, he'd be exactly what the people of Huntley needed.

"Come, Lydia. You must be worn out by all that's happened. Let me take you home to Huntley."

Robert left a bag of coins behind for Gibson and the men cleared out. Some of the crew would return to Huntley, but others had secured lodgings in Ashwyn.

They rode home in silence and after checking on the sleeping child cuddled around a puppy, she slowly walked to her room, so drained of energy that after she unpinned her hair she could only stand next to the mantel, staring into the fire.

She heard Robert enter, felt the heat at her back as he fitted himself to her curves, his hands coming around to cup her breasts through the soft wool of her gown, holding them, cherishing them.

"You need a maid, my dear. Tonight, I will play that role."

He steered her to the chair in front of the dressing table and she sat, looking into the mirror. Robert loomed behind her wearing only his shirt and breeches, feet bare, the shirt unfastened and gleaming white against the bronzed planes of his chest. He leaned over her back and taking her brush off the table, began stroking it through her hair, firm strokes that pulled tension from her even as it worked the day's tangles out.

"Your hair is lovely in the firelight, like a fine burgundy, rich and luscious," he said. "Such glory should be appreciated, not hidden."

He spoke no overt threats against her headgear, but Lydia would not be surprised if her caps went missing again. Her eyes closed as she enjoyed the sensation of a strong hand working through her hair, soothing her after the day's turmoil. It was hard to believe in the space of a few hours her life had changed so, thanks to this dangerous rogue.

"Stay with me tonight, and tomorrow we will start our future together."

"Robert—" She took the brush from his hand and stood, moving away from him so she could think. It was impossible to have this conversation when he was so close to her that all she wanted to do was let him embrace her and take care of her problems. It was a solution, but not the one that was best for her, not anymore.

"You were correct, Robert, removing the threat of Wilson was something you could accomplish that I was unlikely to manage on my own. But after Edwin left me I swore I would never be dependent on a man again. That's why I earn my own way."

"I know. Your strength is part of what drew me to you."

"Then you understand, if I am to stay I can only do it on one condition... Pay me my wages."

"What? Why? You don't need the money, you will be my wife and I will take care of you."

She shook her head slowly, never taking her eyes off of him. "I am a woman grown and I will never be dependent on a man again. Pay me."

He stepped back, away from her, and her heart sank. "This is ridiculous! You don't trust me? I cannot believe you will let money come between us!"

She knew what she was doing was risky, but the pirate St. Armand was too used to taking what he wanted, and she was not pirate booty. He awkwardly tugged at his shirt cuff and she felt her heart soften. He was nervous. Afraid she'd reject him, which in a sense she just had. He would to do anything to keep her, whether it was killing a man, withholding her wages, or seducing her into his bed.

Lydia took a hesitant step forward, then another, until she was close enough to place her hand on his broad chest and look up into those eyes, dark as the midnight skies. With her other hand she brushed back that errant curl falling across his forehead and left her hand alongside his face. She could feel a pulse there, strong and steady beneath her fingers.

"Robert—even if you never gave me a farthing, if I want to leave, I will leave. I will find a way, just as you did when you found your situation here unbearable, just as I did in London. But I will not leave the man I love, and I will not leave my children, and I will not have an affair with the dancing master. You must have faith in me. You must trust *me*, and I will have faith in you if you show me you understand what I need."

His face, usually so full of expression, was unreadable as he looked at her. Then he turned on his heel and left, taking her heart and her soul with him.

Well. She'd gambled, and she'd lost.

Lydia sat on the edge of her bed, her legs unable to hold her. She didn't know how long she sat, listening to nothing but the small sounds of a house asleep, a house she'd thought could be her home after so long. It was better this way. She had to know Robert trusted her, and if he did not, then there was no basis for their marriage. If she stayed there would be some happiness because of Mattie, and having a home, but she'd never have Robert's heart, not fully, not without his trust.

A noise from the doorway made her glance up and Robert stood there, a paper in his hand.

"Here. It is a bank draft. I did not have enough coin on hand."

He walked over to her, put it in her hand, and she did not look at it. She did not have to.

"You have what you asked for, Lydia Burke. You have enough money now to leave, to go back to the islands, to go to Paris or America or wherever you want."

He looked down at her, his heart in his eyes.

"Will you stay?" he whispered.

She set the bank draft facedown on the table next to her bed and stood, taking his face between her hands.

"You are a good man, Robert St. Armand Huntley. Not just a good pirate, you are a good man."

"You are the first person in the universe to make that statement," he said, bemused.

"Notice I did not say you are perfect, or that there isn't room for improvement. Your propensity for solving problems at knifepoint can be addressed."

She brought his head down until their lips were only a whisper apart. "But we can address them another time, my darling."

Her kiss was the answer to his question, the love she had for him pouring out of her, showing him she would stay, telling him he was more precious to her than rubies, than all the gold in London's banks.

He picked her up in his arms and carried her to his rooms, where it was his turn to watch her undress, removing her garments beneath his approving gaze, until she stood before him only in her shift. She put her hands beneath her hair, pulling the mass up atop her head, knowing that the fire behind her limned her body through the cloth, displaying her to his gaze and she smiled at his expression as he removed his own clothes.

"Have I ever told you I adore the gap between your teeth? It reminds me you are as lickerish as the Wife of Bath."

"'Gat-toothed I was, and that became me well,'" she murmured.

He joined her in his bed, the laughter in his face replaced by a gentleness she'd never seen before, a smile unlike the others because he knew now she'd stay with him, forever. He pulled her shift over her head, taking his time, exploring her with his hands, and his mouth, paying particular attention to those areas he'd learned were especially sensitive, moving his way down the length of her.

He whispered French phrases into her ear, telling her how wonderful her responses were, how lovely to see her passion in full play, how fortunate he was to be able to touch her *so* as he eased her legs apart and placed the fur pillow beneath her. It raised her to his mouth, to those skillful fingers working inside her in concert with his tongue, stroking her, and in the quiet of the room the only sounds now were of him loving her and her own moans as the sensations ramped higher until she had to jam her hand between her teeth to keep from waking the house.

When the spinning room righted itself she gasped, "What Oriental technique was that?"

"I forget if that was number sixteen or—who cares?" he murmured, inflicting small, biting kisses on her as he moved up to her side until he was braced over her, his beautiful eyes veiled by his ridiculously lush lashes. He kissed her languidly, open-mouthed, taking his time to know everything about her. She understood why she'd said yes after so long.

She'd been waiting for Robert Huntley, Captain St.

Armand, who swept her up into his strong arms and took her away from her safe and boring existence in the islands to a life full of pirates and puppies and laughter. A life she'd never been willing to imagine for herself after the disasters of London. A life full of all that she'd dreamed of—passion and excitement and adventure. It was the life she was meant for, she'd known that in the constraints of her girlhood, and it was the life she'd chosen, once upon a time.

He pushed himself into her, hard, and it was right, so right, to be taken this way, to release all of her dark desires. He paused, the muscles on his arms straining where he held himself up, looking down at her with burning, black eyes as his chest heaved, sweat gleaming across his face.

"I am going to start moving now, and I am going to thrust deep and fast," he rasped. "Do not fear—when you start screaming in ecstasy I will understand."

Such a comment would normally bring at the very least a snicker, but now his words heated her blood, raising her need to an even higher pitch. He read the expression on her face with satisfaction and a small quirk of those sculpted lips and began to do as he promised. She held on to his hips, her own legs locked over his back, relishing the play of sinew and muscle beneath her fingers as he flexed himself within her. The stark bones of his face were outlined by the tight flesh as he pumped into her with deep thrusts bordering on painful, but it was exactly what she wanted. He kept himself in check, holding back his own release so she would get the utmost pleasure. He was charmingly courteous and considerate for a pirate, and she pulled her legs up and allowed him deeper access, a good move for both of them.

"Lydia," he murmured her name, caressing the syllables, as he moved in her. They said nothing more, words no longer coming between them, no longer necessary as they used their bodies and their passion to show their love for one another.

ROBERT WAS TEMPTED to burn the letter from his cousin Lionel begging for assistance. Not surprisingly, the presumed heir to Huntley found himself without friends or funds once the actual heir returned. Some might consider the weasel a minor annoyance, but Captain St. Armand knew from experience men killed for wealth and position, for far lower stakes than the barony of Huntley. He'd have to deal with it eventually, but he had more important matters to take care of when he went to London, including ensuring there were no untidy ends left from Thomas Wilson's abrupt departure from the city.

Laughter floated out from the window of the nursery to his study. He'd never grow tired of hearing that sound. For too long Huntley Manor had not echoed with the sound of children's laughter, or the laughter of a woman in love. He needed to secure his future with a beautiful (and amazingly imaginative) wife, more children, and keeping Mattie as safe as he could from an unkind world.

Lydia claimed he was a good man. Now he would prove it.

"$\mathcal{M}$iss Burke, there is something wrong with Papa. Is he ill?"

Lydia hugged the motherless child to her chest, knowing the thought of her strong father being ill terrified her.

"No, Mattie, I am absolutely certain your father is not ill. His color is good, he had an excellent appetite at breakfast, remember? It must simply be he is adjusting to life here, just as we had to adjust to walking on land after being aboard ship for so long. You had to learn how to be a member of the *Prodigal Son's* crew, now your papa is learning how to be Lord Huntley."

"I don't like this adjustment," she said with a youngster's honesty. "I want my pirate papa back. And I want knife practice."

Robert had been replaced by a changeling and in lieu of a dashing pirate, the boredom fairies left an English country squire. Serious. Sober. Dressed in browns and grays and muted shades of blue doing little to enhance his appearance. He arose at an early hour and worked all day except to break for luncheon, where he'd quiz Mattie about her lessons.

Bedtime tales of bloodthirsty pirates were replaced with books about good little boys and girls who never did anything bad and were always a shining example to others. Lydia caught herself jerking awake out of a doze after one of these instructional interludes.

Knife practice was suspended, with a suggestion that Mathilde work on her needlework instead. It was a suggestion which would have led to a temper tantrum of epic proportions had Mattie not been as stunned as Lydia by the idea.

Lydia would have enjoyed having the pirate back herself. The man sitting in the big chair in the study still looked like Robert, if you squinted and held your head to the side, but where was the earring? The red satin? The kohl-lined eyes?

Sails was so morose she feared he'd turn to drink if he had to keep dressing Robert as he did.

"Cap'n insists on it, Miss Burke. I didn't even know he had such dull clothes in his wardrobe. I figured they were for dress-up, like when he needs to fool the navy or hoodwink someone like that Wilson. Even the vicar's waistcoat has more style than that garment he wore to supper," he said, shaking his head. "I offered him the purple satin, but he said it was gaudy and inappropriate attire. Inappropriate attire! Never thought I'd hear Captain St. Armand say such a thing!"

When they gathered for luncheon the lord of the manor made an announcement.

"I am leaving for London tomorrow, ladies. Mr. Fuller will be here if any difficulties arise, but my business shouldn't take too long."

"I want to go to London too, Papa! I want to see the Tower where people are kept prisoner and tortured and executed!"

"Such an excitable child," Robert murmured, then raised his voice. "No, Mattie, not this time. I promise we will go to

London together, perhaps in the springtime before the city gets too fetid."

"Miss Burke too? And Jolly?"

"I will rent a house. Now, no more about this. Shall I bring you a new doll from London?"

"I'd rather have my own pistols, Papa."

"Of course you would."

Robert left the next morning, finally looking more like himself. It gave Lydia hope to see him dressed in a coat of blue superfine, buckskin breeches molded to his long, long legs, and black topboots polished by Sails until they reflected the sunlight poking through the leaves. He looked good, despite his duller than usual plumage. Of course, Robert Huntley looked good in nothing at all, though she'd not been graced with that sight either for the past week. He'd politely said good night to her each evening, then retired to his study or his bedroom.

At first she'd worried that something she'd done gave him a disgust of her—possibly that interlude with the feathers and the string of beads—but when she thought further, she just shook her head. This morning when he picked up his calfskin gloves from the table in the hall he'd paused and looked at them thoughtfully before pulling them on, flexing his fingers inside the soft leather, and when he retrieved his riding crop he slapped it lightly against his palm and smiled, a smile much more reminiscent of the pirate St. Armand than the baron.

But he was sober and thoughtful when he bade them farewell. He hugged Mattie to his chest and she threw her arms around his neck and said, "I love you, Papa, even when you are a baron and not a pirate! I will love you always and forever, that's a promise!"

"It pleases me to hear you say that, poppet. I love you too."

"Will you be careful in London, Papa? It is a big town and

you won't have Jolly with you to guide you home if you get lost."

"I will be careful in London, Mattie. And what of you, Miss Burke, will you miss me?"

She leaned closer to him and said into his ear, "I will think of you every night when I play with my toys, my lord."

She was gratified by his dumbfounded expression. His mouth opened, then closed, and he appeared about to say something, but instead mounted his horse and with a final wave, rode off. The ladies held hands and watched until he was out of sight.

It was amazing how empty a big house could feel with the absence of just one man. That night Lydia put Mattie to bed by herself, and Mattie clapped her hands in approval when Captain Johnson's book was retrieved from the shelf, banishing the storybook about the little boy who was horribly good and who kept his room neat as a pin. He probably ate his beets too, Mattie pointed out, good enough reason to push him off a cliff. Lydia didn't remonstrate with her and her eye remained remarkably twitch free.

"Tonight we will read of how Anne Bonny turned to the pirate's life, Mattie," Lydia said, resuming their story. "'Her father expected a good match for her; but she spoilt it all, for without his consent she marries a young fellow who belonged to the sea, and was not worth a groat which provoked her father to such a degree, that he turned her out of doors...'"

Lydia continued reading with renewed appreciation for the pirate through to the end, and both ladies agreed it was better not knowing for certain what happened to Anne over time.

"Pirates take care of each other, don't they?"

"A good ship is crewed by good shipmates, Mattie, and good people watch out for one another. And on that, it's time

THE PIRATE'S SECRET BABY

for bed," Lydia added, listening to the child's prayers. Those took time because they included Mattie's mama in heaven, her papa here, Miss Burke, the entire crew of the *Prodigal* and Jolly, of course.

Lydia tucked the covers around the girl, who held her arms up for a hug, and she embraced Mattie, inhaling her fragrance of fresh air, soap and little girl.

"Good night, Miss Burke. I love you."

"I love you too, my dear."

The dog trotted out with her and the governess left the door slightly ajar. Jolly had the makings of a mouser and Mrs. Farmer was very much in favor of the pup roaming the kitchens at night to keep the rodents at bay, though the dog always ended the evening's rambles in Mattie's bed.

Despite her provocative words to Robert, Lydia wasn't interested in playing with her toys, not by herself. It had been much more enjoyable to use them with her naughty pirate. If it wasn't her bedroom behavior that made him change, could it be her fault in other ways? Hadn't she constantly sniped at him about his piratical ways, about reforming, about not being such a reprobate and setting a better example for Mattie? He was certainly doing all of that now, to her great frustration. She wanted to swing a cutlass at him herself, just to get a good reaction.

Swing a cutlass...

She of all people knew there was truth to the old saying that the pen was mightier than the sword. Now she had to prove it.

The house quiet, the dog off on his midnight rambles, Lydia sat at her desk, sharpened her quill, and began to write.

CHAPTER 28

*R*obert climbed down wearily from his horse, worn to a nub by his hurried trip south. He patted the gelding on his flank and handed him off to Henry, the lad working in the stable. Braxton informed him the ladies were in Ashwyn and expected back before dark. Robert changed his clothing and washed, ignoring Sails mumbled complaints, then went to his study to secure the items he'd purchased in London.

He paused as he was about to sit in the chair he now considered *his* chair, the master's chair. There was a package on it, brown paper tied with string. *For Captain St. Armand* was written on the front in a familiar hand.

Inside was his banknote for a governess's wages, torn in half. The two pieces fluttered to the desk, and he looked at them in dismay. His reputation for knowing what women wanted left him at sea with his Lydia. Figuring her out was like trying to decipher a treasure map, a map that promised reward for a lifetime, but also said, "Here be sea serpents!"

He shook his head and unwrapped the rest of the package. It was a sheaf of foolscap and on the top page was written *The Impetuous Pirate—Memoirs of a Kidnapped Lady*, by Randy Scribe. Intrigued, he sat and turned to the next page.

——

My tale, dear reader, risks offering salacious entertainment to low-minded persons, but it is not for that reason I take pen in hand. I do not write of my adventures in the brawny arms of the lusty pirate Valdez to titillate or arouse base passion. When I write of how his burning kisses inflamed me, how his ivory shaft with its vermillion head made me long to caress it, to feel its prodigious length pierce my tender, warm sheath, to feel those mighty thrusts of delight, over and over again until my journey to love's enchantment was fulfilled, it is not to inspire prurient interest, but rather to edify readers as to the risks inherent in being a young woman adrift in today's dangerous world...

——

When Braxton brought the post to the study he nearly ran into his lordship, on his way out.

"Braxton, I am not to be disturbed. If anyone asks for me I'll—I'll be in my bunk."

"Yes, my lord."

~

"GOOD AFTERNOON, Braxton. Lord Huntley has returned?"

"He was here, ma'am, then he left again just an hour or so ago. He did say he would see you ladies before Mattie goes to sleep, but not to wait supper for him. I must tell you though, he appeared"—Braxton sought the right word—"distracted."

"Really?" Lydia purred. "Distracted? Thank you, Braxton."

It pleased her to know her writing could still distract

men, even if she had no intention of taking up her pen as Randy Scribe for money again. However, when he came to the nursery later that evening Robert Huntley didn't look distracted at all. He was calm, pleasant, asked Mattie about her day, told the ladies about the interesting sights he'd seen in London—not many, as he'd been busy meeting with his man of business and others, but that was all. There was no talk of the future. No mention of what it meant that Lydia'd returned his money to him.

He played jackstraws with Mattie and Lydia tried to read a novel he'd brought from London for her. *Mansfield Park* was by an author she enjoyed, and this novel hadn't made it to St. Martin while she was residing there. She should have been immersed in the story of Fanny Price and the Bertrams, but she was distracted.

Braxton brought in the tea tray and warm milk for Mattie. This was the point in the evening when Captain St. Armand would have reached for the rum bottle to flavor his tea, but boring Lord Huntley only took milk—*milk*—and some of Mrs. Farmer's excellent jam tarts.

"Be careful you don't get overstimulated," she muttered under her breath as she poured.

"Did you say something, Miss Burke?"

"I said, 'More hot water, my lord?'"

The end of the evening was brightened by a new book for Mattie, illustrated stories for children, such as the tale of Dick Whittington and his cat.

"It will help you learn more about your new home, Mattie," her father said, and the child showed proper appreciation, no doubt grateful for a reprieve from the boring pap of her father's own childhood reading. It was no wonder he'd found a pirate's life attractive after that, Lydia mused to herself.

She did her own needlework as Robert read, pausing to

watch the two heads so close together, so similar in expression. It wasn't her pirate reading to Mattie, but it was still a man she could love all her days. She could even put up with a touch of boredom in her life, if necessary.

When they exited Mattie's room Lydia fiddled with the bag that held her needlework.

"Did you have a chance to read what I left you, Robert?"

She looked up at him through her lashes, holding her breath.

"Oh, that. No, I am truly sorry, my dear, but I had so much to do after my journey I had to set your package aside until later. Was it important? I'm sure I'll have time in a few days to give it a glance."

He peered at her in the low light of the hallway, then held his candle high. "Are you well? You look—agitated."

"I'm fine," she snapped. "Good night, my lord."

"Good night, Miss Burke—oh, I have to go out this evening to speak with Mr. Fuller."

Lydia turned and frowned. "At this hour?"

"It cannot wait. I sent a note around to him earlier."

At least she no longer had to worry about whether he'd go off to the Knight's Head to drink and carouse and roll home at dawn smelling of spilled ale! That was behavior for Captain St. Armand, not Lord Huntley, damn it.

LYDIA WASN'T sure what sound woke her, but she was ready when she saw the dark shape in the doorway to her bedroom.

"Neptune's bloody balls!" he yelped. "You could have hit me with that! Who taught you to throw a knife?"

"Mattie, and if I wanted to hit you, I would have. Get out."

The intruder yanked the knife from the doorjamb and

put it in his boot. In his other hand he carried a candle, which he set on the table. She was disappointed his hand didn't shake, but he was probably used to people flinging sharp objects at him. She'd fantasized about it herself often enough since St. Martin.

He sat beside her atop the covers, looming over her in the candle's glow, and she could finally see him—really see him. He wore a greatcoat over his shirt of sapphire satin, the shirt unbuttoned down its front, drawing the eye along its gap down to where it was tucked into leather breeches banded with a gold sash and tucked into tall boots. A matching sapphire the size of an acorn dangled from his ear.

Her midnight visitor wasn't Lord Huntley, but the notorious Captain St. Armand.

"And did Marauding Mattie teach you that once you throw your knife it is no longer a weapon you can use?"

"I'll scream."

He tucked one finger under her chin and raised it, his kohl-rimmed eyes looking deep into hers and she almost—almost—forgot why she'd been upset with him.

"No you won't scream, 'Tessa,' you will follow the script."

"What sc—oh no you don't!"

"It says right on page 22, *'And then Valdez tossed me over his wide shoulder, and I shuddered to think what depredations he might wreak upon my tender and innocent flesh if I were held prisoner in his den of iniquity.'*"

"That's just a story, Ro—eeep!"

Her protests were muffled as he pulled the coverlet around her, wrapping her like a Egyptian mummy, then tossed her over his wide shoulder, humming to himself as he carried her out of the room and down the staircase to wreak depredations upon her.

"Let me go, you, you pirate! You cannot carry me off like baggage! Ouch!"

"'Silence, wench!' Valdez commanded, applying his hard hand to my'…my apologies, that doesn't happen until chapter five, does it? And I don't have a parrot. I couldn't procure one on short notice in the wilds of Lancashire."

"I mean it, Robert! Let me up or I'll spew supper down your back!"

He stopped, and she heard him sigh.

"You are no fun and this is my favorite greatcoat. Very well," he grumbled, putting her on her feet and spinning her around as he unwrapped her, but kept the coverlet over her shoulders for warmth and modesty, also keeping her freed arm firmly in his grip.

She blinked in the lamplight. They were in the front entranceway and Mr. Fuller stood there, shaking his head.

"Help! I'm being kidnapped!"

"Kidnapping women never ends well for you, Captain. Haven't you learned that yet?"

"Third time's the charm, Mr. Fuller," he said cheerfully. "Is everything ready?"

"No, really, I'm being kidnapped—"

Instead of rescuing her he held the door as St. Armand lifted her into his arms, carrying her outside and tossing her atop his gelding.

"Oof. I am sick to death of being tossed like a sack of beans! I demand you let me back into the house, this instant!"

The door to Huntley closed and St. Armand climbed behind her before she could scramble down. The horse, big dumb creature that it was, did nothing to aid her. It was likely thrilled at having some excitement in its life.

He grabbed the reins, then pulled the coverlet around her, wrapping her in his arms as they rode down the path.

"Why are we going to Mr. Fuller's cottage?"

"He won't need it for the next day or so. We will."

"I think not, you scoundrel! Release me at once."

He just snickered and had the effrontery to kiss the top of her head. He truly was the most annoying man in the world, but she relaxed against him as they rode. She'd been bemoaning the lack of exciting pirates in her life and it was being remedied, so other than scolding on general principle, she had to admit great curiosity as to what St. Armand's plans were. If he was using her book as a script, the evening could be quite exciting, with or without a parrot.

A lamp illuminated the cottage, and when they entered Lydia blinked in surprise. Fuller's cottage was rather drab and utilitarian, like his cabin aboard ship, but now it was transformed into a sybaritic den of delights. The bed was strewn with St. Armand's silk and fur pillows, along with more silk scarves and sashes. Food covered the plain small table, a feast of apples, Huntley's own hams, cheeses, savories and small cakes, and there were bottles of wine and rum on the shelf.

"I'll be back after I see to the horse. Do not try to escape my clutches or it will go badly for you, governess."

Escape my clutches? Lydia thought as she stepped closer to the fireplace, discarding her blanket from Huntley. Good thing the man was a pirate and not an author. The cottage was snug and comfortable from the fire, and as the door opened again she smiled to herself, because she knew the flames outlined her form, rendering her cotton nightrail nearly transparent.

There was some throat clearing and a rustle of papers behind her.

"Coming then into his cabin and seeing me lying with my face turned away, without more ado just slipped off his breeches, and laying himself then gently down by me, he applied his belly and thighs close to me and put his member to work..."

He came up behind her and slipped his hands around her waist, holding her against him. "I don't need a script," he purred in her ear. "I can satisfy your desires, all of them. Would you like to know what my cunning plan is?"

He began nibbling on her neck, moving his hands up to grasp her breasts and toy with her nipples when she attempted to squirm away.

"Oh, I suppose," she said, wishing it didn't come out in such a breathless tone.

"My plan, little hedgehog, is to kidnap you, hold you here against your will, ravish you until you swoon with passion, and compromise you within an inch of your life so you will be forced to marry me."

She couldn't help it. She giggled. "*That* is your dastardly plan?"

"I am an impetuous pirate, after all. Isn't that what you expect? Or would you prefer sober, responsible Lord Huntley?"

She turned in his arms. He'd discarded his coat and her fingers glided over the rich material of his shirt as she put her hands around his waist.

"I tried to be the man I thought you wanted, Lydia. You'd had enough upheaval in your life from bad men, men who didn't value you, who only cared for themselves. I was one of those men. But later, when I removed Wilson from your life, I was *glad* I was that bad man, the man who could do those things for you."

"Would you have killed Wilson?"

"I would burn the world for you."

He said it so quietly, in such a grave tone, that Lydia wasn't sure she'd understood him. She looked up into his serious eyes, all the laughter gone from them.

"You still do not understand how I feel about you, do you, Lydia Burke? You were threatened and I could not allow that. You are everything to me."

He stepped back from her and began to pace, his words

pouring out of him. "I never expected this. I never expected a daughter, or inheriting Huntley. I never questioned whether my life had meaning, whether I was a good man before all of this happened.

"I never expected *you*. I kept telling myself that wasn't who I was, the man a good woman could love and want for her husband. But if you know nothing else about me, know this—I love you, Lydia, with all the breath in my body, all the passion in my soul. There are days I feel as if I'm caught in an undertow dragging me out to sea, but when I fear drowning beneath all of this, there you are. You are my anchor."

"You want a mother for Mattie."

"I want *you*. Yes, you are an excellent mother for Mattie, but I am still selfish enough to know the real reason I want you is for myself. I want you in my bed. I want you in my arms. When I have to put on spectacles to admire your bosom, I will still be there, admiring your bosom. I want to sit in front of a cozy fire thirty years from now next to someone who snickers at my bad behavior and outrageous statements."

Robert appeared startled by his words, as if they'd burst out of him of their own accord. He came forward, taking her hands in his, gazing down into her eyes, his grip tight on her. He smelled of citrus and male, and she thought she could hear his heart in the quiet room. It may have been her own heart she heard, for it was surely pounding.

"It's hard for me to imagine life decades from now. I never expected to grow old, my dear. I thought I would be like Bartholomew Roberts in the pirate book, living 'A merry life and a short one,' ending on a rope, or a knife. Now I want my motto to be 'a merry life and a *long* one,' with you, and Mattie, and more children to fill Huntley's old walls with noise and laughter. You are the best wife for me, and you know I always believe I deserve the best. Not that I deserve you—I don't, but you are the best I can ever hope to have."

"Oh, so you deserve the best, but what do I get from this?"

"You get me. I hope that will be enough. And if you need added inducement, there are still five—no, seven secret Oriental tricks I have not yet shown you. I know I'm not perfect…"

A sound emerged from her that from a less refined person would be termed a snort.

"To continue, I know *I'm* not perfect, but dammit, neither are you! You're managing and you sneer at me and I suspect you laugh at me when I'm not looking. But I still love you and want to marry you. If it's Lord Huntley you want and not the pirate St. Armand, I can be him, for you."

Lydia stepped closer to him, and put her arms around his neck, that strong neck and the shoulders as wide as those of her impetuous, imaginary pirate.

"The governess hiding in the islands may have been willing to take less than a full measure, but *I* want it all. Lord Huntley is a good man indeed. One can always count on him to do the right thing, to behave properly in the parlor and in church," she said with a look of her own she knew could match any pirate's for wickedness. "But in my bed I want, no, I demand the pirate. He is the one who makes me feel like Anne Bonny and Mary Read and even Lydia Burke—the real Lydia. Although…" She mused, running her finger down his exposed flesh, following the line of hair as it trailed toward what she wanted. "I can also see an attraction in having Huntley in my bed. He has proven himself most capable. He would put a great deal of effort into making sure all is done properly so that all obligations and expectations are met."

"Then our desires match, madam. I long for prissy Miss Burke in my parlor, in the classroom, but in my bed I want that naughty Randy Scribe who has such an active imagination. Although," he said thoughtfully, running his hands down her back to her bottom and pulling her against him, "there is something to be said for seducing the governess, for submitting to her strict ways and exacting expectations. But there is still one more thing I must ask you."

He went down on his knee, took her hand in both of his, and with utter seriousness and great tenderness said, "Lydia Burke, would you do me the honor of accepting my hand in marriage?"

Lydia almost asked if it was the pirate or the lord proposing, but she knew the answer. It didn't matter. Regardless of how he styled himself or what title he used, he was hers.

"Yes, I will," she said, and she knew from the look in his face that the smile on hers showed what was in her heart for this man.

He rose fluidly to his feet and grasped her upper arms, his eyes ringed with blue fire as they searched her face, and then he pulled her into his embrace and kissed her, enveloping her in his passion and desire. She gave him back full measure, for she too had found an anchor, a safe harbor from her life's turmoil, a home.

"And now," he said, untying the sash from around his waist and skillfully knotting it around her wrists, "there is still the matter of my plans for the rest of this evening."

"Having been kidnapped by the notorious pirate St. Armand, I suppose any reasonable governess would submit to his every whim. As you wish." She sighed theatrically. "Have your wicked way with me, sir, for I can do nothing to stop you!"

"It's always gratifying when my cunning plans fall into place."

CHAPTER 29

$\mathcal{L}$ ydia was pulled out of a boneless sleep by the sound of voices outside the cottage. Weak morning sun filtered through the shutters, but the bed was warm and if she stayed in it, perhaps she'd have some company to begin the day.

"Wake up, slug-a-bed! We have things to do."

She shrieked as the covers were thrown back and the cold air rushed over her naked body.

"Give that back!"

He ignored her and poured hot water into a slipper tub in front of the fireplace, whistling to himself. She looked around the room where pillows lay scattered, one leaving a trail of feathers across the floor, while scarves fluttered from the rafter. The dregs of last night's drink and dining lay on the table and when she reached up to push her disordered hair out of her eyes, there were twinges in her muscles from the previous night's activities.

Was there any better way to wake up? Maybe not, but sleeping for a few hours longer was even more attractive. Robert relentlessly pulled her off the mattress and put her in the tub, but he made up for it by shucking off his shirt and breeches and washing her lovingly, then drying her with the stack of toweling he'd left to warm in front of the fire.

"I could become accustomed to having a beautiful, naked man attend to my toilette."

"My services are greatly in demand, madam. Now we have to hurry. You don't want to be late."

"Late? Late for what?"

He pulled a towel around his waist, then opened the wardrobe. She wrapped herself in her towel and walked to the cabinet while he opened the shutters on the window.

The contents of the wardrobe glowed in the morning light. There was a dress of sapphire velvet, the lower skirt elaborately worked with double flounces of pink satin, and a low crowned bonnet festooned with ribbons and white ostrich feathers making up for years of ugly caps. A sable muff rested on a shelf and she ran her hand over it, shivering at the touch of the soft fur.

"You are creature of sensation," he whispered in her ear, coming up behind her. "You will wear this ensemble today, and think of me every time you brush your hand across the velvet covering your body, every time you look at the fur, and remember."

"Oh but, Robert! It is too fine for me! Certainly too fine for everyday wear in Ashwyn."

"Then I am glad today is not every day."

"It isn't?"

She turned and looked over her shoulder, but he only kissed her ear and said, "Come. I will be your servant this morning and dress you."

He began with her stockings, new silk stockings with clocking, stockings that smoothed up her leg to be tied with garters of wine red satin, her feet slipped into blue kid half-boots.

Of course, there were many kisses and caresses accompanying the stockings, but she tolerated it for he was so skillful with women's attire.

He'd knotted the towel at his waist, but kneeling at her feet she had a view of his sleek back, the muscles working beneath his skin and she reached down and rested her hand atop his hair, the locks gleaming in the morning light.

"I do love you, you know."

He kissed the palm of her hand, then stood and helped her to her feet. Her chemise was of finest lawn, whispering over her body, then he laced her securely into a new corset of the same satin as the garters, a foundation that plumped her breasts over the soft black lace edging the top. It was a wicked, wicked garment, fit for a pirate queen.

No one would know the scandalous garments she wore beneath the elegant velvet, but every time she breathed in she would remember, and feel.

The petticoats were followed by the magnificent dress and then she returned the favor, helping Robert into his attire. He'd brought the red coat crusted with gold braiding, so heavy she thought she'd need help lifting it, but once on him he looked so magnificent it took her breath away.

He tied his own cravat, skillfully, of course, for he was a master of tying knots. His shirt was fully fastened, and the white linen glowed against his sun-darkened skin. Her final act to garb him was to retrieve his gold sash from the bedpost and wrap it around his waist. He tucked a finger beneath her chin and raised it, giving her a soft kiss.

"All day, when I look down and see your knot in this silk, it will remind me of last night—and of thousands of nights to come. But there is one more thing you need to make your ensemble complete."

He took a slim sandalwood chest from his saddlebags and put it on the table, a chest carved with an Oriental design.

"Turn around."

She did, and dipped her head when she felt his fingers at her neck. She felt the weight on her neck, then walked to the small looking glass Fuller'd hung for shaving.

There was a strand of pearls around her neck, each one large, luscious and perfect. She gasped, and fingered them gently.

"They are beautiful! Priceless!"

"*You* are priceless. They are only an adornment for your beauty."

She turned to him, frowning. "I worry that I am being adorned with your ill-gotten gains."

"Nonsense. These were a gift from a grateful sea captain."

"A gift for you not slicing him open?" she asked tartly.

He just smiled, then reached into his coat for a smaller box. "This was my mother's."

He slid a magnificent sapphire onto her hand. The oval stone was ringed with diamonds that caught fire in the morning light and took her breath away.

"I will treasure it, Robert."

He helped her into her jacket, the one Sails made for her, and when she protested leaving the cottage in such disarray, was assured it was all arranged.

"But everyone will know—oh." She frowned. "We must marry quickly, Robert, or my reputation will be worse than yours."

"Not even on the most productive day of your life, Miss Burke, could your reputation be worse than mine. However, that too is arranged."

He escorted her outside and she pulled up her jacket's fur collar against the chill, then stared at the gig. It was decorated with ribbons and fall foliage, and the horse had some late blooming daisies tucked into its mane.

Robert turned to her, took her hand in his and kissed it.

"It is your wedding day, Lydia."

"What? How?"

"I procured a special license in London, and Mr. Castle is waiting for us at Huntley."

Her eyes narrowed as she took it all in. "You are quite sure of yourself, sir! What if I refused?"

His own face was grave. "If you refused and left me, I would take Mattie and go to sea. I could not stay here. Huntley is not a home without you by my side, Lydia. Because you said yes, you will be Lady Huntley before noon, and your reputation is secure. And," he said with his best "charming pirate" smile, "you may wish to know there's one Oriental technique I'm saving for our wedding night."

With that he picked her up and carried her to the gig before climbing in beside her and driving the short distance to the manor.

Today it was a different sight than what she'd first seen when they arrived at Huntley. The shrubbery was pruned, the windows gleamed in the morning light, and Braxton stood at the entrance, looking years younger and bushels prouder than the butler who'd greeted them that day.

"All is in readiness, my lord, Miss Burke. And may I just add how very, very glad I am for both of you—for all of us at Huntley—today."

"Thank you, Braxton," Lydia said. "It is good to—eep!"

Robert came up behind her and picked her up in his arms, carrying her over the threshold.

"That comes after the ceremony!"

"I am not taking any chances on you running away, my little hedgehog."

He continued to carry her up the stairs into the ballroom at Huntley, newly scrubbed and somewhat bare of adornment, but that didn't matter, for it was adorned with people she cared for. He set her on her feet and she looked around the room.

There was the crew of the *Prodigal* who'd stayed on land—Sails, Norton, Conroy, Paget, Turnbull—who honked noisily into a handkerchief while Nash patted his arm—and Mr. Fuller, who met her at the door and said, "I would be greatly honored if you would allow me to escort you down the aisle, lass."

"The honor would be mine, Mr. Fuller." She leaned up on her toes to kiss him on his cheek. "Thank you for taking such good care of my pirate."

He blushed, gave her a wink, and tucked her arm in his. Robert had moved down to the front of the room, pausing to pick Mattie up in his arms and give her a huge buss on the cheek. She too wore a new dress, of the same blue velvet as Lydia's, with a pink satin sash around her middle.

"See?" he said. "I told you I could convince Miss Burke to be your new mama."

"And you wore your coat! I told you she would say yes if you wore your red coat!"

Susanna Castle walked over to Lydia and pressed a bouquet of pink hydrangeas into her hands.

"From my garden," she said, "for the bride."

Lydia clutched her bouquet and looked around the room at her friends, her neighbors, even Jolly, wearing a blue bow and held on a short leash by Nellie, and waiting for her with love in their eyes, her new family.

As she took a deep breath, Mr. Fuller patted her arm, and they walked to the front of the room. She stood next to the two pirates, one large, one small, but both of whom she loved so much, and Mattie said, "Papa said I will have a *maman* in heaven and a mama here too. Does that mean I will be your own little girl now, Miss Burke?"

"You will be my little girl always and forever, Mattie. And that's a promise."

Robert set the child down and she looked up at Lydia and whispered, "I have an important job to do today, but now it's Mr. Castle's turn."

Castle laughed and said, "It is my turn indeed, child, and so I'll begin. 'Dearly beloved…'"

When it came time for the ring Mattie solemnly passed a gold band to her father, and as he slid it onto Lydia's finger and said the words the vicar told him to say, he smiled at her. There was nothing of the "dashing pirate rogue" in this smile, nothing studied or practiced or planned. It was natural, and beautiful, and lit up his face. It was the smile of love as he added his own words to that of the solemn service, "And I will love you always and forever. That's a promise."

He kissed her to the cheers of the assembled pirates, servants, friends, puppies and clergy, beginning their life together.

Had there ever been a better morning in the history of the world?

She thought not.

ABOUT THE AUTHOR

 Darlene Marshall is an award-winning author of historical romance featuring pirates, privateers, smugglers and the occasional possum. She loves working at a job where business attire is shorts and a shirt festooned with pink flamingos and palm trees. Marshall lives in North Central Florida, a convenient location for researching sites of great historical significance, which also happen to also be at the beach and serve mojitos. Her books have been published in English, German and Estonian.

You can learn more about Darlene by visiting her website: http://darlenemarshall.com

Want more of the notorious Captain Robert St. Armand? Read **Castaway Dreams**--*2013 Aspen Gold Reader's Choice Award—On sale now in ebook and print:*

After a lifetime in the Royal Navy, surgeon Alexander Murray knows one cannot exist without a brain, yet Daphne Farnham may be the exception. Her head contains nothing but rainbows, shoes, bonnets, pink frills and butterflies. Even her fluffy dog is useless. But the war with Napoleon is finally over and Alexander is sure he can put up with the cloth-headed Miss Farnham only for a couple of months until they reach England.

Did that naval officer have his sense of humor surgically removed? It is bad enough Alexander has no fashion sensibilities, never smiles at Daphne like other men do and doesn't adore her darling pup Pompom. He had the gall to proclaim her "useless" when everyone knows it's Daphne who's the best at picking out just the right ensemble for any social occasion. Fortunately, she has to put up with the sour Scotsman only for a couple of months until they reach England.

But when their ship goes down, the dour doctor (after a fashion), the dizzy damsel (more or less) and the darling (and potentially delicious) doggy are about to embark on the adventure of a lifetime as unlikely companions, castaway on a desert island. One of them may have fleas, but it's the two humans who will find themselves wanting to scratch a certain itch.

facebook.com/DMarshallAuthor

twitter.com/DarleneMarshall

instagram.com/darlenemarshallauthor

bookbub.com/profile/darlene-marshall